EMPIRE IN CHAOS

THE LANDS OF the Empire are being ravaged by a terrible plague. When Annaleise Jaeger's village is overrun and destroyed by mutants, she and an injured elf captive are the only survivors. As the two unlikely companions fight their way towards Black Fire Pass, Annaliese discovers within herself powers of courage and faith that inspire all around her. With a grizzled witch hunter and a dwarf warrior, the heroes battle alongside the armies of the Empire and the dwarfs, above and below the earth, against greenskin tribes and the hordes of Chaos. Together, they must find their courage and help turn back the tides of darkness, lest all of the Empire be lost.

A WARHAMMER NOVEL

EMPIRE IN CHAOS

ANTHONY REYNOLDS

For Joy, a woman full of life, love and poetry, and the baker of the dreaded curried shortbread.

A BLACK LIBRARY PUBLICATION

First published in Great Britain in 2008 by
BL Publishing,
Games Workshop Ltd.,
Willow Road, Nottingham,
NG7 2WS, UK

10 9 8 7 6 5 4 3 2 1

Cover illustration by Petrol.
Map by Nuala Kinrade.

With thanks to EA Mythic.

A CIP record for this book is available from the British Library.

ISBN 13: 978 1 84416 527 8
ISBN 10: 1 84416 527 2

Distributed in the US by Simon & Schuster
1230 Avenue of the Americas, New York, NY 10020.

See the Black Library on the Internet at
www.blacklibrary.com

Find out more about Games Workshop
and the world of Warhammer at
www.games-workshop.com

Find out more about Warhammer Online - Age of Reckoning at
www.warhammeronline.com

THIS IS A DARK age, a bloody age, an age of daemons and of sorcery. It is an age of battle and death, and of the world's ending. Amidst all of the fire, flame and fury it is a time, too, of mighty heroes, of bold deeds and great courage.

AT THE HEART of the Old World sprawls the Empire, the largest and most powerful of the human realms. Known for its engineers, sorcerers, traders and soldiers, it is a land of great mountains, mighty rivers, dark forests and vast cities. And from his throne in Altdorf reigns the Emperor Karl-Franz, sacred descendant of the founder of these lands, Sigmar, and wielder of his magical warhammer.

BUT THESE ARE far from civilised times. Across the length and breadth of the Old World, from the knightly palaces of Bretonnia to ice-bound Kislev in the far north, come rumblings of war. In the towering World's Edge Mountains, the orc tribes are gathering for another assault. Bandits and renegades harry the wild southern lands of the Border Princes. There are rumours of rat-things, the skaven, emerging from the sewers and swamps across the land. And from the northern wildernesses there is the ever-present threat of Chaos, of daemons and beastmen corrupted by the foul powers of the Dark Gods. As the time of battle draws ever nearer, the Empire needs heroes like never before.

PROLOGUE

THUNDER ROLLED ACROSS the sky and clouds heavy and pregnant with rain hung low over the land. A malformed figure stood leaning awkwardly on a shovel, his thick, mud-caked features set in an expression of idiocy as he watched Udo Grunwald's approach.

Up through the mud and the waste Udo trudged, leading a half-starved mule that struggled beneath the weight of the cart it hauled up the incline towards the temple.

The wretched beast strained as the uneven, swollen wheels of the cart turned laboriously, carving a pair of deep furrows through the mud. A dark cloak of oiled leather covered Udo's large shoulders, and he wore a heavy crossbow upon his back. His shaven head was bare to the elements, and his face was thuggish, his nose having been broken and badly set more than once and his jaw heavy and protruding. The malformed servant of the temple grinned stupidly as he passed. He stared hard at the simpleton for a moment before he turned back to look upon the temple gateway.

Dominating the surrounding landscape with its brutal, martial architecture, the temple appeared more like a small fortress than a place of worship, as befitted the warrior deity it honoured. Carved statues adorned the buttresses, their features smoothed and crumbling from centuries of attack from the elements. These were the saints of this priesthood, warriors all, the devout of holy Sigmar. Each was heavily armoured in mail and plate and bore weapons – hammers and flails.

Through the arched, fortified gateway he walked, under the raised portcullis that hung like an array of deadly teeth, and into the dimly lit cobbled passageway leading to the temple courtyard. He led the mule and cart through the gatehouse, murder holes and arrow slits watching his progress darkly.

Dozens of pairs of eyes tracked his approach, men-at-arms upon the ramparts leaning on tall, broad-bladed halberds, cold-eyed priests with the arms of blacksmiths, and muddy servants of all ages, some crippled and deformed. A heavy-set soldier in studded leather blocked his path; Udo glared at him. After a quick look into the cart, the soldier stepped aside without comment.

Udo stopped in the centre of the courtyard before the great double-doors of the temple. The mule sagged in exhaustion, its bones pushing against its thin skin. Udo strode to the back of the cart, and glanced down upon its flat bed, at the dead body lying there – the dead body of his employer.

Dressed in knee-high black riding boots, uniform black trousers, shirt and vest, and a black shoulder-cloak with a purple lining, the corpse could have been that of any wealthy young Empire noble with a penchant for morbid colours, but it was the combination of these clothes with the wide-brimmed black hat, the pair of ornate wheel-lock pistols on his wide belt and the prominent bronze talisman that hung around the corpse's pallid neck that gave away his true calling.

Witch hunter.

A calling that filled even the innocent with dread and guilt.

Ruthless and without pity, the witch hunters stalked the lands of the Empire, rooting out corruption, sorcery and mutation wherever it was to be found. To even be suspected of infernal dealings was to be subject to the witch hunter's cruel ministrations, and many confessed to crimes they had no knowledge of merely to achieve a swift death.

One of the great doors of the temple creaked open, and an ancient, broad-shouldered figure emerged, his breath turning to steam in the cold air. Adorned in simple robes of deepest red, his only adornment a pin on his breast in the shape of a warhammer, the priest had clearly once been a powerful warrior, but the cruelness of time had robbed him of his strength. His skin was heavily lined and covered with liver spots, yet he moved with an assurance that belied his age.

The priest stepped down the broad steps of the temple and came to a halt before Udo. His eyes were slightly cloudy, but there was strength there still. His face was grim, set in a deep frown that looked like it had not moved in several decades, and he acknowledged Udo's presence with a sour nod.

'I will inform the abbot that you have brought his body back to us,' the old priest said dourly, looking upon the broken body of the witch hunter. Even the dark clothes of the corpse could not hide the terrible wounds that had killed him – the savage tears in his flesh that were caused by no human hand.

Udo thought back to that night, only seven nights earlier. He saw again the painted flesh of the feather-cloaked zealot ripple as *things* clawed within him. He saw again the horrific carnage that followed.

The elderly priest turned to climb the stairs leading within the temple once more. He paused after a step, and turned his rheumy gaze towards the face of the cloaked man.

'Come,' he said. 'Your old master spoke well of you. The Temple of Sigmar has much it wishes to discuss with you.'

BOOK ONE

THE ARMIES OF *Destruction march against the Empire.*

From the east come the greenskin hordes, massing beyond the Worlds Edge Mountains in the Dark Lands, gathering in numbers not seen since the age of holy Sigmar, before the foundation of the Empire. The dwarfs are stalwart defenders, but I fear that even their great, ancient holds will not have the strength to stem the tide.

Far to the west, beyond the Great Ocean, our allies the high elves of Ulthuan are beset by their hated dark kin, hampering their efforts to come to our plight.

And to the north comes the greatest threat of all, for the hordes of Chaos, they who have sold their immortal souls into damnation, are marching upon us once again.

The Raven Host, an army mustered for the sole purpose of the destruction of the Empire, advances against us. Already they have swept through the Peak Pass, and overrun the lands of our allies the Kislevites in the frozen north.

Dispatches from the Tsarina have informed me that the great city of Praag itself is besieged.

War has been met in the northern states, and war parties are pushing south towards the Talabec as I write this. Towns and cities are being sacked even as the electors gather their armies. Already my people are being butchered, but I know that this is merely the beginning of a far greater conflict that threatens to overwhelm us.

Elector Hertwig of the Ostermark struggles to hold back the tide, and von Raukov of Ostland has already lost much of his state army. Todbringer of Middenland musters his forces north of the Talabec, but I fear even his martial skill will do little against the overwhelming hatred driving the enemy. The electors bicker amongst themselves, bringing ancient enmities and feuds to the surface in this our time of greatest peril. The temples of Sigmar and Ulric are at loggerheads, and I fear what shall come to pass if a reconciliation cannot be achieved.

A great plague is sweeping the lands, striking down thousands of my citizens beneath its unnatural pestilence. My agents of the Order of the Griffon are even now investigating the source of this dire sickness, and all fingers point towards its sorcerous nature – it would seem that this is a ploy of the enemy, to weaken our resolve as their first forays strike against us. It has even reached the streets of Altdorf itself – it seems that nowhere is safe from the vile pestilence.

The doomsayers predict that this is the dawning of the End Times. I fear that they may speak the truth.

K.F.

CHAPTER ONE

THE FLAMES CRACKLED, curling around the fresh wood like infernal, flaming tongues. Annaliese Jaeger stared deep into the glowing blaze, lost within its destructive beauty.

Though she could feel the heat from the fireplace reddening her face, it did nothing to dispel the icy chill that pervaded the darkened room of the cabin. No matter how much wood she stacked within the fireplace, no matter how high the flames rose, the intense cold would not lift. It was like the cruel touch of death itself – unstoppable, and so, so cold.

The window in the small room was obscured by a heavy, moth-eaten curtain that had once been a deep green but had long since faded. Beams of cold, grey light slipped through where the moths had eaten completely through the fraying material. The timber beams of the roof sagged as if the weight of existence was too much to bear, and a rug covered the uneven wooden floorboards. There was no furniture within the room bar an old straw pallet upon the floor, and a low chair beside it. In better times, her father would sit in that chair before the fire, lost in his thoughts.

Annaliese tore her dead-eyed gaze from the fire and back to the pale, grey face of her father. She prayed that she would remember him as the powerful man that he had been – not this wasted skeleton breathing painfully beneath the heavy, sweat-drenched blankets. His once strongly muscled arms were now little more than skin and bone, wasted away as the sickness ravaged his body. For four days he had remained in this comatose state, neither waking nor uttering a sound. It was only the nigh-on imperceptible rise and fall of his sunken chest that told her he still lived.

It would not be for long, if Morr were merciful.

Merciful! She almost laughed at the thought. What mercy there was in the world had long since abandoned the people of Averland.

Winter still held the land tightly to its icy bosom, as it had done for almost five months, long after the thaw should have come and gone. Snow was banked up outside. The crops in the fields had long withered and perished in the frozen earth, and none of the hardy, long-coated sheep farmed in the area had survived. Death was prevalent, particularly amongst the elderly and infirm, and there had even been blood spilt amongst the desperate villagers, disputes over the scarce supply of blankets, firewood and food. Adelmo Haefen, the village's quietly spoken miller, had been stabbed in the stomach only two days past after an altercation over a loaf of bread.

But the harshness of the winter was as nothing compared to what had come next.

A deranged, half-naked wretch had come to the village almost three weeks ago. Nails had been hammered into the bones of his arms, and his back was stripped of flesh, the skin hanging in loose, bloody rents. Upon his forehead a crude shape of a twin-tailed comet had been carved, both dried and fresh blood covered his face.

He had screamed and ranted of the end of the world, proclaiming that death was coming and that he was its herald. In accompaniment to his doom-laden, fiery screech, he lashed himself with a flail of leather straps studded with metal barbs.

And the flagellant had been correct, but possibly not in the way that he had imagined, for he had brought the plague with him. He had collapsed within the day, falling into a deathly coma from which he could not be roused.

Within days dozens of villagers were struck down seemingly at random, and it was not long before families who had tolled the land for dozens of generations were packing their belongings into carts usually used to transport goods to market, heading for the ethereal safety of far away cities: Nuln, Averheim and Wissenburg. But gossip said that the plague was rife even on the streets of the Empire's capital, Altdorf, and that is when true panic had set in.

Each day more victims were dragged to the trade guildhall that overlooked the village square. This decaying building with its sunken, uneven roof and perilously leaning walls had long sat unused, and it had been decided that it would be converted into a makeshift quarantined hospice. Its doors and windows were kept locked, shuttered and barred, and warning signs were driven into the ground around its circumference. For those who could not read the Reikspiel lettering on these boards, which was most of the common folk of the Empire, the intention of the signs was made very clear – skulls of dead livestock daubed with the mark of Morr hung from them, along with the rotting bodies of dead rats, black birds, and other grisly trophies warning of plague and pestilence.

The village burgher had fled in the dead of night, abandoning his post and the villagers to their fate. There was no one to bake the bread, for the baker, his wife and his apprentices had all been early victims, and they lay comatose and wasting away within the rising filth of the guildhall. The local butcher, who doubled as the local apothecary and was the closest thing the village had to a healer, had succumbed to the early stages of the wasting sickness. There was now none who dared enter the deathly building to tend to the sick and dying. Each morning the local men of the village drew straws to determine who was to drag the newly discovered plague victims into the building, covering their mouths and noses with cloths as they rapidly dumped their charges inside and relocked the doors.

As yet, it was unknown if any of the plague victims had died, but it was believed that none had awoken from the deathly state that came some three days after the initial symptoms were identified. Certainly there was no one trying to get out of the horrific hospice.

Annaliese looked again at the wasted face of her father. Only a week ago he had been in the peak of health. She had refused to take him to the hellish quarantine guildhall – she would be damned if she would let him spend his last hours rotting in that festering place among the dead and the dying.

The sound of angry voices carried over the cabin from the village below, and Annaliese rose to her feet. She drew aside the heavy, dusty curtains and opened the dirty window to see what the commotion was. Shielding her eyes against the sudden glare that came off the snow, she could see a cluster of men, some wearing the provincial yellow and black uniforms of Averland state soldiers, trudging through the muddy slush. Some were brandishing weapons – halberds, pitchforks and clubs – and their shouting was drawing more onlookers from their homes and their misery.

With a worried glance at her father, she bit her lip in indecision. Strangers to the village had brought nothing but trouble and sadness of late, and she feared what this new drama would bring. Still, she was drawn by a morbid curiosity to witness this new arrival. Her father did not seem to be any worse than he had been for the last two days, so she made her decision. Drawing her sheepskin coat around her tightly, she opened the door to the cabin and stepped out into the winter. She would only be a moment away from her father's side.

As she walked down the hill, the crisp snow crunching underfoot and making her long dress wet where it dragged, she saw men pushing and prodding a bound and gagged prisoner before them. She saw one soldier club the bound figure to the ground where it was brutally kicked by three or more men before being dragged back up to its feet.

She saw a flash of long, silken black hair before the figure disappeared into the crowd again. Some of the men were carrying burning torches, and there were angry, raised voices shouting for blood.

A crowd was gathering in the village square. None stood too close to the guildhall, and many covered their mouths and noses with dirty rags and strips of cloth. Hugging herself for warmth, she went to stand beside Johann Weiss, a portly villager with heavy jowls.

'What's happening?' she asked Johann quietly. He was the innkeeper of her workplace, and she had known him since childhood.

'Three families left the village yesterday, all their possessions packed onto a single cart,' he said, his voice devoid of emotion but his eyes tired and sad. Annaliese nodded fearfully. She had known the daughters of the families well.

'They were murdered on the road. Not even the little ones were spared. This,' he said with a nod of his head, 'is one of those responsible.'

Grief and horror washed over Annaliese, and the innkeeper put a fatherly arm around her shoulders.

The men dragged their murderous captive into the centre of the village square. A solid, ancient gibbet stood there as it had done for countless decades, a blackened metal cage hanging from its crossbar. She had always felt a horrible loathing for the thing, and when she was young had sat aside as other children threw rocks at the condemned.

A skeleton was slumped within the torturous, black iron device, the remnants of a thief who had been placed there a year before as a warning to others. The heavy chains holding the grisly remains aloft were slackened, and the metal cage plummeted to the ground with a crash and a cheer from the crowd.

Leonard Horst, a reed-thin villager with the stilted, stiff movements of a hunting stork climbed onto a rotting bale of hay, waving a hand for silence. He was the village warden, and a man with a reputation for harshness. He had once beaten a trader to death, it was said, for attempting to bypass paying his road tax. Nevertheless, he was a respected man, for none doubted his devotion to the village and its people.

'The farrier Hellmaan and his family, and the families of his two sisters, have been brutally murdered on the road to Averheim,' Horst said, his voice bitter and filled with hatred. Those in the crowd before him held weapons clenched tightly in their hands, their faces angry. The two men holding the captive pinned to the ground tightened their grip.

'We return with one of their murderers: a hateful, black-hearted killer of elven kind.'

There were several gasps from the gathered villagers. Most had come to believe that elves were nothing more than stories told to children.

'An elf?' breathed Annaliese. She stepped away from the innkeeper and inched further down the hill, to better see the captive.

'Hang him!' called a man, and others shouted their agreement.

'Burn him alive!' another roared, a pronouncement that was greeted with a cheer.

'Oh, we shall do much worse than that to him,' said the stick-thin figure of Horst from the rotten hay bale. 'He must be made to suffer long for the savagery that he unleashed upon those poor families.'

His voice rose in pitch, anger and bitterness fuelling his diatribe.

'Let us gag his mouth that he may not incant his vile sorceries or cry out to his hateful gods for aid. Let us raise him in the gallows and pelt him with stones and rocks. Let us cut out his eyes and feed them to the crows! After a week in the cage, let us drag him forth and quarter him, his entrails carried to the four corners of the village. Then he and all his hated kin shall fear us, and know the true vengeance of Averland!'

A huge roar rose from the gathered crowd, and Annaliese was shocked and horrified to see her neighbours, good hearted and caring people, baying for blood and torture, their faces twisted into masks of hatred. She realised that it was fear and desperation that was fuelling this emotion – a need to blame someone for their horrific, hopeless predicament.

She saw the black haired elf pulled to his feet, glimpsing his pale, arrogant profile for the first time. Almost as white as the crispest snow, his face was angular and long, his eyes large, dark and almond shaped. He was aloof and distant despite the bruises and blood upon him, and she saw how he stood against the mob with his head held high.

Screeching metal accompanied the opening of the cage. The skeleton within was kicked free and the elf was dragged towards the vacant iron device. He struggled against his captors. Breaking the grip that one had on him, he smashed his elbow into the man's face, crushing his nose. With inhuman swiftness he kicked another state soldier in the face, and then spun, rolling his wrist so that the arm of the one holding him was turned until the elbow was facing the sky. With a sharp downward strike the elf shattered the joint of the soldier's overextended arm.

A heavy mallet smashed into the back of the elf's head, and his body went limp. Swearing, blood pumping from his nose, the first of the fallen men rose to his feet with a dagger in his hands and murder in his eyes. He stepped towards the slumped elf, but Horst stopped him with a hand on his chest.

'We will make sure his suffering is long and drawn out,' he hissed. The man sheathed his knife with a curse, and spat upon the elf.

The barely conscious elf, blood covering the back of his head, was dragged to the torturous man-shaped cage. He was pushed within the tight confines, and the cage door slammed shut. A rusted old padlock as large as a man's head was clamped shut, sealing him within. He had no room to move. Half unconscious and bleeding, the elf was hauled up into the air. Rocks and rotten food pelted him.

Not wanting to see any more, and anxious to be with her father, Annaliese pushed against the crowd around her, panicked and sickened at the hate, fear and murderous intent she saw on the faces of those around her. Tears in her eyes, she pushed free of the frenzied mob, and ran back up through the snow towards her home.

Annaliese slammed the door behind her, breathing hard, wracking sobs rocking her body. She could still hear the muted shouts of the villagers, a dire sound of venomous hate fuelled by fear and despair.

Moving to the small kitchen adjoining the main room, she plunged her hands into a bucket of water and washed her face. The water was icy cold, and an involuntary shiver ran through her. She brushed her

long blonde hair back away from her face and took a
deep breath, calming herself.

If the elf truly did murder those families, then he
deserved death, she thought – but not a long, torturous
death. That was savage and barbaric.

She took another deep breath. That's when she heard
the first screams.

Running through the cabin, she burst through the
front door to see a very different scene than that she
had just left. People were running in all directions, and
she saw blood splashed across the snow. There was
screaming and shouting, and her first thought was that
the elf had somehow escaped, or that his allies had
come to rescue him. But no, she could still see his
caged form hanging aloft above the bloodshed below.

She saw a warrior dressed in the yellow and black of
a state soldier in the pay of the Elector of Averland
rolling in the slush, fighting with a drably dressed villager. Two other plainly clothed men dragged another
to the ground, their hands around his throat. Others
were knocked to the ground by the press of bodies
seeking escape. What was going on? What madness was
this?

There was a solid thump that shook the floorboards,
and Annaliese started. It had come from her father's
room, and a moment later there was a scrape of wood
on wood, and a crash. It sounded like the chair by her
father's palette being pushed back and toppling to the
floor. Tearing herself away from the insane, murderous
savagery below, she stepped warily into the centre of
the living area to better see into her father's room, her
heart pounding in her chest. Floorboards creaked
beneath her feet.

Dimly she perceived a low hanging mist coiling within the dark room. She saw the dark shape of a man on all fours beside the palette, and her heart skipped a beat. Her father was alive, and up out of his bed!

'Father!' she cried as she rushed to his side. As soon as she entered the room the temperature fell markedly. The fire that had been raging when she had left the cabin earlier had died away completely, and a ribbon of smoke rose from the blackened logs.

Annaliese dropped to her knees, putting an arm around her father's bony shoulders. His flesh radiated an icy chill through the rough linen undershirt covering his skin. His head hung low, and his lank dark hair fell down over his face.

'Father', she said once again, tears welling in her eyes. Days ago she had resigned herself to his passing.

He turned his face towards her. She had a glimpse of blue-tinged lips, and saw that her father's eyes were closed. His skin was grey and ashen, and she could see blue veins criss-crossing within.

Her father's cold blue lips curled into a sickly grin that made her skin crawl, and she felt revulsion and horror run through her for a moment. Then he began to convulse, his wasted muscles tensing as his entire body went into uncontrollable spasms. He fell to his back, and sickly, yellow froth bubbled at the corners of his still grinning lips. Annaliese cried out, not knowing what to do. She grasped her father's head tightly in her arms, holding him to her bosom in an effort to stop him smashing his head against the floorboards in his seizure.

It was over in a moment, and he went completely limp. Breathing heavily with the shock, Annaliese carefully laid her father's head back down against the floor. She could not hear him breathing, and she felt for a pulse on his wasted, scrawny neck. There was none.

Closing her eyes, Annaliese allowed exhaustion and despair to wash over her. She couldn't remember when last she had slept, and her entire body heaved with sobs from the shock of her father's dying fit.

She opened her eyes to see a cold pair of eyes regarding her.

Blue flames flickered within the sunken sockets of her father's face, and Annaliese felt the edges of her sanity begin to fray.

She screamed involuntarily and scrambled backwards across the floor. The thing that had once been her father pushed itself onto its stomach, and began to claw its way across the floorboards towards her, fingernails digging into the floorboards. Its movements were jerky and stilted, as if it were some twisted marionette and someone was plucking at its strings.

Its face was still locked in a hideous grinning rictus, a manic death-grimace, and eyes of blue fire blazed coldly.

CHAPTER TWO

UDO REMOVED HIS wide-brimmed black hat, and ran a gloved hand across his shaven head. If there had been hair growing there it would have had grey in it, as there was in his moustache and the salt-and-pepper stubble that covered his thick jaw. You are getting old, he thought to himself. His legs were sore, and he cursed again the bastards who had stolen his horse.

He had been returning to the tall, black stallion after relieving himself up against a tree when he came upon them. There had been three of them, rough men that had the look of deserters about them, and they were struggling to keep the stallion from bucking.

So intent were they on the powerful steed that they didn't notice the appearance of Grunwald until he calmly killed the first with a bolt through the back of the neck.

The would-be thief was killed instantly and the reins fell from his limp hand. The powerful stallion lashed out with its hooves, slamming another of the men to the ground. Grunwald had stalked forwards then, his dark coat billowing out behind him, dropping his heavy crossbow to the ground. He hefted a heavy, flanged mace in one hand and with the other he drew an ornate, gold-worked pistol – one of the weapons of his former master. The brigand struck by the horse struggled to his feet, and the pistol boomed deafeningly. The lead shot slammed into his head, sending a mist of blood out behind him as he fell.

The third man, a small, weasely individual, leapt into the saddle of the bucking horse, the reins held tightly in his hands.

'It will be better for you if you get off my horse now,' said Grunwald. The outlaw spat in response, and kicked the stallion into a gallop.

It had not been hard to follow his trail across the destitute lands of Stirland.

The three were part of a larger group that were preying on the weakened local people. The plague had desolated much of the region, and the armies of Graf Alberich Haupt-Anderssen, the Elector Count of Stirland, were scouring the land, killing and burning the bodies of those infected by the foul contagion.

The wretches that Grunwald was now hunting were parasites, eking out an existence by taking advantage of the horrific situation that the Empire found itself in. Low-life scavengers, they were looting abandoned settlements and villages, and preying upon those fleeing with all their worldly possessions. Grunwald had learnt from his inquiries that they had been pressed into service in the armies of the Graf to fight the terrible threat that pressed from the north, but had deserted their posts, fleeing into the wilderness rather than stand and fight for the good of the Empire.

Grunwald's face was dark. It sickened him that while tens of thousands of loyal soldiers were fighting and dying in the north to protect the Empire, there were others such as these who were abandoning their posts and preying on innocents. He would ensure that these men were punished for their crimes.

But none of those crimes was as heinous as the one they had committed the day before. They had come across a rural chapel devoted to Sigmar, and in an act of extreme sacrilege, they had stolen the offering pot and knocked a statue of the holy deity to the ground in their haste to leave. By such actions they had doomed themselves. The bruised and battered priest had been shamefaced as he spoke of how he had been overcome by the ruffians, and Grunwald's brutish face was set in an angry expression as he recalled the incident.

He hated this land, Stirland. Always poor, and living in the shadow of the cursed realm of Sylvania, it seemed to breed corruption and wretchedness. The grim landscape, with its fields of wasted crops, oppressive dark forests and bleak mountains merely seemed to feed the feeling of hopelessness that pervaded the life of the Stirlanders.

Darkness was falling quickly, and the thick clouds overhead ensured no light from moon or star would reveal him. Twisted trees loomed like dark, malevolent presences around him, and Grunwald began to crawl forwards through the snow once more, drawing towards the bored sentry.

Rising up behind the man, he placed one gloved hand around his mouth while the other ripped a knife across his throat. He pulled the man down into the snow without a sound, holding him tightly as he convulsed, his warm blood soaking into the pristine white snow.

After weeks of tracking these doomed bandits, he gloried in the feeling of satisfaction as he watched the life slip from the ruffian's eyes.

Concealing the body beneath a fallen log, Grunwald pressed on, slipping between the thick boles of the dense trees. He cursed as he looked over the deserters' camp. There were at least half a dozen of them lounging around a fire, but that was not what made the witch hunter swear.

There were no horses tethered at the campsite – but there was an unmistakable equine shape roasting on a heavy spit over a fire.

A battle trained stallion bred from the line of the finest warhorses of Averland, the horse was worth an Elector's ransom, and these ignorant fools were roasting it.

Grunwald pushed himself flat in the snow as he heard a voice rise in alarm. He readied himself for violence. Had they found the sentry already? That was unlikely – he had watched the camp for almost an hour before he had made his move, and he was fairly certain that there would be no one checking up on him for a good few hours. He strained to hear the muffled conversation.

'…down the path,' he made out.

'…tracking us?' came the reply, a deeper voice than the first. Grunwald carefully elbowed himself forward.

He saw a slight man – the one that had ridden off with his horse – talking to a more solidly built outlaw. Once he might have been well proportioned, but it looked as though his muscle had long since run to fat.

'Don't think so, sergeant' said the smaller man.

'I told you not to damn well call me that!'

'Sorry. Lone traveller by the looks of it. A dwarf, heavily armoured. Got himself a heavy looking pack, too. Must be something in there worth takin' – gold perhaps. Everyone knows his kind hoard it, countin' their wealth while us Stirlanders starve.'

The bigger brigand grunted.

'Would certainly be rude to pass up such an opportunity, 'specially when it appears on our doorstep. Right, let's get moving then, you pack of worthless whoresons,' he said, kicking out at the dozing men.

Grunwald swore once again. He had been planning on moving through the darkness and killing each of the sentries in turn before turning on the sleeping camp. He sighed, and began crawling backwards through the trees, away from the campsite.

THE SHORT, BROAD-shouldered figure of Thorrik Lokrison hummed tunelessly to himself as he sat before a small fireplace. A solid pot of black iron was balanced on top of a small pile of rocks within the fire, and a heavy pack lay in the snow beside him, an object wrapped in oiled leather carefully positioned on top of it.

A round metal shield leant against the log on which Thorrik sat, a stylised embossed bearded face in its centre and intricate bronze weave-work running around the rim, Besides the shield was a single-bladed axe, runes and more intricate bronze-work adorning it.

Belching loudly, Thorrik leant over the steaming broth bubbling away within the iron pot, savouring the aroma of the heavy, stodgy food, before leaning back and resuming his humming.

He had removed his helmet, but was otherwise covered in heavy armour from head to toe. The only exposed skin that could be seen was his forehead, bulbous nose and ruddy cheeks, the rest of his face framed by a finely wrought chainmail coif and a prodigious plaited beard. That beard was woven with bronze wire and hung down over his ornately worked breastplate. The plaits were adorned with metal discs, stylised faces engraved upon them.

With a heavy, gauntleted hand, the dwarf stirred the meaty broth with a chunky metal spoon.

'Smells good, friend,' came a voice from behind him that sounded anything but friendly. Thorrik's features darkened. He had not heard the man's approach.

Rising to his feet he picked up his axe and turned to face this human that was interrupting his supper. Eyes as hard as stone glinted from beneath his bushy eyebrows. His gaze flicked left and right, seeing that there were six men fanning out around him. Two had bows in their hands, while the others were armed with swords and axes, though they were not drawn. He settled on the overweight figure in the centre of the group, the one who had spoken. A towering brute, he wore tattered clothes dyed yellow and green and a heavy fur over his shoulders. Beside him was a slight, pinch-faced man that looked to Thorrik not unlike one of the stinking grobi that infest the depths beneath the mountains, though his skin was not green as were those hated enemies of his kin.

"'Tis a cold and wintry night to be out here alone, friend,' said the overweight man, his voice dripping with threat. 'Would you not like some company? I would dearly like to try that fine smelling food you are preparing.'

'I'd say you have eaten your fair share of food for two lifetimes, manling,' growled the dwarf.

The leader of the group laughed at that, and grobi-face gave a sycophantic chuckle. The remainder of the group made no reaction – their eyes were hard.

'No need for hostility, friend dwarf, though I dare say you are right in your estimation,' said the man, a brutish smile upon his big, jowled face as he patted his prodigious belly. 'We are merely loyal soldiers of the Empire seeking to warm ourselves at your camp. May we? I assure you, we mean you no harm.'

Thorrik tightened his grip on his axe, frowning.

'There is no Stirland state patrol within twenty miles and you 'aint scouts or militia,' he said gruffly. 'I'd say you are deserters. Cowards. Your word is worth less than pig shit.'

The smile dropped from the leader of the outlaws' face.

'Brave words for someone so heavily outnumbered, dwarf.'

His greedy eyes flicked towards Thorrik's pack, and the object wrapped in leather on top of it.

'Give us your belongings, and we will be on our way. No harm need come to you, friend.'

'Call me friend once more, pig face, and I will carve the fat from your bones,' growled the dwarf. 'Where are your companions? I thought it would take more of you cowardly dogs to pluck up the courage to rob a clan warrior of Karaz-a-Karak.'

One of the deserters, grobi-face, looked around him. 'Where's Anton, sergeant? And Valdar?'

'Shut your hole,' snarled the big outlaw. 'The time for niceties is over, dwarf. Shoot him.'

The two archers drew back their bows, and Thorrik roared a war cry in Khazalid, the dwarfen tongue. Hefting his axe, he surged forwards. There was a flash of movement in the darkness further up the trail, and one of the archers fell, a black bolt protruding from his neck. The other archer fired, the arrow streaking through the air towards the dwarf.

Thorrik turned his shoulder into the path of the arrow, and it skidded off one of his heavy gromril pauldrons, unable to penetrate or even dent the thick metal plate. He closed the distance to the leader of the outlaws with surprising swiftness, and the big outlaw swore as he stepped backwards to make more room for himself, drawing a massive double-handed greatsword from his back.

A brigand darted in from the left, a short sword stabbing towards the dwarf's exposed face. With a powerful swipe of his arm, Thorrik deflected the blow with his armoured forearm and slammed his axe into the man's neck, and blood fountained from the mortal wound.

Thorrik saw an ugly brute of a man appear from the darkness and a pistol boomed, shattering the leg of another of the outlaws, who fell screaming to the ground. The newcomer wore a dark great-cloak, and had a broad-brimmed hat upon his head. A heavy black breastplate protected his chest, and his body was criss-crossed with buckles and straps from which hung an impressive array of knives and deadly implements.

Then the newcomer was amongst them, his mace pulverising the face of one who had turned to face this new threat.

Thorrik stalked towards the overweight leader of the outlaws, aware of the axe-man stepping to his flank but keeping his eyes locked on the fat man the other had called sergeant.

'What's the matter, *friend*?' he snarled, his voice gravelly. 'Things not turning out how you had hoped?'

Thorrik saw an arrow fired in haste glance over the shaven-headed man's shoulder, and saw the archer draw a long knife from his boot. The thug lunged, but the dark-clad figure caught his wrist, keeping the knife turned away from him. A heavy mace smashed down onto the brigand's shoulder, shattering it with a sickening crunch. He screamed in agony and dropped to his knees. His cries were silenced as the mace swung in and crushed his skull.

Thorrik turned as the axe-man to his right darted forwards, and he deflected the descending axe blade with his own. Twisting the blade, he knocked the axe-man off balance and into the path of the outlaw leader who had stepped forwards swinging his greatsword murderously. The outlaw pulled the blow with some difficulty, and stopped just short of cleaving his comrade in two.

The dwarf stepped forwards and smashed his axe into the brigand's knee, and he fell heavily.

The leader of the outlaws spun, feeling a presence behind him, turning to see a pistol levelled at his head. He stood frozen for a moment, like a deer caught in the light of a lantern, his eyes wide and staring. Then the trigger was squeezed and the man's head was blown apart in a spray of bone and blood.

There were no more outlaws standing, though several of them were moaning in pain from their prone positions in the snow.

'I didn't need your damn help,' growled Thorrik, squinting up at the shaven-headed man.

'And I didn't come to your aid,' replied the man, holstering his smoking pistol. 'I have been hunting these men for several days.'

'Rob you, did they?' asked Thorrik. The man nodded his head.

'Stole my horse.'

The dwarf grunted in response.

'Get it back?'

'No,' came the reply. The man moved to one of the wounded men who was moaning in pain. Without ceremony he slashed the outlaw's throat with his knife, and moved on to the next. 'These bastards ate it.'

'Ah,' said Thorrik, wiping the blood from his axe head on the tunic of one of the dead men. 'Good eating, horse.'

The man glared at Thorrik, but the dwarf ignored the manling and sat down heavily, stirring his steaming broth.

He glanced up from his now overcooked supper, scowling, and watched as the man found the last of the living outlaws. The injured deserter had tried to crawl away, leaving a bloody trail behind him, and Thorrik watched in silence as the dark-clad man placed his knee in the small of the outlaw's back, and pulled the brigand's head back. It was grobi-face, and he whimpered in fear. Without hesitation, his throat was cut.

LEAVING THE DYING outlaw where he lay, Grunwald picked his way back through the snow and retrieved his heavy crossbow from where he had dropped it before joining the fight in close. The dwarf was sitting smoking an ornate, dragon-headed pipe when he returned.

'May I?' he asked, indicating towards a large stone opposite the log where Thorrik sat.

The dwarf grunted, which Grunwald took as assent. He sat down heavily, and began wiping and blowing the snow from the firing mechanism of his heavy crossbow.

'You fight well,' he said when it became clear that the dwarf was not going to initiate a conversation.

Again the dwarf grunted.

'You as well,' he said eventually. 'For a manling.'

'My name is Udo Grunwald.' He extended a black-gloved hand towards the dwarf, who gave a long puff on his pipe before he extended his own hand, ensconced within his heavy gauntlet. To Grunwald, the dwarf's grip felt like it was crushing the bones of his hand.

'Thorrik Lokrison, Ironbreaker of the mining Clan Barad of Karaz-a-Karak, guardian of the Ungdrin.' Grunwald noted that the dwarf had a strong grasp of Reikspiel, the language of the Empire, though it was heavily accented.

'Karaz-a-Karak...' said Grunwald, forming the strange dwarfen words with some difficulty. Clearly his pronunciation was inadequate, for Thorrik scowled.

'It is the greatest of all the dwarfen holds, the seat of the High King himself. In the tongues of men it is known as the Everpeak.'

'Ah,' said Grunwald, recognising the name. 'That is far across the Worlds Edge and Black Mountains to the south-east, is it not?'

'Such are the names known by manlings, aye,' said Thorrik gruffly.

'You are a long way from home, Thorrik.'

'Thank you for reminding me,' said the dwarf sharply. He took a long pull on his pipe, eyes glittering angrily. He sighed heavily. 'It has been eight years since I have seen the great hold.'

Grunwald's eyebrows rose. 'A long time to be away.'

'To your kind, manling. But aye, it has been too long.'

'What has kept you from returning these past eight years?'

'A throng was raised from Karaz-a-Karak at the High King's order nine years ago. The warriors of Clan Barad responded to this call, and I was a part of their muster. For seven years we have been engaged in the north of your Empire, bolstering your defence against the hordes massing in the north.'

'You have been fighting within the Empire, to protect our border?' asked Grunwald. His estimation of the dwarf and his kin rose steeply.

'Aye. The High King takes the oath sworn by King Kurgan very seriously.'

'King Kurgan…'

He knew the name, for it was said that the king fought alongside blessed Sigmar in his battles against the greenskins.

'That was… thousands of years ago.'

'An oath is an oath,' growled Thorrik. 'Enough talk.' He retrieved a heavy metal bowl, spooned out a generous portion of his stew and handed it to Grunwald, who thanked him with a nod. The dwarf spooned out his own portion, and began to eat noisily. Grunwald stabbed the pieces of meat on the end of his knife. The food was heavy and simple, but flavoursome. Thorrik grumbled about it being overcooked.

'Wasn't much meat on this goat,' he said into his stew. 'Wish it was horse.' He punctuated this statement with a snort, and Grunwald wondered if he were making a joke.

After the meal, Thorrik offered Grunwald a spare pipe, but he politely declined, hoping that was not some breach of dwarfen etiquette. Thorrik merely shrugged and grunted, and took up his own pipe once more.

Cracking his neck to either side, Grunwald pushed himself to his feet, shouldering his heavy crossbow.

'I wish you well, Thorrik Lokrison,' he said. 'And I thank you for the food.'

The dwarf did not stand, but merely squinted up at him. He grunted what may have been a farewell, and took another long pull on his dragon-headed pipe.

Thorrik watched as Grunwald disappeared into the darkness. He seemed solid enough for a manling, and at least he did not talk as much as most of them. They were usually incessant with their inane chatter – as if they needed to cram too many words into their short lifetimes. He had long ago given up trying to understand the ways of the humans, and his eight years in the northern states of the Empire had only reinforced this.

But an oath was an oath.

He brushed the light dusting of snow off the oiled leather that protected the precious item he bore from harm.

Aye. An oath was an oath.

CHAPTER THREE

ANNALIESE SLAMMED INTO the doorframe as she scrabbled frantically backwards. She tried to push herself to her feet, but fell backwards out into the living area of the cabin in her haste to escape the horrific creature clawing its way towards her.

It pulled itself forward upon wasted, skeletal hands. It was still half wrapped in blankets, and it dragged them along behind it. Still it smiled its deathly grin, its eyes blazing with icy fire fixed on her.

'Father!' she cried out as she kicked backwards out of the grasp of the creature as it made to snatch at her leg. 'Father, it's me!'

It spoke then, but the voice was not the one she knew so well, nor did the creature's lips move in time with the words that were spoken.

She could not comprehend the garbled torrent of words, and with horror she realised that it was not a single voice at all – it sounded as though a multitude of creatures were attempting to speak to her at once, their voices blurring and overlapping.

'Tzch'aaaarkan gharbol'ankh'ha mesch'antar'mor,' drawled the strongest of the voices, a sound that made Annaliese's skin crawl.

Rising to her feet finally, she ran into the small, stone kitchen and slammed the heavy door behind her. Her terror granted her strength, and she dragged the heavy wooden counter in front of the door. She backed away and leant up against the shuttered window, breathing hard.

That *thing* was no longer her father. She prayed to Morr and to Sigmar that her father's soul had passed on, that this truly was just his abandoned flesh and that his soul did not live on in torment within the foul creature. The idea was horrific, and she wished she had not thought it.

There was the wet sound of rotten wood smashing, and a cold hand grabbed her around the throat. Splinters of damp wood sprayed in from the window behind her.

Annaliese tried to scream, but found she could not, as the cold strength of the hand tightened its grip. She grabbed at the arm, her fingernails tearing at flesh. She felt her fingers go numb against its unearthly cold.

A sibilant whispering came from behind her. It was the same host of voices that had whispered forth from the throat of the creature, only this was spoken right into her ear.

'Sth'aaark Tzch'aaaarkan,' it hissed.

She scrabbled around frantically as her vision began to waver, and her hand closed on a bone handled knife.

In an instant, she lifted the knife and hacked at the arm that pinned her to the wall, feeling ice-cold blood begin to flow. The grip did not relent, and she sawed frantically against the wrist of the creature. Cold blood washed over her, making the knife so slippery that she almost lost her grip on it. The blood made the creature's hand slippery as well, and with a lurch, Annaliese freed herself from its grasp, pushing away, gasping for air.

A heavy weight threw itself against the door leading to the living area, and the wooden counter rocked from the blow. She threw her weight against it, and turned to stare wide-eyed at the smashed shutters of the window. A heavy arm swept the remainder of the wood away, and she flinched.

She saw the shape of the monster silhouetted against the pristine white snow outside. She could see nothing of its features except for its eyes, blue flames that flickered and burned coldly. It reached forward and ripped the shattered shutters from their hinges, not noticing the thick splinters of wood that pierced its flesh.

'Always have a weapon to hand,' her father had always told her. 'And never allow yourself to be cornered – always have an escape route.'

Yet here she was, backed into a corner with nothing more than a carving knife. She cursed, knowing that on the other side of the wall was her father's precious sword, agonisingly out of reach. No matter how poor they had become, he had never even considered selling the blade, and Annaliese had never broached the subject. It was the last link he had to his former life as a soldier, and she knew that he missed those times. But one accident had taken all of that away from him when the thumb of his right hand, his sword hand, had been severed. There was no soldiering work for a warrior that could not hold a sword.

Flipping the knife around in her hand so that she held it downwards like a dagger, Annaliese leapt forward as the deathly creature began to clamber through the window frame, a ceaseless cacophony of hateful gibberish spilling from its throat. She slammed the knife into the side of creature's neck, the blade sinking to the hilt before ripping it free once again.

What would have been a fatal blow to any man barely slowed its advance. Reaching a blue-tinged arm further into the kitchen, it pulled itself through the window, falling with a limp thud upon the stone floor, dark, matted hair falling over its face.

Still, Annaliese didn't need to see its face to recognise that this creature was once Jonas Scriber, the farrier's apprentice. Its once ruddy, furnace-reddened face and arms were bereft of colour, and it pushed itself heavily to its feet, towering over the slight framed teenage girl. Its face, too, was set in a deathly grin, its broad features daemonically lit by flaming orbs. Its shirt was ripped open, and it bore several wounds, deep gashes in its skin that exposed the red muscle beneath. It lurched towards her, as if trying to embrace her in its massive arms.

She ducked and slashed her knife across its gut, slicing the skin open. She was knocked to the side as the wooden bench blocking the door was wrenched away by a powerful push from the other side of the door, and she stumbled towards the monster that had been Jonas.

One of its heavy arms clubbed her to the ground, the blow numbing her shoulder and arm.

The multitude of voices seemed to get more excited, and they spoke quickly, the garbled words spilling from its mouth in a horrid torrent of foul, insensible words.

Pushing up with all her force, she rammed the knife up into the soft flesh beneath the monster's chin. The blade punched up through the roof of its mouth, sliding on into its brain.

It twitched for a second, transfixed, and with a push with her shoulder she sent the creature sprawling backwards, the gore-covered knife still clasped in her hand.

She felt another presence behind her and turned blindly, her bloody knife slashing out, carving an arc towards the creature that was her father. Too late she realised who it was, and though she tried to pull the blow, the knife bit deeply. Its head was knocked to the side by the force of the blow, and it stumbled into the door frame, falling to its knees.

With a cry, Annaliese dropped the knife and knelt by its side. Its head rolled around to fix on her once more, and she recoiled from its blood-drenched, smiling visage. It reached for her, but she surged up, sprinting into the cabin's living area.

Her gaze settled on her father's short-bladed sword. She pulled it from its display hooks in the log-wall, and turned grimly towards the dark shapes moving towards her, the pale witch-lights of their eyes casting a cold blue tinge across the room. She ripped the scabbard from the sword, and stood with the glinting blade held ready before her.

This was not her father, she reminded herself.

And if this truly was her time to pass into the halls of Morr, then she would be damned if she didn't take these creatures with her.

She stepped backwards to give herself some room, her mouth set into a determined line as she lowered herself into a ready stance, the short-sword held out before her.

'You are not Jonas, and you are not my father,' she breathed as the puppet-like figures staggered towards her.

The unnaturally cold air was filled with the tumultuous din that spilled from the throats of the monsters, a dozen voices whispering and hissing all around her. The twisted, slashed face of the creature that was once her father continued to grin at her as it advanced towards her, and she backed away frantically from its outstretched hands.

Annaliese was far from an expert swordswoman, but these creatures, with their stilted and awkward movement, were far from skilled foes. As the zombie-like creature that resembled Jonas reached for her, she hacked at it with her sword, the blade severing several blackened, frostbitten fingers. The creature's eyes blazed ever brighter, until she plunged the point of the sword into its chest, piercing the heart. The fire flickered and died, and the creature slumped to the ground, a marionette with its strings cut.

A hand, as cold as death itself, grabbed her by her long blonde hair and wrenched her head back, and she saw the creature's slashed face close to her own, its mouth opened wide as it lunged for her throat. The icy chill that exuded from the monster burnt her, and she threw herself to the side in desperation, leaving a handful of hair in its grasp. Annaliese's head crashed into the leg of the heavy wooden table, and pain shot through her.

Voices were all around her, and when her vision cleared, she looked up into the twisted face of the monster. It stood over her hefting a heavy chunk of wood above its head, ready to cave her skull in.

'Father, no!' she screamed in desperation, but if it understood her it gave no indication.

She slashed with her sword, the blow hitting the creature in the shin, splintering the bone. Its leg collapsed beneath it and it fell to its knees. Annaliese was on her feet in an instant, and she lashed out blindly. Her blade hacked into its neck, cutting to the bone. It lodged fast between the vertebrae, and the sword was wrenched from her hands as it fell to the ground.

Shaking frantically, her breath coming in short, sharp gasps, she burst through the door of the cabin and ran outside.

She fled blindly from the cabin, her home, stumbling through the snow, registering that there was the movement of people all around. She fell to her knees as she tripped over something – a dead body. She jumped to her feet with a moan of horror, adrenaline pumping through her.

People ran screaming, clutching their children protectively to them, fleeing in every direction. There was no order to the flight, for there was nothing but panic and terror in these people, and they fought each other in their haste to get away.

Annaliese was knocked to the ground by a middle-aged villager she knew, though she had never seen the look of abject horror on his face before, and he made no sign of recognition or apology as he fled blindly. Bodies were strewn across the ground, blood splattered over the snow and mixing with the muddy slush. There were shouts and screams of pain and fear all around, and she swung her head from side to side, trying to see the enemy, or a safe direction to run.

Some people were defending themselves with drawn weapons, and she gasped as she saw one wildly flailing villager impaled on the shaft of a spear. He didn't stop fighting then, either, but dragged himself further onto the haft of the weapon in his eagerness to get close enough to claw at the warrior.

A woman screamed as she was grabbed from behind. Her throat was ripped out by her attacker's teeth, blood spraying madly from the fatal wound.

She saw a wasted and thin figure crouching over a fallen woman. She began to back away, but as if feeling her gaze upon it, the emaciated creature raised its head. Its eyes were blazing blue orbs of fire and its mouth and chin dripped with blood. Clearly it had been feasting, but it dropped its meal and began staggering towards her, its movements jerky and uncoordinated, but with deadly intent.

With no weapon to hand she knew she was no match for this creature, and she turned and ran through the mayhem. She saw an elderly man screaming and fighting frantically as he was pulled to the ground by two more plague victims, their eyes burning with cold intensity, and she faltered momentarily, seeing the desperate plea in the old man's face. An instant later, his cries were silenced as one of the creatures smashed his head into the ground with a horrible crack.

A terrified looking soldier swung towards her, the long spike on the tip of his halberd pointing in her direction. His trousers were stained where he had clearly lost control of his bodily functions, and

Annaliese raised her hands up before her to show she meant no harm. The point of the halberd wavered dangerously before her, and she flicked a glance over her shoulder at the creature stumbling towards her.

'I'm not one of them,' she said as she turned back, though she may as well have been speaking a foreign language, for the soldier merely backed away from her, his weapon still lowered in her direction and his eyes wide with terror. He tripped over a severed arm, and fell backwards into the snow.

She darted past him and heard a horrible yelp from the fallen soldier. She did not look back. The only thing on her mind now was escape.

She found herself running into the village square. Disoriented amongst the surging crowd, her blind flight had brought her here, and she groaned in fear. The fighting was intense, and she saw that the doors of the guildhall had been smashed down from the inside. As she stood there despairing, she saw one of the boarded up windows blown out, and a pair of grinning, flaming eyed monsters crawled through the rotten wreckage of splintered wood.

The black iron cage still hung from the gibbet, and the dark haired elf was staring out across the madness below with wide eyes. As much as he shook the door of the cage, the rusted padlock imprisoning him within held fast.

Annaliese saw her chance – there was a thin alleyway between the butchers and the Golden Wheatsheaf, the inn where she worked. It backed onto farmland, and beyond were the woods. Seeing no one in the narrow passageway, she ran, sidestepping combatants that rolled in the slush and the grasping hands of zombie-like plague victims.

A heavy set villager, a local huntsman, was fighting for his life against two of the plague monsters, a woodsman's axe in his grasp. He cut one of them down with a savage blow to the neck, but the other one reached for his face. He stumbled backwards to gain more room, swinging the axe over his shoulder.

On his backswing, the head of the axe struck the locking mechanism that held the gibbet cage aloft, freeing the chain and sending the cage plummeting towards the ground. The huntsman lost his grip on the axe, and the creature was upon him in an instant, tearing at his skin and flesh with skeletal hands curled like the talons of a bird of prey.

As he screamed in horror and pain, the black iron gibbet cage smashed into the earth with a clatter, and fell to its side. Several plague victims swung their heavy heads towards the sound, and broke off from their feasting to stagger towards the cage. Annaliese saw the elf shaking the bars of the cage frantically, but the lock held still.

She stopped short, biting her lip, glancing back towards the elf, still struggling against his imprisonment. It seemed an unnecessarily cruel way to die, even for one who had committed murderous, black acts.

Cursing herself, she rushed back into the fray, running lightly towards the cage. Several creatures were close to it now, and she heard the torrent of ungodly voices spilling from their throats raise in tempo in excitement.

Stooping, she swept up the fallen axe from the huntsman who was being eaten alive at the base of the gibbet, and hefted it over her shoulder before dashing towards the cage. With all her force and with a scream of anger and fear, she brought the axe crashing down onto the head of one of the plague victims trying to claw at the elf through the bars of the cage. It cut through its skull, splattering blood and gore over her dress and across the pristine white face of the elf, and the figure fell to the ground.

Annaliese caught the gaze of the elf, and was struck by his alien, defiant eyes. They were not black as she had first thought, those eyes, but had a slight tinge of lavender to them that merely enhanced the impression of inhuman, otherworldliness about him.

Praying she was doing the right thing, she brought the head of the axe crashing down on the rusted lock imprisoning the elf, smashing it asunder beneath the blow. She dropped the axe with numbed fingers, and without waiting to see his escape she turned and ran. She had given the elf a chance – it was now up to him to do with it what he would.

Not pausing this time, she bolted into the thin alleyway, running up its narrow passageway towards the beckoning farmland and woods beyond.

Her foot caught on something and she fell heavily to the ground, the air driven from her lungs. She hadn't even had time to get her hands in front of her to break her fall, and she gasped for air, winded, face down in the snow.

Something was holding onto her ankle, and she kicked out frantically, trying to free herself. Still trying to regain her breath, she gasped as pain flared up her leg. Rolling over in the icy cold slush, she saw a hand clasped around her ankle, blackened fingernails biting through her leather leggings. The fingers of the hand were a bruised red colour, for the blood had clotted in the veins when the plague victim's heart had stopped. She kicked at the hand with her free leg, feeling finger bones break beneath her heel, but still the grip did not relent.

She saw the creature's face then, and it filled her with mindless terror. It was the face of a friend, Ilsa, a barmaid at the Golden Wheatsheaf, though her plump, pretty face was contorted and foul. Her lips were swollen and bloated, and her skin was drawn and so pale that she could see the network of blue veins within her flesh. Sickeningly, the bones of her skull were malformed and warped, a cluster of bony, branch-like protrusions pushing from the flesh on her right temple. As Annaliese watched in horror, the twig-like tips of this mutation waved in air, straining towards her as if they sensed the life in her. Ice-blue flames flared in the girl's eye-sockets, and she opened her mouth wide, exposing blackened teeth. Where there should have been a tongue was a bulbous, staring eyeball, the iris iridescent blue and flecked with gold. That eye blinked slowly as it stared at her, and Annaliese thrashed against the grip of this foul creature, kicking at it again and again.

It did not release its grip, and it began to pull itself up her legs, the staring bulbous eye glaring at her from within the girl's ever widening mouth.

Over the creature's shoulder she saw a flash of movement, and she looked up, absolute panic in her eyes, to see the elf running towards her, the huntsman's axe in his hands. He swung it back over his head, and hurled it towards her.

Annaliese screamed as the axe flew through the air, turning end over end.

The axe blade slammed into the back of the mutant girl's head with a sickening, wet sound. Annaliese screamed again, pushing away from the now limp monster, kicking and scrabbling backwards.

Then the elf was at her side, pulling her to her feet with strength that belied his inhumanly slight, tall frame. His grip around her arm was strong, and painful, and her nostrils were filled with the scent of strange, unearthly spices and herbs.

The horror and shock of the day won out, and Annaliese saw stars of light for a second before she slumped to the ground unconscious, like a limp rag-doll.

Mouthing a curse in his native tongue, the elf stooped and lifted the girl up in his arms. Her head flopped back limply, her long blonde hair hanging to the ground.

Cursing himself for a fool, the elf, carrying the slender form of the human woman, loped away from the mayhem of the village, heading towards the beckoning trees in the distance.

CHAPTER FOUR

UDO GRUNWALD PUSHED open the small, ill-fitting door, lowering his head to avoid the low-hanging lintel and entered the seedy looking inn. It was called the Hanging Donkey, and outside its gateway hung the rotten, snow-covered corpse of said donkey, hanging by the noose around its neck. He wondered briefly what crime the animal had committed, what malefaction it had concocted within its devious criminal brain to warrant such punishment.

It had probably been the lover of the innkeeper's wife, he thought, and smiled to himself. That smile did nothing but make his brutish, ugly face look even more dangerous.

The inn was dark and smoky, and silence descended as soon as he stepped inside. His heavy boots sounded loudly on the wooden floorboards, and he glared around him at the staring faces, daring any of them to say a word.

Udo knew he was an intimidating figure, and he was used to the way that people's eyes quickly turned away from his gaze. Here was no different, though the hostility within the room was tangible, even if none of these farmers and travellers dared look him in the eye.

He could understand the reaction to his presence – none were safe on the roads these days, and the news from the north was grim. Brigands and outlaws roamed the countryside, preying on those fleeing the trouble, and there were whispers of far darker things within the forests that were growing restless. Witches, secret covens, foul mutants and Chaotic beasts that walked upright like men – these were all things to be feared by people of the Empire, and here was no different. Outsiders were regarded with fear and distrust, particularly with the growing rumours of the hideous plague that was spreading like wildfire through the towns and villages.

But more than this, he was a witch hunter, and his occupation was obvious. His presence inspired fear and twinges of guilt even in the guiltless.

The hushed chatter began to reassert itself as drinkers and cold travellers turned back to their private musings and discussions, pulling hats and hoods down over their faces so as not to draw the witch hunter's attention to them. Udo strode towards the bar, removing the wide-brimmed hat and placing it down in front of him. Those standing nearby backed away. He saw one patron try to hide his malformed, club-like hand within his coat, and Udo shook his head slightly. It was always the same – any wretch who had a disability would try to hide it from the eyes of a witch hunter, fearing prosecution. Udo had no interest in burning cripples or those afflicted with birth defects but he could understand the fear of these simple people – there were witch hunters who would see them cleansed in flame.

'What can I get for you, friend?' said the barkeeper, trying and failing to hide his nervousness. He was a pudgy man with eyeballs that protruded a little too far, giving him a goggle-eyed, startled expression like a fish. He also seemed to be sweating heavily, though it was not overly warm within the room. Udo instantly disliked him.

'A room. A meal. But first,' he said, 'I want a drink.'

'If it's no bother, good sir, I would see your coin beforehand,' said the innkeeper, wringing his moist hands nervously. 'I don't mean to be discourteous, but these are hard times, and I'm sure you can understand my reticence at serving a stranger without first knowing that he could pay. Can you, sir? Pay, I mean?'

Udo glared at the little man for a moment, his lip curling in distaste. The barkeeper fidgeted, his protruding eyes flicking left and right. Udo pulled the glove off one of his hands, finger by finger, and the pudgy, sweating innkeeper jumped as he slapped the black leather glove down on the bar. Still staring at the barkeeper, Grunwald lifted a clinking pouch of dark leather from his belt and pulled out a pair coins, which he slammed down onto the bar.

'Will this do?' he sneered.

'Most indeed, gracious sir! Most indeed!' said the barman. The coins disappeared in a flash, and he thrust his hand towards Grunwald. 'I am Claus Fiedler, the owner of this fine establishment. I *am* happy to have such a fine upstanding gentleman such as you staying beneath my roof.'

Udo stared at the innkeeper's proffered, sweating hand in distaste, and ignored it.

'I'll take that drink now,' he said.

'Why, yes, of course sir.' He began enthusiastically pumping a grimy mug with ale, grinning like an idiot, sweat dripping down his brow.

Don't fall in my ale, Grunwald thought, seeing a heavy bead of sweat hanging precariously over his pint from Fiedler's eyebrow. Thankfully, it didn't, though the image had already soured his enjoyment of the drink.

Taking the mug, he turned his back on the unpleasant barkeep. It was probably the barkeeper that had been caught with the donkey, he thought.

He looked for an isolated place to sit, having no wish to engage with anyone. He saw the dwarf he had met three days earlier smoking his dragon-headed pipe in the corner. Thorrik, wasn't it? He inclined his head to the stocky dwarf warrior, who nodded his head solemnly in acknowledgement. He was not surprised to see the dwarf again – this was one of the few inns on the road to the south-east.

Pushing through the stinking crowd of travellers, farmers and local drinkers, Udo found himself a secluded bench in a dark corner, away from the press of bodies. He placed his ale on the table, shrugged off his crossbow which also went down on the table with a heavy thump, and shifted the bench so that it was up against the wall, glaring at the patrons who tutted and huffed as they were bumped out of the way.

He slumped down in the seat with his back to the wall, and cracked his aching neck from side to side.

Lifting his ale, he took a tentative sip. It was weak, but not bad, and he gulped back a mouthful.

He was sore and tired, and he sighed as he rested his aching back against the wall. After the battle alongside the dwarf, he had recovered what coin he could from the bandits and returned to the Sigmarite shrine that they had robbed, intending to bequeath it to the priest there. He had found the priest lying on the floor of the holy shrine, his throat savagely cut and his body filled with stab wounds. For two days he searched for sign of the killers, but had found nothing. His failure to discover the culprits rankled him, and after burying the priest and putting the shrine in order, he had somewhat reluctantly continued on his way. His master was expecting him, and he had already wasted enough time.

It wasn't long before the sweating figure of Fiedler was back at his side, putting a bowl of steaming grey slop down before him and a hunk of bread. It looked incredibly unappetising, and he poked at it with his spoon. Fiedler stood at his side, grinning like an idiot, clearly waiting for some complimentary reaction to his food.

'Go away,' said Udo, and the pudgy innkeeper nodded and stuttered before moving back behind the bar. Udo saw him cuff a servant hard over the back of the head.

'Out of the way!' he heard Fiedler shout, which got a laugh from some of the customers. The servant was clearly a simpleton, his head tilted to the side and his jaw slack. As he shuffled out of the way of his master,

Udo saw that one of his legs was twisted awkwardly beneath him, giving him an ungainly loping gait.

Grunwald ate his fill, dipping the bread into the steaming slop, which wasn't as bad as it looked, though he could not identify the chunks of meat in it. It was probably best that he didn't know, he decided.

Upon the completion of his meal, the simpleton came to collect his plate, limping through the press of people. He lifted Udo's used plate, his fleshy tongue protruding from the side of his mouth in concentration. In an instant, Fiedler was at his side, and he cuffed the servant over the head again, swearing at him, and took the plate from his hands.

'I'm sorry about that, sir, he's not right in the head and shouldn't be bothering you,' he said apologetically.

'What is his name?' asked Grunwald.

'Otto. Idiot son of my dead sister,' he said, lowering his voice conspiratorially, as if speaking to one who would understand his sentiments. 'If he weren't family he would have been out on his arse years ago. Still might be, the way the useless cripple carries on. Upsets the customers.' He chuckled to himself and nudged Udo. 'And we can't be having customers the likes of you bein' upset by the likes of him, family or no.'

Grunwald looked into the eyes of the repugnant barkeeper. 'Touch me one more time and I will break your face,' he said quietly. Fiedler visibly paled. Ignoring him, Grunwald addressed the servant cowering at the barkeeper's side. 'Thank you, Otto.'

The simpleton grinned at him broadly.

'Your presence repulses me, you foetid little man' said Grunwald, addressing Fiedler, who was still hovering at his side. He didn't move away, however, and

Grunwald looked at him, an eyebrow raised. 'Leave,' he said slowly and menacingly. '*Now*.'

Udo sighed. He gained nothing by threatening the man except for spit or something worse in his meal if he ever ate here again. But he wouldn't be eating here again – he would leave before dawn, and would eat on the road. He still had some way to travel, and the sooner he was away from here the better. Briefly he considered taking his money back and leaving, to sleep rough on the road, but the promise of a pallet was too enticing, even if it was in a hovel such as the Hanging Donkey.

Grunwald had just decided to turn in early when a ruckus erupted across the room. A patron's head was slammed into a table, breaking his nose and leaving a smear of blood on the wood.

'We don't want your type round here no more,' shouted a burly, drunk local, lifting the dazed man roughly to his feet. The thug's friends tried to calm him down, but he shook off their hands angrily.

'No!' bellowed the drunk, and he rocked on his heels, unsteady with drink. He slammed a fist into the man's stomach, and he folded under the force of the blow, falling to the ground.

'Now Rikard, that's enough,' said Fiedler, approaching the drunk with his sweating hands held out before him.

'S'alright for you,' slurred the drunk. 'You are gettin' fat off the money of all these travellers. But not me,' he said, tapping himself on the chest. 'They come here – any one of 'em could be bringin' plague. Shouldn't be allowed here anymore, I say!'

A hearty, drunken cheer from more than half the patrons in the bar followed this pronouncement. The travellers, many sitting with their wives and children as they fled the ravages of plague and war, looked around nervously, feeling the hostility within the room directed towards them. Heartened, the drunken local thug kicked the downed man hard in the face.

'I say make a stand – make sure there won't be no one passing through here 'til the plague is long gone,' he bellowed, to another hearty cheer. He emphasised his point by kicking the fallen man again.

'Now Rikard, I think you've had enough for one night. Go home and sleep it off, eh?' said Fiedler, taking another wary step towards the swaying thug. The drunkard fumbled at his belt and drew a short-bladed knife, which he levelled at the barkeeper's throat.

'Keep back with you, or I'll gut you like the swine you are, Fiedler,' he snarled. He nodded his head towards the fallen man. 'I'm gonna string this bastard up. Word'll spread, and there won't be any more damn outsiders passin' through. Pick him up,' he barked to his friends. They immediately lifted the near unconscious man, and followed the drunkard as he stomped outside.

There were scattered cheers, and the sound of chairs being pushed back as more patrons rose to follow the thuggish trio, clearly wanting to witness the outcome of the confrontation.

Udo sighed and stood up. He pressed a coin into the malformed hand of the simpleton servant, Otto. 'Don't let anyone touch my crossbow,' he said. 'And don't tell your uncle that I gave you this coin,' he added. Otto grinned at him, and Udo stalked through the packed inn, pushing people out of his way as he followed the crowd.

Outside, the beaten man was on his knees in the middle of the street.

'Please, Sigmar no!' he pleaded, tears and blood running down his face. 'I am travelling to my wife and child in Averheim! I sent them on ahead! If you kill me, you kill them too! Please, you cannot do this!'

Ignoring his pleas, the drunkard grabbed the man by his hair, pulling his head back for the killing blow. The crowd roared for blood.

Pushing people roughly out of his way, Udo stalked into the centre of the circle.

'Kill that man and you die next,' he said. His voice was not loud, but he spoke with such authority and menace that it gave the villagers pause. Grunwald had drawn one of his ornate, embossed pistols and it was levelled at the drunken would-be murderer's head. The roaring died down, and the fallen man looked up at him, desperate hope in his eyes.

'Who is this?' snarled the drunk, gesturing with his knife towards the dark clad figure of Grunwald, eyes trying to focus on the barrel of the gun pointed at him.

'Grunwald,' he said loudly, his deep voice pitched perfectly to carry to all those crowded around. His next words were said slowly and clearly, so that none could mistake them. 'Udo Grunwald, witch hunter of the Temple of Sigmar.' There was sudden silence, and several within the crowd began to inch away from him. 'And I say again – you kill that man and you will die next. I promise you that.'

Blinking his eyes heavily, the drunk glanced at the crowd around him. His motives were easily read – he was gauging the crowd's reaction, trying to judge if they would tackle the witch hunter if things got more serious. He looked once more at the pistol held before him, and he spat a thick ball of phlegm onto the ground at Grunwald's feet before sheathing his knife.

'This aint over,' he snarled, and turned and stomped unsteadily away. He made to kick the fallen man once more as he left, and smirked as the beaten man flinched. The crowd rapidly dissipated. Grunwald was soon left alone bar the bruised man who was thanking him through his tears. He was surprised to see the dwarf Thorrik standing a few paces away, his axe in his hands.

'Thought I was going to have to come to *your* aid this time round,' he said, his voice grave.

'Glad they saw sense and it was not needed,' said Grunwald darkly.

'Bah. That manling had murder in his eyes. Though I think he saw the sense in not arguing with a loaded gun – even if it is a shoddy weapon made by the clumsy hands of men.'

Grunwald snorted. 'Come,' he said, as the pair walked back to the inn, helping the wounded man inside. 'I'll buy you a drink.'

They saw Fiedler standing in the door of the inn, wringing his hands nervously.

'See that this man is taken to a room and his wounds tended to. If he is not well cared for, I will hold you personally responsible,' Udo said to him. The bar-keeper's face was pale, but he nodded, and helped the man inside.

'Repugnant little troll,' commented Thorrik, his face curled as if he had stepped in something unpleasant.

'A bit unfair, perhaps,' said Grunwald mildly. 'On trolls, I mean.'

The dwarf looked seriously at Udo for a moment before his eyes creased with humour, and he gave a throaty chuckle.

'Aye,' he said. 'You may be right.'

ANNALIESE STOPPED TO rest for a moment, leaning her hand against a tree, her breath ragged. Though it was freezing cold, she was sweating inside her heavy, fur-lined coat. She stared up the steep incline to where the elf stood, his face turned back towards her. He beckoned sharply for her to continue, and she steeled herself for the climb.

She had always prided herself on her physical fitness. She regularly did fourteen-hour shifts at the Golden Wheatsheaf and was on her feet all day, carrying trays of food back and forth from the kitchen and clearing up at the day's end, but she had never been more exhausted than over the past two days. She knew the elf was frustrated at the pace they were travelling. His stamina was astounding – she would not have been surprised if he was able to run for days without slowing. He also moved with unnerving silence, and she had been startled on several occasions by him appearing at her side while she thought she had been alone.

She had no idea where the elf was leading her, but he was insistent, and seemed to know exactly where he was going. It seemed that he could not, or would not, speak a word of Reikspiel, and though she had questioned him as to their destination, silence was his only response.

They were passing deeper into the Westenholz than Annaliese had ever ventured, and in truth perhaps they were already beyond that wood and into unknown territory. These woods were dangerous, a refuge for brigands, wild beasts and worse.

She thought back to the words of the village warden, who had said that this elf was one of the murderers of the family on the road. Was she his captive now? He had not bound her arms, and indeed he had saved her from the mutant back in the village. She shivered. Everything that had happened to her seemed unreal, like a nightmare. But it was all too real.

For a night and a day they had been travelling together in silence, the elf's impatience clear on his inhuman face. Still, he allowed her to stop and rest when she needed it, and he gave her food – strange, savoury flat cakes that stemmed her hunger instantly.

Was she his slave now? Would he take advantage of her once he deemed them far enough away from the village, and beyond pursuit? She had decided that she would not sleep the previous night at all – she would wait until the elf was asleep, and she would escape from him. That plan had come to nothing, for she had dropped into a deep and fitful sleep. She had been plagued by horrible dreams – she saw her father's face, twisted and grinning, burning blue orbs where his eyes should have been. When she had finally woken, the elf was already up and waiting for her.

Tonight, she thought. Tonight I will escape from him.

Having caught her breath, she began clambering up the incline, slipping in the dark, moist earth, the muscles of her legs burning. Drawing near the pale-skinned elf she raised her gaze to meet his, her eyes defiant. His hard, cold, lavender eyes held hers for a moment before he indicated for her to continue up the incline with a quick nod of his pointed chin.

He was tall, taller even than her father had been, though he was inhumanly slender. But not weak, she decided. No, he was far from weak. He was lean and sinewy, like a rangy wolf, and his every move was perfectly balanced and elegant. There was a harshness to him that made every movement he made seem fuelled by bitterness, and she often jumped at his swift, sharp movements.

Dressed in soft, grey leather, he wore a pair of thin, empty scabbards strapped to his thighs. Over his back were two empty quivers. The soldiers had clearly taken his weapons away from him. Still, he did not seem any less dangerous for being unarmed.

His eyes seemed to mock her, to speak of her frailty. Annaliese was determined not to show weakness in front of him.

With her head held high, she moved past him and continued climbing the hill, trying to ignore the pain in her legs.

She rose over the incline and began to move along the ridge. Lost in her own misery, she walked for some time before she felt a hand upon her shoulder. She gasped involuntarily.

It was the elf, of course, and Annaliese cursed herself for showing her fear.

He pointed into the undergrowth, but she couldn't see anything. She shrugged, furrowing her brow, and the elf gave a slight, disdainful shake of his head, and indicated for her to follow him.

They moved some thirty yards through the ferns towards an ancient and contorted oak tree, where the elf halted. He swept off his long grey cloak in a quick movement and threw it over a low-hanging branch, fixing it there with simple leather ties. He pinned the corners of the cloak into the ground, using twigs as makeshift pegs. It had taken only seconds, but he had constructed a basic, yet highly effective one-man shelter. He indicated for her to sit beneath the cloak, but she stayed where she was standing, glaring at him.

After a moment, he shrugged his shoulders, and pulled the twig-pegs from the moist soil and swung the cloak back over his shoulder. He pulled the hood up over his head, so that his face was all but hidden in its depths, his eyes glittering.

A moment later it began to sleet, icy rain coming down in sheets. The water slipped off the elf's hood like oil, and Annaliese pulled her coat around her tighter. She thought she saw a hint of amusement in the eyes of the elf, and she lifted her head high, her mouth set in a grim line.

The elf stabbed a finger towards her, then at the ground. He was telling her to stay here. He repeated the action, and she nodded her head.

Then he was gone, slipping away into the trees like a shadow. In an instant he had disappeared.

This was her chance to escape, she knew. But she had no idea where she was, and if there were more of those monsters lurking nearby. These dense woods were rife with outlaws and killers. There were even some who claimed to have seen hulking creatures here with horns sprouting from their bestial heads and walking like men, but upon cloven hooves. In stories she had heard as a child these woods were haunted by the shades of the criminals hung on its outskirts, and that they walked amongst the trees in the dead of night, seeking the living. Her childhood fears rose within her.

If she died out here no one would mourn her.

She shivered again, and crouched down in the lee of the twisted oak tree, trying to get out of the biting wind and relentless sleet. She pulled her hands within the sleeves of her coat to warm them. She realised that she had nowhere to run. Tears ran down her face, invisible against the icy sleet.

How had she come to be in this situation, she wondered? Her legs were stiff and sore and she sat down on a twisted root, uncaring of the mud. She pushed herself back against the tree and hugged herself tightly. Despite the wind, the sleet lashing the tree and the uncomfortable position she was in, she fell asleep within moments.

ANNALIESE WOKE TO the delicious aroma of cooking meat. The wind and rain had stopped, and dusk had fallen.

She sat up. She was aching from the awkward position she had slept in. Standing, she stretched like a cat, loosening her cold, cramped muscles. She saw the elf tending a small, smokeless fire-pit dug into the earth. He was cooking what looked like a pair of spherical shaped green objects, but the smell coming from them was divine.

Rolling them from the fire, the elf moved them skilfully onto a pair of flat stones with sticks.

He gestured for her to approach, and she did so cautiously. He placed one of the flat stones at Annaliese's side, then sat himself back down across from her on the other side of the small, glowing fire-pit.

She took a seat on a fallen log, and looked at her meal, intrigued. Glancing over the glowing embers, she watched as the elf deftly prized the greenery away with one hand and a stick. A whoosh of steam rose from within. Feeling her looking at him, his almond-shaped eyes rose, and she hastily dropped her gaze to the meal in front of her.

She saw the green ball was a series of leaves carefully woven together and overlapped to form a spherical container. It was beautiful in its simplicity and the obvious care that had gone into it. With her hand and a stick she opened it up, trying to emulate the elf's deft movements, and steam billowed from within. It brought with it the aroma of rabbit and all manner of herbs, many that she did not recognise.

Her stomach groaned loudly, but she hesitated. The elf was picking at his food delicately, watching her. What if it was poisoned, she thought? Then you will be dead, but at least you will die with warm food in your belly, she answered herself.

She tried a piece of rabbit tentatively. It was exquisite, and she smiled shyly to the elf before eating her meal hungrily. The elf regarded her coldly. She didn't care.

Afterwards she realised that she must have appeared like some ravenous barbarian thanks to the speed that she devoured the delicious meal. As she licked her fingers, she found herself staring over the glowing embers at the elf.

Long and black, his hair was drawn over his head and pulled into a tight ponytail, and there was a thin black tattoo upon his cheek. It showed an alien symbol of curling lines and elegantly tapered flourishes. It was beautiful and powerful, and she wondered what it signified. The elf ate his food slowly, delicately picking at the pieces with his long, pale fingers that for some reason reminded her of the legs of spiders – delicate, their movements measured, concealing their deadly power.

Annaliese looked away quickly. There was something chilling about him. She was fearful of him, of that there was no doubt; everything about him was just so… inhuman.

Still, despite her fear, she was curious.

'I…' began Annaliese, realising that she had no idea what to say to him. 'I don't think you can understand me,' she said. He stared at her blankly.

'Did you kill that family? Did you murder those poor little girls?' she said. 'And are you going to kill me as well?'

The elf shrugged his shoulders and stood, moving around the campfire towards her. She recoiled back away from him. He squatted down in front of her, and held out his hands. Looking down, she saw that he was offering her his meal – he had not eaten it all. She felt foolish suddenly, and a blush rose over her lightly freckled face. She shook her head. He offered her his meal again, his face emotionless, and this time she accepted it. She touched his hands as she took it from him – though they looked as cold and hard as the whitest marble, they were warm and soft.

She blushed again, and began to eat as he moved away. After she had finished this second meal, she tried talking to him again.

'Thank you for the meal,' she said. She felt somewhat foolish talking to this silent, aloof figure – it was like talking to a blank stone wall. But she was determined to attempt to communicate. His impassive, ghostly white face gave away not a hint of what he was thinking.

She tapped herself on the chest. 'Annaliese. Annaliese,' she repeated. Then she pointed at him and raised her eyebrows questioningly. He made no movement, merely continued staring at her with his lavender eyes.

'Annaliese,' she said once again, tapping herself on the chest. She pointed at him again and made a questioning motion. He probably thinks I have lost my mind, she thought. He stared at her for a moment longer, and began to turn away.

He turned back briefly, and tapped himself on the chest. 'Eldanair Lathalos ath Laralemenos lo Nagary-the,' he breathed in a carefully enunciated voice, the words clipped and spoken quickly.

Annaliese stared at him. She didn't catch any of what he had just said, and it was clear on her face.

The elf blinked, then spoke more slowly, tapping his chest.

'Eldanair,' he said, then turned his back on her.

'Eldanair,' said Annaliese quietly to herself, listening to the sound of the name as it rolled off her tongue. The way she said it didn't sound quite how the elf had spoken it, but at least she now knew his name. It was a start.

CHAPTER FIVE

THE DARKENED CELLAR was a bloodbath.

Men lay strewn upon the rough cobbled floor, moaning in agony as their lifeblood leaked from fatal wounds. The stench of the dead and dying was overpowering. There were shouts and curses, the ringing of steel upon steel, and the sickening, wet, meaty sound of swords cleaving flesh.

A thunderous voice rose above the din.

'No clemency! Let none leave here alive!'

More soldiers pounded down the stairs, swords drawn. They wore the black, slashed doublets of Nuln, and carried swords and bucklers – their more traditional halberds would have been next to useless in the confined space.

The enemy were not hard to discern amongst the frantic melee, for they wore long silken robes of blues, yellows and purples. They had drawn weapons of their own, and once they realised that there was to be no escape, they fought with a frenzy and lack of self-preservation that was off-putting, even to the most battle-hardened of the state soldiers – they fought like rabid, cornered animals.

'Grunwald! To me!' came the booming voice.

The burly, unshaven sergeant loosed a shaft from his crossbow. It punched through the forehead of one of the coven members who fell to his back, dead.

'You heard the man,' Udo Grunwald roared, hurling the crossbow to the side and pulling his heavy, flanged mace from his belt. 'Push forward! We end this now!'

With a roar, he led a group of black-clad soldiers into the fray. He swatted a blade away from him with his heavy weapon and smashed the mace-head into a cultist's face with his return blow, shattering his lower jaw in a spray of blood and teeth.

Another fell, a sword piercing his stomach, and Grunwald kicked him savagely in the head as he went down. A blade slashed across his shoulder and he grimaced in pain, and brained his attacker, the ridged edges of his heavy mace shattering the skull.

He heard a string of shouted words; phrases yelled in a language that he didn't know.

Hissing against the pain in his shoulder, Grunwald saw the towering, black-cloaked figure of the witch hunter Stoebar battling against a trio of assailants. A consummate swordsman, his sabre flashed out, slicing open the throat of the first, and whipped back quickly enough to block a lethal cut from another foe that would have disembowelled him.

'With me!' shouted Grunwald, and pushed his way through the press of bodies towards the witch hunter, his mace crushing shoulders and breaking limbs.

The soldier to his left died as a spear was thrust into his throat, and another to his right was dropped as a knife plunged into his thigh. Still, the weight of the soldiers smashed the snarling cultists aside, clubbing them to the ground and plunging swords into their prone forms.

A wave of revulsion and nausea washed over them, and Grunwald staggered. He heard a voice chanting in an unholy language, and he felt his stomach contract tightly and painfully.

Again the witch hunter's voice sounded out.

'Sigmar, lend us strength!'

Grunwald felt the pain within him lessen, and he opened his tightly clenched eyes to see a figure standing on a dais, arms raised over its head as its chant reached a crescendo.

The witch hunter Stoebar cut down the last of his opponents and leapt up the stairs towards the figure, and Grunwald staggered after him.

With a shout that hurt the eardrums with its intensity, the figure completed the incantation and dropped his arms to his side. A high collar of iridescent feathers framed the zealot's lowered head. Naked to the waist, swirling blue patterns had been painstakingly etched onto his skin. Grunwald saw the twisted patterns begin to move, rotating in circular motions, weaving new patterns and symbols upon the zealot's flesh.

With a roar of pure hatred and loathing, Stoebar raised his long bladed sabre over his shoulder as he drew near the coven leader, and the sword flashed out to open the throat of the motionless figure.

Throughout the basement, the last of the cultists were hacked down, and the state soldiers of Nuln closed in towards the dais, gripping their bloody weapons tightly as they watched the fateful blow fall.

Half a foot before the blade struck flesh the blow was halted. In mid-air the witch hunter's blade stopped, and he gasped as he strained to complete the killing strike.

The zealot raised its head then, blue fire flickering in its eyes and a smile upon its lips.

The air around the sorcerer seemed to ripple as if with a wave of intense heat, and his flesh bulged unnaturally, as if things within were trying to escape. A line of backwards curving barbs pushed through the skin of his forearms, forming a deadly ridge of horns, and his hands extended into long, cruel talons, like those of some mutated eagle. Mouths screaming in obscene languages opened up all over the zealot's body, ripping through muscle and flesh. Some were filled with needle-like teeth and long, sinuous tongues tipped with thorns, while others were little more than bony beaks filled with tiny, barbed teeth.

Stoebar seemed unable to move, and the creature reached forwards, gripping him by the shoulders. Blood welled where the daemon-possessed zealot's talons bit into his flesh, and it drew him closer to its hideous, maddening form.

Then, merely by willing it so, the Chaos abomination ripped the witch hunter's chest open. As if unseen knives slashed him, the clothes and armour of the witch hunter were slashed dozens of times, and the flesh was turned to bloody tatters. Ribs were snapped as his rib cage was pulled back by invisible hands, exposing the pulsing organs within. His heart exploded messily, and the dead witch hunter was hurled across the room away from the daemonically possessed zealot, landing in a wet, bloody heap at Grunwald's feat.

The daemon's eyes blazed with fire, and it opened its mouth wide, lips pulling back to expose a double set of sharpened teeth. It lifted one pale taloned hand before it, and it began to glow with burning light, as if the fires of the sun were building within its flesh.

Grunwald reached down and grabbed the icon of Sigmar wrapped around the dead witch hunter's hand – a bronze symbol depicting Sigmar's holy hammer, Ghal Maraz. It was burning hot to the touch. He held it aloft by its chain, and he felt the heat radiated by the holy symbol increase tenfold. Blinding light spilled from the hammer icon as Grunwald cried out to the warrior god for aid.

But this is where his dream took a path divergent to what had occurred that night. Five years earlier, the creature had been driven back by the symbol, buying time for the soldiers to surge forwards and kill the daemon's earthly body, sending it screaming back to its own plane of existence.

But not tonight.

No, in Grunwald's dream the daemon merely laughed at him, mocking his pitiful, weak faith. It killed until Grunwald alone was left alive and frozen in place. And then the daemon began to tear at his skin with invisible claws. He felt his ribcage being pulled open, and heard the first cracks as the bones snapped…

He awoke, gasping, sitting upright in his sweat-soaked bed. The pain in his chest lingered for a moment.

That was when he noticed the smoke.

Swearing, he leapt up, throwing off the sheets. He crossed to his door quickly, unbolting it and throwing it wide. He stepped out onto the internal balcony above the bar. Smoke was thick, and he could see the glow of flames.

'Fire!' he roared. In his past life, before he became a witch hunter, he had been a sergeant in the state army of Nuln, and he was well used to shouting loud enough and with enough authority for his orders to be heard and obeyed over the din of battle. 'Fire!' he roared again, and people began to stumble from their bedrooms.

He saw Thorrik kick his door open violently. The dwarf was wearing his armour and brandished his axe in one hand, while his shield was on his other arm.

Grunwald ran back into his room, and hastily pulled on his boots and hitched his belt around his waist, feeling instantly more in control with his weapons at his side. He scooped up his belongings in his arms and quickly left the room. All the rooms were being vacated now, and there were screams and wails from the people trying to flee the rising inferno. The heat and smoke made him light headed.

He saw the terrified, pale face of Fiedler as the plump man ran past him, dressed in his nightclothes.

Stumbling out of the front door, the occupants spilled out into the cold, Grunwald and Thorrik amongst them. The Hanging Donkey was ablaze, flame leaping high up the old, leaning structure. Several people were making ineffective attempts to stem the blaze, throwing pails of water against the wood, and beating the flames with blankets.

There was a group of men standing in the main street out front, flaming brands held in their hands. The drunkard who Grunwald had stopped from killing the innocent man earlier that night stood in the middle of the group, knife in one hand and a burning torch in the other. It was clear that the men had continued drinking, and now they had drunk themselves enough courage to return and finish what they had started, Grunwald surmised.

'What have you done?' wailed Fiedler.

'Shut up, worm,' shouted one of the men. 'It's your damned inn that is bringing people here!'

'Bring him to me!' shouted the instigator of this violence. 'I've come to finish what I started!'

Grunwald, the braces of his trousers hanging by his sides and his undershirt unbuttoned and exposing his heavily scarred upper body, stalked towards the group, his square jaw jutting forwards.

At ten paces he drew his pistol from the holster on his belt and without a word shot the troublemaker in the head. The sound of the pistol was deafening, and blood, bits of skull and brain splattered over the gathered drunk locals, who stood frozen in shock.

Grunwald holstered the smoking pistol and drew his heavy-headed mace, facing off against the remaining ten men.

'You bastard!' snarled one of them, a young man Udo recognised from earlier in the night. He hurled his flaming brand at the witch hunter, and ran forwards with his knife drawn.

Grunwald swayed out of the brand's path and stepped in to meet the man. With a deft side step he avoided the man's drunken, clumsy blow and smashed

his mace into his head, dropping him without a sound.
The others hefted their own weapons, their faces angry
and dark, and Udo realised that he was in some serious
trouble. A gruff, rumbling voice halted the men before
they could launch their attack.

'It's a good day to die, manlings,' growled Thorrik.
'Step forward and see if your time has come.'

The dwarf stamped forward heavily to stand at
Grunwald's side, and the witch hunter saw that he was
fully decked out in his armour as if ready for war. He
held his heavy, circular metal shield over his left arm,
and his head was completely enclosed in a helmet
shaped and worked to represent a stylised dwarf face.
His eyes glittered dangerously within, and his heavy,
short-handled axe was held over his shoulder ready to
hack at the first man that came within range.

He looked absolutely impervious to harm, for there was
not a single inch of exposed flesh on him. Udo had to
admit he was an intimidating presence, despite his height.

The men stood rooted to the spot, indecision clear
on their faces. None of them wanted to die here. He
sensed the change in mood coming over them.

'You two,' he barked, pointing sharply at a pair of
men, making them jump. 'Pick up your friend here and
take him home. He is alive, but his skull may be frac-
tured. And you two,' he said, pointing to another pair,
'see that your dead friend is buried. The rest of you, go
and help fight those fires.'

His voice was commanding, brooking no argument,
and the men responded instantly, the fight having
evaporated from them completely.

'Beardlings,' scoffed Thorrik, his voice muffled
behind the thick metal of his full-face helm.

'Indeed,' said Grunwald, judging it was an insult by the tone of the dwarf's voice. He walked back towards where he had placed his possessions, shortening his strides to allow the dwarf to walk alongside him, clanking in his heavy armour. He buttoned up his undershirt and pulled his braces over his broad shoulders.

The villagers were battling the flames, though it was impossible to tell if they were winning. Udo saw the barkeeper wringing his hands and hopping from foot to foot, doing little to help.

The pair aided the villagers, Grunwald organising them into worker teams to more efficiently tackle the blaze, and as the dawn began to light the sky, the last of the fire was put out. It had gutted the kitchen and a good portion of the common area, and the exterior was blackened, but the structure was more or less intact, though it would doubtless need months of work.

Grunwald's face was blackened with soot. He approached Thorrik as he sat on the stoop smoking his pipe. 'I'm leaving,' he said.

'Aye, sounds like a plan. I've had my fill of this stinking place.' He glared up at the fire-blackened inn. 'That's what comes of building with wood,' he remarked. 'Only thing wood is good for is burning. Build something out of stone and it will stand for generations.'

'I can see the merit in that,' said Grunwald.

'I don't understand you humans, you know,' said the dwarf, looking up at the brightening sky.

'Oh?'

'Your Empire is at war, and your people are suffering from starvation and plague. And yet still you fight amongst yourselves. Have you no honour?'

Grunwald thought about this for a moment, and shrugged his shoulders. 'Precious little these days, it seems. Still, don't judge us all by the actions of the weak and cowardly.'

'I don't understand you humans,' said Thorrik. 'I'm not sure that I ever will – and I will be glad of that.'

He stood up, and ensured that his pack was tightly secured. With dutiful care, he tightened the leather straps that held the long, oilskin wrapped object upon the pack, and tied his shield protectively over it.

'What is that you carry?' asked Udo as the dwarf hefted the heavy looking pack to his broad shoulders.

'Never you mind,' said the dwarf brusquely, shoving his helmet over his head. 'Always wanting to know everyone else's business, you humans,' came his voice, muffled behind the thick metal of his helm. Udo noted that the helmet even had a stylised metal moustache upon it. The helmet alone must have been worth a fortune, with all the intricate, bronze-gilt knotwork around its rim, let alone his entire set of armour.

Udo shrugged again, and Thorrik began to walk away, each heavy footstep leaving a deep impression in the muddy ground. He walked ten paces before he paused and turned back towards the witch hunter.

'Where you headed?' he said gruffly.

'I am returning to my temple, to seek the counsel of my superior. Near Black Fire Pass.'

The dwarf huffed in response.

'Well, come on then,' he said eventually. 'I'm heading to Black Fire myself.'

ELDANAIR KNELT IN the undergrowth. He placed a hand to the ground, carefully and precisely reading the signs.

To even a trained woodsman there would be nothing here to see, but to the elf the ground was like an open book, and he could read its stories effortlessly. Those that had left the tracks were not unskilled – indeed they displayed a skill that he found surprising this far from Ulthuan. No human could move through woodland and leave such a faint trail of its passing, and his unease grew. This was not the mark of one of his party, and he knew of no other Asur moving through this area, but he could not shake the belief that this was the spoor of one of his kin. Unconsciously, he brushed a wisp of long, dark hair behind one of his pointed ears, his eyebrows drawn together in thought upon his ivory forehead.

The human woman, Annaliese, stood behind him, watching him with interest. She showed spirit, this woman, though to his eyes her movements were painfully clumsy, slow and noisy. She had slowed his progress considerably, but he had bound himself to see her safe. And the safest place for her now was with his kin. The seer would know best what to do with her.

He moved on, picking his way silently through the trees. He paused again, touching his fingers to the cold earth. He lifted them to his nose, sniffing delicately. His concern grew.

These were not human tracks, he was sure of that now. Nor were they made by any of the foul creatures that existed within the dark, foreboding forests that engulfed the Empire.

Urging Annaliese to hurry, he began to run lightly through the trees. Swift and silent, he leapt over fallen logs and ducked beneath low hanging branches, leaving no trace of his passing. Decades earlier he had mastered the art, and he now he did not break even a single blade of grass with his soft footfalls. None would be able to track him.

The same could not be said for the human woman however. She crashed along behind him, and he had to pause often so that she was not left behind. He shook his head slightly at the noise she made as twigs and sticks cracked beneath her heavy footfalls. He glanced back sharply, irritation and impatience flashing in his eyes, and she looked up at him apologetically. It was unfair to blame her, he knew, but that didn't make it easier to accept her inept blundering.

For three hours he pushed on, allowing Annaliese little time to catch her breath. He couldn't explain to her what he feared these tracks portended, but she seemed to understand his need for urgency. He was still confused by the tracks, but a deeply unsettling feeling had settled in his stomach.

He cursed himself for a fool. If the elven patrol had been ambushed by enemies, then he knew that he and he alone was to blame, and that he would carry the burden upon his shoulders. If he had not gone to the aid of the human child, then none of this would have happened.

His mind drifted back to the fateful events. The shame of his capture still cut him.

He had been scouting a wide range in front of the advancing senthanos. The group had been made up of a dozen of the Asur, led by a powerful seer. Eldanair was the scout for the senthanos, their Shadow Warrior, and it was his duty to ensure the paths they travelled were clear of the enemy.

There had been a scream, the high-pitched cry of a child, and he had dropped to his haunches amongst the low-lying ferns. The birds in the dark canopy far above had gone silent, and there was no sound but the icy howl of the wind whipping through the skeletal boughs of the trees, the creaking of branches that longed for the thaw to come.

A second scream carried to him on the wind. Spitting a curse, he had risen from his crouch and raced through the woodland towards the sound. To an onlooker, he knew that he would have appeared as little more than a shadow as he ghosted through the trees, moving at great speed.

What he had discovered had been sickening. It was the sight of a massacre. Human bodies were strewn across the road, blood pooling beneath their still forms. They had been savagely mutilated, and dozens of wounds covered each of the corpses so that they were almost unrecognisable, little more than hacked-apart meat. There were puncture wounds in most of the bodies, and Eldanair knew that that was where arrows had been pulled from their flesh. Or crossbow bolts, he thought darkly.

The eyes of each corpse had been cut out, and by the evidence of the ripped open chest cavities, it looked to Eldanair as if they had all had their hearts removed. Even the mule hitched to the wagon had been killed, its throat slashed open and its eyes torn from their sockets.

A girl, probably less than five human years old, was standing on the back of the wagon, her face pale as she looked around at the devastation that had been wrought. She must have hidden when the attack had come.

Eldanair had approached the girl, speaking sooth-ingly, and she stared at him with the frightened eyes of a doe, her body trembling. He approached slowly, and his voice was soft and calming. He placed his bow down upon the ground, and walked towards her with his hands outstretched.

Her eyes flicked over his shoulder, and then she screamed again, loudly and piercingly. He spun around to see a score of rough looking human soldiers moving out of the trees to encircle him. He cursed. In his haste, he had not heard or smelt their approach.

The men stared at the carnage with despair and outrage, their weapons levelled in his direction. When they looked upon him again, he saw the hatred, the fear and the anger written in their eyes.

He had lifted his hands up, showing he was unarmed, but they clubbed him to the ground anyway, and had dragged him back their village. He hadn't seen the little girl again.

Shaking himself from his reverie, Eldanair motioned to Annaliese to halt, and to be silent.

He ghosted up a rocky escarpment, crouching low to the ground. Nearing the top, he dropped to his stomach and wormed his way to its edge. He was careful to keep himself concealed amongst the wet ferns and not make any of them move, giving away his position.

What he saw below made his blood run cold.

He had found his companions. He had found the senthanos.

They were dead.

Their broken corpses lay strewn across the protected clearing, their white and blue cloaks and robes torn and slashed, stained dark with blood. Sorrow, shock and guilt fought for dominance within him, and he swallowed dryly.

He almost cried out when he saw the form of the seer, his slender frame hanging against the trunk of a tree. Crude wooden nails had been hammered through his wrists and ankles, and the robes had been torn from his chest. His ribs were splayed open, exposing his internal organs, and his heart was missing. By the look of agony on the dead seer's face, Eldanair guessed that his death had not been quick.

The human woman, Annaliese, had crawled up beside him, and her eyes widened in horror as she looked down upon the sight of the massacre. Her mouth opened to scream, but Eldanair clamped his hand over it tightly, holding her firmly in his arms. His eyes were locked on a shadow on the far side of the clearing.

The shadow was moving, so slowly at first that it was almost impossible to discern. But Eldanair's eyes were far keener than the eyes of a human's, and he could see the movement, even if Annaliese could not.

It was a slim figure, clad from head to toe in black, and it wore the darkness around it like a cloak. Shadows seemed to follow it, clinging to its rangy form like living creatures, and every muscle in Eldanair's body tensed with a deep and all-consuming hatred.

The black clad figure stepped gingerly over the corpses, turning its head from side to side as if sniffing the air. Black cloth covered the lower part of its face, and a deep black hood covered its head, but Eldanair caught a glimpse of the figure's face, and he burnt its visage into his memory.

The face was delicate and fine-boned, with high cheekbones that gave it an arrogant and graceful appearance, and Eldanair saw that it was female. Her flesh was as pale as his own, and her eyes were wide and cruelly, seductively curved. A small crossbow was held in one hand, and he made out a teardrop tattoo beneath her left eye before she turned away.

She dragged the concealing shadows with her as she left, and Eldanair cursed that he did not have his bow to hand. It would have been so easy to have killed her then and there. In an instant she had disappeared, melting into the darkness beneath the trees, and Eldanair tensed himself to go after her, hatred and the need for vengeance burning within him. He would hunt down and kill every one of the cursed murderers.

He glanced to his side and saw Annaliese's eyes wide and filled with helplessness and fear. To leave her was as good as a death sentence, and he cursed softly in elvish.

They lay unmoving for almost an hour before the elf deemed it safe to move from their position.

His heart heavy with sorrow and grief, he climbed down towards the mutilated bodies of his kin. Annaliese came down with him, tears in her eyes as she surveyed the carnage.

She said something to him, but he didn't know what her words meant.

Fixed in his mind's eye was the face of his enemy.

'Druchii,' he said to himself, the word spat with such venom that Annaliese looked at him sharply.

Dark elves were moving within the Empire.

CHAPTER SIX

FOUR DAYS HAD passed since they had left the site of the massacre. Eldanair's eyes were dark and brooding, and despite their inability to communicate verbally, Annaliese could see that a heavy burden weighed upon him.

If possible, he seemed even more distant, more cold and removed, than he had done previously. Nevertheless, the bond between the two had certainly strengthened, and Annaliese no longer feared him as she had done. She was convinced that he had not been one of the murderers that slaughtered the poor family on the road, for it seemed to her that the same killers were the ones to have set upon his own people.

Eldanair had worked tirelessly to give his people a simple burial. In shallow graves he had arranged their bodies carefully, crossing their arms over their chests. In death they looked ghostly and ethereal, yet at peace once Eldanair had cleaned away the blood from their flesh, and covered their wounds with draped cloaks. Annaliese was surprised to see that several of the party were female, yet garbed for war in the same manner as their comrades. Their weapons and personal belongings were placed alongside them, and the mourning elf had sung a soft, haunting song for them in the moonlight. With Annaliese's aid, he had gathered rocks and stones that he carefully piled onto the graves, forming a dozen cairns spread in a semi circular arc that clearly had some significance, though its meaning was unclear to her.

Tears had run down her face as Eldanair bid his comrades farewell, speaking quietly in his lilting, lyrical tongue. Though she could not understand his words, there was a deep and profound sadness about them.

Eldanair had armed himself, whispering to the fallen as he took up the weapons. A powerful recurving longbow of pale wood was now never far from his hands, and a slender longsword and matching knife were sheathed at his side.

Annaliese had felt honoured and moved as the elf had solemnly presented her with a weapon from one of his fallen kin – a slim-bladed shortsword of beautiful artistry. It was surprisingly light in her hands, and the blade was so thin that at first she thought it would shatter with any solid blow. It was far stronger than it looked – indeed, she now believed that it was far stronger than any of the broad, heavy blades that her father had on the walls of their cabin. Perfectly balanced, it felt comfortable in her hand. Even its scabbard was a work of art – simple and functional, yet highly elegant.

She longed to question Eldanair, about his people and about the murderous figure cloaked in shadows that she had glimpsed. It had not been human, she knew that much, for it moved with a sinister grace that no human could replicate. It moved, she noted, in the same way that Eldanair did, though the sheer malice and hatred the creature had exuded had been palpable. Being unable to communicate was proving frustrating, though the elf seemed content to remain in silence, lost in his own brooding, grim thoughts.

Annaliese was unsure of exactly where they currently were, but she guessed that they were nearing the border of Averland and Wissenland, heading towards the Upper Reik that divided the two states. It was the furthest she had ever been from her home, and it made her simultaneously scared and excited. Where Eldanair was now leading her was beyond her, and she wondered if he even had a destination in mind. Earlier he had been focused on escorting her to the camp of his kin, but now she did not know where he was taking her, and his movements lacked the urgency that had previously marked their travel. She could sense that he wanted to go after the shadow-cloaked figure, doubtlessly to enact his vengeance, and he was clearly in two minds. Sometimes she found him staring at her, with eyes angry and full of pain.

She wondered if he was taking her to a place of safety, to free himself of the burden of her presence. In honesty she could not guess at his thoughts, for he gave little away, and his ways, she reminded herself, were alien.

They travelled through woodland when they could, though this was not always possible, for these lands had long been dedicated to farming, and great expanses of trees had been felled generations earlier. The great forests that swathed most of the Empire were far to the north-west, and even the densest woodland in the south-eastern states was utterly unlike the claustrophobic, dark and dangerous Drakwald.

Eldanair was clearly uncomfortable travelling across the open fields, though they saw few people, and those were far away and easily avoided. They came across many abandoned farmsteads, and passed through icy fields that had long been neglected and left to ruin.

They paused to eat beside a natural spring. She guessed it was around midday, though it was hard to judge – heavy clouds threatened overhead, making the light dim and gloomy, and thunder rumbled ominously.

They ate a simple meal of berries and mushrooms they had collected while travelling. Eldanair pointed out edible foods as they passed, as well as indicating which mushrooms and toadstools were poisonous. Where she had viewed the snow-covered land as lacking in nourishment, she now realised that there was abundant food all around if you knew where to look. They drank from the spring, the mineral laden water tasting slightly metallic but not unpleasant.

After they had eaten, Annaliese slid her thin, elven blade from its scabbard. The metal was bluish-silver, without a hint of tarnish, and she held it reverently in her hands, savouring its weight. Eldanair motioned for her to stand, and she did so warily, sword in hand. He unclasped his flowing grey cloak and placed it on the ground before drawing his own blade and stepping backwards to give them some room. With a nod, he made an overly slow attack towards her.

She parried the blow with an overhead defence, as her father had taught her, and gave a swift riposte. Smoothly he parried the blow with a deft flick of his wrist, and he nodded at her, seeing that she had at least some skill. She felt a sudden need to impress the silent elf, and she whipped another attack towards him, throwing more weight and speed behind it.

He stepped swiftly to the side and angled her blade away from him. She stumbled, off balance, and she felt a flush creep over her face. He had been so balanced and swift. Frustrated and embarrassed she attacked again, her sword cutting left and right.

Eldanair's blade moved like liquid silver, darting back and forth, effortlessly deflecting her increasingly powerful blows, and the sound of steel on steel rang out sharply as each strike was turned away. He was not launching any attacks of his own, and Annaliese felt her frustration grow. She pulled her arm back to launch a yet fiercer attack, but Eldanair stepped away from her, raising his hand, a slight smile curling the corner of his lips.

Feeling foolish, she dropped her arm, breathing heavily. Eldanair walked to stand by her side and raised his sword into a defensive ready position before him. He nodded to Annaliese. When she didn't understand his meaning, he motioned more emphatically for her to raise her own weapon into the same position.

He ran through a series of strikes, correcting her technique and posture as she tried to emulate his crisp, sharp movements. He massaged her shoulders for a second, motioning to her to relax. She felt awkward, and the blush returned to her face.

Eldanair imitated her, swinging his sword in a wild arc, putting too much power into the blow and stumbling theatrically off balance. Annaliese's mouth opened in mock indignation.

'I don't look like that,' she said, half insulted and half laughing. Eldanair nodded at her.

'Right, well show me how to move like you, all balanced and everything.' She knew he could not understand, but it felt strange to her to remain in silence.

They practised for over an hour until Annaliese's arm felt like a leaden weight. Still, she had begun to feel more comfortable with the sword, that her movements were a little more controlled and sharp. She was now acutely aware that it would take her many years of practice to be classed as a decent swordswoman. She had been humbled, for she had regarded herself as at least competent with the blade, but that fact was now doubtful, she realised. She blew a strand of hair away from her face, and smiled broadly at Eldanair.

'Thank you,' she said, as she sheathed her blade. She collapsed onto the ground in mock exhaustion.

When she opened her eyes she saw Eldanair standing looking into the distance, his posture alert and his expression intense.

'What is it?' she said, sitting up. Eldanair held up a hand for silence and cocked his head to the side, listening intently. Annaliese could hear nothing but the gentle babbling of the spring. The light had dimmed further, so that it resembled the shadowy half-light after sunset.

Tense and cold, his eyes hard, Eldanair urged Annaliese to her feet swiftly, speaking sharply, and he led her quickly to the east, climbing the gentle rise away from the spring.

A distant horn sounded, and Eldanair broke into a loping run, nocking an arrow smoothly to his bowstring. Annaliese felt a wave of fear wash over her at the horrible sound. It was the sound of victorious hunters closing on their prey.

But what, or who, was the prey?

They travelled swiftly across the countryside, Annaliese struggling to keep pace with the elf. Dimly, she heard shouts and a shrill scream, accompanied by what sounded like the snarls and roars of wolves, or bears, though there was also the bleating not unlike that of goats, though deeper and more powerful. It made her feel instantly uneasy, and a shiver ran down her spine. There was the clash of weapons, and the hunting horn blared again; two long, hard notes.

As she struggled to the top of a steep rise, Eldanair pushed her roughly to the ground. She opened her mouth to voice her protest at his rough treatment, but held her tongue as he dropped to one knee and raised his bow. In one smooth action he pulled the bowstring taut and fired; the arrow hissed through the air away from him. In a flash he had another arrow drawn and nocked, and he fired it seemingly without pause to aim.

She followed the path of the arrows with difficulty through the dim light, and saw a powerfully muscled figure clad in furs stagger as an arrow slammed into its lower back.

It fell to its knees but struggled back to its feet, pulling the arrow free. Another arrow thudded into its head, and it fell motionless to the snowy ground.

It had been running with astonishing speed towards a train of wagons, and Annaliese saw that there were women and children crowded within them – more people fleeing the plague, most probably.

Forming a desperate ring around the wagons were a score of uniformed men, dressed in the black and yellow of Averland state troops. She heard a barked command, and four of the men fired their long arquebus handguns, the cracking sound of their fire echoing across the sky. Flame flashed from the barrels of the unwieldy weapons, and smoke obscured them from view.

These soldiers were accompanied by a rag-tag bunch of men hefting a motley array of axes, pitchforks and spears – the husbands, fathers and sons of the women-folk within the wagons.

Hurtling through the snow from either side of the wagons came their attackers, big men dressed in furs – they seemed to Annaliese to be wearing bestial faced, horned masks as well, and she was momentarily stunned by their bizarre appearance. They streamed towards the wagons and a fusillade from a second group of handgunners boomed, dropping several of them, dark blood misting out behind them.

Eldanair dropped another of them with an arrow through the base of his skull, and Annaliese heard three sharp blasts from a hunting horn. At the sound, Eldanair instantly rose, dragging Annaliese to her feet, and began pulling her by the arm down the hill, cutting left away from the wagons. She lost sight of them as she was half-dragged around a raised hillock covered in twisted thorn bushes and rocks.

Annaliese shook free of his grip.

'We have to help them!' she shouted, pointing towards the wagons. Eldanair said something sharp in his own tongue, and made to grab her wrist once again, but she stepped away from him, her face defiant.

'No!' she shouted. 'We are going to help them!'

A stream of words spat from Eldanair's lips, and he made an encircling motion that she did not understand.

'These are my people,' said Annaliese. 'I have to help them.' She turned away from Eldanair, and began moving around the hillock back towards the wagons.

A monstrous bestial roar, something akin to that of a bear but filled with malice, echoed loudly down into the dip, and Annaliese faltered, looking around her fearfully. Scanning the area with wide eyes, she saw a pair of the fur-clad figures standing on the ridge they had just left, their horned heads scanning the area. One of them snarled as it spotted her, and the pair of them began leaping down the incline towards her, kicking powdery snow out around them.

They were not wearing furs, she realised, and they were not human. The one in the lead was roughly the same size of a man, but its face was a bestial mockery of humanity. A pair of short horns jutted from its forehead, and small, feral eyes fixed hungrily on her. It whooped in excitement, exposing an array of stubby fangs, and began closing the distance to her with terrifying swiftness. Its two legs were back-jointed like those of a goat and covered in shaggy, dark fur.

And yet, it was not some mindless, mutated beast of the forest, that much was clear. Its baleful eyes blazed with animal cunning, and there was the hint of a feral intelligence working there, and it wore a semblance of clothing. A loincloth of rough leather was secured by strips of sinew tied around its waist, and tokens and bones hung from this crude belt. Bracers of beaten copper protected its forearms, and in its clawed hands it clasped a pair of weapons – a savagely barbed spear decorated with plaited hair soaked in blood, and a rusted cleaver.

The second of the creatures was much more heavily built, and thick matted fur hung down over the rippling muscles of its torso. It stood easily a head taller than six feet in height, and its brutish face was broad and hateful, a pair of thick horns covered in beaten copper curling from the side of its head. Around the thick, corded muscles of its neck hung strings of bones and teeth. An obscene symbol had been smeared in blood upon its massive chest, and it carried a massive axe in its hands. Its skin, the colour of wet earth, was pierced with studs and rings of metal, and it bellowed deafeningly as it charged towards her, hefting its axe over its heavy head.

The first creature drew back its arm and hurled its heavy spear.

Eldanair slammed into Annaliese from behind, knocking her to the ground, and the deadly missile streaked over her head to imbed itself into the snow. He was up instantly, loosing an arrow from his bow.

Annaliese scrambled to her feet, her shaking hands fumbling for her sword. The first creature fell as if poleaxed as Eldanair's arrow thudded into its neck, but the second was barely slowed as another arrow embedded itself deep into the slab-like muscle of its chest.

Then it was on them, towering over Eldanair, swinging its axe down in a powerful blow that would have split him in two had it connected. He ducked beneath the wild swing and leapt past the creature, rolling neatly and coming up to one knee, an arrow nocked. He fired, and such was the power of bow at close range that the arrow sank almost to its feathered flight into the creature's back, and it roared as it was knocked forward a pace by the force.

Still it did not fall, and it swung towards him, spittle dripping in thick ropes from its maw.

With a scream, Annaliese surged forwards and the blade of her elven shortsword pierced the creature's side. With one hand upon the pommel she drove the blade in with all her strength and weight, pushing it deep into its body. Blood, dark and hot, poured from the wound and the creature roared in pain and fury. It spun around and the haft of its giant axe caught Annaliese a glancing blow to the side of the head, sending her reeling backwards into the snow. It stepped over her, axe raised for the killing blow. The beast shuddered as an arrow punched through the back of its skull, piercing its brain. It toppled into the snow beside Annaliese, blood leaking from its wounds.

Annaliese rose shakily to her knees, wincing as she touched a hand gingerly to her temple. She felt a wave of nausea overcome her, and she coughed and retched the contents of her stomach onto the pristine white snow. The stink of the creature was overpowering.

Three sharp blasts were blown on a hunting horn, and Eldanair loosed several more arrows, though Annaliese, her head pounding, could not focus on what he was firing at. She gathered a handful of snow and held it against her head; the cold numbed the pain.

Wiping her mouth, she stared bleary-eyed at the corpses of the two creatures. Shuddering, she looked away. Eldanair was kneeling at her side, concern on his face, and he gently pulled her hand away from the rising lump on her head, inspecting the wound carefully. Apparently satisfied, he nodded his head, and went to the bodies of the dead beastmen, wrenching his arrows free from their dead flesh and studying their tips, testing them on his thumb. He pulled free Annaliese's sword, and wiped the gore from it with a handful of snow. Spinning it around in his hand, he presented it hilt first to the fallen woman.

When she was able to stand, her legs shaking, Annaliese saw that the battle was over. Milling people surrounded the wagons, and she heard the wailing of women and the cries of children. She motioned to Eldanair that she was going towards the wagons, and he nodded, pulling the hood of his cloak over his head to hide his elven features. He moved out across the open ground to retrieve his other arrows.

As she drew close, she saw women crying over the bodies of dead men: husbands, brothers or fathers. Others were binding the wounds of those lucky enough to have survived, and a team of soldiers was struggling to get the lead wagon moving, as it was stuck in a snowdrift.

She saw a flicker of movement, and cried out when she saw a small boy, no more than five years old, crawling through the snow towards a corpse on the ground. Fresh blood was trailing behind the boy.

No one was moving towards the child, and Annaliese ran to him. The man he was crawling towards had the look of a farmer about him, and his head had been all but severed from his body by a vicious blow to the back of his neck. Blood soaked the snow around him.

Kneeling, Annaliese took the boy in her arms, carefully turning him over. He cried out, straining to see the corpse, and Annaliese felt tears spring to her eyes as she saw the blood soaking the child's tunic and the expression on the child's face as it contorted in pain. She clasped him to her, tears rolling down her cheeks, soothing him with gentle words.

'Da?' gasped the boy, his wide blue eyes fearful.

'Shh,' soothed Annaliese, wiping her hand over his brow, brushing back his sandy hair.

'Where is Da?' the boy said again, blood frothing on his lips.

'At peace,' said Annaliese softly. The boy cried out in pain, and Annaliese's heart wrenched. 'Be brave, little warrior,' she said.

She closed her eyes and prayed then, silently mouthing words to Sigmar. Angry and bitter, she raged against the cruelty of the world, and beseeched the warrior-god for mercy, tears running down her face.

When she opened her eyes she saw that the boy was asleep, his heart beating strongly against her.

Annaliese laid him back against the ground, and ripped open his blood-drenched tunic. She rubbed her hand across the flesh of his stomach, expecting to find a deep wound, but the skin was unbroken. Her eyes widened in shock.

'You should leave him,' said a voice. 'I saw the cursed spear strike him. It was a cowardly blow, but not even a full grown man could have survived it.'

Annaliese looked up into the sad, grim eyes of a farmer and smiled. 'He is not even wounded,' she said

breathlessly, shaking her head. The farmer stared at her
as if she were mad.

'I saw it myself, girl,' he repeated, a pitying expression
coming over his face. She shook her head, and wiped
away more of the blood on the boy's skin.

'Look – there is no wound! The boy lives!' she said,
louder this time. She was certain that the boy had been
close to death, but she could now see the rise and fall
of his chest as he rested peacefully.

The farmer looked at the boy, then at her, fear in his
eyes.

'Witchcraft,' he muttered.

'What?' said Annaliese. 'What are you talking about?
It must not have been his blood. The spear must have
missed him!'

'Don't look at me, witch!' cried the farmer, shielding
his eyes from her gaze. More people looked over at her,
fear and suspicion on their faces. They muttered
beneath their breath.

Annaliese stood up, wiping the tears from her face.
'No,' she said emphatically, shaking her head. 'You are
mistaken. The boy is well.'

'Where did she come from?' said a fearful voice. Several of the soldiers tightened their grips on their
halberds uneasily, stepping towards her.

'She wasn't with us before the attack. She led them to
us!' declared an elderly woman, to the accompaniment
of angry mutterings.

Lifting the boy protectively in her arms, she stepped
backwards away from the angry group, shaking her
head. She felt the reassuring presence of Eldanair
behind her, his bow in hand.

'Leave her be,' snapped one of the soldiers. 'She and
her companion killed several of the beasts.'

'That child was dead, I tell you. He should be journeying to the halls of Morr, alongside his father,' said the first farmer, his voice raised. 'She brought him back to life! She's a witch!'

'Enough,' roared the soldier. 'There will be no more bloodshed this day. Go get those wagons moving.' The farmer stared at the man darkly. 'Go!' the soldier barked. Then he marched towards Annaliese.

'Thank you,' she said breathlessly. 'I... I don't understand it. I too thought he was close to death. But... I must have been mistaken.'

The soldier was middle-aged, and his armour dented and scarred from use and repair. His face was grim, and his eyes dead as they flicked from Annaliese to Eldanair, who tugged his hood down lower over his face. He shrugged.

'I don't want to see any more people hurt,' he said. 'Where are the boy's parents?'

'His mother died in childbirth. Her father lies dead at your feet. He has no family.'

'Someone must take him in,' Annaliese said. The soldier looked at her blankly.

'He has no family,' he said slowly. 'There is no one to take him in.'

'Surely someone amongst these people will care for him? Some relative, or friend?'

The soldier shook his head. 'These people are starving,' he said, his voice lowered. 'There are not enough provisions as it is – he is just another mouth to feed, another back to clothe. There is no one, I'm sorry.' He turned away from her, and began marching back towards the wagons.

'But you cannot leave him here to die!' she said, going after him. The soldier turned back to her, his face hard.

'It might have been better for him if he *had* died,' he hissed. 'I saw him struck as well – it was a mortal blow. I don't know what power it was that you used to heal him, but I will not allow you or the boy to travel with us. Care for him yourself.'

The anger faded from him and he seemed to slump, exhaustion overcoming him. He sighed, running a hand across his unshaved jaw, and Annaliese realised that this was the real reason why they would not accept the child – they feared that she had healed him with sorcerous power, and that perhaps he had been tainted by the power of Chaos.

'There is a temple of Shallya, some twenty leagues to the north-east. Follow the road, and you will find it. The gentle sisters of that order will take the boy in. I wish you well.'

With that, he turned away.

ELDANAIR GLARED AT the humans from within his deep cowl, and loosened the tension on his bowstring, though he kept an arrow nocked. He couldn't understand the words spoken during the exchange, but he guessed at their meaning. These humans were barbarians, he thought, turning on each other in their ignorance and fear.

He had hoped to escort the woman to her people, to see her safe and then he could return to hunting the Druchii and enact his vengeance. He touched a long finger to his cheek, following the thin black tattoo design. *Thalui* was the name for the rune and it represented hatred and vengeance. Many of his people, the Shadow Warriors of ruined Nagarythe, bore such symbols so that the atrocities perpetrated by the hated Dark

Elves, the Druchii, would never be forgotten. But he saw now that she would not be safe with these people, for they clearly could not even protect themselves.

To see the beastmen herd so far from the dense forests where they bred was surprising. To see them emboldened enough to venture forth, and in daylight no less, spoke of the threat that the human realm was in. With the human armies engaged elsewhere, the beasts of the deep forbidden places where man feared to tread had become bold, striking out against ones likes these, weakly protected and vulnerable. He doubted that many of the humans even realised that their world, their Empire, teetered on the brink of destruction.

Guilt wracked him. Had he been with his kin, he would surely have seen signs of the Druchii war party. His kinsmen would not have died. If he had not gone to the aid of the human child, then he would never have been captured. If he had left Annaliese to her fate, then he would have covered the ground back to his kin far swifter, and their massacre would have been averted.

The weight of their deaths was upon his shoulders. Annaliese had lived at the expense of his kin, and for that he may have hated her. But he did not. No, if she were to die, then the deaths of his kin were for nought, and he now swore to himself to protect her, to see her safe until such a time as he deemed her ably protected.

A human would have difficulty understanding his honour, he knew, but that mattered little to him. They were a strange people, and before he met Annaliese he had discounted them all. But she was different, he saw that, and as much as he desired his vengeance against the Druchii, he knew that it could wait. When the human woman was safe, then he would resume his blood-quest against them. Only then, when all those who had slaughtered his kin had perished, would his soul be unburdened by guilt and remorse.

He would take Annaliese to the south. War wracked the north – though, as they had seen, no place was safe – the southern lands of the Empire would be the least affected in the dark days to come. He sighed, for she seemed to have adopted the human child. Though it would slow their progress further, he could not expect her to abandon the child, as it seemed the others had done.

'Annaliese,' he said, indicating that they should get moving. He was wary of the beasts of Chaos nearby, and he reckoned that once they had recovered their nerve, they would attack again, probably under the cover of darkness. With certainty, he knew that the humans with the wagons would be dead by sunrise.

He motioned again for her to come, to resume their travel, but she merely shook her head, pointing along the road, to the east. It was the direction that the wagons had come from. What was she thinking? He shook his head, but saw the determined set of her mouth, and knew that she would not relent. By the gods of the Asur, she was a headstrong woman.

'Upon the spirits of my murdered brothers of the Asur, I swear that I shall see you safe,' he snapped in his native tongue. 'But I cannot protect you from your own innate human stubbornness, child.'

She pointed fiercely to the east, and he shook his head resolutely. She snapped something in her crude, guttural language, and turned to watch the wagons rolling away, shifting the weight of the sleeping child to her hip, his head on her shoulder. They could have been mother and child, he thought, for they both shared the same sandy blonde hair.

How old was she? Perhaps eighteen? Long past the time when most human women would have spawned children of their own, he thought with some distaste. Rare was it amongst his own people for a child to be born of an elf maiden less than a hundred and fifty years old. Humanity is a race of children, no wonder they bickered and turned on their own with such frequency. It was also no wonder that they were so susceptible to the wiles of Chaos, he thought darkly, for with their foreshortened, largely futile lives, the tempting lure of a shortcut to power must be attractive.

When she turned back to him, there were tears in her eyes. She indicated to the sleeping boy, and pointed to the east once more, though this time the movement lacked anger. Eldanair did not move a muscle. Annaliese stepped in to him, and raising herself up onto her tiptoes, she placed a sad kiss upon his pale cheek. She said something else that he guessed was a parting goodbye, and she turned away from him and began walking along the road, heading to the east.

Thunder rolled, and vast arcs of lightning could be seen flashing in the sky. Vaul was at his anvil, as was said amongst his people of Nagarythe to describe such weather.

He glared at the departing figure of Annaliese, and began walking to the east, following in her wake.

CHAPTER SEVEN

Udo Grunwald swore and gritted his teeth as the gruff voice behind him continued its slow, rhythmic, mournful song. *If* that dire sound could be classed as song, he thought.

He didn't understand the words of course, but it sounded like some relentless requiem that droned on and on monotonously without end. When occasionally it stopped, Grunwald closed his eyes and listened to the blessed silence. It never lasted long.

They had covered tens of miles on foot, and he wasn't sure if his travelling companion had merely started the chanting song over again after these small breaks, or if it really was some torturous drone that truly had no end. He wouldn't be at all surprised if that were the case.

This wasn't the only thing that grated on Grunwald's nerves. His companion seemed incapable of moving without alerting every living soul within a ten-mile radius of their position. Every heavy step of his nail-studded, metal encased boots was accompanied by the clanking of metal and the jangling of buckles and chainmail.

Grunwald turned around to look upon his companion, his deep baritone voice still booming out from beneath his helmet.

Thorrik stood just over four feet tall, a decent height for his kin, and he was almost as wide as he was tall. He probably weighed twice that of a full-grown man, and that was before you included the heavy armour that he wore. Gromril, Thorrik had called the metal it was forged of, and it was unlike any metal that the witch hunter had ever seen. Stronger than steel, the dwarf claimed, able to deflect all but the most powerful blows, it was sometimes known as silverstone or hammernought. Within the lands of the Empire, it was called meteoric iron, and that was a name familiar to Grunwald, though he had never seen the fabled metal before.

Only Thorrik's glittering eyes could be seen beneath his fully enclosed helmet. Beneath this spilled his real beard, his pride and joy, a billowing mass of red hair that had been drawn into a dozen plaits with thin wire twisted through them and each decorated with a circular metal icon depicting a stylised dwarfen face. Ancestor deities, Grunwald had learnt.

He had no idea how the dwarf moved within such an immense amount of armour, let alone marched and fought. And it wasn't as if the armour was the only load that the dwarf bore – he carried a heavy looking pack across his shoulders, along with the mysterious large shape wrapped in waterproofed leather. On one arm he carried his solid gromril shield, and he carried his axe. Such a load would have been a heavy burden for a mule, let alone a man, but the dwarf bore it without complaint, and he seemed easily able to march all day despite the weight.

Seeing that Grunwald had halted, Thorrik ceased his baritone singing and planted his feet in the snow, glaring up at the taller figure.

'What's the problem?' he growled, his voice deep and rumbling. 'Why are you stopping?'

'What was that you were singing, anyway? You have been singing it non-stop for days now,' said Grunwald.

'It is a traditional marching chant of Clan Barad, from Karaz-a-Karak,' Thorrik replied. 'It was the chant the armies of Clan Barad would march to war by in the time of my great-great-grandfather. It recounts the deeds of those slain during the siege of Karak Drazh, when Clan Barad came to the aid of our besieged kin. Rousing, is it not?'

'That's not the word that I was going to use,' said Grunwald. 'Can you not travel more... quietly?'

'I do not hide from my enemies. I have no need to travel silently.'

Grunwald turned away from the dwarf and began striding through the snow up the ridge. Thorrik wasn't singing, but still each footstep was accompanied by the clank of metal. In the distance, the mountain range came into view.

The Black Mountains – sharp and inhospitable peaks with barren, sheer cliffs of iron-hard rock, they had a dangerous reputation. They towered up into the clouds, though Grunwald knew that even their dizzy heights were far surpassed by the immense Worlds Edge Mountains that butted up against them to the north-east. That range climbed higher than he could conceive.

The mountains surrounded the Empire on most sides, and Grunwald knew that his people had grown strong thanks to their defensive borders. Though the enemies of mankind were many and powerful, were it not for the towering mountains the Empire would have long ago become merely a footnote in the histories of the dwarfs.

A flutter of movement caught his eyes, and he halted, squinting into the morning sunlight that had finally managed to pierce the ever-present clouds.

'What now, manling?' blurted Thorrik. 'You try my patience!'

Without speaking, Grunwald pointed into the distance. The vanguard of an Empire state force could be seen, rounding an area of coppiced woodland. Banners flying the black and yellow of Averland fluttered in the sharp breeze, and the sound of drumbeats could now be heard, carrying across the open ground.

The soldiers marched in perfect unison to the beat of the drums. In a long, thin column they snaked from behind the coppice, following the road that led from Averheim. Tall halberds rested on the right shoulders of the front regiments, and many of the soldiers wore long black feathers in their helmets and cloth caps that bobbed in time to their disciplined march.

The smaller road that Grunwald and Thorrik travelled along, little more than a pair of deep furrows carved by the wheels of wagons loaded with goods, intercepted the larger road that the Empire troops marched along some three hundred yards from their position.

'Looks like they are heading in the same direction as us,' said Grunwald.

He estimated that there were around eight hundred men already in view, and the State army continued to emerge from behind the woods. Alongside the column were several contingents of knights riding powerful warhorses bedecked in lacquered black and bronze barding. Elegant plumes topped the helms of the fully armoured knights, and pennants rippled from the tips of their lances.

Grunwald squinted to make out the details of their banners – a bronze sun device on a black background, surrounded by intricate scrollwork.

'Knights of the Blazing Sun,' he commented. 'An entire temple's worth by the looks of it.' He grunted and frowned. This was an army of considerable force, all heading towards Black Fire Pass. Surely they would be of more worth deployed in the north, he thought.

'Wonder if they would spare a horse?' he added.

'Hateful beasts,' grumbled Thorrik.

One of the contingents of knights broke into a canter and wheeled off the road, heading towards Grunwald and Thorrik. The witch hunter reached beneath his tunic and pulled out a bronze icon hung from a chain around his neck so that it hung outside his dark clothes. It was a weighty pendant shaped to mirror the holy weapon of Sigmar Heldenhammer, the great war hammer Ghal Maraz, and it was the symbol that denoted him as a servant of Sigmar's temple. It had previously belonged to the witch hunter Stoebar, before Grunwald became one of the order.

He saw that Thorrik was tense as the powerful destriers of the knights closed the distance, pounding across
the rough ground and kicking up great clods of earth as
they went.

They were an impressive sight, and Grunwald was
thankful that their lances were held aloft rather than
lowered for the charge. A charge by these seasoned
knights would be terrifying.

As they drew closer, he saw that a brazen icon topped
the heavy fabric of the standard, depicting an eagle
clutching a spear in its talons. This was a variation of
the symbol of the foreign deity Myrmidia, patron goddess of the human realms to the south-west of the
Empire. Though he was suspicious of this god, for it
was not a deity traditionally honoured within the
Empire, Grunwald respected the martial traditions of
its followers and the strict code of honour it was said
they abided by.

The ground shook with the thunder of hooves, and
they pulled up in perfect unison before the pair of travellers, displaying remarkable horsemanship and control.
Horses snorted and shook their heads, jangling their bri-
dles. The armour of the knights was wonderfully crafted
– immaculate burnished bronze edging rimmed their
gleaming, black lacquered plate mail.

One of the knights, bearing a wreath of bronze-leafed
ivy around the crown of his helmet, lifted his visor. The
knight's face was surprisingly young and clean-shaven.

'Who are you, and what business have you in these
parts?' the young knight said, looking down at the pair,
his voice strong and authoritative.

'What business is that of yours?' snapped Thorrik,
and Grunwald glared at him, holding a hand up to

hush him. He shook his head slightly before looking up at the young knight.

'My name is Udo Grunwald, and I am a holy templar of Sigmar,' he said. 'I am travelling to the temple of my order near Black Fire Pass. This is my travelling companion, Thorrik Lokrison, of Everpeak. And you, knight of Myrmidia, what is your name and purpose here?'

'I am Karl Heiden, preceptor of the Knights of the Blazing Sun. We travel with an army of Averland to the defence of Black Fire Pass.'

'The defence of the pass? What is this you speak of? The war is in the north.'

'Some amongst us will travel from Black Fire Pass to the north. But the war is all around us,' countered the knight. 'The pass is threatened.'

'The pass is guarded by the clans of my kinsmen,' growled Thorrik. 'Do you doubt the strength of the dwarfs, beardling?'

The knight turned his gaze upon the bristling figure of the dwarf ironbreaker. 'I intend no slur or disrespect with my words,' he said. 'But if Black Fire Pass falls, it is Empire lands that will be ravaged, not those of dwarfen kind.'

'To guard what manlings call Black Fire Pass was an oath sworn by the forebears of all dwarfs,' growled Thorrik, his gravelly voice thick with outrage. 'It was an oath sworn of blood, and as long as a single dwarf lives, no enemy shall attack the Empire through the pass.' Grunwald sighed.

'I commend your vigilance and pride, master dwarf,' said the knight carefully, 'and I believe you would speak the truth, if times were different. But war threatens the dwarfen holds as well as the Empire – we come to bolster Black Fire Pass at the behest of your High King himself.'

Thorrik's eyes narrowed.

'What do you speak of when you say war threatens dwarfen holds?'

'The greenskin tribes are massing beyond the mountains. It is said they threaten the Everpeak itself.'

'Bah!' snorted Thorrik. 'Impossible!'

The knight shrugged his shoulders, a movement all but hidden by his thick, black lacquered armour.

'Is the temple of Sigmar intact and secure?' asked Grunwald sharply.

'I regret that I do not know,' replied the knight. He raised his hand, and the knights snapped to attention. The first regiments of foot troops were passing along the road now, the thump of their footsteps echoing loudly.

'You say that some amongst your force will travel to the north from Black Fire – why travel here if your destination is in the northern states? That's a long way out of your way, templar,' said Grunwald. The knight merely grinned.

'You haven't heard of the steam engine of the dwarfs, then?'

Grunwald frowned, but the preceptor continued, not giving him time to query his words.

'We march to Black Fire Pass. Travel with us if you wish,' said the knight. 'Speak to supplies officer Siegfried at the rear of the column. You may request a steed from him, tell him that I have authorised it. He may even be able to find a small pony for your friend to ride,' he said, his eyes shining with humour though his face was serious. 'Or a large dog.'

With that, the knights turned and wheeled away, leaving Grunwald smiling and Thorrik apoplectic with rage.

'I should stick my axe so far up his arse that it severs his tongue for that insult,' he raged, his face turning a deep crimson that matched the colour of his bristling beard.

'I'm sure he was just trying to be helpful,' commented Grunwald.

'Helpful? The stripling, beardless whoreson bastard...' Without pausing for breath the dwarf switched to his native language and cut loose with a torrent of bile-fuelled phrases. Grunwald didn't know what he was saying, but he winced at the acidic, barbed and vengeful tone of voice. It slowly descended into insensible muttering.

'So, what *do* you think of dogs?' asked Grunwald, trying to hide his smirk. Thorrik glared up at him suspiciously, trying to see any mockery in his face. Satisfied, he grunted loudly before making his answer.

'Good eating,' he said, finally.

ANNALIESE WAS EXHAUSTED when they finally reached the brow of a hill and saw the temple of Shallya in the distance. She walked hand in hand with the boy. After two days he had finally spoken, though he said nothing more than his name.

'Look Tomas,' she said, pointing towards the crooked spire that topped the temple of Shallya. 'The sisters are kind. If you are lucky, you might even get a hot bath this evening!' She leant down and sniffed at him, then reeled, her face a mask of exaggerated disgust. The boy giggled, his facing lighting up. He copied her, sniffing her and then gasping.

Annaliese laughed. 'I guess I could do with a bath too, young Tomas.' It had been too long since she'd had anything to laugh at.

It took an hour to walk down to the temple. She carried Tomas part of the way, until he felt like a leaden weight in her arms. The sky was dark overhead, clouds hanging too close to the ground, making the air claustrophobic and heavy. Still, it was a little warmer here, either because she was further south than her village – or perhaps the winter was finally breaking.

There was still snow piled in drifts up against rough stone walls and hedges, but the fields were relatively clear. The grass was muddy and dead, but it would grow back.

Tomas made her laugh as he spotted a mouse and sprang after it as it ducked into a hedgerow to escape from him. The boy emerged a moment later, sticks in his hair, grinning, crunching happily through the snow back to her side.

Eldanair appeared silently, the hood pulled down low over his face. Tomas instantly hid behind Annaliese, and she put her hand comfortingly upon his shoulder. The elf pulled off his hood. His face was grim, and Annaliese looked at him in growing concern.

She heard the ugly cawing of crows.

The temple of Shallya had been ransacked, and gutted by fire. Worse, it had been defiled, and crude symbols had been daubed on its walls in what looked like blood. There was no sign of the sisters.

There was an animal stink that assailed their nostrils as they approached the temple, as if a herd of wild dogs had used the place as a refuse pit, and despite the cold the buzzing of flies filled the air. Annaliese lifted

Tomas, hugging him against her chest and keeping his head turned away from the desecrated place. He began to cry, and she rocked him in her arms, making soothing noises.

Eldanair held his hand up for her to remain outside, and with an arrow nocked to his bow, he stepped lightly through the shattered doors of the temple.

Annaliese surveyed the carnage with sad eyes. The windows had been smashed in, and the smell of faeces and urine was strong. Her eyes were drawn to the crude symbols painted on the pale stone walls of the small chapel, and she felt revulsion pull at her.

She walked around the outside of the chapel grounds. There was a small vegetable garden around the rear of the structure, but it was trampled and kicked apart. There were small icon shrines positioned on low poles in front of small wooden benches, places for silent, isolated communion. They had all been smashed down. She stopped before one of these shattered icons, seeing a small woodcarving of Shallya kneeling. Carefully so as not to drop Tomas, she bent over and lifted the carving out of the snow. It looked as though an axe had removed the head of the carving. She dropped it back into the snow with a sigh.

Rounding the shrine, she lifted her eyes and gasped. She had found one of the gentle sisters of the goddess of healing.

She was spreadeagled across a wagon wheel and nailed to its wooden rim. The wheel had been lifted into the air and its broken axle driven into the ground, so that she lay looking up into the sky.

Carrion birds hopped over the body, flapping their wings and cawing loudly as they fought over the tastiest morsels. Annaliese felt bile rise in her throat, and she began to shake uncontrollably. Tomas wailed, and tried to squirm out of her grip, but she covered his eyes with her hand and kept him clasped to her tightly. She ran blindly away from the nightmarish scene, round the corner of the shrine and straight into the arms of Eldanair.

She cried into his chest as his arms closed around her awkwardly, as if he were uneasy with such contact. At last she pulled away, hugging Tomas to her with one hand as she wiped the tears away from her face.

Eldanair indicated for her to follow him, and he led her around to the front of the shrine and through its shattered door. She almost gagged at the stench inside, and Tomas began to cry loudly once more.

The elf led them to the back of the temple, past smashed pews. Glass crunched underfoot, and Eldanair finally pointed down a stone staircase that led beneath the temple floor, down into the crypt.

She looked at him in concern, but he nodded encouragement, and led the way down the narrow, worn steps. It was icy cold as she descended, but it was not as dark as she had imagined, as light illuminated the crypt through carved recesses, shafts that led up to windows in the shrine.

There were carved statues of reclining women, and each had a plaque before it. She looked at one, but she could not read, and it meant nothing to her. The stubs of candles protruded from candelabras that may have been lit in honour of the temple's deceased priestesses, but thankfully it seemed that the marauders had not discovered this area, and the stench was not as strong down here.

The hair on the back of Annaliese's neck rose as she heard a scrape against the cold stone flooring, and she froze. A shadowy shape dashed away from them, and Eldanair motioned for her to approach.

Peering into the gloom, she saw that there was a person crouched behind one of the tombs. She saw a glimpse of long hair and pale robes, and understanding dawned on her. She placed Tomas onto the ground and knelt before him, looking into his tearful eyes.

'I want you to be a brave boy, and to stay with Eldanair for a moment. I won't be long.' The boy whimpered and clung to her. 'I promise I will be back in a moment, I am just going to talk to the lady over there.'

She began to move towards the woman, but Tomas continued to cling to her desperately. She sighed, and picked him up again. Eldanair shrugged. 'All right Tomas, you can come with me. Come on.'

She moved slowly towards the woman. 'Hello?' she said. 'My name is Annaliese, and we are not going to harm you. You are safe now.'

She stepped around an ancient stone tomb. The woman cowered in the corner, her face mostly hidden beneath an unruly mass of dark hair. She was wearing the robes of a priestess.

'You are one of the Sisters of Shallya, aren't you? It's alright; there is nothing here now. They have gone.'

She moved closer, and dropped to her knees, steadying Tomas onto his feet. He stared at the woman curiously.

'Where are the others of your order, sister?'

The woman looked her in the eyes then, and they were filled with pain and fear. Her face was dirty and

streaked with tears, and she began rocking back and
forth.

'Gone,' she said, shaking her head. 'They've all gone.
Just Sister Margrethe and I left…' She looked up at
Annaliese frantically. 'I don't know where Sister Mar-
grethe is. I…I heard her screaming.'

'She is not in pain anymore,' said Annaliese, and the
woman slumped down against the wall.

'I prayed for her. They are gone?' she said fearfully.
'They are truly gone? They were animals, they attacked
us, braying and shouting…'

'Shh,' said Annaliese softly, hugging Tomas. Seeing
the boy the woman's eyes seemed to clear a little and
she smiled through her tears.

'And what is your name, young man?'

'Tomas,' he replied shyly.

'Tomas – a strong name for a strong boy,' the woman
replied.

'You don't need to cry,' said the boy, and the priestess
laughed, wiping away her tears.

'Bless you, boy,' she said. Annaliese stood and
offered her arm to the woman, who took it and
allowed herself to be helped to her feet. 'The strength
of the innocent is a wondrous thing – here am I, old
enough to be his grandmother and I have gone to
pieces, yet a boy not more than five years old can
still smile.'

'How FAR IS it?' asked Annaliese to the priestess, whose
name was Katrin. With her face and robes cleaned,
Annaliese could see that she was a handsome woman
of middling years, and though her eyes were haunted,
she had a way with the child.

'Two days' walk, no more,' Katrin answered. She turned and smiled at Annaliese. 'You have travelled far – I am grateful that you are escorting me to the temple. I do not think I could have faced it alone – to be honest I do not think I would ever have summoned the strength to leave the crypt.'

'I am glad that we found you,' she said, staring up at the towering Black Mountains before them. 'Though I am sorry we did not arrive sooner.'

'There would only have been more pain and death had you arrived any sooner,' said Katrin.

'We might have been able to stop them.'

'Maybe. Maybe not. Either way there would have been more death and violence, and that is anathema to our order. It would have made the goddess weep.'

'Is not your order dedicated to life? To living?'

'Of course it is, but not at the expense of the life of another, Annaliese,' she gently chided. She sighed deeply. 'I already miss Sister Margrethe greatly – she was a gentle, simple girl.'

'I'm sorry to remind you, sister,' said Annaliese.

'Pff,' said Katrin, waving away the apology. 'Grief and sadness is a part of life, and not something to hide from,' she said, looking into Annaliese's eyes. The girl looked away quickly, her hand resting on the hilt of her sword.

'The boy is strong and healthy,' said Katrin, judging Annaliese's mood and changing the subject. The boy was running ahead, looking back anxiously to see if they were still following. 'Though there is pain hidden away inside him that will take a lifetime to heal. If it ever does.'

'You are good with children,' said Annaliese.

'As are you. You are what – seventeen years? You have no children of your own?'

'No. I… never married.'

They walked on in silence. Eldanair was out in front, an indistinct grey shadow a hundred yards ahead.

'You certainly keep strange company,' commented Katrin, shaking her head. 'An orphan and an elf.'

Annaliese smiled, and nodded.

'Why did your order leave your temple, Katrin? Why was it only you and Margrethe that were left behind?'

The older woman sighed again.

'The Empire is beset by foes, surrounded on all sides by enemies deadly and jealous. The head of my order was visited by a vision of the Lady Shallya herself in a dream. The goddess was weeping, for she knew of the horrors yet to come. When the head sister awoke, she ordered the others to ready themselves to travel to Black Fire Pass, to the temple of Sigmar there. That was where we would be needed in the dark days to come,' Katrin said.

'But why were you chosen to stay behind?' asked Annaliese.

'In truth? I requested it. I am tired, Annaliese, and I have seen much horror in my life. Though I know the head sister wished for me to be at her side, I asked to be the one to remain behind, to tend the weeping shrine until the order returned.' She shook her head with a sigh. 'Strange how things turn out, but it is not my place to question the will of the gods.'

'It must be peaceful, living within the temple,' said Annaliese. She immediately went red. 'Under normal circumstances, I mean,' she hastily added.

'Peaceful? Yes, I was never more at peace than I have been in the years since joining the order. Sad? Yes. Difficult? Yes. But you are correct; I am at peace in myself.

'You could join the temple, Annaliese,' Katrin said after a pause. 'You would find a home amongst us. And I can see that you have the healing touch within you.'

Annaliese blushed again. Lightning flashed above the Black Mountains.

Katrin sighed to herself. She had spoken the truth, and the girl could find a home amongst the Sisters of Shallya, but she would never become one of their order.

Another god had already claimed her as his own.

CHAPTER EIGHT

THE LIGHTNING FLASHING across the skies above the mountains in the distance made the mood of the camp grim. In Grunwald's experience, soldiers were a superstitious bunch, and seeing the flashes in the direction they were travelling could be seen as a bad omen.

He had no time for omens and he was far from a superstitious man, even when he had been a regular soldier in the army of Nuln. He had always been devout, and was careful to pay due respect to the gods – invoking Manann whenever he stepped aboard a ship, and giving thanks to Verena whenever justice was rightly served – but he frowned upon the ignorant, uninformed rural practices, oaths and lucky charms that many claimed warded against bad omens and spirits. Such things had the reek of infernal practices, and they were a way that one could inadvertently slip towards damnation.

The state soldiers had picketed in orderly lines, with eight men to each simple canvas tent, and the air was filled with the smells of cooking and the chatter of men. Merchants and whores moved around the encampment, selling their wares – camp hangers-on were common when an army marched, for it provided safety as well as willing customers with little else to spend their money on. Not that there was much money to go around – he had learnt that these soldiers had not seen a coin for months.

In the centre of the camp were the lavish tents of the officers and nobility, flying pennants and banners high. Each was larger than the house of an average Empire citizen, and their fabric was decorated with gold and heavily embroidered, as if each was trying to outdo the other, which was probably the case. It made Grunwald sick.

He had glimpsed the military commander of the state troops, a foppish inbred noble said to be the second cousin to one of the contenders for the disputed position of Elector Count of Averland. The noble wore weapons glittering with jewels and ornamentation, and wore a gold-plated breastplate moulded to represent a heroic, muscled torso. A limp-wristed fop who played at war, was Grunwald's assessment. Averlanders generally had a reputation within the Empire for extroverted displays of wealth and ornamentation, yet this nobleman took that to a whole new level.

The Knights of the Blazing Sun had no overt political association with the state, nor with any other, and they were picketed separate from the Averlanders. Grunwald had learnt that the temple that these knights had come from was within Stirland, and there was little love lost between Stirlanders and Averlanders. Nonetheless, they had come at the behest of the Emperor himself, and they were utterly devoted and honourable servants of the Empire.

'I am still intrigued as to how travelling to Black Fire gets you closer to the battlefields in the north,' said Grunwald. The preceptor laughed.

'The dwarfs have some machine here that will shorten the journey,' he said. 'I will need to see it with my own eyes to believe it, but it is said to be a monstrous creation of steam and metal,' he shrugged.

A pair of Averlanders, clearly more than a little drunk and with their arms draped around a trio of women reeking of cheap perfume, staggered past Grunwald's campfire, laughing raucously. As they caught sight of the glaring witch hunter they fell silent and hurried on their way.

'You know, I think your presence is making the state soldiers nervous,' remarked Karl.

'Only the guilty need fear my presence,' replied Grunwald. Karl smiled from across the campfire at the grim witch hunter.

'My, you are an uplifting, positive character to have around, aren't you?' he said, his eyes full of humour.

'Being uplifting and positive doesn't really go hand in hand with my occupation,' said Grunwald, scowling. In truth he liked the young knight – he was easy company after spending weeks on the road with the dour ironbreaker, Thorrik. The dwarf lowered his bulk and sat down noisily alongside the pair, and within moments was puffing on his dragon-headed pipe.

The witch hunter liked the fact that the knight seemed utterly unfazed by him – he was not cowed in the slightest by his appearance, manner or occupation, and he found it a refreshing change.

'You should try it sometime though,' continued the knight. 'It might put people more at ease – and when people are at ease, *that's* usually when they'll say something wrong and implicate themselves.'

'People are pretty good at implicating themselves when they are very much *ill* at ease,' said Grunwald in reply, twisting his knife in front of him before eating the hunk of meat off its tip.

'I'd imagine that is correct,' said Karl. He was a handsome, blue-eyed man, probably in his early twenties, Grunwald gauged. His wavy hair was fair, and hung to his shoulders now that he wore neither his chainmail coif nor his black-lacquered helmet. Vain, thought Grunwald – long hair had a tendency to catch painfully in chainmail. Long hair, in his opinion, was impractical for warriors at the best of times. It gave the enemy something else they could use against you. Still, he was certain that many of the younger women camp followers were besotted with the dashing young knight, so longer hair clearly had some benefit. He snorted at his own line of thinking.

'What?' asked Karl.

'Nothing. I was just thinking that you make me feel old,' Grunwald said.

'Yes, you are getting a bit long in the tooth, grandfather, and there is more than a bit of grey in your moustache. You must be pushing, what, thirty?'

Grunwald snorted again. 'Thirty-three, and you should learn to respect your elders – I'm not so old that I couldn't break that pretty nose of yours.'

'Thirty-three,' guffawed Thorrik. 'Ha! I remember thirty-three! Barely past suckling at a teat!'

Karl burst into laughter, and Grunwald smiled.

WEARY BEYOND WORDS, Annaliese climbed the high mountain road, the sleeping form of Tomas clinging around her neck. Night had long fallen, and they travelled in silence. Eldanair stalked out in front of them, bow in hand, his every movement sharp and wary. Katrin walked at her side, the hem of the sister's robes dirtied from days of travel.

The rough road had been hewn into the side of the mountain, and to her right it rose steeply, covered in dense fir trees. To her left the ground fell away sharply, the mountainside rocky and steep.

Far below in the dark valley glinted the lights of the small settlement, Priesterstadt, and on the far side the mountains rose against the dark sky. The valley fed into Black Fire Pass itself, and though nothing of it could be seen in the darkness, merely being in such close proximity to the hallowed place filled her with awe. It was said that the earth had spewed forth molten rock and fire which had cooled and hardened and filled the valley with the craggy, black surface that gave the pass its name. Annaliese was unsure of the truth to the story – rock that ran like water and burned like wood sounded even more far-fetched than the idea of giant rats that walked upright like men and lurked beneath the surface of the world.

At Black Fire Pass the mighty Sigmar had stood with the united human tribes and their dwarfen allies and fought the greatest battle ever to have taken place in the Old World. A horde of greenskins the likes of which had never before been seen was set to pass through the valley and into the fertile lands beyond – it would have spelt the end of human civilisation. Sigmar stood against this force and fought it to a standstill for days on end. He slew the mighty greenskin warlord and the unity of the orc and goblin tribes was shattered. It was the most important victory in the history of mankind, and it heralded the dawning of the Empire itself.

Annaliese had listened as a child at the knee of her father, her mouth agape as he recounted the tale of Sigmar's victory. She never grew tired of the story, and would beg her father each night before bed to retell it. He would embellish it and invent new, super-human exploits for the blond warrior-god, but the essence of the tale was always the same. A single man refusing to be beaten that brought about salvation for all.

A single man was all that stood between victory and defeat, her father had always said. If just one warrior had turned to flee that day, it would have caused an unstoppable rout that would have been the end of the Empire before it was even formed – but none ran, even though most must have believed that their doom had come. And they held only because of their belief in a single, brave warrior.

All it takes, her father would often say, is one person to stand up against oppression and overwhelming force for others to stand with them – just one person to show bravery in the face of death for others to overcome their fear. This, he said, was the most important lesson he could ever teach her, and he would repeat it often. The smallest things win battles, he said – a single man turning and running, a single man standing tall and defying the enemy when all seemed lost.

There was the distant howling of a wolf, and she shivered, glancing back at the way they had come.

In the far distance, there was a score of tiny flickering lights. More travellers coming late at night to Black Fire Pass?

The vista would have been stunning in daylight, and she wished that she could see it. Still, it mattered little – she had decided that she would stay at the temple to aid the Sisters of Shallya in their sacred duty. She would have many days before her to witness the grandeur of Black Fire Pass.

She felt a sense of calm come over her as she thought about the years that lay ahead having made the decision. To spend her years dedicated to the goddess of mercy tending the ill and the wounded would be both heart wrenching and satisfying, she thought. And it would allow her to remain with Tomas and Katrin, and that in itself made her pleased.

Her long journey was almost over, and she was glad of it. She felt stronger than she ever had done, and she had travelled Sigmar knew how many miles across the Empire, but her journeys had brought her to where she felt in her heart she was meant to be; a pilgrimage of sorts.

They came upon an impassable, crenelated wall that protected the approach to the temple. A powerful, squat gatehouse was positioned squarely in the road, its massive gate barred and a black iron portcullis standing before it.

Sentries stood upon walls lit with burning braziers, and Annaliese saw the glint of metal from the tips of halberds. One of the sentries gave a shout as the weary travellers approached, and crossbows were aimed down at them through the crenelations. Even this could not dampen Annaliese's feeling of well-being, and she felt a shiver of anticipation as she saw the bronze icon above the gate of a twin-tailed comet, the symbol that was said to herald the coming of Sigmar himself.

Eldanair loosened the tension on his bowstring as more crossbows were aimed towards them, and he lifted his hands into the air to show his weapon was not readied.

'Who goes there?' came a shout, and Katrin stepped forwards so that the light of the braziers fell upon her.

'I am a Sister of Shallya, come to rejoin my order who have come to the temple to give aid where it is needed,' she said. This was met with a muffled conversation, and Annaliese could hear the sound of a heavy bar being lifted by several men. A small door inset into the massive double-doors of the gate was opened and a sleepy looking warrior appeared. He blinked as he saw Katrin standing before him, and cast a quick eye over Annaliese and Eldanair, who had drawn his hood over his head. He nodded, yawning.

'You will have to wait for one of the priests, I am afraid, good sister. None may pass through here after dark without their express permission.'

Katrin nodded her assent, and the wooden door closed. It was opened a moment later by the same sentry.

'Can I get you anything, sister? Water? Bread? It's nothing fancy, I'm afraid.'

'Thank you but no,' she replied. 'We will wait until I am rejoined with my sisters to take refreshment.' The door clicked shut once again.

Ten minutes passed before the sound of turning gears and levers heralded the lifting of the spiked, iron portcullis. One of the large double-doors opened with a heavy groan of wood to show a powerful warrior priest waiting for them, leaning on an immense double-handed hammer. He was thickly set, and dressed in armour of plate steel beneath his robes. He looked every inch the veteran soldier.

'Sister, it is late to be travelling these parts,' he said, his voice surprisingly soft as he ushered her forwards. 'There are dangers abroad.'

'Thank you, brother,' said Katrin. 'These are my friends and they seek refuge within the temple.'

The warrior priest nodded, and his eyes flicked to Eldanair, then to Annaliese and her young charge, then back to the hooded elf.

'The girl and child we welcome with open arms. But I would see the face of the warrior before allowing him to pass,' the warrior priest said softly.

As if he understood the words, Eldanair pulled the hood from his face, his bearing proud and noble as he looked into the priest's eyes. One of the warriors of Sigmar's eyebrows rose slightly, though his expression did not change. He held up a hand towards the elf, and Annaliese felt a flutter within her, as if something ethereal and invisible stirred within.

'Your heart is pure and that of a brave warrior,' said the priest. 'Nevertheless, I regret that you may not pass within these gates.'

'What?' said Annaliese sharply. 'If it were not for him, we would all have perished. I was not aware the temple was so unwelcoming.'

The priest turned his gentle eyes towards her, and she felt an aura of strength and calm descend over her.

'Would we humans be allowed within a temple of elven kind? Would we be allowed within the ancestral halls of dwarfenkind? It is not through being unwelcoming that I bar his entrance. It is merely out of respect to the temple.'

Annaliese glared at him, pushing away the feeling of calm that he was exerting.

'Fine,' she snapped, and turned towards Eldanair. With hand signals and gestures, she quickly made the situation known. She tried to communicate that she would come back out once Tomas was safe. He shrugged slightly, and looked down his nose at the Sigmarite priest. Turning swiftly, he pulled the hood down low over his face, and melted into the fir trees.

'The temple will provide food and firewood should the elf require it, lady,' said the priest softly. Annaliese flashed him an angry glance.

'He would not accept them,' she said. The priest merely shrugged in response, and turned to lead them through the gatehouse. Gravel crunched underfoot as they made their way back onto the road beyond.

It seemed like a dream to Annaliese when they finally rounded a bend and saw the glory of the temple of Sigmar, and her foul mood evaporated instantly. Braziers of warming fire welcomed them, and lights could be seen through the small, high windows that had been constructed with as much thought to defence as to architectural beauty.

In the dim moonlight, Annaliese could see that at the apex of the domed roof of the temple glittered a golden statue of man, a mighty hammer in his hands. Her mouth opened in awe. With the coming of sunrise, the statue would be lit up as if blazing with divine light.

The doors of the temple creaked open, and warmth and light spilled out. Annaliese felt a surge of well-being as she entered.

'I am home,' she whispered.

UDO GRUNWALD WALKED his horse alongside Thorrik, giving the tired beast a rest. It was skittish, and he could feel it trembling as wolves howled in the distance. It must have been nearing midnight, but he was determined to press on to the temple. It was around three hours further on, he estimated – they should reach it an hour or so before dawn.

Karl Heiden, preceptor of the Knights of the Blazing Sun, was leading the column, and the night was filled with rhythmic clopping of hooves on the black rocky ground that gave the pass its name. There was but a score of the knights accompanying them, the remainder of the order having set up camp just outside the valley, so as to enter at dawn. Grunwald and Thorrik had both been keen to continue on, and Karl had requested permission from the Templar Master of his order to escort them. It was a noble gesture, and Grunwald was thankful for the company. Every fourth knight carried a burning brand aloft in his armoured hand, letting off a warm, flickering glow.

The mountains rose up on either side of the valley, and the trees were thick on their slopes.

'Good road, this,' commented Thorrik, lowering the burning brand he held towards the ground. Grunwald grunted in response. He hadn't paid the road much notice. 'Made by my kinsmen before the War of Vengeance.' He stamped one of his feet solidly onto the stonework, making Grunwald's horse shy. 'Good, solid, dwarf work,' continued Thorrik. 'Will last until the end of the world, when Grimnir himself will return to us.' The dwarf glanced up at Grunwald. 'We must part ways soon, lad. I must deliver this,' he said, indicating with a thumb to the wrapped item on his back. 'I am oathbound to one now drinking in the halls of the ancestors,' he said gruffly, obviously uncomfortable with such talk. He cleared his throat. 'I won't be around much longer to keep saving your neck.'

The witch hunter smiled. In truth he would miss his dour companion. His horse shied again, whinnying sharply and tugging at the reins in his hand. 'Hush,' he said, patting it on the neck as Thorrik glared at it hatefully from beneath his helm. The horse pulled at its reins again, more forcefully, its ears flat against its head.

'What is wrong with that confounded beast?' grumbled the dwarf as Grunwald tried to calm it.

'Something's spooked him,' said Grunwald, struggling with the horse. He saw that the knights' horses were uneasy as well, though their training kept them from acting up. He saw Karl raise his hand for the column to halt, and Grunwald held a hand to his trembling mount's neck, whispering quietly to it. Its eyes were wide.

There was another howling of wolves, closer this time, and he heard Thorrik hiss as he swung to stare into the dark fir woods that walled the roadway.

'Have you never heard wolves before, dwarf?' scoffed Grunwald. His grin slipped when more howling sounded, closer again than before.

'Grobi,' snarled Thorrik, dropping his heavy pack to the ground and hefting his axe in one hand, the other still holding his burning brand aloft.

'What?' said Grunwald.

'We are being attacked!' roared the dwarf as the first shape streaked from the darkness of the trees, hurtling towards the column of knights.

Teeth bared and a feral growl emanating from deep in its chest, the huge wolf bounded across the uneven ground. A green-skinned creature clung to its back, grinning broadly to expose a fearsome array of needle-like teeth.

Before the knights could react to Thorrik's warning, the wolf leapt at the closest warrior of the Blazing Sun. The wolf was immense, easily the size of a small horse, and it closed its slavering jaws around the steed's armoured neck. The horse screamed in terror and fell beneath the weight of the wolf, as the creature perched upon its back thrust its crude spear into the chest of the knight, denting but not piercing his breastplate. Nevertheless, his legs were crushed as the weight of his panicked, barded steed fell upon him. The hateful green-skinned creature leapt from its mount onto the knight, ramming the spear tip through the knight's vision slit, as the blood-hungry wolf killed his horse.

'Goblins,' snarled Grunwald, as more of the creatures swarmed from the concealing darkness of the tree line, bounding towards the column. He released his grip on his horse's reins, and it reared, hooves flailing, before a hurled spear drove into its chest. It bolted, its lifeblood pumping from the mortal wound.

At a shout from Karl, the knights wheeled their steeds to face the threat, maintaining their discipline despite the confusion that was erupting.

Thorrik roared a dwarfen war cry and hurled his burning brand into the face of one of the charging creatures before hefting his axe in both hands and slamming it into the side of the head of a wolf that leapt towards him, caving its skull.

Grunwald drew and fired one of his pistols, sending a goblin flying from the saddle, blood spraying out behind it. He threw himself to the ground as the monstrous wolf leapt at him.

The knights flailed around them, discarding their lances in favour of their heavy cavalry blades. They hacked down at the wolf riders, killing several, but other knights were being knocked from their steeds as more wolves launched themselves at their warhorses.

As he rose to his feet, Grunwald slipped his mace from its belt, and leapt at a wolf that was tearing at a fallen knight. It turned as he closed on it, baring its teeth and its feral eyes filled with animal ferocity and hunger. The mace smashed into the side of the creature's head, smashing teeth and bone, and it fell with a whimper.

Grunwald heard Karl trying to organise his knights, barking commands and orders. He saw a hurled spear slam into the side of Thorrik's helmet, and his head jerked, but the blow could not even scratch his gromril armour, nor did it knock him back a single step. He merely turned, cursing in his own language, and cut down another leaping wolf, his blade smashing it to the ground.

The witch hunter snarled as a jagged blade cut across his forearm, and he spun, smashing his attacker from the back of a wolf. The goblin hissed at him as he leapt at it, its scrawny limbs kicking out at him. Grunwald slammed a boot into the creature's head, hearing a satisfying crack as its neck broke.

He saw Karl then, battling like a hero of old, his sword cutting down goblins and his horse shattering skulls with its flailing hooves. A diminutive greenskin leapt from the back of its own mount onto the saddle behind Karl, spider-like fingers scrabbling at the knight's helmet, a serrated dagger held in its other hand. His warhorse reared; both the knight and the goblin fell to the ground, and Grunwald lost sight of the preceptor.

He hefted his mace and took a step back to get a better footing as a pair of wolf riders leapt towards him, tongues lolling from the maws of the massive grey-furred mounts. One of the goblins tumbled forward off its steed, and the wolf of the second rider yelped in pain and collapsed to the ground, its back legs giving way beneath it. The witch hunter saw a metal crossbow bolt protruding from the hindquarters of the wolf, and the air was suddenly filled with a second flight of bolts fired from the tree line.

The wolf that had lost its rider leapt at him, huge paws slamming into his chest, jaws widening as it sought his throat. He was knocked backwards onto the ground, and he felt the rancid, hot breath of the foul creature on his face. Desperately he held its jaws at bay with a gloved hand clamped around the beast's throat, but the strength and weight of it was immense.

His sight was obscured as hot blood sprayed into his eyes, and he felt the monstrous creature go limp, collapsing on top of him. With a surge of adrenaline-fuelled strength he pushed the dead weight from him, and rose unsteadily to his feet, wiping the thick gruel of viscous gore from his eyes.

A short, stocky figure turned away from him, hefting a double-headed axe.

A throaty war cry sounded all around him, Grunwald saw a host of the stocky figures trudging forward, hefting axes. Grunwald grunted with exertion as he clubbed his mace into the head of a goblin half-crushed beneath its dead mount, smashing it like a piece of fruit, and watched as the dwarfs descended on the goblins, vitriolic hatred guiding their blows. Their axes carved a bloody swathe through the greenskins, and the last of the wolf riders were soon fleeing into the darkness, the sound of their howls growing ever more distant.

Grunwald wiped the blood and brain matter from the ridges of his mace as Thorrik greeted his kinsmen dourly, speaking in their own rumbling, guttural tongue. He looked around and caught sight of Karl, swearing profusely as he brushed the mud from his armour.

'How many?' he asked the preceptor as he drew alongside him. The knight looked up, his eyes angry.

'Too many. Six knights, and four horses. One more horse will have to be destroyed.' Even as he said the words, the pained screams of a horse were silenced. 'Damn it, things must be bad if there are goblins raiding the entrance to the pass.'

'Aye,' said Grunwald.

'You alright? Got yourself cut?' asked Karl, seeing the blood dripping from the witch hunter's arm. Grunwald glanced down at the wound.

'Nothing much. Should have seen it coming,' he said dismissively.

'I'm glad *they* turned up,' muttered Karl, nodding his head towards the dwarfs. The leader of the dwarfs was conversing with Thorrik while the rest of their number got to work piling up the dead goblins and wolves. It looked like there were over two dozen of the wretched corpses all told.

They were not as heavily armoured as Thorrik, he noted. Each of them wore a heavy coat of mail and a thick furred cloak, and carried axes and sturdy crossbows. They moved about their work with diligence and within minutes they had a large blaze going, and the air was filled with the stench of burning flesh.

The witch hunter and preceptor walked to Thorrik's side, and the dwarf he was talking to turned his stony gaze towards them. He looked older than Thorrik, though it was hard to gauge his age, and his grey-streaked beard would have touched the ground if it had not been tied up and folded back on itself in a series of intricate braids. He had a pipe in his mouth, and blue smoke puffed from his nostrils.

'I thank you for your timely arrival, sir dwarf,' said the knight. 'I am Karl Heiden, preceptor of Myrmidia, and this is Udo Grunwald, templar of Sigmar. Had you not arrived when you did, I fear that my losses would have been considerably higher.'

The dwarf grunted in reply, and said something in his native language, pipe-smoke billowing around him.

'It seems that you spoke the truth,' said Thorrik gruffly, addressing Karl, his face dark. 'The hated green-skins are massing in numbers not seen since the time of King Kurgan himself. They smash against the walls of Kolaz Umgol and the Grimbeard Station like a living tide, and it is said that even Karaz-a-Karak is threatened. This is a grim day indeed.'

'But these outriders slipped past the defences of the pass,' said Grunwald, concerned. 'Others may have done so as well. The temple of Sigmar may itself be under attack.'

'Aye, it may be so, manling' said the leader of the dwarf rangers, still puffing at his pipe. His voice sounded like boulders grinding together, stony and hard. 'These stinking grobi,' he said, removing his pipe to spit on the ground at the mention of the greenskins, 'are not the only of their kind moving out there this night. I can smell their stink on the air.'

Grunwald felt his anger grow. He turned towards Karl, rage and concern in his eyes.

'I must get to the temple. It must not be defiled by the likes of these foul creatures,' he said indicating towards the burning pile of goblins. Karl nodded his head.

'The Knights of the Blazing Sun will ride with you,' said the preceptor, his face unusually serious.

'Manling,' said Thorrik, and the witch hunter turned towards the dour, dependable warrior.

'I cannot accompany you this time,' said the dwarf. 'My oath binds me. Here our ways part.' The pair shook arms, hands locked around the other's forearm in the dwarfen manner. Then, with no more than a gruff nod in farewell, the dwarf turned and began marching to the east with his kinsmen.

Silently, Grunwald wished the dwarf well.

'Come,' said Karl. 'I will find a steed for you.'

In the distance, wolves howled.

ANNALIESE LAY THE sleeping Tomas down on a pallet thick with straw, deep within the temple of Sigmar and decided to rest alongside him. Just for a moment, she told herself. She felt like a different person having bathed, washing the grime from her skin. As she washed, she had been pleased to see that the muscles of her legs were defined and strong, before she laughed at herself for her vanity. She would rest her head on the pillow for just a moment, she told herself. Instantly she fell into a deep, restful sleep, her arm protectively round the sleeping boy.

Somewhere close by, wolves were howling, but she ignored them, feeling blessedly safe deep within the stone fortress. Dimly she registered the pounding of skin drums, but she pushed these intrusions away, thinking they were a part of her dreams.

They seemed to fade, and she found herself walking in the sunshine through a golden field. Strangely, she was dressed in armour of shining brilliance, but she felt completely comfortable in the war gear. She smiled as the sun beat down upon her, and she brushed her hands through the crops gently swaying in the light breeze.

A bell sounded close by, sharp and loud, and Annaliese woke with a start.

The room was dimly lit, for someone had turned the lantern down low, though she had never heard anyone come into the room. The bell tolled urgently, and she rolled from the pallet and dressed herself quickly. She noticed that Tomas was no longer asleep on the bed, nor anywhere else in the room.

The bell rang frantically, and she heard the howling of wolves. She had heard that sound before, in the wilderness hunting with her father.

It was the sound of wolves closing in for the kill.

CHAPTER NINE

ELDANAIR PULLED THE arrow from the goblin's neck as he swept past the dead creature, nocking it to his bowstring. He ran swiftly through the trees, a shadow in the darkness. He made no sound nor left any mark of his passing bar the corpses of the slain as he cut between the dense firs, running hard.

He came upon a small clearing on the edge of a cliff face and sprang lightly up a rocky outcrop, until he stood on its edge, unfazed by the thousand foot drop below him. From here he could see across to the temple of the human god in the distance. The sound of the warning bell tolled out across the valley, and with his keen elven eyes he could see dark shapes swarming towards the temple.

Cursing, he broke into a run again, leaping lightly from his precarious position on the rock face and striking out towards the building.

Having been denied entrance to the human temple, Eldanair had merely scaled the walls, unseen and unheard by the sentries. Such dull senses they had! he had mused. Dropping down to the ground within the compound, he had melted into the shadows, ghosting after Annaliese.

Despite his ease at circumventing them, he had been impressed with the temple's defences. High walls and gates guarded the approach to the temple from the north and the south, while the east was protected by sheer cliff that dropped away to the valley far below; the west was guarded by equally impassable cliffs that towered above.

Distant howling that would have been impossible for a human to discern had carried to his keen ears, and he caught a whiff of a familiar, hated scent on the wind. Without pause, he had scaled the north walls and set off into the trees, hunting the greenskins.

Hearing pounding coming up the road, Eldanair cut to his left, towards the sound, and he dropped into a crouch beside the bole of an ancient tree. Eldanair let out a long even breath, waiting for his moment, before he stepped from his concealment onto the road, and fired.

The arrow slammed into a thick, sloping forehead, punching through the bone and into the brain of the hulking creature. It toppled from the ridged back of a snorting war boar. The beast swung around to viciously gore its fallen rider with tusks as long as a man's forearm. A second arrow punched into the neck of another rider, but it merely bellowed in rage and yanked its mount brutally in Eldanair's direction.

His third arrow sank into the orc's crude wooden shield, and the creature roared again, its mouth impossibly large and filled with thick tusk-like teeth. It hefted a cleaver of huge proportions, and Eldanair rolled neatly out of the way as the frenzied boar charged him. The orc's weapon slammed into the trunk of the tree, a hair's breadth from Eldanair's back as the elf rolled to his feet and he sent two shafts slicing just behind the boar's shoulder, seeking the heart. The creature smashed into the ground, dead, its jaw and furred snout digging a deep furrow in the earth. The greenskin leapt from its back, turning towards Eldanair.

It might have been of a height equal to the elf had it stood straight up, but it was stooped, its broad, brutish head buried squarely between its massive shoulders. Its arms were as thick as tree stumps, and it roared as it leapt towards Eldanair, spittle dripping from its gaping jaws.

He put two arrows into the creature before it reached him. With its wooden shield it smashed him to the side, and he staggered to avoid a lethal swing of its massive weapon. Seeing him off balance, the creature roared again and charged him, slamming its meaty shoulder into his chest, and he was knocked to the ground, wincing in pain.

Still, he recovered with inhuman swiftness and grace. His hand flashed out as he rose to his knee, and a knife embedded itself to the hilt in the orc's eye socket. It fell with a groan to the ground, twitched once and was still. Eldanair swiftly retrieved his knife and broke into a run again.

More greenskins pounded up the road heading towards the temple, and Eldanair cut to the right, striking out through the fir trees. Keeping off the road, he made good time, zigzagging through the maze of trees with impossible swiftness.

At last he saw the dark shadow of the wall rising up before him and he broke from the tree line, throwing his bow over his shoulder as he darted towards the sheer wall almost fifteen feet high.

He sprang onto the wall, his fingers finding purchase between the rough-hewn rocks. Praying there was no sentry on this section, he climbed up, his muscles straining and hissing at the pain in his fingers.

Reaching the top, he threw a leg over the crenelations, and dropped onto the ramparts in a crouch. Drawing his bow, he glanced along the defensive wall, seeing the corpses of sentries hacked apart by vicious blows. Crude ladders were leaning up against the walls, and he saw a goblin cutting the ears from one of the sentries. Eldanair dispatched the creature with an arrow through the back of the neck.

Eldanair dropped silently to the ground inside the wall, hugging the darkness. He darted forwards and crouched beside a covered well, hidden in its shadow. From here he could see that the portcullis of the gatehouse had been raised, and jammed open with tree-trunks. The heavy wooden door had been shattered, and more greenskins were streaming through the now open portal.

He heard a dull, rhythmic pounding sound and knew instantly that it was a battering ram being used on the temple's entrance.

'Annaliese,' he hissed, and broke from his cover, heading in the direction of the temple.

'TOMAS!' ANNALIESE SHOUTED, hearing her own voice disappear in the cacophony of shouts and screams. She ran up the corridor towards the temple proper, passing beneath severe archways and the cold stare of Sigmarite saints, frantic with panic. The tolling of the bell continued to resound deafeningly from somewhere high overhead.

Servants of the temple and the devout who had come to the temple on pilgrimages were bursting from dormitories on either side of the passageway, fear on their faces. They clutched icons of Sigmar and wailed. Annaliese tried to ask several of them if they had seen a little boy, but she was buffeted by hurrying people, and no one wanted to listen to her.

A deep, commanding voice bellowed down the corridor. The milling, scared people were silenced by the authoritative tone, and they began to shuffle towards the speaker, a tall warrior priest adorned in armour and robes.

'The temple of our lord is besieged,' the priest said, his voice loud enough to carry to everyone gathered. 'Any man able to fight should remain here to aid in the defence of the temple. I want all the women and children to come to the front now, and you will be taken to the undercroft.' The corridor suddenly erupted in a cacophony of noise, people crying out in fear, and assailing the priest with questions.

'Enough!' he roared, silencing the crowd. 'There will be no argument here! Initiate Alexis here will guide you to the undercroft. I want women and children to go with him. Now! Take nothing with you, you go with what you are carrying now.'

People began to bustle and push, and the sound level rose quickly once more.

'Be silent!' raged the priest. 'You are all children of Sigmar – do not dishonour him with weakness and tears! Go now, in silence, and Alexis will lead you in prayer once the undercroft is sealed. Go now!'

Women made hasty farewells to nervous looking husbands and fathers, and an argument broke out between a boy and his mother.

'You are too young!' the mother said severely, cutting him off mid-sentence. The tall priest placed a hand on her shoulder, and she turned tearful eyes up at him.

'The boy has Sigmar's fighting spirit – let him stand alongside us and defy these enemies,' he said, his voice stern. Tears began to roll down the woman's face, and she hugged the boy to her chest, sobbing.

The young initiate Alexis, who could not have been older than eight years old, took the woman's hand and led her away with the others.

The tall priest turned his green eyes towards Annaliese, who was craning her neck, trying to see Tomas in the crowd.

'Go with the others,' he said. She merely shook her head, ignoring him as she continued to scan the corridor. He gripped her arm firmly, urging her towards the departing women and children.

'I will not,' she snapped, shaking her arm free. She glared at him fiercely, tears welling unbidden in her eyes. 'I cannot find… there is a boy… Tomas.'

'There is no time for this, girl!' barked the priest. 'Your child is probably already down there, with the gentle sisters.'

'The sisters…' muttered Annaliese. That must be it! Tomas had gone to find Katrin. 'The sisters are already down there?'

'Yes, yes they are,' said the priest, distracted now. 'Now go! Hurry!'

She left the priest who barked at the wide-eyed men to follow him to the armoury. Running lightly, she headed in the direction that the women had been ushered in. She passed through several corridors, hearing a rhythmic pounding in-between the ringing of the bell.

She ran out of an archway and came upon the central chapel to Sigmar, lit with candles and braziers and she gasped in awe.

It had been darkened when they had been bustled through earlier that evening, but now that it was lit, she gazed around with her mouth wide open.

The room was immense, the walls rising impossibly high and disappearing into darkness above. Statues of Sigmar's warrior saints lined the walls, standing within arched alcoves twenty feet above the ground. They posed heroically, holding mighty weapons and standing on top of slain enemies. Each statue was the size of a giant, and candlelight flickered over their forms, giving the illusion of movement.

But the statue of Sigmar himself in the centre of the domed temple, standing on a plinth and surrounded by statues of fierce horsemen, took her breath away.

Braziers lit the mighty golden statue from beneath, forming deep shadows upon its heavily muscled torso as the representation of the warrior god lifted his war hammer Ghal Maraz high into the air. His hair was long and flowing, and upon his face was an expression of utter determination – it was the expression Annaliese imagined the man-god had worn when he defied the endless hordes of greenskins in the blackened pass nearby, and it spoke of awesome strength and nobility.

Clockwork cherubs circled around the statue, metallic feathered wings clicking as they flapped jerkily and raised trumpets to their pouting lips.

Her attention was distracted from the awe-inspiring statue as a trio of heavily armoured warrior priests hurried past. One of them was the gentle-spoken priest that had escorted her to the temple earlier that night, though she almost did not recognise him wearing his open-faced helm, and he stopped at her side.

'You should be with the others,' he said gently, his eyebrows furrowing in concern. 'Come,' he added and began to hurry her towards the back of the temple.

'I can fight,' she said defiantly, standing her ground. The priest paused and smiled, transforming his face. He was very handsome, she thought, and felt a blush coming over her cheeks. The priest placed a heavy hand on her shoulder. The metal of his gauntlet felt cold.

'Of that I have no doubt,' he said. 'Someone needs to guard over the women and children. Come.'

She knew he was humouring her, and she felt her blush deepen, but she allowed herself to be led to the entrance leading beneath the temple. It was a narrow staircase spiralling down into the rock. Light flickered up weakly from below.

There was a resounding boom that echoed through the temple, followed by the sound of splintering wood.

'We are breached!' came a shout, followed by the sound of weapons clashing. A blood-curdling, bestial roar resounded across the temple, and a warrior cried out in pain.

'I must go,' said the priest. He squeezed her shoulder briefly, and turned away, holding his hammer in both hands, his face grim. She bit her lip as she looked at the spiralling, stone steps. Seeing her indecision as he glanced back, the priest shouted to her, all softness gone from his voice. 'Go now!' he commanded.

She heard a roared prayer to Sigmar, accompanied by a flash of golden light from across the temple, and the roars and bellows of inhuman foes. A man cried out in pain as Annaliese began the descent beneath the temple.

Down and down the staircase spiralled. She passed a landing where a burning torch burnt in its brazier. She touched an ancient shield emblazoned with the twin-tailed comet that hung on the wall, and continued further down in near darkness, feeling the way along the smooth walls with her hands. Sounds of battle filtered down from above, and her breath was heavy – it felt like the walls were closing in on her, and she imagined herself tripping and falling headlong down the treacherous steps into the darkness.

At last she began to be able to see again, and she stepped onto a wide landing carved out of the rock. Torches burnt on the walls, and she began to dash down the wide corridor towards the heavy door at the other end, passing by numerous shrine-alcoves holding the bones of saints.

She paused at one of the shrines as she passed, seeing a skeleton in highly polished, ancient armour lying on a plinth carved into the wall. A gleaming shield hung above the long dead warrior's resting place, and a hammer was clasped in skeletal hands over his chest. Faded parchment hung upon the walls, doubtlessly speaking of the deeds of the warrior priest, and strips of velum hung beneath sconces of candles, covered in intricate writings. She turned away as a horrible death scream echoed down from above, and ran to the door at the far end of the corridor.

It was a heavy door of oak, reinforced with iron strips and spikes. She hammered on its surface.

'Please,' she cried. 'Please open the door.'

She realised then that she was not wearing the sword blade that Eldanair had given her, and she cursed herself. If the enemy did manage to slaughter the warrior priests above, how was she going to defend the women and children down here?

Still cursing herself, she spun on her heel, eyes flashing around for a weapon. She noticed a dull light emanating from one of the alcoves, and she stepped warily towards it.

She barely noticed the sound of a heavy bar being lifted, for she was certain that something was drawing her towards the resting place of this ancient warrior.

'Annaliese!' hissed a voice as the door behind her was opened, and dimly she registered the voice of the Sister of Shallya, Katrin. 'Annaliese, come inside, quickly! Tomas is with me here!'

In a daze, Annaliese ignored the woman, and stepped into the alcove.

Where all the other shrines had been painstakingly maintained, the armour and weapons of the deceased being highly shined and free from dust, this warrior was covered in cobwebs, his ornate platemail rusted and tarnished.

Shadows seemed to play at the corner of her vision, and Annaliese thought she heard a gentle whispering, like a voice carried on a breeze. Spiders scuttled away from her as she approached what she guessed could only be a revered warrior priest of another era, and the whispering seemed to get stronger, though she could not make out any words.

A deathly chill descended, but still she drew closer to the skeleton as if it were calling to her. She knelt in dust undisturbed for centuries at the venerable warrior's side, and looked at its face. The flesh had long wasted away from the bones, and the lower jaw hung half loose from the skull, but she was not horrified or scared.

Dimly she heard a voice frantically calling her name, but it seemed like it was coming from a long way away, and she ignored it.

The skeleton wore a circlet of tarnished metal around the crown of its head, and tufts of hair remained on the skull. She glanced down at the warrior's hands. Clasped in each hand was a hammer covered in dust and cobwebs, crossed over a plain, long-rusted breastplate. The hammers were of simple, functional design – a short, plain metal haft that ended in a solid twin-head. The only ornamentation upon them was the twin-tailed comet relief set into the sides of the hammer head, but even these were far from ostentatious.

Driven more by instinct than rational thought, her hand closed around the haft of one of the hammers. A finger bone snapped as she lifted the brittle hand and slid the hammer from the grasp of the long dead warrior priest. Carefully she replaced the hand upon the chest and marvelled at the weapon clasped in her hands. She wiped away the dust and spiderwebs, feeling the strength within the killing weapon.

Leaning forward, she planted a kiss upon the forehead of the skeletal warrior priest.

'Thank you,' she whispered, and rose to her feet.

Sound crashed in on her. A woman was screaming in her ear, and pulling upon her arm. The stamp of heavy feet echoed through the passageway, accompanied by the scrape of metal on stone and monstrous growls and guttural words barked in some crude, brutish language.

As if waking from a dream, Annaliese saw Katrin's tearful face close to hers, begging her to go with her.

The sound of pounding feet came from the stairway, and she realised then that the enemy had arrived. She stared with wide eyes at the hammer held in her hands.

Feeling a sense of peace and calm come over her, Annaliese lifted her head and smiled at Katrin.

'Go inside and seal the door behind you,' she said to the frantic woman. Katrin shook her head, tears running down her face, and tried to pull her bodily towards the safety of the doorway. Beyond the open portal Annaliese saw the frightened faces of women, and the young priest initiate wearing an expression of astonishment.

'Go, Katrin,' said Annaliese firmly, love and strength in her voice. Katrin stopped her sobbing and looked deep into the teenage girl's eyes, seeing the resolve there, but seeing something else as well. Somewhat reluctantly she released her grip on the girl, and with a last forlorn kiss on the cheek, she ran back through the doorway.

'Seal it,' Annaliese heard the sister order, and she registered the door slamming shut as she turned calmly away from it. Bolts were slid into place, and the heavy bar behind the door was locked into position.

Walking slowly up the corridor, testing the weight of the hammer in her hands, Annaliese stared grimly at the spiralling stone stairs.

She felt the presence of the long dead saints of Sigmar alongside her, and as the first of the enemies appeared, she let out a furious shout. With hammer raised high, she attacked.

SURROUNDED BY SHARDS of coloured glass, Eldanair knelt on the tall windowsill, surveying the carnage in the temple below. The window was some ten feet above the tiled floor, and the stained glass set within it had depicted the human god, Sigmar, until it had recently been smashed by a hurled spear.

The main expanse within the lofty, domed temple was seething with combatants. A knot of heavily armoured humans fought back to back against the horde of greenskins rushing in against them. The enemy smashed against them like a raging torrent, and though they stood firm, they could not hold back the living tide, and orcs and goblins were running rampant through the temple, smashing statues and kicking over tall candelabras, whooping and roaring.

An arrow shattered as it struck the old stonework of the arched windowsill not more than a foot from Eldanair's head, and he saw a sharp-featured goblin frantically nocking another barbed arrow to its short bow. He sent a shaft through the creature's chest, knocking it to the ground, and leaped from his vantage point, landing lightly on the stone slabs flooring the temple.

He fired another arrow that slammed into the shoulder of an orc towering over one of the humans. It was knocked off balance from the blow, and the human stepped forward and clubbed it to the ground with a powerful blow of his double-handed hammer.

'Annaliese!' shouted Eldanair as he felled another orc with an arrow in the lower back. 'Annaliese,' he called again, and darted through the melee, dodging spear thrusts and wild slashes from broad cleavers.

He had no idea where the girl could be, but he was desperate to find and protect her. On the blood of his fallen kin he had sworn to see her safe, and he would die before he failed once more in his duty.

He rounded a towering pillar of white stone, the string of his bow pulled back and an arrow readied. He came face to face with a green-eyed warrior, his face splattered with blood, and fired. The arrow sliced through the air past the warrior's ear and slammed into the orc looming behind him, the shaft flying into the greenskin's wide mouth and punching through the back of its neck.

The human caught his own blow before he crushed the elf with his massive war hammer, his eyes wide is surprise. Eldanair was past him then, flitting across the temple floor.

'Annaliese,' he shouted again, and he turned as the warrior priest called out. The human shouted something that he could not understand, but he made out the name Annaliese within the garbled stream of words, pointing towards the rear of the temple.

Eldanair gave a shout of warning, but it was too late, and a roaring orc slammed a pair of giant cleavers into the back of the human. With a grimace of pain, the warrior slammed forwards to the ground, the victorious orc whooping like a frenzied beast, blood dripping from his weapons.

He sent an arrow slamming into the creature's neck, but it ignored the blow in its bloodlust, and leapt away towards the other human warriors.

The elf darted towards the rear of the temple, coming up short as he reached the back wall. Mouthing an obscenity, he turned around on the spot, wondering if he had mistaken the meaning of the human's words.

He heard a muffled roar and his eyes snapped towards a thin set of stairs spiralling into darkness, half obscured behind a pillar.

'Annaliese,' he called out once more. There was no response, though the sounds of battle were filtering up from below.

Throwing his bow over his shoulders and drawing his long elven blade, Eldanair launched himself down the stairs.

THE KNIGHTS CHARGED through the breached guard-house with lances lowered, the thunder of their mighty warhorses deafening. At their head rode Karl Heiden, the preceptor urging his warriors urgently onwards.

The past hours had been a blur, as the knights rode hard up the winding mountain road towards the temple. The blare of horns and the howling of wolves had become more frantic and loud as they had neared their destination and Grunwald had prayed they were not too late. A single bell tolled frantically, a desperate warning that pealed out across the valley.

Goblins screamed as they scurried out of the path of knights pounding up the road. Several of them were impaled on the end of lances, and Grunwald saw one piteous creature lifted high into the air, spitted on Karl's masterfully guided lance.

The witch hunter was not trained to fight from horse-back, and his estimation of the knights of Myrmidia rose. They engaged the enemy with lance and shield, forsaking the use of reins now that battle had commenced, guiding their warhorses expertly with their knees.

The wedge of knights thundered up the road, smashing aside all resistance. Once lances had snapped or become embedded in the bodies of the greenskins they were discarded, and the templars fought with cavalry sabres and blades, slashing down onto the skulls of the foes as they pounded past.

Grunwald was unused to riding a fully trained warhorse bedecked in armour, but he found the steed instantly responsive to his commands. It snorted and lashed out at fallen orcs, trampling them beneath its hooves.

With the black and gold banner of Myrmidia flying high, the knights kept their momentum, charging up the tree-lined road, foam flecking the mouths of their steeds. The temple of Sigmar suddenly loomed large before them, imposing and martial, and Grunwald swore to see its great doors smashed asunder, and greenskins piling through the hallowed archway.

With a shouted command, the knights split into two groups, the smaller of the two heading towards the temple itself while the other galloped hard towards the largest cluster of orcs running towards the besieged structure.

Seeing the greenskins milling within the wide entrance to the temple, Karl guided his splinter group of knights straight up the broad steps, ploughing into the rear of the enemy.

Swords rose and fell, carving bloody arcs through the air. Grunwald brought a pistol to bear, it boomed loudly as the lead shot punched through the iron helmet of an orc, dropping the creature instantly.

The knights' charge took them into the main nave of the temple, the horses' hooves slipping on the smooth stone. One of the steeds screamed and fell as it ran onto a planted spear, the shaft snapping off as it embedded deep in its chest. Another knight fell as a hurled cleaver slammed into his chest, and Grunwald struggled to stay in the saddle as his steed reared, kicking out at anything nearby. He saw Karl reel back in his saddle as an arrow thudded into his shoulder, but the preceptor did not fall.

'Sigmar lend me strength!' came a shout, and the witch hunter's eyes locked onto a handful of warriors battling against insurmountable odds. He saw a tall, white-haired figure in the midst of the priests, wielding twin blades, one short and wide for defence, and he recognised his fierce superior. Thanking Sigmar that he was still alive, Grunwald kicked his warhorse sharply, urging it on into the press of green bodies.

A huge orc wrapped its massive arms around the neck of his warhorse, which began thrashing around madly, bucking and kicking. Another orc leaped forwards and hacked its blade into one of the horse's exposed rear legs and the whole armoured beast fell to the ground with a resounding crash.

Lucky not to have had his leg crushed, Grunwald staggered to his feet, and deflected a wild swing with his mace, smashing the orc in the face with the weighted butt of his pistol. Before the greenskin could recover, a pair of hooves connected squarely with its forehead, killing it instantly.

He saw Karl rip his dented helmet from his head, before he led his steed deeper into the press of bodies, his sword blade hacking left and right as he carved a path towards the beleaguered warrior priests. Another knight was dragged down, and Grunwald smashed his mace into the bony head of an orc that leapt towards the knight. The impact cracked the orc's skull, but sent a shudder up the handle of the mace that jarred the witch hunter's arm.

He fought his way to the warrior priests.

'You took your time getting here, Grunwald,' snarled the witchfinder general as he reached the knot of warriors, smashing a goblin down from behind.

'Something ate my horse,' grunted Udo in response, falling in beside the taller, older witch hunter.

With Karl and his knights hacking down the greenskins, the tide was turning, and some of the orcs turned to flee. The preceptor dismounted so as not to further risk his mount slipping fatally on the smooth stones. Deftly he turned aside a brutal swinging blade and sent a deadly riposte that tore out an orc's throat.

'My humblest apologies for entering your temple on horseback,' he said with a roguish smile.

'Under the circumstances, I think we can forgive it,' snarled one of the priests, a powerful figure hefting a pair of gore-covered hammers as he stepped forwards and smashed both weapons into the face of another greenskin.

'The women… and children,' groaned a fallen priest from the ground, his lifeblood leaking out onto the stone slabs from numerous wounds.

'What?' said Grunwald.

'Some of the desecrators got past us…' He paused for breath, wincing in pain. The witchfinder general cursed.

'Where are they?' he asked.

'The undercoft,' said another of the priests as he despatched another of the enemy.

'Hold them here,' Grunwald said, and turned towards the back of the temple. Karl ran at his side, clanking in his armour. Grunwald knew the temple well, and he paused at the top of the descending spiral stairs.

'The way is steep and narrow,' he said. 'Be careful.' He had visions of the heavily armoured preceptor slipping and falling headlong down into the undercroft. 'Maybe you had better remain up here.'

'There are women down there, are there not?' he said, flashing a smile at the witch hunter. 'I'm sure I will manage it.'

Grunwald snorted in response, and descended the stairway, taking the steps three at a time. He almost tripped over several bodies on the stairs, orcs that had been killed by some neat blade work from behind – it looked as though the orcs had not even turned towards their attacker, as if they were unaware of him until it was too late.

He leaped the last steps and burst into the wide tomb corridor. The stench of the orcs was great here, and the stink of death hung heavily in the air.

There were bodies on the ground, but half a dozen orcs remained standing, arrayed in a half circle around a pair of warriors.

Grunwald blinked, as if his eyes were deceiving him.

An elf, and a girl with a Sigmarite hammer.

As he hesitated, he saw the elf cut down one of the brutish greenskins with a lightning riposte. Karl almost crashed into Grunwald as he half-ran, half-fell down the stairs. His eyes widened as he surveyed the bloody battle ensuing in the corridor, and he stared in unabashed admiration at the hammer-wielding girl.

She lifted the hammer up before her with a defiant shout, and it seemed that the orcs covered their eyes and shied back from her. She leapt forwards and slammed the hammer into the head of one of the creatures, pulverising it in a spray of blood.

Together, the witch hunter and the preceptor surged forwards, roaring wordless war cries. The rearmost orcs swung towards them, but Grunwald saw a pair of the creatures launch themselves at the girl.

As fast as the elf was, he was not quick enough to block the blades that swung towards the girl from left and right, though he threw himself in the path of one of the orcs, turning its attack aside smoothly and nearly decapitating the greenskin with his return swing. The other cleaver hacked into the side of the girl with a wet crunching sound.

The girl was knocked back against a wall, and slumped lifelessly to the ground. The elf knelt instantly at her side, uncaring of the danger, his long, angular features twisted with despair.

'She was amazing,' breathed Karl as he cut down the last orc.

'Yes,' said the witch hunter, looking at the motionless girl bleeding on the floor. 'She *was*.'

CHAPTER TEN

THORRIK WAITED IN the stone antechamber, his thoughts grim, despite being back amongst his people and within a proper, dwarf-made stronghold. Shields on the walls bore the faces of ancestor gods: Grimnir, Valaya and Grungni amongst them. He marvelled at the stonework – it was wonderfully, lovingly crafted and put shoddy human workmanship to shame – but even that could not shake free his dark musings.

The dwarf holds were once again besieged, he had learnt. Karaz-a-Karak itself was assailed by the hated greenskins – indeed, it looked as though the grim times of the goblin wars long past had reasserted themselves, and the long war had begun once more.

He grumbled to himself and shuffled his feet, his gauntleted hands gripping the carved stone armrests of his chair tightly.

A pair of hammerers stood to either side of the thick, engraved steel doors, helms bearing tall feathered wings of hammered bronze on their heads. They stood motionless with gloved hands resting on the hafts of their mighty hammers, motionless sentinels that guarded the entrance to their thane's audience chamber.

At last the ornate, solid doors were opened, and an ancient greybeard nodded for him to enter.

With his helm held under one arm, Thorrik entered the audience chamber. Grim statues lined the long room, stylised dwarfen warriors bearing axes and hammers, helms carved with runes upon their heads. Thorrik clomped across the stone flooring, following the ancient dwarf whose beard trailed behind him, his eyes fixed on the dwarf seated behind a carved stone table ahead of him. The thane's head was lowered, and his desk was strewn with parchments, maps, stone tablets and thick, steel-bound books.

The thane did not raise his head even when Thorrik came to a halt before him. The greybeard moved around the table to his lord's side, and cleared his throat loudly.

'Thorrik Lokrison, Ironbreaker of Clan Barad of Karaz-a-Karak, guardian of the Ungdrin seeks audience, my thane.'

The thane grunted and looked up from his study, a deep frown upon his face and his eyes narrowed in concentration. His beard was as black as pitch, except for a streak of white growing from scar tissue on the left of his face, and ringed with bands of gold and gromril. He nodded in greeting to Thorrik, who nodded respectfully back.

'Ironbreaker of Karaz-a-Karak,' he said, his voice deep. 'I bid you welcome to Grimbeard. You come at a dark time. We could use an additional ironbreaker here – we are hard pressed.'

'So I understand, thane,' said Thorrik. 'And if I were not oath-bound I would gladly fight alongside the clans here.'

The thane grunted. 'Oathbound, eh. What is it you need?'

'I come to deliver an heirloom to a warrior stationed here. It is from his father, who dwells now in the great halls beyond.'

'There are many stationed here,' said the thane bluntly. 'Though far fewer after the past two months of fighting. What is his name and clan?'

'His name is Kraggi Ranulfson, of Clan Bruzgrond of Zhufbar.'

The thane looked over at the greybeard with his eyebrows raised, and Thorrik realised he must have been the loremaster. The old dwarf turned a lock upon a massive book, and the wheels and cogs of the book's cover clicked and turned, allowing the tome to be opened. The greybeard began leafing through the pages.

'Of Clan Bruzgrond, you say?' he muttered.

'Aye,' replied Thorrik.

Finding the correct section of the tome, the dwarf lodged a magnifying monocle in his left eye and began squinting at the tiny rune-script on the pages, tracing down with his finger.

'Ah,' he said at last in triumph. 'Here he is. Kraggi Ranulfson of Clan Bruzgrond of Zhufbar.' The greybeard squinted up at him with a grin, the monocle making his left eye seem of alarming size, before he lowered his head once more. 'Right where is he.... oh,' the dwarf's words trailed off and he popped his monocle from his eye-socket, his face grim.

'What is it, loremaster?' said the thane. 'No need to be so dramatic.'

'It is just that... well,' began the greybeard.

'Spit it out,' said the thane.

'He has taken up the slayer oath,' said the loremaster, and Thorrik lowered his head, covering his face with one of his gromril-encased hands, groaning in despair and sadness. Out of respect neither the thane nor the greybeard spoke, leaving Thorrik to his grief.

Deeply proud individuals, dwarfs who suffered some terrible tragedy, loss or deep blow to their honour would become inconsolable and take up the slayer oath. With great lamentation they would throw off their armour and dye their hair so that all might recognise their shame, seeking out battle wherever it could be found. Their honour could only be restored upon their death in battle, and so the slayer would hunt out the most dangerous of foes to combat to ensure his oath was met.

At last Thorrik gave a deep sigh, and raised his gaze to the greybeard, his eyes profoundly sad.

'And has he succeeded in his oath? Has be passed into the halls of his fathers?' asked Thorrik grimly, his voice thick with emotion.

If Kraggi had already died in battle, then if he had a son, the heirloom Thorrik bore would be passed on to him. But as far as he knew, the young slayer had no son – he was the last of his bloodline. If he had already passed into the halls of his ancestors then there would be no way for Thorrik to achieve his oath.

'He is not with us any longer,' said the old greybeard solemnly, reading from his weighty tome, having wedged his eyeglass back in place. Thorrik felt the bite of shame deep in his belly. Hurriedly, the ancient dwarf continued. 'By that, I do not mean he has succeeded in his oath, though he may yet have done so,' he said, making Thorrik look at him with narrowed eyes, not understanding.

'Oh, spit it out, you wattock,' snapped the thane.

The loremaster cleared his throat, and glared at the thane before squinting back down at the tiny rune-script. 'Beardling,' he muttered under his breath. 'Ah, here we are. It seems that Kraggi has left Black Fire Pass, journeying north through the mountains towards Karak Kadrin, there to join with others of the slayer cult beneath the flames of Grimnir. He left here forty-three days past. There is no further record of him.'

Thorrik gave a long sigh. 'It would seem that I will be making the journey to Kadrin then,' he grunted.

'The way through the mountains by foot is blocked,' said the loremaster, squinting over the table at Thorrik. 'The greenskins of Karak Varn and Mount Gunbad have arisen once more in force, and are laying siege to Zhuf-bar. The way past Black Water is cut off, and we have had no communication from Zhufbar for a month.'

The once proud dwarf halls of Karak Varn and Mount Gunbad had long ago fallen to the greenskins after earthquakes shattered them over three and half thousand years earlier. The dwarfs of the remaining holds still lamented the fates of these ancient halls, and long had been the oaths sworn to reclaim them from the hated hands of the grobi. But in the past three thousand years, the wars against the many enemies assailing the last remaining dwarf holds had been such that no reclamation expedition had yet been successful.

'Thankfully,' said the thane, '*Grimgrandel* still runs. It leaves on the morn – that would be your most direct path to Kadrin, ironbreaker.'

Thorrik nodded his head, his heart as heavy as stone in his chest. 'If such is the way I must go, then so it is.'

The thane stared at him wearily from across the desk. 'The war here is escalating – never in my lifespan, nor that of my father or grandfather, have the greenskins massed in such numbers. It is as though some dire power binds them together and keeps them from their usual infighting. I am disheartened to see that you will not stay to fight here, ironbreaker, but an oath is an oath. I wish you well with your task.'

'I thank you, thane,' said Thorrik, and nodded again to the two dwarfs before turning and marching from the room. The door shut solidly behind him.

THE WITCHFINDER GENERAL Albrecht Horscht passed back and forth before the open fire. There was a fresh wound on the side of his face that ran from his ear to the side of his mouth, red-raw and stitched closed. Still, blood and pus wept from the painful wound. If anything, Udo thought, the pain of the injury merely made the witchfinder general more irritable and caustic than usual.

He was a tall, white-haired individual, and his ruthless ways made him both feared and respected throughout the church of Sigmar and beyond. Thousands of heretics had been burnt at the stake at his command, and with spike and maul he had received the confession of hundreds of witches before executing them in cleansing fire.

'So, what do you think, revered Sigmund?' he said, speaking out of one side of his mouth to avoid reopening his wound further. 'Is she truthful, or is she an agent-pretender of the enemy? Will she bring ruin down upon us if she lives?'

Sigmund, the holy patriarch of the temple of Sigmar at Black Fire, furrowed his brow and scratched at the whiskers on his chin. He was an elderly man, yet was still a powerfully built warrior priest. He lay on his pallet, with bandages wrapped tightly around his chest. There was a slight hint of blood on these wrappings, and a pair of gentle Sisters of Shallya fussed over him. He had come very close to death during the battle against the greenskins, and they tutted and glared at the two witch hunters for disturbing their patient, unfazed by their grim reputations.

'Leave me, please, sisters,' said the elderly priest, his voice strained and ragged. With a reproachful expression upon her face, one of the women opened her mouth to protest. 'Please, Sister Katrin,' he repeated, wincing under her withering gaze. In any other circumstances Udo would have found it almost comical that this powerful priest, a veteran of hundreds of holy battles, could be told what to do by a woman.

The priestess, her raven hair streaked with silver, swung towards Grunwald and his superior and levelled a finger towards them. 'I'll give you ten minutes,' she snapped. 'No longer. He needs his rest.' With that, the two Sisters of Shallya left the room. Sigmund gave a long sigh.

'I am not sure,' he admitted finally. 'The girl – Annaliese, is it not? I am yet to be convinced either way. I need more time for communion with Sigmar, to ask his guidance.'

'I saw her myself, wielding a hammer of the saints against the foe,' said Grunwald. 'I felt the light of Sigmar was with her.'

'It could have been a trick of the enemy,' hissed the witchfinder general. 'If she recovers, which is doubtful, I say that we submit her to trial.'

'That will be the end of her, whatever the outcome,' said the old priest.

'And if she is innocent, then she will go to be with holy Sigmar, her name honoured and cleared of wrong-doing' said Horscht, shrugging. 'A truly devout woman of the temple could hope for no more.'

'To subject her to trial now will be demoralising,' said Sigmund. 'Initiate Alexis is not the only one to be convinced of her saintliness – half the temple believes that she is a holy warrior of Sigmar. If you subject her to trial, they will lose faith. They will lose hope.'

'Then they are not truly devout,' snarled Horscht.

The old priest sighed, closing his eyes. 'Many of my warrior priests believe in her,' he said with a tired voice. 'You would suggest that they are not truly devout?'

Horscht spun on his heel and began pacing back and forth once more.

'The histories tell of the Sisters of Sigmar of the cursed city that Sigmar smote beneath his hammer. They tell us that he grew angry with their temple and did strike it down with his twin-tailed, fiery comet of vengeance.'

Grunwald frowned and shifted his feet. He had read that the temple of the Sisters of Sigmar had been the only thing to remain *untouched* by the comet, but he had no wish to contradict his superior.

'If we let her live without trial,' continued Horscht, 'do we not risk harkening our own doom? Might

Sigmar not be displeased to let her be proclaimed as a warrior sister of his church?'

'I have no intention of proclaiming her anything,' wheezed Sigmund, his eyes angry. 'I merely suggest that you stay your hand for now. If she lives, then you can watch over her like a hawk – if you see anything that could make her claim doubtful, then she can be put to trial.'

'To be fair to the girl, I do not believe she has claimed anything,' said Grunwald. Horscht scowled at him.

'It matters not if she verbally claims it!' he said. 'The fact that by her actions *others* claim it is enough.'

Grunwald nodded slowly, conceding the point.

'It is true that she fought with the hammer of saintly Brother Trenkner, long thought lost to us,' said Sigmund. 'For five hundred years it has remained little more than a myth – it had long been said that brother Trenkner's body lies entombed beneath the temple, but none have ever discovered its whereabouts. The fact that she fought with one of our ancient Brother's weapons in her hand counts in her favour.'

'But how did she find it when none other, not even you, revered one, had been able to?' said Horscht, his voice accusing. 'She could have been guided to it by devilry, or by the restless dead.'

Sigmund scoffed at the remark. 'Come, Brother Albrecht, such things could not come to pass within the walls of the temple.'

'The enemy had breached the temple when the initiate claims she discovered the hammer,' said Grunwald. 'They smashed statues and breached the sanctity of our temple – could that not have allowed such witchcraft to be performed within its walls?'

Sigmund frowned, making the lines of his face deepen. 'That is a possibility,' he admitted.

'Anyway,' said Horscht. 'She is unlikely to survive the night, so this conversation may prove to be of little consequence. It may be that all we will need to decide is the manner of her burial – that of a saint, or as a devil.'

'We shall cross that bridge when we come to it,' said Sigmund.

On that note, the witch hunters took their leave, allowing the wounded patriarch to rest.

'How is she?' asked Katrin as she entered the small room. Annaliese lay beneath sheets heavy with perspiration. A young sister of the healing goddess of mercy knelt over the girl, cooling her forehead with a damp cloth. The hammer the girl had used to fight the greenskins lay upon the bedside table next to her. So she took up the path of the warrior, Katrin thought sadly.

'She is stable,' said the sister. 'But I cannot yet say if she will live or not.'

Katrin smiled at the elf standing sentinel over Annaliese's bed. He inclined his head slightly in response, and she shivered. He made her nervous with his cold demeanour and otherworldly distance. She knew that he made the other Sisters of Shallya uneasy as well, yet he had stood watching over the girl without sleep since she had been struck down. It was impossible to gauge his emotion, for his pale, thin face gave away nothing.

There was another in the room as well, a tall, powerfully built knight whose face was filled with concern.

'You should rest, sister,' he said to her. He was handsome, she saw. His face was strong, and his eyes clear and green. His hair was sandy blond and hung to his heavily armoured shoulders. Oh to be twenty years younger, she thought fleetingly.

'I will rest when there is none that need my care,' she said in reply.

'Then you will not be resting for a long time to come,' he noted.

ANNALIESE WALKED THROUGH a field of gold, the sun beating down on her skin, and she smiled. It was a radiant day, and she felt utterly content despite the roiling black clouds that were clawing across the sky to the north. Red lightning flashed in the gathering darkness, crackling across the sky.

The warmth began to seep from her body, and she shivered with a sudden chill. The sun had disappeared. Overhead, the writhing clouds were thickening. Annaliese hugged herself tightly as her bones were chilled. She felt pain then, and cried out.

She looked at the hammer held in her hands. It glowed with warm light, but it was nothing more than a spark in the overwhelming darkness swallowing the sky.

Annaliese opened her eyes with a shuddering gasp, and the pain of her wound crashed in on her. She saw concerned faces crowded around her, but she looked past them all at a figure standing apart from the others, and she smiled.

'She is delirious,' said a voice.

'I must go,' she said suddenly, struggling to rise. 'The darkness is rising in the north! My place is there! It is His will!'

'Hush,' said a gentle voice, and she felt a cool hand on her forehead. She sank back into the bed sheets, feeling as though there were heavy weights that pulled her eyelids down.

'My place is in the north,' she muttered. 'The griffon aflame. That is where I am bound.'

She felt the presence of Sigmar with her then, and warmth flowed through her.

Annaliese sank into a deep and dreamless sleep, a smile upon her face.

She had a purpose.

BOOK TWO

THE NORTHLANDS ARE *in ruin. Ostland is overrun and will fall any day. Its lands are rife with enemy forces, and they have taken control of the north bank of the Talabec River. They push into Talabecland, though our defences are holding there thus far.*

I have received little word from Elector Hertwig of the Ostermark, besieged as he is in Bechafen. If the Ostermark falls, then the Empire is wide open and vulnerable – the enemy will be able to strike at the rear of the armies defending the Talabec, overwhelming them for they cannot hold against two fronts. Once they fall, the enemy will march into the very heart of the Empire, and will be within striking range of Altdorf itself. I dread the day that such news is brought to me. I pray to Sigmar that the Ostermark holds.

The plague has claimed great swathes of the Empire, entire towns and villages fallen beneath its spell. These

*places are overrun with blood-frenzied degenerate beings –
the enemy is turning our own people against each other with
its sorcery. It is certain now that this sickness has been
spread by agents of Chaos. The Order of the Griffon is vigilant, and is hunting down the perpetrators – but the damage
has already been done.*

*Word has come from the High King of the dwarfs that the
Everpeak itself is besieged, a disastrous turn of events for we
can expect no aid against the despoilers of the north from
our mountainous allies while their own kingdom is so beset.*

*A feeling of dread has descended on the populace and our
armies, and many of the electors have succumbed to hopelessness. This cannot be allowed to continue, for all the
Empire has is the resolve of its people.*

*This is indeed a dark era. I pray that I have the strength
to maintain control.*

K.F.

CHAPTER ELEVEN

UDO GRUNWALD HAD seen many strange and terrifying sights in his years as a soldier and a witch hunter. He had borne witness to scenes of madness and bloodshed, had seen foul magick performed that twisted the essence of reality, and had seen men possessed by daemons. But nothing prepared him for the sight of the hissing, steaming monstrosity that rolled inexorably forward as it passed through the arched entrance into the massive stronghold that was the Grimbeard Station.

'Lady of mercy,' swore Grunwald. Annaliese was equally awed by the beast that approached.

As they marched through Black Fire Pass en route to Grimbeard, across earth on which Sigmar himself had walked, he had begun to assess the girl. She seemed pure enough on first impressions, though he knew that such things were often carefully feigned masks. These thoughts slipped away as he gaped at the monstrous machine before them.

Only the elf, who Grunwald had learnt was named Eldanair, seemed unimpressed – he watched the proceedings with a look of distaste on his long, pale face, and held a section of his cloak over his mouth and nose to block out the acrid smoke. Though Grunwald knew that Eldanair had no knowledge of the long argument that had taken place for the dwarfs to even *consider* allowing the elf within Grimbeard, he was irritated by his reaction to this wonder of the dwarfs.

The trio stood with their backs up against the smooth stone wall as the steaming behemoth came closer. The platform was a hive of activity, as dwarf engineers and workers bustled to and fro, but the witch hunter's eyes were fixed on the colossal machine as it drew to a halt, steam and smoke billowing from its iron-encased belly.

Borne upon dozens of steel wheels, guided upon massive metal tracks fixed to the ground, the steam-powered machine was a riot of deafening noise and motion. Pistons hissed super-heated steam as they rose and fell, and huge gears and levers rotated and clicked as they moved. Smoke, black and sooty, spewed from the four chimney stacks on the top of the ironclad body of the beast. Whistles blew painful blasts as they vented steam, and bells rang as mechanical hammers struck them.

The circular front of the mechanical engine was dominated by a metal-bearded ancestor face taller than a man, the image painstakingly inlaid with criss-crossing lines of gold and bronze. Each turning of the massive machine's wheels was accompanied by a deep rhythmic sound like the breathing of some ancient forge-god, and dozens of coupling rods hissed and screamed as they rose and fell.

With a screech of protesting metal, the giant beast slowed, and Grunwald was enveloped in a cloud of black smoke. He coughed, blinking tears away as ash and soot assailed his eyes. The laboured breathing of the machine stopped altogether, replaced by a deep exhalation of venting steam. When the smoke cleared, he saw that there were soot-covered dwarfs swarming all over the cabin of the engine, oiling levers and gears and ensuring everything was in correct, working order.

Huge crane-structures swung above the snaking carriage behind the engine that was still exhaling steam, and a huge quantity of what looked like coal was dropped into an open tray. A flexible hose the width of a man's body was manoeuvred into position, its metal clamps fixed onto the curving body of the engine, as water began to pump into the belly of the beast. Steam rose into the air, and the beast seemed to hiss in contentment as its thirst was quenched.

Grunwald had of course heard of the wonders created by the School of Engineers in Nuln, but according to Thorrik, the skills of the Empire's finest engineers paled in comparison to those of even the lowliest dwarf apprentice. Seeing this monstrous machine, he could well believe the dwarf's claim.

There were engines powered by steam and fire within the lands of men – twelve mighty steam tanks protected by thick sheets of metal and kitted out with dangerous experimental technologies, steam powered cannons and such – but even they were no comparison to this behemoth, for it dwarfed them in size. This titanic creation that was able to journey through the heart of the mountains to link the dwarf holds was truly immense. It was easily the height of a two-storey building, and the engine-carriage itself was over fifty yards in length. Hitched behind this hissing engine were six carriages – it was a long caravan train made of metal, pulled by a fire-breathing beast of burden of immense power and strength.

'Behold the wonder of *Grimgrandel*,' said the young apprentice engineer who had been assigned as the humans' guide and chaperone, pride in his thickly accented voice. He was clearly pleased at the open-mouthed astonishment that the humans were showing.

'I have never seen anything like it,' said Grunwald eventually. The apprentice snorted.

'And nor would you have,' he said. 'There is nothing in the world that compares to *Grimgrandel* – and certainly not in the lands of men!'

The elf had a dark look of distaste and loathing on his face and he brushed at the soot on his clothes and long black hair, in a futile effort to remove the black marks. The dwarfs bustling around the group gave the elf dark looks, muttering under their breath.

The elf seemed to have adopted an air of superiority and he looked around with his delicate nose turned up in repugnance to the goings on. He stuck close to Annaliese, and his eyes flicked around warily towards any who approached too close to her. A strange girl, he thought, to inspire loyalty in such a disparate group.

The elf was clearly protective of her, even though he was unable to speak Reikspiel, and the folk in the Temple of Sigmar had clearly adopted her as their own – they had showered her with gifts that they could ill afford upon her departure from the temple. She had blushed and refused many of the gifts as impractical for travel – but the clothes she now wore were gifts that she had been grateful to accept. She barely resembled the rural serving girl that she had been – it was as though she had thrown away her past and reforged her image after her near-fatal injuries.

She had shorn away her flowing blonde hair and she now wore it at a more practical shoulder-length. Outfitted from the armoury of the temple itself on the instruction of the old patriarch, Sigmund, she wore a long dress of chainmail beneath a heavy robe of red and cream. This armour was heavy, but provided good protection, while still allowing great freedom of movement, and the girl was stronger than she looked. Her shoulders and neck were protected by a high gorget of stiffened leather and thick leather also protected her forearms. A twin-tailed comet medallion hung around her neck over her chainmail and robes, and the girl's smooth-skinned face shone with devotion.

If she was false, then she was a damn fine actor, he would give her that. She spoke of Sigmar with believable reverence, and though it was clear her knowledge of the great deeds of the deity were limited, she was eager to learn.

'I am to come with you upon your pilgrimage to the north – to guard over you and to school you in the ways of our lord Sigmar,' he had lied, watching closely for any sign of fear or displeasure. She had beamed with joy at his proclamation.

Still, Grunwald knew that the external veneer that people wore was only that – an image, surface-deep, that could hide foulness within. How many servants of the Ruinous Powers wore the guise of nobility and servitude to the Emperor? How many foul witches and mutants paraded themselves within Empire society as devout adherents to Sigmar's ways? The enemy within was the most dangerous and cunning enemy of all, and it was the duty of the witch hunters to root out and unveil these hated foes wherever they were to be found.

'Do not let her know that you suspect her,' the witchfinder general Horscht had instructed him. 'For that would be to alert her to your motive, and she would only become more careful and conniving in her ways. Be a friend to her – be her guardian and her confidant. But always beware the guiles of the enemy, and watch for signs of corruption. And once there is valid proof expose her for what she truly is and enact Sigmar's vengeance upon her with the full power vested in you.'

'I will be ever vigilant in my duty,' Grunwald had vowed. In truth he hated such a duplicitous approach – he had been embraced as a witch hunter due to his brutal, forthright and direct approach, not for his subtlety. While others of his order specialised in infiltrating and unearthing covens of dark worship from the inside, with admirable success, Grunwald had always frowned upon such practice. Descending on the foe with all the brutal power his position could muster, to force a confession from the lips of his suspects – that was his preferred way. And he had been lauded for the success he had already had in his young career. This task left a sour taste in his mouth.

'Come,' said the dwarf apprentice, ushering the trio towards the steaming beast. Udo felt distinctly uncomfortable with the idea of travelling over the mountains hundreds of miles to the north within the belly of this giant metal serpent. He would have been much more comfortable riding the distance on horseback, or even walking, but this was certainly the quickest mode of transport available and Annaliese had been insistent. A vision drove her onwards, she said – Sigmar wished for her to travel to the north with all haste. Grunwald found such claims doubtful, he had been a servant of the warrior god for some years now and had never received a vision. He knew that some in the order had received such visitations, but they were usually priests of particularly high standing – not an untrained peasant.

They followed the young apprentice as he marched up the platform that was raised some ten feet above the ground, passing the hissing steam engine of the giant machine he had called *Grimgrandel*. Dozens of engineers, many with long beards that would have been white if they were not blackened with soot, stood arguing loudly near the cabin of the machine. The group ducked out of the way of two master engineers stalking towards them. The engineers were engrossed in heated conversation, and they carried huge spanners upon which were fixed arrays of steam-powered tools of arcane design. One of them lost the flow of his diatribe when he caught sight of Eldanair, and he spluttered in outrage, his face reddening. Swiftly, the apprentice ushered the trio past the revered engineers, blushing a deep red. He was clearly uncomfortable being a chaperone, Grunwald realised.

Tons of coal were being dropped into the vast tender behind the lead engine. Grunwald found himself gaping, and almost bowled an aged dwarf over as he looked around the frantic activity around the platform. The dwarf huffed and barked an insult, as the witch hunter was hurried on his way by the shame-faced apprentice, who apologised profusely to the old dwarf.

Warning whistles blew loud and shrill, and with a hissing of steam and the clanking of levers, sections of the carriages began to unfold. Gears and cogs ground as the sides collapsed outwards onto the platform with a resounding crash amidst venting smoke and steam.

Hundreds of dwarf warriors bustled from the carriages, their weapons and armour clanking, their heavy steps pounding rhythmically upon the unfolded metal carriage sides. Mule-sized spluttering engines were fired up, belching choking smoke, and they dragged behind them lines of war machines – cannons, organ guns and other more esoteric devices that Grunwald did not recognise. Sweating engineers guided these steam-powered hauling engines as they puttered out from inside the carriages, directing them down ramps leading into the main stronghold of Grimbeard. Reinforcements from other dwarf holds, Grunwald figured.

Scores of grim dwarfs marched past, who were ignored completely or regarded with looks of scorn. Most were cloaked in heavy green fabric, and they marched resolutely behind bronze standards depicting horned ancestor-heads. Wonderfully crafted guns were carried over the broad shoulders of many.

'Clan warriors from Karak Hirn,' said the young engineer apprentice, ushering Grunwald to the side so as not to block the way.

Legions of dwarf warriors waited in the wings of the Grimbeard platform alongside the monstrous engine, and they nodded their heads to the warriors filing past them. When the last warriors had marched from the carriages, and the final war machines had been disembarked, horns were blown, making Eldanair wince.

'You will be travelling in the third carriage of *Grimgrandel*, quite separate to the clan warriors,' the apprentice informed them as he began leading them through the press once more. 'Much care must be taken to ensure rival clans do not embark within the same carriage, I might add.'

They neared the third carriage, and the apprentice halted. 'Here you are,' he said. He nodded to Grunwald and Annaliese, studiously ignoring Eldanair, and without further ado he turned and hurried away from them. Grunwald shrugged, and stepped inside the metal hull of the carriage.

THORRIK MUTTERED TO himself as the sides of *Grimgrandel* slammed shut with a burst of steam and a belch of smoke. He tutted to himself at the delay of leaving Grimbeard. Had he not been waiting for *Grimgrandel*, he could have been two days ahead on his journey – but that journey would have taken many weeks, and by all accounts this journey would take but days. But still, he didn't trust this new-fangled creation of the Engineering Guilds.

The inside of the carriage was not unlike a dwarf hold, he thought, though on a far smaller scale. The ceiling of the carriage was almost hidden in darkness overhead, and lanterns built into the curving rib-like support beams blazed with warm light. The enclosed air was filled with pipe-smoke and small groups of dwarfs drank ale from ornate metal flagons. A rowdy group of warriors further up the carriage stamped their metal-shod boots against the steel floor in time to their chanting, while the scrape of metal sounded as other dwarfs sharpened already flawless axe-blades with whetstones.

There was a riot of bustling movement within the carriage as dwarfs stowed weapons and equipment in heavy steel lockers located within the backrests of the benches, but the area around Thorrik was an island of calm. Ironbreakers were highly respected warriors, and none would wish to give offence to the veteran.

A contingent of thunderers holding their beloved black-powder weapons protectively across their laps sat nearby, talking in low tones amongst themselves. He recognised from the uniform metal discs each wore around his neck that they were holdless clan warriors whose ancestors had come from Karak Varn – a hold lost by natural disaster and subsequent skaven and grobi attacks over four thousand years earlier. Though generations of the survivors lived within the other dwarf holds, they could never truly be at home or fully accepted in any of them. Most of these grim thunderers were meticulously cleaning the mechanisms of their priceless guns, oiling cogs and shining their barrels.

There were even a few slayers within the carriage, lost in their own misery. They were instantly recognisable; they wore little in the way of clothing and forsake any form of armour. Their bare skin was covered in spiralling blue tattoos, and the sides of their heads shaved. Their hair, stiffened with lime and grease, was spiked up in large crests and both hair and beard were dyed a bright orange so that none may mistake the oaths of death they had sworn.

No dwarf approached these grim figures, and they in turn kept their eyes downcast, chuntering away to themselves, fingering the hafts of their axes. The fire of disgrace burnt fiercely within them, and it could only be doused with their own honourable death in battle.

Thorrik's face darkened as looked upon the doomed slayers. He sighed deeply and thought of the heirloom he carried wrapped within oilskin. The only remaining member of the family, the rightful owner of the artefact, had taken up the slayer oath. Thorrik's heart was heavy.

He looked up from his position seated on one of the three aisles running the length of the carriage to see a tall, dark-clad shape leading a pair of other tall figures through the press of dwarfs. He recognised the broad-rimmed black hat worn by the witch hunter Udo Grunwald, and he nodded in greeting as he caught the human's eye.

'Thorrik Lokrison,' said the witch hunter once he had picked his way through the press.

'Didn't expect to see you here, manling,' said Thorrik gruffly. The witch hunter gave a curt shake of the head.

'Didn't expect to be here,' he replied. 'You are heading back to the north?'

'Aye, to Karak Kadrin,' said Thorrik, squinting up at the big man. He couldn't quite see the two behind the witch hunter. 'Sit yourself down, manling, I am getting a crick in my neck from looking up at you.'

Thorrik nodded in thanks as the thunderers made room for the new arrivals.

'This is Annaliese,' introduced Grunwald, gesturing towards the human girl dressed like one of their warrior priests of Sigmar. 'And this is her… companion.'

'Eldanair,' said the girl, introducing the third figure, who was cloaked and hooded. Thorrik stiffened at the name, and peered into the gloom beneath the figure's hood.

'Elf,' he spat. Several dwarfs nearby glanced around sharply, scowling. Thorrik's face hardened, and he turned back to Grunwald. 'You keep unwelcome company, manling.'

'He can handle himself in a fight,' shrugged the witch hunter.

'Doesn't mean he fights on *our* side though. An elf fights only for himself – they have no concept of honour or oaths of friendship.'

'Eldanair has been a devoted protector and friend to me,' said the human girl, her face reddening in anger. 'I will not have you or anyone else speak ill of him.'

Thorrik gave the girl a withering look, but to her credit she did not baulk beneath his stony gaze. 'Remember your words, lass, when he deserts you and flees from danger in the dead of night.'

'He would never…' started the girl, her voice rising, and the elf touched her on the shoulder, shaking his head.

'Oathbreakers, all of them,' declared Thorrik loudly, turning away from the girl and the elf. 'Never trust an elf.'

'Glad to see you have mellowed in our time apart,' commented Grunwald.

Thorrik swore in Khazalid as he saw another tall figure moving though the crowd down the aisle towards him. This human was wearing plate armour, and had a broad grin on his face.

'Another friend of yours?' said Thorrik. The witch hunter looked up in surprise.

'Karl Heiden!' he said, standing and gripping the man's armoured forearm in greeting.

'I heard that there were other humans on board this marvel. If I'd known they were quite so pretty, I would have dressed up,' the knight proclaimed, winking at Annaliese, who blushed.

A whistle blared, and *Grimgrandel* shuddered into movement, almost knocking the human knight off his feet.

Grimgrandel pulled out from Grimbeard, the massive engine steaming and smoking as the pressure within the boiler grew. Pistons began to rise and fall, and searing pipes and valves began to shudder. With a final whistle, the massive steam-powered engine began to pick up speed. Within the hour, it entered a massive tunnel that bored straight into the side of the mountains, and began hurtling through the darkness, cutting straight through the heart of the Worlds Edge Mountains.

CHAPTER TWELVE

THE CARRIAGE JERKED suddenly, shaking Grunwald awake with a start. It was dark and his ears where filled with ungodly, unfamiliar sounds and the air was hot and stifling. For a moment he imagined that he had died, and was on his way to Morr's underworld realm, but he shook off these maddening thoughts as he regained his bearings.

With bleary eyes he glanced around the gloomy interior. Lanterns rattled and shook as the carriage shuddered through the darkness far beneath the mountains. In the dim light he could see that many of the dwarfs were sleeping, their loud snoring all but drowned out by the rattling carriage, the relentless hissing and pounding of pistons and coupling rods, and the screech of the metal wheels upon steel tracks.

The heat within the carriage was almost unbearable, the air thick with smoke, both from the massive coal stacks at the front of the hauling engine and from pipes. The stink of coal and oil filled his nostrils, and his breathing was laboured. His eyes stung from ash, and he blinked heavily.

It truly was an infernal machine, this steam engine, he thought. It seemed that it ploughed down into the heart of the world. This was not a place for man, he decided. Just the idea that there were hundreds of thousands of tons of rock hanging over their heads, ready to collapse and crush them at any moment, made his breathing quicken and sweat trickle down the back of his neck.

Thorrik was sleeping, his head tipped back and his mouth wide open. Annaliese slept as well, her legs tucked up underneath her and her head lolling on the elf's shoulder, though he could not tell if the elf was awake. He wore a strip of cloth tied around his mouth and nose, and had his hood pulled down low, concealing his eyes and pointed ears, and though he made no reaction to Grunwald, that was not to say that he was asleep.

Karl Heiden was nowhere to be seen – soon after the steam engine had begun its journey he had returned to his men, who were travelling within the carriage behind theirs. He had told the witch hunter that the dwarfs had kicked up quite a fuss when he had tried to board the warhorses of the knightly order, and the thoroughbred steeds had whinnied in fear, stamping their hooves despite their training. But such was the agreement that the humans had with the dwarfs – they were travelling to the northern battle zones of the Empire, and the quickest route was by this steaming monstrosity – and the dwarf High King had pledged its availability to the Emperor himself.

Half of Karl's order was travelling northwards on board. Though there were rumours of armies of darkness massing beyond the Peak Pass, which Karak Kadrin guarded, from latest correspondences the way from the dwarf hold into the Empire was clear. How long it would remain so, however, was another matter.

Feeling a need to stretch his aching back, the witch hunter stood warily, holding onto the side-bench for stability. The dwarfs certainly eschewed comfort, and he winced as his back clicked alarmingly. The travelling benches were cold and hard, leather over steel; no wonder the dwarfs were such a taciturn race if this was how they lived.

Seating himself once more, Grunwald stared at Annaliese, as if trying to penetrate her sleeping thoughts. Was she true, or did the touch of Chaos itself, linger within? Even if she did not yet realise it, she could still be tainted and thus deserving of death. Usually such a taint would eventually manifest itself physically, through mutation however slight – webbed toes, knobbly growths protruding from the spine, additional fingers – but these might not necessarily have yet had time to develop in one so young. Or, he thought darkly, she was able to control the powers of Chaos to such an extent that she was able to restrain such outward markers of her sin.

Once again he felt his frustration grow. This was not his way – he was a man of action and directness. If there was suspicion of witchery and Chaos taint, then there would be a trial. If the individual proved to be innocent, then their death cleared them – for all who were tried received death, guilty or no. There was no remorse, and Grunwald felt no guilt for the innocent dead – better to die with your purity ensured than to linger with doubt.

He flicked his gaze from the girl to the elf. He felt with certainty that Eldanair was not asleep, but rather was watching over the girl. Perhaps he was her familiar, thought Grunwald darkly. He shuffled in his seat. He must test her, he knew, but he must also do as the witch finder general commanded – he must determine her innocence or guilt without her knowing his motive.

The train lurched, and Annaliese awoke with a gasp, her eyes wide and fearful. She looked around and caught the witch hunter's gaze – she smiled sleepily to him. Grunwald fingered a water bottle at his belt, thinking. Then he unscrewed its cap, and took a small swig. He offered the girl the bottle.

'It's just water,' he assured her. Nodding her thanks, she unfurled her long legs from beneath her, stretching herself like a cat. Grunwald stood up and stepped over to her. The train rocked again and he stumbled. A small amount of water splashed over Eldanair and Grunwald felt the elf's dark eyes boring into him. Apologising, he handed the girl the bottle. She gratefully took a long swig, and smiled her thanks.

Re-seated, Grunwald sealed the bottle of sanctified holy water once more. It was precious – certainly not drinking water – but it should have been like acid to a devotee of the Ruinous Powers. But then, that meant nothing. The enemy was cunning.

There was a screech of metal on metal as the wheels of the steam engine locked. Those few dwarfs who had been standing were knocked from their feet and fell to the floor of the aisle heavily, cursing. Equipment and rucksacks fell from overhead shelves, crashing down upon those still seated, who slid along the bench seats towards the front of the carriage. Grunwald caught hold of the bench as he began to slide, but lost his grip when Thorrik's immense armoured weight slammed into him, and was almost crushed against an ornately crafted bronze armrest in the shape of a rearing dragon.

Annaliese half fell from her seat and would have flown up the carriage if Eldanair hadn't grabbed her arm with preternatural speed and pulled her to safety. Grunwald winced as the weight of Thorrik pressed against him, and he was sure that his ribs were going to break. With a final grinding screech, the engine halted.

Muttering, the dwarf picked himself off Grunwald and stood, brushing his beard with his hand. Grunwald just glared at him, shaking his head, his ribs aching.

'You alright?' he asked Annaliese, and the girl nodded back at him. The elf was speaking to himself, his voice scathing, as he looked through the slats upon the side of the carriage into the darkness beyond. The dwarfs through the carriage were huffing and stomping their feet, their voices rising in tones of anger and accusation. Many looked half asleep as they straightened helmets knocked to the side and retrieved fallen stowage.

'Why in the name of the gods did this thing stop?' he asked Thorrik, who glared back at him with humourless eyes. He coughed something in his crude language.

'How should I know, manling?' snapped the dwarf in Reikspiel.

'I wonder where we are,' said Grunwald, joining Eldanair in peering out of the metal slats. 'And what time of day it is. Such notions as day and night mean nothing down here.'

'Well, I would say it is around midday on the surface,' said Thorrik as he began to load his pipe from a pouch. Grunwald gave a snort and looked at the dwarf incredulously. Not a sliver of light penetrated this far beneath the mountains – it was like some hateful, stygian abyss.

'And how could you know that?' he said derisively.

'I'm a dwarf, manling,' snarled Thorrik, his eyes blazing in the flickering lantern flame. 'You wouldn't understand such things.'

Grunwald snorted again, and turned back to peer out into the darkness. Now that the engine had halted, there was no movement of air, making it feel even more heavy and oppressive.

'Judging by the time that has passed and the speed of *Grimgrandel*, I would guess we are almost half way. Somewhere between Zhufbar and Mount Gunbad. Possibly beneath Black Water.'

'Beneath what?'

'Black Water – the inland sea of the mountains.'

'So you are saying that above us is not only miles of rock, but also a sea?'

'Aye, lad. No need to get so worked up. This is dwarf engineering – built to last.'

Great, thought Grunwald, shaking his head. He looked back out through the slats, squinting his eyes to see something, anything outside. Nothing. It was as if the world ended a foot beyond the carriage. He turned his head to say something to Thorrik, but as he opened his mouth to speak, a black arrow hissed past his head. It struck the metal roof of the carriage and ricocheted down into the press of dwarfs milling around on the next aisle over.

More arrows slipped through the slats of the carriage, clattering loudly, and dozens more shattered on the outside of the carriage. One of the arrows slammed into the leather backrest a hair's-breadth from Thorrik's face. The dwarf pulled the arrow from the leather, his face furious as he looked at the crude black dart – its tip was of sharp stone, bound to the wooden shaft with sinew, and the flight was stringy and frayed raven feather. Thorrik's face reddened.

'Grobi!' he bellowed in a thunderous voice. He slammed his helmet down over his head, and leapt to his feet, scrabbling for his shield and axe. 'Grobi!' he yelled again.

The dwarf handgunners primed and readied their weapons, and within seconds they took up places at the side of the carriage. Though Grunwald had been unable to see anything in the gloom beyond, the dwarfs clearly were more adept and within seconds the air was filled with the deafening booms of the guns firing. Smoke filled the carriage. Eldanair fired his longbow out into darkness, and Grunwald, hunkering down away from the slats through which arrows still penetrated, dragged free his heavy crossbow.

Annaliese was beside him, crouching down away from the windows, her eyes fearful.

'Stay down,' ordered Grunwald. He then hefted his crossbow pointing it out through the slats. Lanterns had been turned out into the darkness, and he could see the reflection of hundreds of eyes out there. He could hear them now too, their cackling and their screeches. He fired, sending the crossbow bolt slamming between two of the glimmering reflections, which disappeared instantly.

A sharp whistle rang out along the line of carriages, and venting steam hissed out of dragon-headed vents along the top of the carriage. The angled metal shutters running the length of the carriage began to close, and the sound of arrows striking them from the outside echoed dully within. Gears and heavy metal cogs ground, and the sides of the carriages began to unfold outwards, like mechanical drawbridges being lowered.

Dwarfs stepped forwards side-by-side, locking their shields together as the carriage-walls were lowered. The arrows of the enemy shattered against shield and helmet, and Grunwald ducked down behind the armoured wall of dwarfs, re-loading his crossbow.

Eldanair was standing on the bench beside him, firing arrows over the heads of the dwarfs into the darkness. He swayed to the side as an arrow streaked towards his head, his face impassive, and sent an arrow back in response.

The heavy stabilising columns of the carriage sides boomed as they hit the ground, and with the grinding of gears and the hiss of steam, the slats rotated from their closed position, forming broad sets of stairs onto the ground of the tunnel.

There was a deep bellowing war-cry and Grunwald saw one of the unarmoured dwarfs with bright red spiked hair step forward, elbowing his way through the shield wall to stand alone and defiant. He raised his axe up over his head and roared incoherently. An arrow slammed into the meat of one of his powerful, thick upper arms, driving through the flesh to protrude out the other side a good six inches.

He grabbed it in one meaty fist and pulled the length of the arrow through the bloody wound, teeth clenched and hissing against the pain, before tossing it dismissively to the ground. With another roar, he hefted his axe and thundered down the metal stairs, lumbering at the enemy now revealing itself as it stepped forwards into the light blaring from focused lanterns on the engine.

Another red-haired berserker warrior launched himself towards the foe creeping forwards, and as the line of dwarfs stepped down the stairs to meet them, each pounding footstep in unison, Grunwald got his first look at them.

They were small, shorter even than the dwarfs advancing towards them, and their green-skinned frames were weak and spindly, all but hidden beneath black robes and pointed hoods. They held a veritable wall of barbed spears out in front of them, and they hissed and screamed at the dwarfs.

Grunwald stepped alongside the dwarf handgunners, who stood still within the carriage, laying down a wall of fire over the heads of their advancing kin. Dozens of the deep-dwelling goblins were ripped apart by each volley, but their bodies were trampled uncaring beneath the feet of the others pushing forward. Hefting his now loaded crossbow to his shoulder, he fired. The bolt slammed into the forehead of a wildly screaming goblin whose black robe was rimmed with yellow stitched dags, and who had been waving a leg bone over his head from which dangled all manner of teeth, hair and a strange likeness of a grinning moon. The goblin fell without a sound, and was lost amongst the leering crowd of goblins.

The red-haired dwarf berserkers reached the line of the enemy, and they splintered the spears angled towards them with wild swings of their axes before ploughing into the midst of the foe, cutting and rending. Their weapons traced bloody arcs through the air, and they cut down dozens of foes before they were overcome, falling to their knees and bleeding from a score of wounds. They were lost from sight as the black-robed goblins swarmed over them, jabbing with blades and spears.

A moment later a goblin pushed to the front, a severed dwarf head held up above his head. He screamed incoherently and hurled the head towards the dwarf line. As the goblins advanced, one of them kicked the bloody head across the floor, and others bustled against one another to continue the game.

Grunwald heard a rumble of outrage rise from the dwarf ranks, and they closed towards the goblins with renewed determination.

''WARE THE BEASTS!' roared Thorrik as the advancing rank of night goblins before them parted. A group of powerful creatures, little more than gaping mouths on legs, were pulling their diminutive retainers forwards, who were trying to maintain some control over them with chains and spiked goads. As he watched, one of the creatures broke away from its master and turned on it, ripping an arm from its socket with one crunching bite.

The other creatures had their cold, black eyes focused on the dwarfs, and needed no encouragement. Their handlers released them, and they came bounding across the stone floor of the tunnel towards the dwarfs.

'Hold the line!' roared a voice as the dwarf warriors continued their relentless advance, stepping shoulder to shoulder, their overlapping shields creating a near impenetrable wall of steel.

Thorrik was in the front rank, and he focused on one of the beasts leaping towards him, its gaping mouth exposing thousands of crooked, serrated teeth. Little more than a reddish ball of muscle, the creature was all mouth, and it barrelled towards him at a great speed. Thorrik had fought these war beasts of the grobi many times in the tunnels he and his kin guarded, and knew they were dangerous foes.

Still, he had learnt a thing or two about them in his years as an ironbreaker, and as it launched itself at him, he waited until he saw the large black irises of its eyes roll backwards, a moment before impact. Then he took a quick step forward, and smashed the boss of his gromril shield into its face, shattering teeth and halting it in its tracks. It felt like he had slammed the shield into solid rock, and Thorrik was forced back a step. His axe sang out, and he sank the blade into its bulbous head, killing it instantly.

Others were not so experienced, and the reddish creatures chomped down upon shields, ripping them away with brutal shakes of the head, severing more than one arm in the process as their jaws snapped viciously.

Arrows flashed in as shields were ripped down low, and several dwarfs groaned in pain as the shafts sank into exposed necks, and pierced mailed chests. An arrow struck Thorrik in the forehead, but no goblin weapon could hope to pierce the precious gromril that protected him.

The dwarf to his left was struggling with one of the beasts, pulling his shield down, shearing through the metal with its powerful jaws. Blood began to flow as teeth bit into the arm strapped behind the shield, and the creature began shaking its head to and fro furiously as it tasted it. Thorrik smashed the creature between the eyes twice before it went limp, but even in death it did not release its grip. The dwarf, gritting his teeth against the pain, hacked at it until it was cut nearly in half before he was able to rip his arm free.

Seeing a flash of movement above, Thorrik yelled a warning as one of the beasts descended from above, a screaming goblin clutching its back. A white-fletched arrow thudded into it as it fell, but it slammed down amongst the dwarf line, its overextended jaws engulfing a warrior to the knees. Blows rained down on it, scoring deep wounds in its side and cutting its rider down, but it bunched its powerful legs and leaped up into the air once more, dwarfen legs and boots protruding from its mouth.

But then the lines of dwarfs and goblins struck, and the killing began in earnest. Thorrik hacked left and right with his axe, scything down goblins, carving through the flesh of the diminutive creatures. They snarled hatefully, baring sharp teeth and their eyes flashing, as they stabbed at him over their shields with spears. Barbed blades jabbed at him and he was struck a dozen times, but not one of the blows was able to pierce his armour.

His axe smashed into one of the goblin's wooden shields, splintering the wood and shattering the arm behind. With his return blow, he drove his axe blade into the goblin's leering face, and dark blood splashed out as its skull was caved in. The dwarfs to either side stepped forward with him, pushing into the goblin masses and hacking with their weapons. The dwarfs were heavily outnumbered, but the goblins died in droves before them.

Setting their shields against their shoulders, the dwarfs began to physically push the goblins back, heaving forwards to the beat of a metal drum that started up. With each solid step, the dwarfs stamped their feet into the ground and grunted heavily, creating a deep pounding echo through the cavern. Goblins were cut down and trampled beneath the heavy boots of the dwarfs as they pushed forwards.

The dwarfs were as unrelenting as rock itself, and the goblins were being crushed, trampling each other to death in the press of bodies. Thorrik ground forward, pushing with his shield and his shoulder. He stamped down on the neck of a goblin, and pushed forwards, stepping over the bodies of the slain.

Crushed between the dwarfs pushing forward and the weight of other goblins behind them, the enemy panicked, and tried to flee. Still, there was nowhere to run, and the axes of the dwarfs rose and fell repetitively, killing and maiming. There was no skill needed here, now – it was like chopping wood. Thorrik hacked into the terrified, hated goblins, his weapon covered in gore. The slaughter was immense – hundreds of bodies lay crushed behind the advancing dwarf line.

GRUNWALD FIRED A last bolt into the fleeing masses and lowered the crossbow from his shoulder. The dwarf casualties had been few – it was an impressive display of strength and order. He had been a soldier for long enough to know that if the dwarf line had been breached, then the goblins would have pushed into the gap and surrounded the dwarfs. And in such a fight, their sheer numbers would have swayed the battle – every last dwarf would have been cut down in the resulting chaos.

But the dwarfs had not faltered and Grunwald was impressed with their unfaltering resolve. They fought as one, and it seemed that there was not a hint of doubt within them, not a thought of retreat, or even of the possibility of losing.

They seemed incapable of fear and failure was something that seemed unacceptable. Grudgingly, he had to admit that he felt more secure now in the knowledge that these grim warriors were the ones who guarded the mountain passes of the Empire – but if a foe could best these hard fighters, then surely the Empire was doomed.

He saw Karl Heiden walking towards him, the visor of his helm raised, and a smile upon his face. A trio of knights marched behind him. Blood was splattered over their platemail, and the broken tips of several arrows were embedded in their shields.

The witch hunter nodded to the knight as he strode up the stairs.

'Not much of a fight,' said the knight. Grunwald grunted in reply. It could have gone much worse, he thought.

Karl's gaze flicked past the witch hunter towards Annaliese, and he smiled at her. 'Survived the battle then, lady?' he said.

'As you said, it wasn't much of a fight,' the girl replied, holding her head high.

'True, and I am glad to see that you are unharmed,' he said. He looked around, at the darkness of the cavern. 'This truly is a marvel of engineering,' he said, shaking his head. 'To think the dwarfs carved this tunnel out of solid rock, all the way through the mountains. It's an astounding feat.'

Grunwald grunted. The dwarf warriors were returning to the steam engine, cleaning their axes of goblin blood. There was a sharp whistle, and the warriors began climbing the stairs into the carriages once more. There was no song or boasting amongst their number – the dwarfs remained grim and dour, even in victory.

'Makes you wonder what stopped this engine,' remarked Karl.

'The cursed grobi caused a cave-in up ahead,' said Thorrik, climbing the stairs into the carriage with heavy metallic steps. '*Grimgrandel* would have been derailed had it not halted. The engineers are clearing the way.' His words were followed by the sound of detonations – the sound of the dwarfs blasting the way clear.

'You and your kinsmen fought well,' said Annaliese, looking at the ironbreaker. The dwarf huffed in reply, deflecting the praise.

'The grobi have no fight in them. Take the battle to them, hard. Kill a bunch of them. The rest will run,' he said, shrugging. 'It is in their nature.' The dwarf eyed the weapon held in the girl's hands, and his eyes gleamed greedily.

'That is a fine hammer you wield, lass,' he said.

'It is a holy weapon of Sigmar,' she said, holding it up before her. Her eyes were bright with passion and fervour. A blush spread over her face. 'I fear I am unworthy to wield it.'

'Certainly not,' said Karl smoothly. 'You are a vision, lady. Like a warrior-woman of old.'

'You are kind,' Annaliese replied, looking down demurely. She gripped the hammer more tightly in her hand, and her eyes rose looking into Karl's, who stared at her appraisingly still. 'Many would say that a woman has no place in war.'

'They are fools,' said Karl earnestly. 'A woman is capable of far greater strength than any man. Men are filled with unbridled aggression, a need to destroy, to assert themselves over the land and each other – women are creators and fight for purer ideals – to protect that which they love: their children, their future, their home. And in such a fight, she is stronger than a man – for she has more to lose.'

Thorrik snorted and turned away. Karl threw his retreating figure a dark look. Annaliese was looking at him with wide eyes, and he flicked his earnest gaze back to hers, and continued. 'The goddess of my order, Myrmidia, is wise, strong and fierce. Her enemies fear her skill in battle, and her friends are awed by her discipline, her mercy and compassion. She is an inspiration, an ideal, that no man can hope to match.'

The whistle blew once more, and the steam engines hissed. Karl lowered his head in a half-bow to Annaliese, nodded to Grunwald, and hurried down through the press of dwarfs to rejoin the trio of knights awaiting him on the tunnel floor.

Grunwald saw Annaliese's eyes follow the handsome knight as he led his comrades back towards their own carriage, and he shook his head slightly.

An explosion of steam burst from valves and cylinders, and with the turning of gears and levers the sides of the carriage began to close.

Within the hour, *Grimgrandel* was moving once more, plunging through the darkness beneath the mountains, grinding its way inexorably towards Karak Kadrin.

CHAPTER THIRTEEN

THE CARRIAGE ROCKED back and forth as it continued through the darkness. Annaliese unconsciously toyed with the symbol of Sigmar around her neck, biting her lip. She stared blankly at the slatted side of the carriage, her mind filled with doubt.

'You are troubled,' said a deep voice, making her start. She looked around to see the Sigmarite witch hunter, Udo, staring at her. His eyes were dark, his face serious. She smiled lightly at him.

'I'm sorry, I was miles away. What did you say?'

'I said you are troubled,' he repeated, his dark eyes intense. 'What are you thinking of?'

Annaliese sighed. 'A week ago, after I had awoken in the temple, I felt like my purpose was clear. My vision had been so strong. But now? I am doubting myself. What purpose could Sigmar have for me? I'm no warrior – I don't know anything of real battle. I don't know… I don't know what good I can do.'

The witch hunter frowned. *He* looked like a warrior, Annaliese thought. Big, strong, brutal. Scarred.

'Describe your vision to me.'

'I saw a griffon – powerful, majestic and dangerous. It was beset on all sides by enemies – savage dark men dressed in furs and black metal. It tore and ripped at them, cutting them down – they couldn't touch it. Their swords bounced off its body, and their axes were blunted against its hide. But then the proud beast caught fire – its fur and its feathers were ablaze, and its wings were flaming. It screamed in pain.' Annaliese shuddered with the memory. She could smell the stink of burning feathers, could hear the painful cry of the creature tearing at her heart. 'The blades of the enemy could hurt it then, and they plunged lances, spears and swords into the body of the griffon. It fell beneath the dark tide surrounding it, and I cried out.'

'I ran forwards, and the sea of enemies parted before me. I was surrounded by blinding light, and they recoiled from me, clearing a path. I knelt beside the dying creature. I cradled its heavy head in my arms and stared into its unblinking, piercing eyes. The flames died, and the griffon grew strong. It reared up, its wounds healed, and the enemy fled before it.'

Annaliese shivered, and looked up at Grunwald with a frown. 'I… I can't remember the rest of it. It's fading with every passing day. But I know that I have to find the griffon – and I know that it lies in the north. A week ago I knew this was my destiny, but now – I doubt myself. What if it was nothing more than a meaning-less dream brought on by my injuries? What if I go north only to find death, destruction and war? What good can I do? I am but a girl. I cannot affect anything.'

The witch hunter was silent, his face thoughtful. 'I don't know if it was a vision from Sigmar or not,' he said eventually. 'But a single person can make all the difference. Sigmar himself was a single man, and yet he united the scattered tribes and defied the enemy. Magnus the Pious was a single man, and yet he defied Chaos at Praag. The Emperor himself is but one man, and he holds the Empire together.'

Annaliese gave a cold laugh. 'These are the great and mighty, witch hunter. Individuals yes, but not individuals like me.'

'They were not always great and mighty. They each were born as helpless babes, crying and suckling at their mothers – by their actions they were made great and mighty. The actions of a single man – or woman – may yet determine the fate of all of us.'

'Forgive me, witch hunter, but I cannot see how the actions of a simple girl of seventeen summers could affect the outcome of the war.'

'I'll put it another way,' said Grunwald. 'Battles are won and lost by the decisions of single men. Often these are the decisions of the so called "great and mighty" – generals, commanders and elector counts. But more often it is the decisions of the average soldier that determine the outcome of the battle. An individual decides to stand and fight. Others are inspired by his resolve, or driven by shame not to run when this man stands defiant. And so the army stands. On the other side, amongst the enemy, a single individual chooses to run. His fears overcome him – he is thinking of his wife, his child, his mistress or his fortune – he doesn't want to die, and so he flees. Others see him fleeing, and they are filled with doubt. Was there a call to retreat that they did not hear? Did this soldier know something that they did not? By that one soldier's decision to run, he has doomed his entire army. Others turn and run with him – and if everyone is running, where is the sense in standing alone, or the loss of honour if they too flee? There is none. And so the day is lost. That first man to run is like a single rock falling from a mountainside – soon others join it, until there is an unstoppable avalanche. But if that first man held, if that first rock did not fall – would they have been victorious? Would the mountainside have collapsed anyway? Perhaps. Perhaps not.' The witch hunter shrugged.

'You sound like an orator,' said Annaliese.

'Ha!' scoffed Grunwald. 'Far from it. It is a speech I heard once, when I was a soldier, and my retelling is a far poorer version. But it is true nonetheless. One man choosing to hold against the enemy, one man choosing to run – that is the difference between victory and defeat. Good commanders know this – they make sure that there are strong, heroic warriors scattered throughout the ranks who will stand defiant and who will either shame or inspire their soldiers to do the same.'

'My father used to say something similar,' said Annaliese.

'A wise man then,' said Grunwald. He stared at her for a moment, and she felt a shiver run through her. His eyes were intense, and there was violence within them. Still, he was a templar of Sigmar.

'I am honoured that you are coming with me,' she said. 'Though in truth *why* you are accompanying me is a mystery.'

The carriage jerked, and Thorrik's snoring was interrupted. Grunwald saw the elf's eyes flick towards the slumbering dwarf, his face unreadable. Thorrik began snoring again a moment later.

'You are... unusual,' said Grunwald, picking his words carefully. 'The young acolyte at the temple claimed to see an aura around you when you somehow retrieved that hammer of yours – a hammer said to have been lost for centuries. And it is claimed that you healed the boy you brought to the temple with your touch. Such claims are rare, and are in need of investigation.'

'I never claimed to have healed Tomas,' said Annaliese quickly. 'And there was nothing mystical about me retrieving the hammer. It was just there, and there were enemies that needed to be faced.'

'You do realise that there was no mortuary alcove where you claimed to have retrieved the hammer,' said Grunwald softly.

'What?' said Annaliese, alarmed. Hearing the tone of her voice, Eldanair looked at the girl then at Grunwald, his face cold. 'That is not possible.'

'No matter,' said Grunwald. 'And the boy? You say that you healed him – how did you manage such a feat with no training?'

'I never claimed to have healed him. I thought he had suffered a mortal wound, but when I held him I realised that he had not.'

'So you say.'

Annaliese smiled ruefully. 'You think I am a witch, Grunwald?'

'If I thought that you would already have been burnt alive at the stake,' he replied. 'You wear the symbol of

Sigmar around your neck, and you wield a weapon of a long dead priest. Yet you have had no religious training – it is in the best interest of the church for you to be accompanied by a member of temple. To instruct you, to guide you and to protect you should your... talents be true.'

Annaliese stared hard into the witch hunter's eyes. 'I have never claimed to be anything, witch hunter.'

Grunwald smiled, which if anything made him seem more dangerous. 'And I am not claiming you *are* anything, Annaliese. Think of me just as... someone watching over you. Helping you make the right choices. In Sigmar's name, of course.'

She heard the threat in his words, but felt suddenly calm. She smiled. For all his words and his occupation, she felt that there was little guile within Udo Grunwald.

'I like you, witch hunter,' she said, as surprised by the truth in her words as he was, judging by the look on his face.

'Why?' he said simply, looking at her as if she were mad.

'I think I know where I stand with you,' she replied. 'Which is something.'

THE CARRIAGE GROUND to a halt, amid blasts of venting steam and the groan of metal.

'What's this?' growled Grunwald, the sudden lack of vibration waking him.

'We are at Karak Kadrin,' said Thorrik dourly.

Grunwald glanced out the slats in the carriage walls – it was still dark out there and he wondered for a moment if night had fallen – he had completely lost track of time beneath the ground.

'Is it night?' he said out loud, voicing his thoughts. The dwarf snorted.

'Manlings,' he scoffed. 'It nears mid-afternoon. We are still below ground – we travel the last distance to Kadrin Keep by foot – we shall not see the surface until we leave Kadrin.'

'We?'

'Aye, we. I'll deliver this,' he said, patting the oil skin wrapped object that had barely left his side the entire journey, 'and then I'll be on my way back to rejoin my clan – in the state of Ostermark.'

'What does he keep so well hidden, wrapped in leather?' asked Annaliese later, as they walked down the metal steps away from the hissing steam engine of *Grimgrandel*.

'I'm not sure,' said Grunwald. 'Some kind of heirloom, he says. Something that he is oath-bound to deliver.' He gave the girl a look. Her face was bright, and she looked rested and curious of the goings on around her. The resilience of youth, he thought. He felt sore, tired and irritable. 'The dwarfs seem to take their oaths particularly seriously.'

'Maybe its some magical relic of old,' said Annaliese, her blue-grey eyes lighting up, making her look even younger than she was.

'Perhaps,' said the witch hunter noncommittally.

They waited for Karl and his thirty knights, who led their snorting warhorses from their carriage. The young preceptor smiled broadly at them as he approached. His steed stood a massive twenty hands tall at the shoulder – a purebred Averland destrier. Its eyes were wide, and its ears were pulled back – it was a fierce beast, but it clearly did not like the unnatural hissing of the steam train, nor being underneath the ground.

'Well that was a much shorter, if more uncomfortable, journey than by horseback. Over five hundred miles! That would have taken weeks – but here it only took what – three days? Truly a marvel this steam engine. Imagine if these were constructed all across the Old World! Our troops could be transported from Altdorf to Kislev within days. Much faster than by ship even.'

'All the coffers of your Emperor would be emptied a thousand times over to fund such an undertaking,' growled Thorrik, who had turned back to them to hurry them up. 'But come, enough of such foolish talk. We must make haste. There is grim news – the keep is besieged. Peak Pass is contested.'

PEAK PASS WAS one of only two ways through the towering mountains that formed the nigh-on impenetrable eastern border of the Empire. Over five hundred miles to the south lay Black Fire Pass. The only other clear route through the Worlds Edge Mountains lay almost six hundred miles further north, in the uppermost reaches of the inhospitable lands of Kislev, the Empire's northern neighbours. There lay the High Pass, through which the Chaos forces spilled during the titanic Great War two hundred and fifty years earlier.

The three passes were the key to the defence of the Empire. Thus was the message hammered home into would-be military commanders and their subordinates. The passes meant life or death, and if they fell, so would the Empire.

But if even one of the passes fell to the enemy, then it spelled disaster. The Empire was almost destroyed during the Great War, and in that time both Black Fire Pass and the Peak Pass had held strong – through the High Pass the bloodthirsty hordes of Chaos erupted, overtaking northern Praag and spilling southwards.

If two passes fell, or Sigmar forbid all three, then there could be no hope for the Empire of man. Grunwald's thoughts were dark as he marched along the cavernous dwarf under-road leading into Kadrin Keep.

It was a marvel of old fashioned dwarf engineering, and Thorrik pointed out the details of the massive expanse with pride in his voice. The way was lit with thousands of torches and oil-burning lanterns, and massive arches rose hundreds of feet above them. The scale of the place was beyond comprehension – indeed the highest building within any of the great cities of the Empire, even Altdorf, would be able to sit within the archways with hundreds of feet to spare above the highest parapet.

Bearded, horn-helmed faces glared down at them, totem-heads that rose as high as a castle tower. Beneath arched, braided moustaches gaped open mouths broad enough to allow ten carriages to pass side-by-side. Columns perfectly square, each side easily a hundred feet in width, rose into the darkness overhead. Square-cut balconies and platforms were hewn into their sides, betraying the fact that they were riddled with rooms and stone chambers.

They passed beneath arched bridges, vast passageways that led to other parts of the hold. Everywhere there were titanic statues and pillars, all intricately carved with spiralling patterns and weaving lines that formed depictions of battles, warriors and the dwarf ancestor-gods.

The sheer scale of the place stunned Grunwald, and Annaliese stared with her mouth wide in astonishment and awe. Thorrik seemed pleased by their reactions. For nearly a mile they walked along the underway, towards one towering statue that rose even higher above them than anything else they had seen so far. Filling the arched expanse, hundreds of feet high and hundreds of feet wide was a giant carved likeness of a fierce dwarf warrior, his deep eye sockets hidden in shadow. Stone braids hung down from his face, curling around themselves and falling to the ground. They hit the ground and extended out before the grand statue to form high-sided walls that reached hundreds of feet before the statue. The statue seemed to grow larger as they approached it, rising into the air above them. Indeed, it seemed as though the arched roof far above was supported on the shoulders of this mighty king – that he bore the weight of Kadrin Keep itself.

The statue's chest and legs were heavily armoured with overlapping plates of rune-inscribed armour, though his muscular arms were bare except for powerful bracers that encircled his forearms and coiling dragon-torcs that wrapped around his massive upper arms. The stone that was carved to form this armour had veins of gold running through it, so that the statue glittered and shone in the torchlight. Over his shoulders he wore a cloak of dragon scales and fur.

In one hand the behemoth held a stone helmet. Giant scaled stone wings extended up from it, merging into the ceiling almost a thousand feet above, forming pillars and supports. The front of the helmet was carved in the likeness of a dragon's roaring visage. The dragon's wide jaws would frame the warrior's face, and there were dozens of sharp teeth carved of pure white stone that protruded from the monster's gums. In his other angular, thick-fingered hand the king held a hammer of giant proportions, engraved with blocky dwarf runes lit up from within, glowing with orange light. Similar runes blazed upon the warrior's helmet, as if the fury of a furnace burnt inside it.

Scores of dwarf warriors bowed their heads and ran their hands over thick strands of stone hair that formed the giant braids that hit the ground, intoning oaths and sacred words of greeting or praise. The passageway continued beneath this mighty statue. Grunwald saw that the dwarfs walking beneath the statue struck their fists upon their chests, above their hearts, and began chanting as they walked, a deep throated, mournful drone.

'Behold mighty Grimnir, ancestor-god of courage and mighty deeds,' spoke Thorrik, his voice solemn and reverential. 'Karak Kadrin guards the Shrine of Grimnir. It is a place of great reverence, and thousands of dawi-kind travel from their holds to pay homage to the ancestor-god here every year.'

'How do those runes glow with light?' asked Annaliese, her voice full of wonder. 'Is it magic?'

'Magic? Pfah!' snorted Thorrik. 'The dawi – dwarfs as you know us – have no use for magic in the way you mean. No, it is something more mundane, yet no less impressive for that. The most skilled stonemasons of Karak Kadrin carved them but the stone of those runes of courage, kingship and battle is as thin as parchment. There is fire behind them that will never grow dim until the dawi are no more, and it is the light of those flames that you see through the stone.'

Annaliese raised her eyebrows, clearly impressed. 'Stone as thin as parchment... Surely it would shatter?'

Thorrik chuckled. 'Aye lass, if carved by any but dwarf hands, it would. None in all the world can match a dwarf in craftsmanship.'

'I can believe that looking upon this,' said Annaliese softly.

'For such short folk, you certainly build tall,' said Karl. 'Almost as if you were making up for your lack of height.'

Grunwald smirked involuntarily but was amazed at the knight's lack of tact for daring to say such a thing, however apt, in the presence of Thorrik and his kinsmen, before such an awe-inspiring statue of one of their great gods. It was clear that the knight had little experience of dwarfs.

Thorrik rounded on the knight, glowering with rage. Karl was forced to halt, and the giant steed he led snorted and stamped its hooves. Though the preceptor towered over the dwarf who came barely to his chest, Annaliese and Grunwald breathed in a little and backed off a step from the simmering rage that threatened to overwhelm the warrior.

'Utter such a remark again, beardling, and as Grimnir is my witness I swear that I will cut the legs from under you so that you will look at the world from the same height as I,' growled the ironbreaker, his hand closing on the haft of his axe threateningly.

Several of Karl's knights frowned and their hands reached for their own swords, but Karl raised his hand to stop them. His eyes still glimmered with humour, but his face was serious.

'I apologise – to you and your gods – brave warrior. I mean no disrespect. This place is… beyond words, and I fear my mouth ran away with me. My deepest apologies, once more, Thorrik Lokrison,' he said earnestly.

Thorrik grunted, pleased by the human's words but his face still burning with rage. He cleared his throat. 'Kadrin is not a place for what might pass amongst you humans as humour. I warn you now, once. So much as *think* such a disrespectful thought, and the Slayer King will have you gutted and left upon the mountainside for the crows to pick at. Kadrin is not the place for levity, and you had best remember that.'

With a final glare, Thorrik swung back around and continued to lead them down the broad passageway. Grunwald shook his head incredulously at Karl as he caught the knight's eye, and the preceptor gave him a quick shrug of the shoulders, a look of mock grievance upon his face. 'You are an idiot,' Grunwald said softly, before turning to follow Thorrik.

'I didn't know he would be quite so touchy,' said Karl to himself.

Annaliese shook her head slightly, her eyebrows raised in reproach, though there was a hint of a smile on her lips. She patted Karl on his armoured shoulder as she passed.

The knight watched the girl walk away from him, her short-cropped blonde hair seeming to glow with a light of its own. He had at first been disappointed when he had seen that she had cut her flowing, wavy hair, but he had to admit that her shorter style was growing on him – it showed her face better, and made her seem a little older. His eyes lingered on her slight figure, the sway of her hips beneath her robe and chainmail that fell almost to the ground.

He whistled softly through his teeth, and shook his head at himself. Then he led his thirty Knights of the Blazing Sun on, passing beneath the statue of Grimnir and into the mighty, besieged, Kadrin Keep.

CHAPTER FOURTEEN

FOR FIVE DAYS they had been stuck inside the keep as the enemy attacked it night and day, and Grunwald's patience was frayed to the point of breaking.

'We should never have come by the damn steam engine,' Karl snarled. 'By now I could have been more than half way to the Ostermark. But here we are trapped like mice inside this accursed dwarf fortress, with no chance of breaking out.'

'I thought you liked the journey,' remarked Grunwald.

Karl glowered at him. 'I am ordered to bolster the ranks of my order in Bechafen. They are dying out there fighting against the damn forces of Chaos, and here we are locked inside a castle in foreign lands.'

'Yes, I know, Karl! You haven't let any of us forget it in the last three days.'

'I am sick of the sight of you, witch hunter. But there isn't really any way that I can avoid it.'

Grunwald rose to his feet, his face dark. Karl remained seated, his face bitter and resentful.

'What are you doing here anyway, Grunwald?' snapped Karl. 'Following the girl around like some lovesick fool? Giving her Sigmar's guidance, my arse. Not really a job befitting a witch hunter, is it? She's hardly some evil sorceress. What is it? You want to rut with the girl or something?'

Grunwald's fist cracked against Karl's cheek, throwing him backwards off the barrel he was sat on. He scrambled to his feet, his face angry.

'What, is that it? Hit a nerve, did I?' he spat. 'You are old enough to be her father, and ugly enough to scare off a dwarf maiden. You think she would ever dream of bedding one such as you?'

'Quiet! I have no such intentions or delusions. I have no such interest in the girl.'

Grunwald glared at the knight for a moment, before sitting back down, rubbing his bruised knuckles.

The knight remained standing, glowering in anger.

'I am not trying to seduce the girl,' said the witch hunter. He sighed. 'I was married once, you know. A beautiful girl, with the sweetest nature a man could ever dream of.' He snorted. 'Never knew what she saw in me.'

'What happened to her?' said Karl, still standing.

'She died in childbirth. The babe was lost, too. It was a girl. Would have been about Annaliese's age by now.'

'Ah,' said Karl, sitting down, rubbing his cheek where the witch hunter had struck him.

'It's not like that,' said Grunwald.

'Like what?'

'I know what you are thinking. That I lost my wife and daughter, and that Annaliese lost her parents. You think I am adopting the girl – a surrogate daughter to replace the one I lost.'

Karl frowned. 'You could do worse.'

'Perhaps.'

'What do you mean by that?' said Karl, his voice sharpening once more. His eyes narrowed. 'What *are* you doing here, Udo?'

'Watching out for the girl. Ensuring she is no danger. To the Empire… to herself.'

'A danger?' Karl huffed in derision. 'What possible danger could she be? You think she is what… a heretic? You templars of Sigmar see much where there is nothing.' His voice was heavy with scorn.

'No,' said Grunwald forcefully. 'I don't. But that does not mean she could not be dangerous.'

'Explain.'

Grunwald sighed. 'The girl had a vision. True or not, it doesn't matter to me, but others believed her. The temple of Sigmar is placed in a tricky situation – either it refuses her, and risks causing dissent at a time when unification is needed, or it accepts her claims and allows her to go north to fulfil her vision.'

'I fail to see the danger in that…'

'Think about it, man. What is the purpose of the devotees of Sigmar? His warrior priests? They are to inspire strength, unification, resilience and courage in the soldiery. A man who might flee will not do so in the presence of his warrior god – it would be an act of shaming cowardice. Thus, the priests of our order are trained from childhood – to ensure that they will not run in the face of the enemy, to make them hard, able and fearless warriors.'

'I understand – it is similar with Myrmidia in the realms south of the Empire. But how does that relate to Annaliese? She is no warrior priest.'

'No, she is not, but that *is* the point. The church does not allow the average Empire citizen to wield the weapons of a priest or carry forth the word of Sigmar.'

Karl leant back, understanding dawning on him. 'I see. So, she is a special case – soldiers would not see her any differently than any other priest – indeed she would probably be the focus of more attention, what with her being a woman. A man would be even less likely to run in panic in front of a *woman* representing his god. That would be shameful indeed. So, you are here to make sure that she doesn't do something that would weaken the resolve of the soldiers – that she herself does not baulk in the face of danger.'

'Something like that,' said Grunwald. He was still unconvinced of the girl's purity, but letting the knight know that would be utmost foolishness.

'Seems like a strange job to give you,' remarked Karl. 'Surely you would be better placed rooting out necromancers and cultists.'

'Aye,' said Grunwald. 'But I am not here by choice – this is a task I have been ordered to perform.'

Karl sat rubbing his cheek thoughtfully for a moment. 'If a woman priest would be more inspirational to soldiers than a man, then why does the church of Sigmar not promote more female priests? I cannot recall seeing a single one.'

'There is a very good reason for that,' said Grunwald. 'Because they have in the past been hunted down by witch hunters such as I and burnt as heretics and witches.'

Karl's jaw dropped. 'What? Why?'

'Hundreds of years ago, there was an order of female priests. But Sigmar smote the city that housed their temple, levelling it with a flaming comet that fell from the heavens. It is believed that their existence angered him. There is fear amongst the church that to allow women to become priests would encourage Sigmar's rage once more.'

'So, why let Annaliese live then, wearing the garb of a priest?'

'Why indeed?' said Grunwald darkly. He thought of the witchfinder general's last words before he left the temple in Black Fire Pass.

'It would be for the best, Grunwald, if the girl had an *accident*. Out on the road somewhere, away from prying eyes. She would be forgotten, and the church would continue as it always has.'

Grunwald had nodded, uneasy with this task that seemed far from noble, but trusting his superior.

Now, he was not so sure.

Kadrin Keep, which Thorrik would often refer to as Slayer Keep, was a grand, powerful bulwark – the kind of structure that seemed to Grunwald to be impossible to destroy. It would have been easier, he thought, to destroy the mountains themselves. Indeed the keep was more mountain than fortress, or perhaps more correctly it was both.

Carved from the hard rock of the craggy peaks, the keep rose high above Kadrin valley, just to the south of the Peak Pass itself. The passages and halls of the fortress-hold riddled the mountain. Vast hall upon vast hall, the hold was larger than any city of the Empire. It delved deep below the earth and rose to the peak's highest point.

It was an immense city beneath the surface, and all the necessary components were housed within it.

Thousands upon thousands of dwarfs dwelled within, split amongst their various clans, and there were vast areas dedicated to breweries, smithies, stores, eating and drinking halls, barracks, mine-workings, libraries of ancient lore, storehouses and anything else that the hold could ever possibly have need of for survival. The witch hunter realised that a dwarf growing up within the hold need never step outside, need never glimpse the grey skies overhead or feel the icy bite of the wind upon the mountainside.

He never saw more than a tiny fraction of the hold, yet was in awe at its scale, its majesty and the sheer care the dwarfs took in their craftsmanship, wherever it was to be found. Even the smallest, least-used passages had intricate knot-work carved upon their sides, leering faces of ancestors jutting from walls and painstakingly chiselled runes arching around the groined support arches overhead.

And it was not a dark place either, as he had expected. The hold was filled with light, though there were invariably many areas of menacing shadow. Lanterns and thick, greasy candles burnt at all hours of the day. Ingenious lamps fuelled by strong alcohol pumped through intricate arrays of pipes and valves ensured that they never burnt low. In the larger halls giant hollow wheels of steel hung from mighty chains, their circumferences pitted with holes through which tongues of flame lit the area.

The sounds and smells of industry pervaded every vast chamber within the hold, and the pounding of hammers, the mechanical turning of vast gears and toothed-wheels, and the hiss of venting steam pressure – all were a constant hubbub of productive noise.

Grunwald had seen the forges of Karak Kadrin, and had been awed at their scale. Giant hammers the size of a castle tower pounding at great sheets of super-heated metal, driven by pistons and hissing boilers, and thousands of sweating smiths worked tirelessly through night and day to provide armour for the armies of the Slayer King.

'It is a tragic tale,' said Thorrik to Annaliese when she asked about the strange title for the monarch of Karak Kadrin. 'Generations past a mighty king, Baragor the Proud, suffered a terrible loss that drove him to take up the slayer oath – only in death would his shame be annulled. But the king faced a terrible dilemma, for if he were to seek his death, as a slayer must, then he would be abandoning his oath of kingship, his oath to oversee and protect his hold, and to do such a thing would be a dishonour far worse than death. It was an impossible dilemma, and one that haunted him until his dying day – indeed one that continues to haunt his line, and will do until the day of reckoning comes, when Grimnir comes back to us.'

'What did he do?' asked Annaliese, her eyes wide. Grunwald and Karl leaned in to listen to the dwarf's grief stricken words.

'His oath to his hold was stronger than his slayer oath. And so, he became the first of the Slayer Kings, and the shame of being unable to fulfil his slayer oath would carry down to his heir. In turn, his heir became the next Slayer King, and his after that. King Baragor built the Shrine of Grimnir, and Kadrin became the centre of the slayer cult. Slayers from all across the dwarf holds would make the pilgrimage here, to mourn and lament before the grand statue of the ancestor-god, who is their patron. He grants them the strength and the fearlessness to go to their end with their heads held high, never to take a backwards step in the face of the enemy.'

'The statue that we saw beneath the mountain?' asked Karl.

The dwarf gave the knight a pitying look. 'No. That is but a pale shadow in comparison to the great shrine, out in Kadrin valley, near Kazad Gromar.' He let the impact of this statement sink in.

'The Slayer King who rules today is Baragor's descendant of blood, King Ungrim Ironfist, and he too bears the shame of his forefather.'

'The slayers, they… scare me,' admitted Annaliese.

'As well they should, lass,' said Thorrik. 'They make even the most doughty dwarfen warrior uneasy, for a broken oath or a personal tragedy could come to us all – leaving us hungering for battle, lamenting life in all its forms and forever seeking the final relief of death.'

Grunwald saw Annaliese shiver, and indeed he felt a chill at the dwarf's words himself.

'And now, Karak Kadrin itself is besieged,' continued Thorrik, his face subtly changing, his mournful expression changing to one of anger. 'The enemies arrayed against it are many. The Bloody Sun tribe, they are called. Greenskins arrayed in such force that they make the mountains tremble beneath their step, and are like a carpet of foulness from horizon to horizon. It is said that this is the self-same tribe of greenskins,' he said, spitting onto the ground, 'that assail Black Fire Pass. And far off Karaz-A-Karak, the seat of the High King himself.'

'How is that possible?' said Grunwald. 'Orc tribes ally uneasily – how is it that one tribe holds dominance over all the others?'

'It is something that I have learnt is troubling the greybeards much,' replied Thorrik. 'They suspect some foul sorcery, some trickery is at play – some power that binds the orc and goblin tribes together. Whatever it is,' he added, 'if it is not broken, the lands of the dwarfs will be overrun. Not this year, probably not next – but if the greenskin hordes do not fracture, I cannot see how the dwarfen holds can withstand such hateful, protracted attack. We live in the shadow times – the end of the dwarf nation draws close.'

'Your people cannot falter!' said Karl fiercely. 'If the holds are lost, then the Empire is lost with them.'

'Aye, I would guess as much,' said Thorrik.

The companions sat in silence for a moment, their mood dark. The sounds of industry rang out around them, and dwarf warriors marched past them, tucked away in the corner of the vast hall where they had made their camp.

'I am going to check on the horses,' said Karl at last, breaking the silence. 'Would you care for a stroll on this most fine evening, young lady?' he asked of Annaliese, bending his knee theatrically and extending his hand. 'Or morning? Or whatever time it is in this… place?'

'I would be most honoured, noble sir,' said Annaliese with a laugh and a curtsy. Eldanair too rose up silently from where he sat cross-legged on the stone floor.

'*He* doesn't need to come,' said Karl.

'Oh hush, leave him be,' said Annaliese.

With her hand resting lightly on his armoured forearm, the pair strode off, ghosted by Eldanair.

'Good girl, that,' said Thorrik gruffly.

'You are troubled, my friend,' said the witch hunter. He had been trying to get some time alone with the ironbreaker for days now. When they had first arrived at Karak Kadrin, Thorrik had been full of energy, for his task was almost complete. He had rushed off to try to discover the whereabouts of the young slayer, so as to deliver unto him the ancient heirloom he bore. But when he had returned, his mood was dark, and Grunwald saw that he still carried the leather-bound relic.

'It's nothing,' said the dwarf. 'You would not understand.'

'Try me,' suggested Grunwald.

'It is this siege. The orcs rising. It portents of bad times to come,' said the dwarf gruffly.

'Undoubtedly. But they have done so before, and together man and dwarf has defeated them. It is something else, is it not? Something to do with your… oath.'

Thorrik sighed and pulled out his dragon-headed pipe. Grunwald did not say anything as the ironbreaker lit up and began puffing away. Tendrils of blue-grey smoke rose from the fanged maw and nostrils of the snarling serpent pipe.

'Aye, you are right, manling,' he said. He cleared his throat. 'I am unable to complete my oath.'

'Unable…' said Grunwald, frowning. 'Ah,' he said finally. 'The young slayer completed his oath, then?'

'Aye,' said Thorrik gruffly. 'He feasts now in the halls of the ancestors, his pride restored. He fell against a stone troll – a mighty foe to be bested by, indeed. He slaughtered more than a dozen greenskins before the fell beast cut him down, so it is said. A good death.'

The witch hunter could see that the dwarf was in pain, but had not the depth of understanding of dwarf culture to fully comprehend the importance of what he said. Thorrik's oath could not be fulfilled. What happened to a dwarf who was unable to complete an oath? Grunwald watched as a painted slayer walked past, gnashing his teeth and pulling at his spiked, orange hair in lamentation. He looked sharply back at the proud ironbreaker, concern on his face.

'What happens now?' he asked, dreading the answer.

'Just as kings have sworn oaths of duty to their hold, an ironbreaker swears oaths to his clan. They cannot be lightly set aside.

'I must head back to my clan, in the Ostermark,' said Thorrik, his eyes weary. 'And once there, I must request from my clan-thane that I might be allowed to take up the slayer oath.'

DAYS PASSED WITHIN Karak Kadrin. Thorrik was gone much of that time, and Grunwald's mood was heavy. Even Annaliese was growing restless and short tempered, eager to be on her way. She snapped at Eldanair one day, frustrated with his silence and his ghostly presence. Indeed he did seem even more distant and cold since being here within the hold of the dwarfs, but then that was understandable – the looks of loathing, mistrust and often outright hatred directed at him from the dwarfs was relentless. To his credit, he never lowered his gaze from the challenging stares, though he never did anything that could have provoked a reaction, for which Grunwald was thankful. The last thing they needed was to have bloodshed within the group. When the girl snapped at him, he merely regarded her coldly, making no reaction to her at all. When she stalked away from him, he merely continued to follow her, much to her frustration.

Still, whenever Annaliese rested, Eldanair sat watching over her. Her sleep was plagued with dreams and nightmares – he heard her cry out often, and the elf would place a hand on her forehead, speaking soothingly in his singsong voice. She would invariably fall back into restful sleep.

Grunwald couldn't work out the elf, and that concerned him. He was deeply intuitive with people – he had a knack for feeling when someone was lying, or concealing something – though he was generally quite happy to let those around him see him merely as a brute. It served his purpose well, for people often lowered their guard around him. But the elf was blank to him, and he never left the girl's side. When the time came for Grunwald to ensure the girl suffered her *accident*, it would be more than likely that he would have to deal with Eldanair as well.

Finally Thorrik returned.

'There *is* a way out,' he said, and everyone's attention snapped onto him. 'But it will not be without risks.'

'Finally,' said Karl. 'Why has it taken so long for you to find this information?'

Grunwald raised a hand to forestall any argument, glaring at Karl.

'And you will not be able to take your precious horses,' said Thorrik, staring the knight squarely in the eye.

'What? Preposterous! We are knights, and we will not leave our destriers here in this dark hole.'

'Then you will stay here in this dark *hole* as well then,' said Thorrik.

'Tell us more about this way out,' said Grunwald.

'There is a final mineshaft that has yet to be sealed. It leads into the mines of Baradum, which have long been abandoned to the enemy. They crawl through the darkness like vermin, seeking an entrance into the slayer keep from below, since their armies are smashing uselessly against its walls. This way is to be sealed tomorrow at midday. At the same time King Ungrim Ironfist's son, the war-mourner Garagrim, will lead forth an army of slayers, to clear the Great Bridge and push back the enemy. It seems that orc and goblin hordes are erecting their crude war machines with which to pound the keep. Kadrin lacks the cannons to effectively pummel these emplacements, and so Garagrim has tasked himself with destroying these threats.'

Thorrik stared around at the humans, ignoring the elf.

'When the war-mourner and his slayer army sallies forth, the enemy will be drawn to them like moths to a flame. That is when we will enter the mines of Baradum. We make our way through them – one of its exits is some distance down the valley, and all being well, we will be able to make a clear run through to the Empire.'

'All being well?' snapped Karl. 'What if the armies of the greenskins are *not* all drawn away? What if they are waiting out there in the valley for us?'

Thorrik looked at the knight, his eyes heavy but his face expressionless.

'Then we die,' he said.

CHAPTER FIFTEEN

CURVING HORNS FASHIONED in the likeness of mighty serpents and wyrms boomed, their resounding blare echoing through Kadrin Keep and out into the valley beyond. Dozens of horns sounded, deep and monotonous, deafeningly loud. Each instrument was the size of a tree, and fixed to the stone walls of the massive gathering chamber with giant bands of iron. Those dwarfs who blew them stood in sunken alcoves built high into the walls, and Grunwald could feel his eardrums reverberate at the colossal din that made the rock beneath his feet shudder in response.

He stood at the side of Karl Heiden, the preceptor knight fully decked out in his ornate armour. He wore his plumed helm and his thirty knights were arrayed behind him, their armour freshly shined and glimmering brightly in the firelight of thousands of torches and lanterns. Their standard was unfurled and resplendent,

and each knight stood to attention, motionless, powerful and silent.

Grunwald wore his full uniform of office. His breastplate was freshly covered in new black lacquer, and he
had affixed several passages from the books of Sigmar
to it, thin parchment scrolls held in place with wax
seals bearing the twin-tailed comet impression of the
large bronze signet ring he wore on his left hand, on
top of his elbow-length black gloves. On his broad-
rimmed black hat he wore a large, freshly shined
wreathed-skull badge, and twin baldrics crossed his
torso upon which were strapped the tools of his trade
– silver-tipped stakes, vials of holy water, powder-horns
and a small, padlocked book of Sigmarite holy passages. His pistols were holstered on his belt, and an
array of knives and bladed 'confession tools' were
sheathed about his body – at his side, strapped to his
knee-high black boots, on his forearms. His trusty
flanged mace hung loosely at his side. Over his shoulders he had drawn his heavy black coat.

Next to him was Annaliese, who looked for all the
world like a true acolyte priest of Sigmar in her robes of
cream and deep red that were worn over her floor-
length robe of chainmail. She held her head high, an
expression of pride and strength on her face. Her holy
Sigmarite hammer hung at her side, and the symbol of
Sigmar was prominent on her breast.

Standing before them was Thorrik, the ironbreaker,
stone-still and radiating strength and resilience. His
reddish beard was freshly braided with copper wire,
and his gromril armour was shined to perfection.

It was a great honour, he had told them, to be
allowed to witness the official muster and blessing of

the Slayer King upon the army that would within hours push out to meet the enemy head on. Only Eldanair had been barred from the official ceremony.

The humans, accompanied by Thorrik Lokrison, had been escorted to a high balcony to oversee the proceedings below, and the sheer scale of the gathering had stunned Grunwald.

The cavern was immense, even greater than any he had yet seen within the dwarf hold, and behind it rose the colossal doors that formed the gateway out of the mighty hold.

Those doors were hundreds of feet high, and giant clockwork wheels and cogs were constructed into their design. Giant idle pistons, levered arms and immense anvil-like counter-weights were built into the grand pillars astride the doors, and Grunwald guessed that it was these mechanics that would open the doors when the time came for this mighty dwarf army to sally forth.

Grunwald had been surprised that he and the other humans had been allowed to bear weapons to such an august ceremony, but he saw now that they could pose no threat to the dwarf king, armed or not.

Spread out on the terraced chamber floor was the army that Garagrim was soon to lead through those great doors, and it made Grunwald's mind boggle to see such numbers arrayed below him.

Thousands of clan warriors of Karak Kadrin had been mustered, and they stood in serried ranks behind their thanes and chieftains. Banners of beaten metal and beautifully crafted icons were held aloft on steel poles, the standards bearing clan symbols and runes.

But these dwarf warriors were outnumbered easily five to one by the garishly painted slayers, who stood

with hands resting on the heads of the axes, their
silence unnerving. A sea of orange, spiked hair and
painted faces, the slayers stared solemnly towards the
arched entranceway through which their patron king
would emerge.

Grunwald studied the faces of the closest slayers –
they had been daubed with blue and black inks and
dyes, and intricate coiling patterns and runes covered
their flesh. Eye sockets had been smeared with ash,
making the slayers' menacing eyes appear to peer out
of darkness. Some held aloft the heads of mighty enemies that had been bested in battle – trolls, massive
greenskins, scaled beasts and furred creatures that
defied name. Many of the slayers towards the front of
the mass array of force were covered in scars and old,
healed wounds, and these ancient warriors bore
weapons gleaming with jewels, gold and throbbing
runes of power.

'Those unable to achieve death,' whispered Thorrik.
'For while all slayers seek to attain their honourable
end, a slayer must fight with all his strength and ability
in battle, else he will not be allowed within the drinking halls of our ancestors. So it is that the mightiest
slayer warriors find their deaths hard to achieve, and
they seek out the most powerful foes on the field of
battle, striving to one day meet the enemy that they
could not overcome. They are truly tragic figures. Giant
slayers, dragon slayers, daemon slayers – tragically, for
some the quest for death is never ending.'

Grunwald estimated that there must have been in the
region of eight thousand slayers gathered below, each
warrior utterly fearless, as hard as stone and eager for
battle. It would have been terrifying to face such a foe,

and yet it was said that the armies battering upon the fortress from the valley beyond was numberless.

The deafening horns sounded again, deep and reverberating, and the alcove doors below were thrown open. The Slayer King and his son marched forth. They were closely followed by an entourage of doughty warriors bearing huge two-handed hammers and wearing armour inlaid with gold, and by dozens of dwarfs holding tall banners and icons aloft, but it was the king who drew Grunwald's eye.

As broad as he was tall, the Slayer King was borne upon a broad round shield of gold, carried by four powerfully built warriors. His fierce head was lifted, and a deafening roar rose from the gathered dwarf warriors, accompanied by ten thousand feet stamping in unison. The booming resounded through the chamber, and the Slayer King was carried onwards through the din. A long cloak of gleaming dragon scales was fixed to his shoulders and hung down over the shield bearing him to trail onto the flagstones behind. He wore a glittering horned crown of gold studded with precious stones, and his mighty beard, dyed bright orange, was tied in intricate braids that looped back upon themselves, such was its length. Above his crown rose a tall crest of spiked orange hair, worn in the same manner as the thousands of slayers before him. Unlike them, however, he wore heavy and ornate armour – the armour of his office as king of Karak Kadrin – and it glowed dully with hundreds of runes.

Before the king walked an honoured white-bearded dwarf, his face lined with age and his beard trailing in his wake. Despite his age, this revered ancient one had arms as thick as tree-stumps, and he held above his head a large golden platter draped in rich cloth, upon which lay the kingly weapon of his lord – a giant double-bladed axe that seemed to shimmer and vibrate with barely restrained power.

Walking steadily beside the shield-bearers that bore the Slayer King was the king's heir and son, Garagrim Ironfist. *War-mourner* was his title, Thorrik had told Grunwald, though the full import of this title was lost on him. This fearsome warrior stalked forwards, arrayed for battle in the manner of the slayers, eschewing armour and treading across the stone floor barefoot. His orange beard was hung with icons of Grimnir, and his heavily muscled forearms were wrapped in chain. These chains were fixed to a pair of axes he carried, perhaps to ensure that he was never rendered weaponless in the heat of battle. His face was streaked with ash and his arms covered in coiling blue ink.

The kingly entourage drew to a halt, and the shield-bearers lowered their liege gently to the ground. He stepped forward, off the golden shield, and stood at the top of a raised stone tier looking over the steps across the host of Karak Kadrin, and silence descended.

Then the king spoke, his deep-throated voice carrying across the entire gathered force thanks to the acoustics of the architecture. None stirred, not a single warrior or slayer shuffled, and his words were met with stony silence. Though the humans could not understand Khazalid, the guttural, harsh language of the dwarfs, they picked up on the spirit of the speech, and it was filled with pride, strength, doom and anger.

It was not a long, drawn out speech as it would have been in the Empire – rather it was curt, short and to the point. Garagrim knelt before his king and the mighty Slayer King of Kadrin lifted him to his feet and placed his forehead against that of his son's, uttering an oath of clearly great importance. A pair of brimming steins of ale were brought forth, and the king and his heir drank deep before throwing the vessels to the ground and crushing them beneath their feet. Grunwald winced as the bare foot of Garagrim bent the metal stein out of shape.

With a final nod to his father, the War-mourner walked down the steps towards his army, and a great clamour of chanting, stamping of feet and the blare of horns sounded out.

'And so the throng of Karak Kadrin goes to war,' said Thorrik, turning away from the spectacle. With the grinding of gears and the venting of steam, the giant doors of the slayer keep opened, and daylight bright and sharp speared inside the hold, bringing with it ungodly screams and the smell of fire. Thousands of crude drums beat from the valley outside – the pounding of the enemy.

A flight of single-manned, steam-powered flying machines lifted from the chamber floor, their rotary blades spinning in a blur of motion, setting the hair and beards of those below flapping with the wind they generated. The gyrocopters flew out through the slowly opening portal, up into the grey skies that were almost blinding after so long without seeing sunlight.

With a roar, the army of Karak Kadrin readied itself for battle, turning towards the ever-expanding archway of light.

'Come,' said Thorrik, his voice gruff. 'It is time.'

* * *

THEY DESCENDED INTO darkness, travelling deeper and
deeper into the heart of the mountain and the mine-
workings that created a labyrinth of passageways far
beneath the surface. The sound of chains running out
was deafening, as was the heavy repetitive clunk and
pounding of the steam engine that lowered the steel
platform down into the abyssal darkness below.

Karl was clearly still angered at having to leave his
beloved warhorse back in the dwarf hold. The faces of
his knights were similarly grim. Eldanair looked
directly upwards, his long, emotionless face turned
towards the distant light at the top of the mining shaft
that was getting ever smaller with every passing minute.

The air was hot and stifling the deeper they went, and
Grunwald found himself sweating profusely beneath
his breastplate and he took his hat off to wipe his brow.
Apart from Thorrik and the miner-turned-slayer Abrek
Snorrison who was to act as their guide, the only one
that seemed to remain calm as they descended deeper
beneath the ground was Annaliese. Her fist was clasped
tightly around her symbol of Sigmar, and she spoke the
simple prayers that Grunwald had taught her like a
mantra. Her face was serene and tranquil. The shuttered lanterns seemed to create a halo-like glow around
her, her blonde hair shining in the darkness, luminous
and golden.

It seemed to Grunwald that their descent was never-
ending, and he would not have been at all surprised to
have found themselves transported to the fiery underworld at journey's end.

Finally, the platform hit solid ground, and the boom
of it striking rock echoed up the sheer shaft that led
into Karak Kadrin.

The grim slayer Abrek indicated forward with his bearded chin, and barked something in Khazalid to Thorrik. The slayer hefted a massive mining pickaxe in one hand, while in the other he held a lantern, its light blinding, focused with polished metal and shutters to project its light in a single beam.

'This is it,' said the ironbreaker, his voice muffled behind his gromril helm. 'Abrek and I take the lead. The rest of you follow, two abreast. We move now. This last mine entrance will be sealed within the hour.'

Karl organised his men, his orders crisp and brooking no argument. He took up position with one of his knights as the rear guard. They all held their swords drawn, and all but those holding dwarf-made alcohol-fuelled lanterns wore their shields strapped to their arms.

'Daughter of Verena, let your light be our guide in the darkness,' said Karl, invoking Myrmidia, the goddess of the Blazing Sun. Grunwald walked at the side of Annaliese in the middle of the party, with Eldanair ghosting their footsteps a pace behind, an arrow nocked to his bow, his face alert and tense. The witch hunter had loaded and primed his wheel-lock pistols, and he walked with one of them held in his left hand – his brutal mace in the other. Annaliese, radiating calm, walked with her hammer held in both hands.

Into the labyrinth of abandoned mining passages they went, lanterns lighting the way. Through twisting corridors hewn of solid rock they marched, the humans pointing their lanterns down dark passages criss-crossing their route, their eyes straining. Some of the corridors they passed were broad, and steel tracks like those of the steam engine were laid on the stone floor.

Within minutes, Grunwald had lost his bearings, utterly and completely. If Thorrik and Abrek fell, then they would have little chance of ever making their way out. It was a veritable maze, with passages leading everywhere. They passed shafts that rose higher into the mountain and others that sank still deeper. The concept of time had no meaning down here.

The ground began to shudder, and Thorrik halted the column of marching warriors. There came an echoing boom reverberating up the passageway, and rocks and dust fell from the ceiling onto the column. Grunwald shielded his head with his arm. A heavy rock fell onto Thorrik's helmet, but it cracked as it struck him, and the pieces fell around him. The dwarf made no reaction. Exactly which direction the sound came from was impossible to discern, as was its distance. Rumbling crashes boomed and rocked the earth beneath their feet. More rock and debris fell, cracking sharply against the knights' armour, they all looked fearfully around them, feeling the weight of the mountain pressing down upon them.

'What is it?' Grunwald hissed, voicing the thoughts of all the humans.

Thorrik's voice ghosted back to his ears, sounding distant and faint. 'Earthquake?'

'The shaft is being sealed by engineers behind us. What you hear are controlled blasting charges closing off the mines so that the enemy may not find a way into the keep.'

'No way back then,' muttered one of the knights behind Grunwald darkly.

'We shall make it through,' said Annaliese, her voice calm and strong. 'Sigmar is with us.'

The last detonations died away, rocks settled and they were surrounded once more by an oppressive silence. Dust continued to fall for several minutes, until that too ceased. Grunwald took off his broad hat, and brushed the stone dust from its rim.

They began to march once more, through twisting passageways and climbing up and down steps hewn from the rock.

'Annaliese,' said Eldanair, making Grunwald jump with shock at the voice at his ear. He had heard the elf speak only a handful of times, and he was not used to the strangely alien, singsong voice of the warrior. Annaliese turned towards the elf, who was as tense as a taut bowstring. The elf gestured sharply to his ear.

'Thorrik,' said Annaliese, understanding Eldanair instantly. 'Stop the column. Can you hear anything?'

The column drew to a halt, and Karl barked sharply at his knights to silence the sound of their clanking armour.

At first they could hear nothing. But then, very faintly they too could hear what it was that had alerted Eldanair.

Very distant, very faint, there was the sound of drumming. A dull roar echoed from afar, and the sound of metal striking metal, in time with the drumming – the sound of blades being rhythmically crashed against metal shield-rims.

Abrek snarled something in the dwarfen tongue, and seemed ready to begin running straight towards the sound. Thorrik nodded his head but said something in an authoritative tone, holding the slayer at bay.

'The greenskins are near,' said Thorrik, his voice filled with anger, but perhaps also a hint of eagerness, Grunwald thought. 'Drawn to the sound of the detonations.'

Several of the knights swore, and Karl barked once more, silencing them.

'If they come, then we fight them,' said the preceptor.

'Oh, they come,' said Thorrik, his voice menacing and full of growing enthusiasm. 'And we *will* face them.'

'Our main aim is to get out of these mines – to get to the Empire,' said Grunwald, his voice containing a warning. 'We fight if we must – but we do not seek battle here.'

Abrek began speaking, harshly and quickly, his voice rising in anger, punching the air with his pickaxe to make his point. Though Grunwald could not see Thorrik's face, hidden as it was in darkness, he could feel the tension in the dwarf, the conflicting desires. At last he said a single word in his language. When the slayer raised his voice to argue, Thorrik barked this one word again, more forcefully.

'Aye,' said the ironbreaker, turning towards Grunwald. 'It is as you say, manling.'

The column began moving once more. In the distance, the sound of the greenskins grew louder.

CHAPTER SIXTEEN

THEY TRAVELLED THROUGH the stygian darkness for what seemed like days in the claustrophobic tunnels, trusting that the dwarf slayer Abrek knew where he was leading them. It was not a clear, direct route they took, but rather it meandered left and right, up and down, and Grunwald lost count of the number of intersections and cross-passages they passed.

They halted several times to rest and eat, chewing the dried, salty meat that Thorrik had acquired from Kadrin Keep. They ate in silence and in darkness. Strange sounds seemed to come at them from all angles, the sounds of metal on stone, odd scraping sounds, dull roars and the sound of falling rocks.

The drumming had faded, and Grunwald hoped that they had managed to bypass the greenskins moving somewhere within the abandoned mines, though in truth he found that being unable to hear the passage of the hateful creatures was even more worrying. The humans jumped and started at the odd reverberations that echoed up to them from the depths of lower passages, the scuttling sounds of creatures scratching just beyond the lantern-light, and at the strange winds that seeped from cracks and fissures in the passage walls.

Hot air was exhaled from the deep, blasts of steaming, wet breath that wafted up from below. Small rocks tumbled down from the darkness above them as they passed through vast caverns carved, Thorrik said, thousands of years earlier by the writhing of monstrous beasts of the underworld that the ancient ancestor gods had wrestled. Giant stalagmite columns rose from the uneven ground, climbing high into the darkness, glistening with moisture and gleaming with a cold light of their own.

Clusters of glowing pinpricks of light speckled overhead, numbered in their tens of thousands, an imitation of the stars that pierced the heavens at night.

In some places there were oddly glowing patches of foul-smelling fungus. Swearing, Thorrik and Abrek angrily kicked and stamped the bloated, palid growths into nothingness and great clouds of spores rose from them as they deflated. The humans and the elf covered their mouths and noses so as not to breathe in any of the foetid spores.

There was much evidence of mining activity in the passages and corridors, and in many places the roof and ceiling was supported with great iron beams. The rock faces were rough and broken, and the passages twisting and convoluted as they followed seams of precious metals.

There was no warning when the first attack came. They were passing through an open area that might have once been a dwarf encampment, and there were numerous entrances and side-passages that opened into the room. An arrow streaked out of the darkness and took one of the knights, who had raised his visor against the heat, squarely in the face. An instant later there was a braying sound of a horn, seeming to come at them from all sides. Other arrows whistled in at the column, striking the shields that the knights raised defensively, and clattering off the stone floor. More distant horns and the sound of heavy feet pounding on stone began echoing all around them.

And then the enemy was upon them, bursting from side corridors, roaring and beating their weapons against their shields. Some carried crude torches of dripping, stinking pitch, and the flames lit up their brutish, savage faces starkly. There was no time for thought as frantic combat erupted on all sides. Grunwald fired his pistol into the face of a hulking orc that launched itself at him with a pair of massive cleavers and fire burst from the barrel of the gun. The orc fell to the ground, but others leapt over the corpse, their gaping maws filled with thick tusks, roaring as they set upon the column.

Karl yelled orders, and the Knights of the Blazing Sun met the charging enemies with shield and sword. They stepped forward, their broad-bladed swords cutting and stabbing frantically. Steel sang through the air as blades sliced into thick-muscled green bodies, cutting through limbs and hacking into necks as thick as a man's body. The savagery and suddenness of the attack was staggering. Blood began to flow freely, and the sound of roars and screams echoed deafeningly over the din of clashing swords and shields.

A monstrous figure stalked out of the darkness towards Grunwald, a massive orc warrior, encased head to toe in crude, heavy armour. Its helmet was all-encompassing, fashioned to house its massive, protruding jaw, and curving tusks emerged from square, steel mandibles. It bore a jagged, steel shield and swung a heavy, thick bladed cleaver at Grunwald as it stepped forwards.

The witch hunter swayed back and the lethal blow whistled past his face. Drawing his second pistol, he fired it at close range into the chest of the hulking greenskin, the sound painful to the ear. The lead shot smashed though the steel plates of the beast and deep into its body, knocking it back a pace. Stepping forward quickly, Grunwald smashed his mace into the head of the creature. With a sickening crunch of metal and bone, the beast took the blow, its heavy head knocked to the side, but it recovered quickly, slamming its shield into Grunwald's face, making him stumble backwards, his head ringing.

A knight plunged his sword deep into the beast's side and it roared, backhanding the knight to the ground before turning towards Grunwald. The witch hunter smashed his mace into the orc's cheek, crushing metal and fracturing bone.

Ignoring the injuries that would have dropped any man, the armoured orc drove its knee up into Grunwald's stomach, and he doubled over, the air forced from his lungs. The orc followed up the attack with a brutal elbow that struck him on the side of the head, and the next thing he knew he was flat out on his back, his vision hazy, and with the creature looming over him.

A white-fletched arrow thudded into its eye socket and it roared. Then a golden hammer smashed into its head, knocking the creature to its knees. A second hammer blow crushed its skull and it sank finally to the ground, dark blood welling from the mortal wound.

White dots of light shimmered before Grunwald's eyes, but he pushed himself to his feet, his head ringing.

'We have to move!' shouted Karl. There was just too many of the enemy attacking from too many sides for the knights to be able to mount an effective defence.

'Back!' roared Thorrik from the head of the column. 'Back to the tunnel!'

Step by painful step, the column retreated from where it had come, swords flashing and blood spraying. Wounded knights gritting their teeth against the pain were half-carried half-dragged back by their comrades, while other knights and the pair of dwarfs formed a protective arc around them.

Eldanair launched arrows through gaps between the tight packed warriors, each fired with deadly accuracy. Karl fought like a man possessed, his broadsword carving a bloody swathe through the orcs launching themselves at him. He turned their heavy blows with his battered shield, and sent lightning ripostes that ripped throats open and severed vital arteries. Grunwald, his head buzzing, repacked his pistols with shot and powder, and they boomed loudly in the enclosed space as the knights backed into the corridor.

With only one route of attack coming against them now, the numbers of the orcs meant nothing, and

Thorrik and Abrek stood side by side in the narrow entranceway, cutting down every enemy that surged against them.

Abrek was bleeding from dozens of cuts, and he snarled like a beast as he fought. Blood was splattered all over his face, chest and arms, giving him a daemonic appearance, and he fought with the wild frenzy of a berserker. The slayer gave no thought to defence, merely intent on attack. His pickaxe was covered in gore, and he swung it murderously, slamming its spikes through skulls and puncturing chests with brutal rage.

Thorrik was as resilient as the mountainside itself, and though dozens of blows rained down on him, few made more than a scratch on his powerful gromril armour. With every blow that struck against him he seemed to grow more powerful, his axe-blows falling with greater strength and speed. Nothing seemed able to breach his defence, and the orcs began to fall back, demoralised and frustrated.

The greenskins pulled back, and a flight of arrows whistled through the air towards the pair of dwarfs. Though they clattered off Thorrik's armour and shield, they sank deep into Abrek's muscled flesh, and he snarled against the pain, drool and blood dripping down over his beard. Two arrows protruded from his chest, one from his thigh and another from his shoulder. Another arrow sliced into the bunched muscles joining his shoulder and his neck, passing cleanly through and out the other side. Uncaring of his wounds, he seemed ready to throw himself back into the fray, but a sharp word from Thorrik held him back.

Drums and howls from the greenskins seemed to announce the arrival of some new terror, and there was a blood-curdling roar that erupted from the darkness. Abrek's gaze snapped up, his eyes mad and eager, and Thorrik spoke to him again, quickly and loudly.

The slayer seemed to ignore him, and only a heavy hand on his shoulder restrained him from hurling himself back into the abandoned arena of battle. He turned then and spoke quickly and forcefully, and Grunwald saw Thorrik's armoured head nod in response. Eldanair sent shafts streaking into the room, and there were muffled roars as they struck home. The bellow of something far larger than an orc reverberated once more, and a monstrous, hulking shape loped into the firelight.

Standing almost eleven feet in height, the creature was hunched and long limbed, its gangly, powerful arms hanging almost to the ground. Its head was large and its features exaggerated, a large bulbous nose sprouting from beneath a pair of malicious yellow eyes. Big flaps of skin hung to either side of its face, over-grown ears studded with crude bone decorations, and its mouth was a wide slash with thick, slab-like teeth.

It was naked but for a loincloth of matted fur, and its flesh was the colour of foul water. In each taloned hand it carried a long bone ending in a bulbous lump, and as it saw the dwarfs standing in the passage entrance it roared once again, thick ropes of spittle splattering from its gaping maw. It broke into a loping run, and Abrek said some final words to Thorrik, before the ironbreaker slapped the slayer on one meaty, bloody shoulder and turned away.

'Come! We must be quick!' shouted the heavily armoured dwarf as Abrek screamed incoherently and threw himself towards the troll closing towards him.

His pickaxe was raised high over his head as he ran to his death.

Quickly Thorrik led them down a series of twisting corridors and side-passages, and Grunwald pushed past the knights to his side.

'He will surely die,' said the witch hunter.

'Aye, if Grimnir favours him,' replied Thorrik curtly.

'You know the way out?' he asked.

'Aye,' replied Thorrik, though he ventured nothing more. The witch hunter dropped back to Annaliese's side. It seemed the elf had fallen back as a rear guard, for he was nowhere to be seen.

In the distance they heard the roar of the troll, though whether they were bellows of pain or victory was impossible to discern.

'May you find peace at last, Abrek,' intoned Thorrik.

FOR ANOTHER DAY and a half the column wound through the endless twisting corridors. They encountered few enemies, though the sounds of them were all around. Thorrik led them relentlessly, his stamina seeming boundless. Eight of the knights had been killed in the battle against the orcs, and another had died on the flight through the darkness, slipping and falling hundreds of feet from a sheer precipice. Karl was angry and sullen, and he travelled in silence, nursing his own brooding thoughts.

They should be nearing the exit of the accursed mines, Thorrik had said. Two hours, perhaps three, he estimated. How the dwarf navigated through the maze he didn't know, but he was thankful he was with them still.

Thorrik drew the column to halt with a raised hand, and after a few minutes of silence all could make out the dim flickering of torchlight and hear the scuffling of many feet. The light came from the passageway ahead, and Grunwald thought back, trying to picture how far back the last intersection had been – over an hour, he thought.

'We must go around,' hissed Grunwald.

'This is the only way,' replied Thorrik.

'Then we go through them,' said Karl, having made his way to the front of the column.

The ironbreaker nodded, and Karl ordered his men to be ready. Lanterns were dimmed, and Thorrik led them forward to a dogleg turn in the passageway. There they waited in darkness, hearing the stamp of feet and the brutal laughter of the enemy drawing ever nearer.

In the dim, flickering light of the nearing torches, Grunwald saw Annaliese leaning against the cold stone wall. A multi-legged insect as long as man's forearm crawled down off the wall and onto her shoulder but she managed to catch her scream before anyone heard her. Hundreds of barbed legs worked in unison, moving like a series of rolling waves, and the creature crawled down over torso, over her left leg and onto the ground. Breathing out slowly, she regained her composure.

As the scuffing of approaching feet seemed to be almost on top of them, Thorrik and Karl stepped out around the corner, sword and axe cutting down the lead greenskins whose eyes opened wide in surprise as they died.

Grunwald was a step behind them. 'Sigmar smite you!' he shouted as he gunned down a pair of the enemy with his booming pistols. They were goblins, diminutive and easily overcome, but the witch hunter could see the larger, more menacing forms of orcs behind them.

The Knights of the Blazing Sun surged forwards to support their preceptor, and they smashed into the press of greenskins like a battering ram, crushing limbs and trampling over the fallen. Thorrik and Karl led the push, hacking at the frantic goblins, severing limbs and splitting skulls.

There came a strange tingling sensation that Grunwald recognised well, accompanied by a repulsive metallic sensation on the tongue. Even as he heard the ghoulish chanting, the hairs on his arms pricked up, and he roared a warning.

'Sorcery!' he shouted, as the first incantation was completed. There was a sharp sucking sound, as all the air in the crowded corridor was suddenly removed, as if by the inhalation of some infernal beast. Then it was exhaled sharply, and a force of extreme power surged down the passageway. Goblins were crushed, their bodies hurled aside and it struck the knights. Ornate breastplates and shields were crumpled by the ghostly green energy, and Grunwald felt something like a rock-hard fist slam him into the wall.

Knights fell, their helmets bent out of shape by the nigh-on invisible, pummelling blows, and he saw Thorrik stagger back. Whooping and cackling madly, the goblins redoubled their attack, and pushed forwards against the knights, uncaring that they stamped upon their own fallen comrades.

Orcs, big brutes in thick iron armour and wielding heavy cleavers, pushed through the press to lend their weight to the attack, and even Thorrik was pushed back by this sudden surge, his feet sliding through the thick layer of rock-dust upon the floor.

The knight before the witch hunter fell as a cleaver slammed down into his head, hacking though metal and bone. Hefting his mace in both hands, Grunwald smashed the weapon onto the orc's arm, shattering it, and stepped in to deliver a return blow that crushed the orc's face.

It fell, but the greenskins pushed forward relentlessly, and another knight was cut down by a brutal hacking blow that cut his arm off at the shoulder. Malicious goblins jabbed at the fatally wounded knight with spears, and he fell amongst them. They cackled gleefully as they ripped his helmet free and clawed his eyes from his sockets. The cries of the knight were sickening, and still the greenskins pushed them back.

'There must be another way!' the witch hunter shouted.

'There is none!' came Thorrik's bellowed reply, as he smashed his axe into the back of a fallen orc, severing its spine. 'This is the only way!'

Bodies were piling up on the floor, and more friends and foes alike were falling with every passing second. Karl drove the point of his sword through the face of a leering orc, though the blade got stuck and he could not immediately dislodge it. A cleaver slammed into the pauldron protecting his shoulder and he staggered, losing his grip on his weapon. An armoured fist cannoned into the face of Thorrik's helm, and the dwarf staggered back a step, losing his footing on the corpses underfoot. With a curse, the dwarf toppled backwards, and the greenskins surged forwards.

He heard the chanting of the greenskin shaman, and he tensed himself for whatever horror would be unleashed. They needed a miracle to win through these foes, or even to survive, Grunwald saw.

'Sigmar, lend me strength!' came the cry and Annaliese stepped over the prone figure of Thorrik, her hammer held high in her hands. The voice of the shaman stumbled, and petered out into a garbled curse. Annaliese smashed her weapon into the first orc before her, driving it back with a strangled cry. Bones were shattered and a smell like burning flesh rose from the mortal wound. Grunwald thought he saw a glowing halo of light surrounding the warrior-woman for a moment, but he blinked and it was gone.

The orcs backed away in a semi circle from this fury of battle, and with a cry she was amongst them, wielding the hammer two-handed. It hissed through the air, and smashed aside a crude wooden shield, breaking the arm holding it.

The Knights of the Blazing Sun pushed to her side, their blades slashing out, clearly inspired and awed by her fearless attack. Karl was at their fore, having picked up a fallen weapon, and he skilfully deflected blows aimed at the girl, protecting her from harm. Eldanair stood at her other side, a long, thin blade of elven design in his hand, the point darting back and forth in a blur.

With skilful swordsmen protecting her from both sides, Annaliese pushed on, her hammer rising and falling, crushing bones and shattering swords.

'For Sigmar!' she roared as she shattered the skull of a goblin that turned to flee, its head crushed like a ripe fruit, splattering blood and brain-matter. Gore dripped from the head of her weapon, and speckled her cheeks and brow. Where before the expression upon her face had been serene, now she was vision of righteous anger.

The fury and aggression soon drained out of Annaliese and she slumped, exhausted and weary, but the damage had been done. The greenskins were falling away from the vengeful knights, and Karl and Eldanair stood protectively over the girl as she knelt on the ground, her eyes closed and her cheeks wan.

The orcs and goblins were cut down mercilessly, and it was Grunwald who clubbed the life out of the small, hunchbacked goblin sorcerer, breaking first its limbs and then its neck with a last, savage blow. He cut the pallid, purplish tongue from the creature's rancid mouth so that even in death it could not utter any of its vile magic, and set its corpse ablaze so that nothing but ashes would remain of its passing.

THREE HOURS LATER the battle-weary warriors stumbled from the mine, out into the cold, clear night. The gibbous silver moon of Mannslieb shone brightly in the heavens above, overlapped by the smaller, green-hued moon of ill omen, Morrslieb. That glowing green orb seemed surrounded by distant flames of viridian, and Grunwald made the sign of Sigmar as protection against its malevolent effects.

There were only a score of Karl's knights remaining, the others having been lost in the nightmare darkness of the abandoned dwarf mine. Of those, all sported injuries and wounds of varying seriousness. Indeed, none had escaped unharmed. Annaliese was bleeding from several cuts, including one deep wound upon her

left cheek. Eldanair's left arm was strapped where a
crooked blade had pierced his bicep, and Karl's shoulder was bleeding profusely beneath the twisted gash in
his pauldron. Even Thorrik had suffered wounds where
the enemy had found gaps in the nigh on impenetrable
suit of armour he wore. Grunwald's head was still ringing, and his legs were shaky beneath him as he walked
out into the night.

They walked over the snow-covered ground, an icy
wind whipping at them as it roared across the immense
Kadrin valley spreading out before them.

Tens of thousands of fires blazed in the night – an
army of greenskins that was beyond comprehension.
And yet, if the dwarfs' information was correct, and
Grunwald had no reason to doubt them, this was but a
fraction of the immense army of destruction that was
pushing ever nearer to the Empire.

In the distance, battle raged, even though it was long
past the witching hour of midnight, and the moons
were sinking towards the horizon. The immense bridge
leading to the mighty gates of Kadrin Keep that
spanned a vast chasm was heaving with bodies, tiny figures moving in the distance. Fire burst from cannons
high in the cliff face, and giant winged beasts armoured
in green scales turned in the skies. As they watched in
silence, a giant wooden siege engine, the crude carved
representation of a greenskin deity's head at its top,
toppled from the bridge to fall into the darkness of the
chasm beneath, flames blazing up its side. Hundreds of
dark figures fell with it into the gloom, and a distant
cheer went up from the dwarfen defenders.

Thousands of warriors fought against each other, the
lines surging, and hundreds would be dying with every

passing minute. Had they been fighting without rest since they had descended into the mines? Grunwald presumed that this was so.

The arms of trebuchets of immense scale flicked forward, driven by giant counter weights of carved stone, hurling rocks lit with sorcerous green fire towards the dwarf keep. They shattered against the mountainside, showering those below with burning shards.

A pocket of perhaps a thousand dwarfs could be seen fighting in a large square formation on the far side of the bridge. As they watched they saw the formation inching towards the enemy war machines.

But the foe arranged against them seemed utterly limitless in number. As the knights turned away from the epic battle zone, Grunwald could not fathom how the dwarfs could hold such an enemy at bay. Karak Kadrin would fall, and the Peak Pass would be held by the greenskin hordes. And without the dwarfs blocking their progress, the savage tribes would descend on the Empire, slaughtering and butchering everything in their path. They did not come for land, or for food, nor even for the spoils of war. They came to destroy, driven by the urge to kill and to maim, to rip down the cities and towns of the civilised and to wipe mankind from the face of the world.

The witch hunter could sense the tension and anger in Thorrik, and he placed a hand upon the ironbreaker's heavily armoured shoulder.

'Come,' he said at last. 'We must move with swiftness into the Empire.'

'Kadrin will not fall, manling,' said Thorrik, as if he had been reading the witch hunter's mind. Still, his voice did not sound convinced, and Grunwald was shocked to hear the doubt in the resolute dwarf's voice.

'I pray that it will not, for all our sakes,' said Grunwald.

'If Kadrin falls, it heralds the end of the dwarfs,' continued Thorrik.

'The end of us all,' added Grunwald.

The pair turned their backs on the war being waged within Kadrin valley. To the east they marched, towards the rising dawn and the lands of the Empire.

CHAPTER SEVENTEEN

THREE HOURS INTO the march away from Kadrin Keep, Eldanair sighted the first of their pursuers. The elf stood tall on a rocky bluff, a silent and brooding sentinel staring to the west. Dawn had risen, bathing the land in cold light, and a freezing wind howled up the mountainous slopes, blowing his long ebony hair around him like a dark halo.

Little grew on the sharp crags of the valley save for low, hardy grasses and thorny bushes – there were few places to hide. With narrowed eyes Eldanair watched as the greenskins picked their way down a slippery slope of shale, a path treacherously close to a sheer drop that they themselves had descended but an hour earlier.

The elf cursed as he saw the greenskins were gaining on them, and that there were too many to be able to face in battle. There was a spindly goblin leading the group as a scout, a pair of bulbous beasts straining at chains wrapped around its hand. They were similar to the massive-jawed creatures that had been unleashed against the dwarf steam engine far beneath the ground, being little more than balls of muscle dominated by massive slavering jaws, with a pair of powerful, short legs that carried them forward. These appeared to have large, overdeveloped slits for nostrils, and they snuffled on the ground, no doubt following the scent of those they pursued.

Behind this goblin and its pets came other greenskins, a motley array of goblins and orcs – Eldanair could see over fifty figures picking their way down the treacherous slope. Even as he watched, one of them, a bare-armed, hulking giant of an orc wearing a furred hat, lost its footing on the loose shale and slid over the precipice. It caught itself before it fell, gripping a sharp outcrop of rock while its legs swung over the thousand foot drop below.

None of the other creatures went to its aid, but it seemed as though they found the incident highly amusing, slapping their legs and their bodies shaking with crude laughter. The orc managed to pull itself over the edge back to safety, and it clobbered a smaller orc over the head with one meaty fist before launching one still giggling goblin off the edge of the precipice. The flailing figure disappeared into the fog hugging the mountainside.

Black carrion birds circled and weaved lazily in the air above the greenskins, riding the winds pushed up by the sheer cliffs. Clearly they followed the orcs, knowing that they would supply them with a feast of death. Eldanair regarded these birds with cold eyes, and for a moment he could hear their raucous cries carried to his sensitive ears on the winds.

He leapt easily down from the rocky escarpment, stepping lightly on the snow, his bow held in his hands.

With hand movements and silent actions the elf conveyed the number of the foe pursuing them to Annaliese, and managed with some difficulty and increasing frustration to communicate the idea that they were an hour behind. The girl nodded and passed on the information to the others.

'I say we stand and fight,' growled Thorrik, and though Eldanair could not understand his crude words, he understood their meaning. 'I will not run like an elf away from battle.'

An argument developed, and strong words were spoken amongst the humans, the dwarf speaking sullenly in short, curt sentences. At last the group began moving once more, the dwarf looking angry and unhappy about the situation. Eldanair glared at the short warrior, the disdain clear upon his face.

The dwarf said something sharp and crude as he stomped past the elf, his eyes glittering from beneath his full-faced helmet. Eldanair snapped back a retort in his own language, the words scathing and arrogant, making the dwarf round on him, hefting his axe. Eldanair stared down at the glowering warrior, an arrow nocked to his bowstring. The dwarf took a step towards him and the bow came up, the bowstring taut.

There may well have been blood spilt then, but Annaliese stepped in between the pair, speaking swiftly, her words laced with anger. The dwarf turned away with a snarl, and stomped away from the elf. Annaliese gave Eldanair a reproachful look, and she too turned away and continued along the path.

The elf's eyes narrowed as he watched the departing figure of Thorrik marching heavily through the snow. He lifted his head high, and began walking back in the direction of the orcs and goblins that were nearing the base of the shale trail behind.

'Where is he going now?' voiced Karl as he watched the tall figure of the elf moving away, and Grunwald shrugged his shoulders.

'Probably covering our tracks, or some such thing,' he replied.

'Makes my blood run cold, that one,' said the preceptor. 'The way he haunts the girl's steps. It's not natural.'

Again Grunwald shrugged. The knight was watching the figure of Annaliese as she picked her way across the rough ground up ahead. Her hair shone brightly in the rising sun.

'She is a beauty though, isn't she?' said Karl, his eyes locked on the figure of the girl.

Grunwald merely grunted in response.

The knight smiled broadly, his features handsome and unmarked. How unlike his own, Grunwald thought, scratching idly at his heavy, stubbled and scarred jaw.

'The mountain air, a beautiful woman at my side… Under different circumstances this might have been a pleasant journey,' said the knight.

'She's not your woman, Karl,' Grunwald pointed out.

'Not yet,' said the knight with a lascivious wink that made the witch hunter snort.

'Good luck with that,' said Grunwald. 'It will come to nothing.'

'You underestimate me, my friend. Women the length and breadth of the Empire rejoice when I come to their towns and cities and cry rivers of tears when I leave. My skills in the bedchamber are legendary.'

'Spread by you, no doubt,' said Grunwald, laughing as he shook his head. The knight gave him a look of feigned hurt.

'We shall see,' he said, his eyes bright with passion.

For the better part of the day the group marched, winding their way down lower as the valley began to spread out before them. Eldanair returned some hours later, silent and ghostlike, and Annaliese told them that he had been laying some sort of traps for their pursuers. They heard witness of one of these traps as the sun began to dip low towards the mountains behind them, a clatter of stones and a strangled cry, though what manner of trap the elf had constructed was unknown.

Through the night they continued their trek, and sign of their pursuers could be seen by all – torches bright and flaming in the darkness followed their path unerringly, despite all the efforts of Eldanair to throw them off the scent.

They ate in silence as they walked, chewing the hard, salted meat. It was strangely filling sustenance, but none of the group was at ease as the hour grew late. The air was freezing, and they struggled through a snowstorm, each step agonising and laboured. At last the storm passed by them, and then they could see the stars once more, millions of tiny lights that pierced the heavens.

Still the enemy came after them – if anything, they seemed to be getting closer.

'Don't they need rest too?' grumbled one of Karl's warriors. The group was slowed by the knights, whose heavy armour was more of a hindrance than a help on the long march. Still, not one of the knights would have considered stripping off and abandoning their armour, and no one mentioned the idea.

They were weary and aching as the first light of dawn began to seep across the skies. They stopped for a short break, sitting down on the rocks gratefully, passing the water-skins around between them.

'Where is the elf?' said Karl, and the others glanced around, realising that he was nowhere to be seen. Annaliese frowned and stood up, turning fully around, concern clear on her face.

'Never know with one of them,' said Thorrik. 'Probably left us to fend for ourselves while he is making a run for it.'

'He would *not* abandon us,' said Annaliese fiercely.

'I wouldn't put it past him,' said the dwarf matter-of-factly. 'It's in their nature to be deceitful. No understanding of honour, elves.'

'Thorrik, hold your tongue,' said the witch hunter, while Annaliese glared at the dwarf hotly. The iron-breaker merely shrugged his shoulders.

'I'm sure he is fine,' said Grunwald to the girl. 'And it does us no good to wait here for his return. We must push on.'

Grunwald marched at Karl's side as the group resumed its march.

'You really think the elf will come back?' said Karl. 'I think there is something in what the dwarf said, you know.'

Grunwald looked over at the knight. 'He'll be back.'

'So certain?'

Grunwald sighed. 'If it were just you, me, your knights and the dwarf, then no, I don't think he would be back. But he will not abandon Annaliese.'

They walked for some minutes in silence. Glancing over at the knight, Grunwald saw the warrior's face was dark.

Where was the elf?

ELDANAIR CROUCHED LOW behind the rocks, all but invisible in the darkness. His face was hard as he listened to the sounds of the pursuit drawing closer. At last he rose from his position, aiming swiftly.

The first arrow slammed through the left eye socket of one of the foul beasts led by the goblin, and it fell to the ground heavily, stubby legs twitching.

The creatures seemed able to follow a scent in the manner of hunting hounds their nostrils wide and flaring as they snuffled along the ground. No matter what efforts the elf took to conceal the trail, these creatures led the greenskins unerringly, and so they had to die.

The goblin screeched loudly and released the chain of the other creature, and it began to bound up the rocks towards Eldanair, its jaw hanging open widely and a feral roar emitting from its throat.

The goblin screeched again, no doubt calling for aid, and launched an arrow from its short bow towards the elf. Eldanair didn't flinch as the arrow shattered against rocks at his feet. Aiming carefully, he loosed his own arrow. It thudded into the cheek of the ravening beast leaping up the rocks, though it did not slow its frantic approach.

He sent another arrow, this one passing between its gaping jaws and cutting through the back of its cavernous mouth. Still it came on, and another arrow whistled through the air towards Eldanair. He swayed to the side and it hissed past his ear. A pair or heavy-set orcs appeared, stamping down the trail behind the goblin, roaring and bellowing as they sighted the elf.

A final arrow sank into the bulbous head of the creature as it leapt from rock to rock towards Eldanair, though again it did not slow the blood-frenzied creature. Eldanair drew his long-bladed sword and waited for the monster to leap. Spittle flying from its expansive maw, the creature bunched its legs and propelled itself at him, thousands of curving teeth exposed within its widespread mouth. The stink of rancid meat and what smelled like rotting fungus reached his nose, and he almost gagged. As the creature snapped at him, he slashed a long cut down its thick-hide.

Bunching its legs again, it leapt at his throat. Eldanair stepped neatly to the side and scored a deep wound up its side as it hurtled past him. Growling and barking madly like a hound, its jaws snapped shut at his trailing black hair as it soared out into empty air. For a moment it seemed to hang in the open expanse, legs kicking madly, before it plummeted two hundred feet down into the darkness, still growling and yelping.

There was an anguished scream of hatred, and Eldanair felt a sharp pain at his neck as the arrow sliced past him, scoring a stinging wound. He grimaced as he felt hot blood on his neck, and he leapt away from the orcs closing on him, jumping lightly from rock to rock.

He rounded a massive boulder and jumped, clearing an area of untouched snow some six feet across. Landing in a roll, he spun as he came up to one knee, an arrow nocked to his bowstring. As the orcs rounded the bend he loosed, the arrow thudding into the first orc's chest. Without thought it tore the arrow from its flesh, hurling it to the side, and with a roar threw itself towards the elf, its cleaver high.

The two orcs surged forwards, but the ground suddenly gave way beneath them. With great care, Eldanair had constructed the light platform of gorse and sticks, before covering it with grass and snow. The orcs bellowed as their weight collapsed the flimsy structure, and they slipped down, disappearing into the gloom. Four seconds later there was a distant clatter of metal as the bodies struck the sharp rocks far below.

Eldanair was off again, racing through the snow, a ghostly apparition that plagued the greenskins for the rest of the night. Several more died from his cunningly laid traps and snares. Tripping a concealed line of twine, sharpened stakes of wood swung around on a taut green branch to slam into the chest of one orc. Two hours later several more died as Eldanair caused an avalanche of rock to fall upon them, forcing the survivors to find a different route.

An hour before dawn, Eldanair killed another two, rising from beneath the snow to launch a volley of arrows into them, fleeing again as the survivors charged at him. They were more wary of him now, though, and checked their pursuit quickly.

These attacks were not without risk though, and as dawn rose he limped back to his companions, a black-feathered arrow embedded deep in his side.

'Eldanair!' called Annaliese as she sighted the elf, and the girl ran to him, catching the exhausted elf in her arms. She forced him to sit, and stripped off his clothes around the wound. He saw the young human knight scowling. The wound was ugly and red, and Annaliese bathed it with water, clearing away the excess blood from his skin.

He would have pulled the arrow loose himself, but the goblins used wickedly barbed arrow tips that would rip at his skin as he tried to pull it loose. This was no doubt what the humans were discussing as they looked upon his wound. One of them, the ugly, brutish, black-clad one called Grunwald made a pushing motion.

'Yes,' said Eldanair in the language of the elves, nodding at the man. He nodded back, understanding, and offered Eldanair a piece of leather to bite upon. The elf looked at the leather strip in scorn, and shook his head. Shrugging, Grunwald took of his hat, and wiped the back of his hand across his brow.

Placing one hand on the elf's shoulder, the witch hunter got a good grip with his other hand on the feathered shaft of the arrow. Without ceremony, he pushed hard upon the arrow, pushing its head deeper into his flesh. Blood welled from the wound, and Annaliese's face was pale. Eldanair winced against the pain but did not cry out. Grunwald pushed harder, and at last the cruelly barbed arrowhead burst from his back. Swiftly the witch hunter pushed the arrow through the elf's flesh, wrapping his hand around the arrowhead and pulling the length of the shaft through the wound.

Eldanair passed out briefly, and in that time the wound was cleaned as best it could be, and bound with cloth. When he awoke, he hissed in pain, probing at the dressing with his long, pale finger. Nodding his thanks, he pushed himself to his feet, and indicated that he was ready to continue.

* * *

HE WAS TOUGHER than he looked, thought Grunwald.

For a time, it seemed as though they had left their pursuers behind, and the group began to think they had finally outrun them. They were nearing the lands of the Empire, the ground levelling out beneath them, leaving the high mountains behind. They were still high, and the wind was icy cold, but they could see the landscape beginning to change. Trees, albeit small and tough, were more frequent here, and the group felt almost deliriously buoyant. Still, they had not slept for days, and the exhausting race through the mountains was taking its toll. One knight almost stepped off a rocky precipice, his face ashen, and he had to be pulled back from the brink. He had not even registered the danger.

'We need to find a place to rest,' said Karl, voicing the exhaustion of the group.

'Up on the rock face,' said Thorrik, pointing. There was a series of heavy overhangs a few hundred feet up a scree-covered ridge. 'There might be caves there,' he said. 'Or at least protection from the wind.'

'There is no escape route up there,' said Karl. 'We will have our backs against the wall when the enemy comes at us.'

Thorrik waved a hand dismissively. 'I've had enough of running,' he said. 'Better to be warm and rested and face the enemy than to continue on and be too weak to lift a blade when they come.'

'I thought the dwarfs were hardy folk,' said Karl, making Thorrik scowl deeply.

'I could march for another week if need be,' said the dwarf, 'but I don't think any of you beardlings will last another hour.'

There was truth in what the dwarf said, and Grunwald knew it.

'I think the dwarf speaks true,' he said. Annaliese nodded her head, too tired to speak. Finally, Karl nodded his assent, and the dwarf led the way up the slope, carefully studying the rock face.

'I would expect there to be caves there,' he said, indicating a little further around the ridge. Grunwald trusted him – the dwarfs certainly seemed to have a deep understanding of the mountains and the rocks.

He was exhausted almost beyond words, and at that moment he almost didn't care if the greenskins pursued them still – all he could think about was rest.

Wincing as he held the wound at his side, Eldanair placed a hand on Grunwald's shoulder. The witch hunter saw a dark patch upon the elf's tunic where the blood from the wound had soaked through the bandages, but it was not this that the elf drew his attention to. He raised his hand, pointing into the distance behind them.

There they could clearly see their pursuers, still doggedly following their trail. Grunwald swore.

They continued to climb the slope, until they reached the overhanging rock face that leant out above them, giving them a modicum of protection. Thorrik was still convinced that there would be caves further around, and so they made their way around the cliff face, keeping a wary watch on the approaching greenskins.

'Do you think they have seen us?' said Annaliese, her face drawn.

'Most certainly,' said Grunwald. The reflections of the setting sun off the knights' armour would be seen for miles, as red as fresh blood.

'Ah!' came Thorrik's voice, filled with satisfaction. He stood before a yawning cave-mouth, the interior dark and expansive. A flight of small bats burst out. The days had blurred together into one nightmarish march, and he flopped to the ground, as tired as he had ever been.

Eldanair said something curt, eyeing the cave with distrust, sniffing at the air. There was a faint odour emanating from within, something almost imperceptible. Perhaps it was rotting meat, Grunwald thought. Yes, that was it – the cave had probably been the refuge for some wild animal; wolves or a bear.

'How long?' he asked Karl.

'Two hours before they reach us, I'd say,' replied the preceptor.

'Wake me when they come,' said Grunwald, and promptly fell asleep on the rock.

IT WAS DARK when he was shaken awake. He saw Annaliese's face hovering above him.

'They come?' he said, and the girl nodded her head. She looked determined and ready for battle, for all that she was exhausted.

He stretched sore and tired muscles as he rose to his feet. He saw Karl staring down into the valley and joined the knight.

'Have you had any rest?' he asked.

'A little,' said the preceptor. His skin was drawn and pale – indeed it must have been agony to have trekked so far in his full suit of armour, wounded as he was.

'So, what's the plan?' Grunwald said.

'The plan? We hold them here, or we die,' replied the preceptor, his voice emotionless with exhaustion.

'Good plan,' replied Grunwald, which got a weary smile. They waited half an hour as the enemy gathered below. There were almost sixty of them – a force that they had little hope of besting, and the mood was grim.

Annaliese came to join them as they sat watching the orcs' preparations.

'My stomach is churning,' admitted the girl.

'The hours before battle are always the worst,' agreed Karl, smiling at the girl. 'It gets to the point when you just wish they would come at us and get it over with. It never goes, no matter how many battles you fight in. Stick with me and you'll be alright.'

'I know I will be alright,' said Annaliese with conviction. 'I have faith. Sigmar would not lead me to the north only to have me die on some snow-swept mountainside.'

'The gods work in mysterious ways,' said Grunwald.

'Maybe *I* should stick near *you*,' said Karl, winking at the girl. 'Maybe your god will protect me too.'

'Do that,' said the girl as she rose to her feet. 'I'll protect you.'

Karl laughed and winked at Grunwald behind Annaliese's back, and whistled through his teeth as she walked away.

'Gods above, she is some woman,' he said.

It took the best part of an hour for the orcs and goblins to ready themselves for battle, as the last of their number arrived. There were almost a hundred of them gathered on the rocky plateau below them now. The largest of the orcs was clearly displeased with the delay, and his bellows and roars echoed up the slope, along with the clashing of weapons, and groans of pain as the target of his wrath was cut down and thrown over the huge bonfire the orcs had set blazing.

'Maybe they will kill each other and forget about us,' ventured Karl.

When they came, there was little warning. Drums began booming through the mountains, and the entire host of greenskins let out a war cry before racing straight up the rock-strewn slope. There was no strategy to their advance, they merely attacked in one surging wave. There was little need for strategy – they would charge up the hill, some would die, and then they would slaughter us all, thought Grunwald.

But he would be damned if he didn't exact a high toll on the green-skinned bastards.

'Sigmar, give me the strength to kill in your name,' he whispered to himself, wishing that his faith was as strong as Annaliese's seemed to be.

He listened for a response from the god, some sign that his words were heard – a flash of light, a warmth in his heart, a shooting star, anything. But there was nothing, just the savage roars of the enemy as they surged up through the night, intent on slaughter.

The long night of bloodshed had begun.

CHAPTER EIGHTEEN

UNDER KARL'S INSTRUCTION, dozens of flaming brands had been scattered around the perimeter of the cave mouth, held upright by piles of rocks. Larger stones and boulders had been rolled to form a crude, arcing wall, and it was here that the knights made their stand.

Annaliese was at the apex of the defensive position, standing tall, her hammer ready in her hands, the elf at her side. As the greenskins began to race up the steep slope he pulled himself onto the rocks and began to fire, his white fletched arrows slicing through the darkness.

Thorrik stood on the rock wall, hurling abuse at the approaching enemy in the dwarf tongue, his words scathing and hate-filled. He seemed unfazed about the sheer number of the foe, and Grunwald wondered if he welcomed a noble death in battle. He himself didn't think there was anything noble about death, however it was achieved. Death was cold and dirty, full of pain and regret.

A heroic death in battle? He almost laughed at the notion. It sounded fine in grand speeches by commanders and leaders of men, and when surrounded by friends and family, an ale in hand, far from the true ravages of war. Death wasn't noble. No one who had smelt the aftermath of a battle, the stink of blood and faeces, of flesh and spilt brains, could say there was anything noble about it. No one who had heard the screams of a man as he took three days to die from a gut wound, or the terrified pleas of a soldier begging the chirurgeons not to amputate his legs could think there was anything glorious about battle.

And yet here he stood, his crossbow bolts stuck into the ground beside him for ease of loading, awaiting his own 'glorious' death against innumerable foes. He stood behind the low boulders, and fired into the mass of greenskins, his first shot taking one in the shoulder. Swiftly he reached for another bolt. Without a miracle, they *would* all die here, but there would be no one to record their deaths. It was not that Grunwald feared death – far from it – but he did not welcome it like some last great achievement. No, he would die kicking and spitting, refusing Morr's grasp as long as he was able.

Karl walked within the perimeter of the crude defensive wall, shouting orders and encouraging his men with the virtues and strength of the goddess Myrmidia. The knights stood grim and weary, waiting for the enemy to reach their lines.

They didn't have long to wait.

The first orcs were cut down mercilessly as they scrambled over the boulders, their necks slashed open and their limbs hacked from their bodies. Thorrik stood resolute and fearless on the wall, his axe carving a bloody swathe around him as he hacked the blade down onto the greenskins' heads, splitting through helmets and skulls alike.

Annaliese called on Sigmar as a greenskin vaulted the boulders, landing before her with a massive blade in each hand. She almost smashed its head from its shoulders with her attack, the orc's skull pulverised to mush.

Grunwald fired another crossbow bolt into the enemy at close range, punching a burly greenskin off the rock wall, falling amongst his comrades pushing forward from behind. Dropping the black-framed heavy crossbow to the ground, he drew his pistols, and another orc died as its head was shattered by lead shot. Another orc lurched towards him from the left, and his other pistol swung around and boomed, and the creature fell back, blood spraying out behind it.

Holstering the pistols, the witch hunter drew his mace in his right hand and a hunting knife in his left. The face of an orc was crushed with a heavy blow of his flanged mace, the sound of metal shattering bone sickening to his ears. Eldanair continued firing his arrows at close range, the shafts sinking deep into thickly muscled green flesh – indeed he fought with such grace and fluidity that you would not have known he carried an injury except for the growing patch of blood on his tunic where the arrow had struck him the previous night.

A massive greenskin, its flesh almost black, roared and jumped heavily down off the rock wall, the ground thumping beneath it. Apart from its brutal face, it was completely ensconced in thick metal armour plates, and it carried a giant barbed blade in its hands, a weapon nearly as tall as the creature's seven feet of height.

Grunwald yelled a warning as the monstrous creature stalked towards Annaliese, the witch hunter struggling to defend himself against a pair of snickering, spear-wielding goblins.

Eldanair, hearing his shout, swung neatly around and fired – the arrow punched through the metal plating of the creature's chest, sinking deep, and it turned its attention to the elf. Standing his ground, the elf fired again, his shot punching through the metal at the orc's throat, but then it was on him, swinging its weapon in a lethal arc.

Eldanair ducked beneath the blow, stepping neatly to the side, but the massive orc anticipated the move and its iron-encased fist swung out in a wild roundhouse punch that almost decapitated the elf. He was thrown through the air to smash against the inside of the rock wall, where he slumped to the ground lifelessly.

'Eldanair!' shouted Annaliese desperately. She smashed her hammer into the side of the orc's brutish helmet, shattering one of the horns protruding from it, and sending the beast reeling. It regained its balance and swung towards her, snarling as it cracked its neck from side to side.

It towered over the girl, each of its arms the same diameter as her entire body, but she stood defiant and unafraid. With a roar, it hurled itself at her.

Three armoured shapes intercepted the massive orc, as Karl and a pair of his knights raced in to cover the breach in the defence. One of them died instantly as the massive cleaver of the orc carved down through his shoulder with a squeal of metal, the blade cutting all the way through to the hip. The two parts of the knight fell to the ground amid a torrent of blood, even as Karl drove his blade into the orc's chest, and his comrade smashed his own blade down onto the beast's arms.

Covered in blood, Karl turned from the dead monster to see if Annaliese was hurt, but the girl was looking towards the fallen figure of Eldanair. Her hammer sang through the air as she hurled herself through the melee towards the elf. Swearing, Karl was a step behind her, desperately fending off attacks thrown towards the girl. He slammed his shield into the face of an orc as it slipped to one knee in a pool of blood, and lunged to intercept a blow from a cleaver that would have killed Annaliese from behind.

The girl threw herself to the ground at the elf's side, checking for a pulse, as Karl stood defensively over her, his sword flashing out at any greenskin that drew near.

Grunwald rammed his knife up into the throat of another foe, and heaved with all his strength to knock the dying creature to the side, where it flopped onto the ground. A fist cracked against his chest, and he saw a blade flashing towards his throat, but it was intercepted at the last moment by an axe.

Nodding his thanks to Thorrik, he swung back into the attack, which was now devolving into little more than a deadly brawl, as more greenskins vaulted the boulders. They would be surrounded within minutes, and then they would be massacred.

'Pull back to the cave!' came Karl's shout, and Grunwald realised that the knight too had seen the danger.

'Come, Annaliese,' shouted the preceptor.

'He lives! We must take him with us!' shot back the girl, and she began trying to drag the elf back from the battle. Grunwald ducked through the fray to aid her. A blade hacked into his shoulder and he winced, stumbling. The killing strike did not come, however, and he saw a knight surge past him, ramming his sword through the orc's throat, the blade sliding in deep. Before he could offer his thanks, the knight was impaled upon a barbed spear from behind, lifted up into the air by the strength of his killer.

Grunwald half ran, half stumbled through the battle to Annaliese's side. He gripped one of the elf's legs and began to drag him back, Karl walking backwards before them, protecting them as best he could.

'Thorrik!' shouted Grunwald as he saw the dwarf still battling furiously on the stone wall. 'We need you!'

Karl was deflecting blows aimed at him with his now battered shield, but it was clear the knight was tiring.

'Knights of the Blazing Sun!' he roared. 'Back to the cave!'

A blow smashed into his shield, knocking the preceptor back a step, though his return blow ripped the throat from the savage greenskin, who died with dark blood bubbling from its throat.

Then Thorrik was at his side, lending the strength of his arm, and they fought a retreat inside the dark cave mouth. The entrance was wide, but it narrowed sharply. They would make their stand here, and fight to the last.

The echoing of the feral roars of the greenskins reverberated around the cave, bouncing off the sloping, natural walls.

Dropping Eldanair's leg to the ground, Grunwald leapt back into the fight. But just as any forlorn hope of victory seemed to fade, the orcs began to pull back. Their faces were fearful, and they seemed indecisive and unsure of themselves.

A massive greenskin roared its fury, and violently shoved the orcs forward, but they resisted. Alone the orc chieftain stomped forwards, and its warriors edged forwards at his back.

Karl and Thorrik stepped out to meet the orc head on. The monster swung a pair of huge cleavers, and Karl was knocked to his knees from the power behind the blows. Thorrik lashed out at the orc's legs, but his blow was deflected and the orc kicked out, knocking the dwarf back.

A shot rang out and smoke spewed from the barrel of Grunwald's pistol. The orc staggered back, blood pumping from its neck, and Karl and Thorrik surged forward. A blow from the chieftain sent the preceptor reeling, but Thorrik's blade found its mark, sinking deep into the greenskin's groin. It roared in fury and slammed a cleaver down onto the dwarf's shoulder, bashing the super-hard gromril metal out of shape, driving the dwarf to one knee. Surging upright, Thorrik's axe hammered up into the orc's chin. The giant orc staggered, and his warriors faltered.

Karl's blade buried itself in the chieftain's chest, and the massive orc fell. With one downward sweep of his axe, Thorrik decapitated the beast and raised the severed head above his own, roaring his defiance to the horde of greenskins. Their will to fight was broken, and they turned as one and fled from the cave.

It was then that Grunwald once again noticed the stench on the air. He had thought it was rotting carrion at first, and there certainly was something akin to that deeper within the darkness, but there was something else, something that niggled at the edge of his mind.

The power of Chaos.

'There is something here,' he said, his voice deep and sepulchral in the sudden silence.

As ANCIENT AS the mountains themselves it awoke in the depths of cave, roused from slumber by the sound of steel on steel, the screams of the dying, and the delicious taste of blood on the air. It had once been a normal creature, but it had long ago been twisted and corrupted by one of the great gods of Chaos, and its nature altered. For millennia it had slumbered, waking occasionally to kill and feed. It had grown powerful and strong over the years, and its furred hide was stronger than steel.

It felt the presence of the great god, the feathered lord that had given it strength, and it could feel that the power of Chaos was strong – far stronger than it had ever experienced before. The creature could taste the coiling winds of magic on its long tongue, and it breathed in deeply, inhaling the luxurious scent deep into its lungs.

It was called many things – among the dwarfs it was known as the *Dum Thaggor*, though the mountain kin had no records of it having awoken for countless centuries, and its existence was all but forgotten. Before the coming of Sigmar, in the times before the Empire, the local tribesman had dubbed it *Tefalbar*, while to the orcs and goblins it had no name, but they believed it was some primal aspect of one of their deities, and left it offerings of corpses and gold.

The sounds of battle came again, echoing down through the darkness, and the mighty creature lifted

itself up on massive clawed feet. Lips drew back from
its huge jaws, exposing a fearsome array of teeth, and
eyes and smaller mouths pushed through the flesh of
its muzzle, rippling the skin, blinking soundlessly
open before merging back into the living flesh once
more. Its own eyes blinked, irises black and ringed with
flickering blue flame.

Lifting itself onto its hind legs it roared, the sound
deafening and making the air ripple with change. It
dropped down to all fours, and began climbing up to
face the intruders of its realm, claws ripping great
chunks of rock from the cave walls as it ascended
towards the surface.

'WHAT IN THE name of Sigmar was that?' said Annaliese,
her face pale as the sound of the ungodly roar echoed
through the cave.

'Something that the greenskins feared to face,' said
Karl, turning around warily with his sword in his hand,
looking into the darkness surrounding them. The other
knights too circled warily, licking their lips in uncer-
tainty. 'I don't think this is the safest of caves to rest in,'
the preceptor added.

'You don't think?' snapped Grunwald.

'How is the elf?' said Karl.

'Not fit to travel,' said Annaliese. Eldanair had regained
consciousness, but was clearly unable to stand.

'Perfect,' said Karl. 'So we just sit here and wait for the
beast of the underworld to appear then?'

'I will not leave Eldanair here,' snapped Annaliese,
'and it lessens you to even think it.'

Karl swallowed hard, but had the grace to look
shamefaced. 'I'm sorry,' he said, 'I spoke out of anger.

Of course we cannot leave him. But could we not carry him?'

'The orcs have set up camp below,' said one of the knights, walking back into the cave. 'They have sentries watching the entrance.'

'Well I guess that answers that,' said Karl.

'Have you ever heard of any beast haunting this area?' Grunwald asked Thorrik.

The dwarf shook his head. 'But I do not know this place, manling, and do not know its local legends.'

'Let's get a fire banked,' suggested Grunwald. 'If it is any natural beast, it will fear the flames.'

'There wasn't anything natural about the sound of that roar,' muttered Karl, but the preceptor organised his men swiftly to do as the witch hunter said. Doing *something* was better than just sitting waiting for whatever was coming for them.

THEY SMELT IT before they saw it. It stank of rotting meat, but there was the nauseating, cloying vapour of Chaos hanging about it. The stench was strong, and as one they rose from their seats around the bonfire, drawing weapons. Grunwald felt his stomach clench, and tasted bile upon his tongue.

'Gods, what an unholy stink,' said Karl, spitting, and Grunwald knew that the power of Chaos was clawing at all of them. He alone amongst them had often faced the minions of the dark gods and felt this sickening, corrupting essence of Chaos. 'I can feel it… twisting inside me.'

'Speak aloud the prayers of your order,' said Grunwald to the knights. 'Your faith will be your shield.'

As one the knights began reciting a prayer in the language of the men to the south of the Empire, from where the faith of Myrmidia originated. Grunwald began speaking a prayer of Sigmar aloud, and Annaliese joined him, their voices speaking together. Eldanair was clearly distressed, and he tried to rise to his feet, but sank back to the ground, sweat appearing on his forehead. Only Thorrik seemed unaffected, standing still and grim, awaiting whatever drew near.

The air seemed to shimmer as if with heat, though they could see coiling shapes writhing in the corner of their eyes, ghostly figures that lunged at them with widespread mouths and clawed, long-limbed arms. The knights spun left and right to face these daemons, but when they looked straight at them there was nothing there. Disturbing and ethereal, these images seemed unable to harm them, for they turned to smoke as they reached forward, though strange cackling screeches and giggles could be heard all around them.

The warriors closed together in a circle around the fire facing outwards, their eyes darting back and forth at the maddening images surrounding them.

'They are nothing,' said Grunwald, trying not to be distracted by these apparitions. 'Creatures of shadow – they cannot harm us.'

Still, it was impossible to ignore the shifting shapes that writhed, blurring and mutating just beyond their vision. But they were merely heralds of the beast that came forward out of the shadows. Indeed even as they watched, more of the wisp-like spirit-creatures were exhaled from the giant beast, flowing from its nostrils to encircle the group.

The ground shook as it stepped forth, and it rose up on its hind legs, standing almost twenty feet tall. It was covered in thick, matted black fur, though its underbelly was furless, the heavily scarred skin an icy blue colour. It raised its legs high into the air, each tipped with long scythe-like talons, and bony spikes and protrusions extended from its forelegs, gleaming and deadly. Its head may once have been that of a bear, but it had grown and mutated out of all proportion, spikes of dark bone erupting from its brow like a crown, and immense curving tusks protruded from its slavering maw.

It opened its jaws, which seemed to have a double set of hinged joints so that they opened far wider than any natural creature's, and when it roared the air shimmered before it, and the warriors staggered, nausea washing over them, and their vision wavering. Spines jutted from its chin, and as the monster bellowed, Grunwald could see that blue fire flared from deep within it. Its eyes too, small and round, were rimmed with this fire, which was blotted out for a moment as they blinked shut, four eyelids closing over each of the hateful orbs.

It roared again, and several of the knights staggered to their knees, grabbing at their heads. Grunwald too felt light-headed, as if he had drunk too much wine or imbibed noxious, mind-altering fumes. The shadow-spirits circling around the group closed in, as if feeding on this confusion, fear and disorientation. They began to circle madly, creating sickening patterns with their ethereal bodies, forming hateful, ruinous symbols, and mesmerising shapes.

'Begone, foul beast of Chaos!' roared Grunwald, breaking the spell abruptly. He levelled one of his precious wheel-lock pistols at the towering monster, and the sound of it as it fired cut through the ghostly whispering of the dim manifestations of Chaos.

The shot impacted with the beast's cheek, but it ricocheted off its flesh as if it had struck stone, leaving not a mark or a weal. The creature drew in a deep, rattling breath, and the spirit creatures were sucked back through the beast's nostrils, disappearing in an instant. However, they were not gone – they could be seen within the beast's flesh now, pushing against the skin of its chest and belly, forming mouths and eyes and clawed limbs in its flesh.

It dropped to all fours, and charged at the group, the stone cracking beneath the impact of its massive clawed paws. Grunwald leapt to the side of the monstrosity, firing his other pistol as it closed the distance with sickening swiftness. The shot took it behind its left foreleg, but again he may as well have been firing on stone, and the lead shot dropped to the ground, flattened, as if it had been fired against a wall of stone.

One knight was too slow to react, and the beast drove a tusk through his body, the thick bony spur punching through the metal of his breastplate and out the other side. He was lifted high into the air, and hot blood splattered into the roaring fire, making it spit furiously. The beast shook its head, hurling the dead knight far across the cavern to smash into the wall before sliding to the ground.

Karl roared a battle cry as he drove his sword at the flank of the beast, and his knights too surged towards its rear, swords slicing through the air. They clanged off the beast's haunches. Redoubling their effort they attacked again, but the beast seemed impervious to harm.

The beast swung around, tusks knocking two men flying, and another was swatted to the ground beneath a sweeping foreleg. The monstrous creature reared up onto its hind legs as it turned on the fallen knight, lifting him towards its maw. With one savage bite, the warrior was bitten in half as the other knights fell back from the monster, rising panic on their faces.

Thinking quickly, Grunwald lifted a burning brand from the fire and hurled it end over end towards the beast. It struck the creature in the small of its back, and the thick fur caught fire instantly. The stink of burning hair filled the cavern, and the monster dropped back to all fours, snarling fiercely, thick rivulets of blood and saliva dripping to the ground. The flames on its back rose for a moment, but then changed hue from orange to blue, then to purple, and then they faded altogether.

Thorrik and Annaliese charged at the beast. Thorrik swung with all his strength, but his blow rebounded. Annaliese smashed her hammer into the creature's leg, and it seemed to feel some pain, though it was far from truly injured. It swung around viciously, talons lashing out. The blow caught Thorrik in the chest, the span of the beast's paw reaching from his neck to his groin, and he was sent flying. He took the brunt of the blow, but Annaliese too was sent hurtling backwards, striking her head hard against a rocky outcrop, and she fell limp to the ground.

'Annaliese!' shouted Karl, and he charged back at the beast, and Grunwald joined him, screaming a prayer to Sigmar. With his mace held in two hands the witch hunter attacked, and he grunted as put all his weight behind the blow. It was like striking a castle wall, and he staggered back, the blow jarring all the way up his arms.

The creature rounded on him, and he hurled a vial of sanctified water into its face. The glass shattered on impact, showering the contents over one side of the beast's face. The flesh blistered and sizzled as it burnt, and he saw one of the creature's eyes dissolve in a liquefied mess of tissue.

The beast roared in pain, and staggered, shaking its head. It crushed a knight underfoot as it stepped backward, and lashed out blindly at another, the knight barely avoiding the slashing paw.

'Got any more of that stuff?' shouted Karl.

'No,' replied Grunwald. His other vials on his person were shattered from the fight against the greenskins.

'This is it then,' said Karl, as he stared up at the monstrous beast that was clearly readying itself for another charge.

'Looks like it,' replied Grunwald.

The beast exhaled, and the ghostly creatures surged around them. One of them reached for Grunwald but pulled its hand back as if burnt, and it was then that he realised the pendant hung around his neck was glowing faintly.

He gripped the pendant tightly in his hand, and prepared himself for death.

THORRIK BLINKED HIS eyes and pushed himself to his knees. It felt like several ribs were broken, but he ignored the pain. His axe was gone. He glanced around and saw the witch hunter hurl the vial into the beast's face, saw it reel backwards, and heard the swift exchange between the two humans.

His eyes locked on something propped against the cavern wall, something he had placed there before the fight against the greenskins outside. An object wrapped in oilskin.

He flicked his gaze back to the beast, and saw a pair of knights reel back from it, their weapons useless. One of them died a second later, ripped in two as it was caught in the massive paws of the Chaos-warped beast. His gaze flicked back to the ancient heirloom he had carried across the Empire and back, and he swore as he realised what he needed to do.

He scrambled across the cavern floor towards it, and lifted it in his hands, discarding his shield. Whispering the forgiveness of the ancestors, he ripped the oilskin from the shape and held the ancient warrior heirloom *Karagaz* reverently in his hands, awe upon his face.

It was a beautiful, immaculate, rune-inscribed war axe, forged six generations past by the finest war-smiths of Zhufbar, and inscribed by the runesmith Beorik Silverfist. It was a double-headed axe, its thick haft inscribed with runes of power and inlaid with gold and gromril. The axe blades themselves were forged in the likeness of twin dragonheads, and they gleamed in the firelight. Never would such a weapon need sharpening, and never would the axe blades tarnish or chip.

Many were the old tales of beasts of the deep that were immune to all but the strike of a rune weapon, mighty wyrms of the dark places and dragons of the treacherous elves.

With a heavy heart he lifted the revered blade, turning it before him, and his eyes fell on the massive beast of Chaos. The monster dropped to its four legs and charged at the few remaining standing humans, and Thorrik felt the fire in his belly become a roaring inferno of rage.

Crying out to Grimnir, Thorrik charged at the beast, swinging the gleaming rune-axe back over his shoulder as he ran. The runic script up its haft blazed into light, white hot and eager, and with one mighty blow, Thorrik severed one of the beast's back legs. Hot blood sprayed from the wound, and spirit-wraiths poured from the wound, their emaciated, ghostly faces twisted in pain and fear. They faded into nothingness as they dissipated into the air, and the monstrous beast collapsed to the ground, a piercing roar of pain bursting from its throat.

Chanting the war cries of his clan and hold, Thorrik stepped closer to the thrashing beast, and hacked deep into its neck. Then he stood back away from the mortally wounded monster, still chanting, and watched as the life slipped from it.

Blood boiled and spat upon the stone cavern floor, pouring from its wounds as it continued to thrash madly. Claws ripped up great rents in the stone, and more spirit shapes poured from the wound at its neck, screaming faintly and disappearing into the air.

The beast's flesh rippled as uncontrollable mutation went through it, and spiked bones burst through the skin over its backbone, twisting and coiling together. A gaping mouth complete with teeth and a pair of whip-like tongues opened up on the flank of the dying beast, and one of its forelegs melted to become a grotesque, bloated flipper that slapped against the stone floor, splattering bubbling blood. The blue skin on its chest peeled away to expose ribs and pulsing organs covered in a film of blue fire, and this fire rose up high as the beast let out a final dying roar, spiderwebs of mutating flesh spreading across its face.

At last it was silent, and the blue flames died away. All that was left was a foul lump of rancid smelling meat and fur, a sickening corpse that spoke of the horrid touch of Chaos.

'Burn it,' said Grunwald, his voice hoarse, and he joined the others in stacking wood around the foul creature before hurling flaming brands upon it.

With his heart heavy, Thorrik stomped away from the others and began to meticulously clean the powerful rune-axe, his face grim.

To use this weapon, the heirloom that he had sworn and failed to deliver to its one and only living rightful owner, was a sacrilege that he would be forced to atone for. He polished the weapon in silence until, at last satisfied, he rewrapped it in oiled leathers, binding it tightly with knotted twine. Then he placed it back against the cave wall, and drew his pipe.

Surrounded by smoke, he sat in silence, brooding and lost in his own dark thoughts.

As THE FIRST rays of dawn pierced the cave mouth, the knights ventured cautiously outside. The orcs and goblins had gone, leaving behind crude totems perhaps to honour the beast of the cave. Their dead were left where they had fallen, and the cawing of carrion birds was loud in the morning's silence as they fought over the richest pickings. Many of the knights' corpses had been mutilated almost beyond recognition.

Exhausted and bone-tired, Karl ordered his templars to scout the area, and they found another cave, thankfully free of the sickening stench of Chaos. There they transferred their dead and their wounded. Those who had perished were laid to rest at the back of the cave, their hands grasping their swords, and the wounds of the injured were tended. Then the group rested, falling into a dreamless, healing sleep, the watch rotated every three hours.

Thorrik couldn't sleep, and he sat in the cave mouth smoking his pipe as he watched the passage of the sun overhead. Finally even he succumbed to his weariness, and he slept.

BOOK THREE

THE GREAT CITY of Praag, in the lands of our Kislevite allies, has been taken by the foe. It is as if history is repeating itself, and the world is beset as it was during the Great War. Then, Magnus the Pious rode forth and confronted the enemy at the gates of Kislev, but alas, I cannot do the same – for the shadow of the enemy reaches far, and its vanguard cuts ever deeper into our lands.

Half of Talabecland has fallen to the foe – even the mighty Talabec has proved to be an ineffective barrier against their hatred and power. The ranks of Talabecland are supported by the armies of Reikland and Stirland, but still the enemy is barely held at bay.

However, if the Ostermark falls to the enemy then all will be lost.

Bechafen still holds out against the hordes of Chaos surging southwards, but its days are numbered, and almost all of the Ostermark has fallen to the enemy. The last Imperial armies there are desperately holding back the tide from sweeping behind our defences in Talabecland, but I fear they cannot resist for long.

If the enemy bursts through these lines and descends on our rear in Talabecland, then it will only be a matter of time before the war comes to Altdorf itself. I dread to think what would happen if our shining capital fell to the infernal enemy. The resolve of our armies would be shattered.

I cannot allow such a thing to come to pass, and as such the Ostermark must hold, at any cost. I have dispatched the Reiksmarshal, Kurt Helborg, and a full demi-legion of Reiksguard knights to lead the Order of the Griffon to bolster that region. This weakens Reikland considerably and was met with much opposition, but I feel that it is necessary. I just pray that the Ostermark can hold until their arrival, for alone they will not hold against the Raven Host forces there.

And for all this, I know that what we suffer now is but the opening phase of the long war to come – the Raven Host has not yet unleashed its full strength against us. They seem determined to destroy Kislev utterly, so that when they do send their full strength against us, they would not have the threat of an enemy upon their rear.

But hope is not lost. I have ordered armies to push north into the lands of Kislev. They march on Praag, for if we can reclaim that city of the damned, then the forays of the enemy will become stalled. I pray that by making a positive, aggressive move we will take the enemy by surprise and weaken him at his heart. There was dissent amongst my Electors at the decision, but the weight of their counsel was with me – the result of many months of negotiations.

It is a dangerous gambit, for marching north leaves our own lands less well defended, and the wolf is already in our midst. However, I feel that it is a necessary risk, and our only chance of success. I pray that my instincts prove to be the right course of action – there shall be none left alive to denounce me should it fail.

I go to Talabecland myself now, so as to be seen to be fighting on the front line. The resolve of our armies is a fragile thing, the gap between victory and defeat narrow. Joining the fight personally will make a more forceful statement to the soldiers and commanders of the Empire than months of politicking here in Altdorf.

I pray that the Ostermark holds, for the balance of the war hangs on it being able to weather the storm of Chaos until the Reiksmarshal arrives to bolster their strength.

May Sigmar be with us in these dark times. I truly fear the End Times draw near.

K.F.

CHAPTER NINETEEN

UDO GRUNWALD STOOD over the twisted corpse. It was emaciated far beyond human endurance, and its ribs pushed against its grey, dead skin. Once it may have been human, but its shape was mutated and contorted, its flesh altered so that it truly could not have been called so when it died.

Its hands were no longer those of a man, but more closely resembled the hunting talons of a great bird of prey. In death, those talons had clenched tightly, the thick black claws digging into its own flesh. The skin of the talons and forearms were yellow and scaled like a bird's, but there was also other evidence of foul, Chaotic mutation – soft, downy black feathers had burst through the flesh of the creature's neck, forming a strange collar, and a bony spur of bone had split through the skin at the base of the creature's neck, extending up along the skull like a sharp ridge.

But it was the creature's face that was truly horrific, all the more so for it was almost perfectly human. The corpse's face was drawn in a horrid expression of what might have been ecstasy, or glee – a smile that was chilling and horrific. Its eyes were wide and staring, the pupils and irises completely white. When the girl Annaliese saw the face of the corpse she backed away quickly, horror on her face, and Grunwald guessed that she had seen similar corpses before, just as he had.

'How long ago did it die do you think?' asked Karl. Grunwald shrugged his shoulders.

'Hard to say. The carrion-eaters won't touch them. Very wise.'

It was easy to see what had killed the plague victim. Its arms were covered in sword cuts, and there was a deep gash in the figure's head, but from his own experience Grunwald knew that these alone would not have stopped the foul creature – but the sword still protruding from its heart had done the job.

The witch hunter rose to his feet. They stood in the centre of a small village, thirteen hard days' march from the base of the Worlds Edge Mountains. He didn't know the name of the place, nor even if it had a name, for it was little more than a group of five shabby buildings. The plague had originated in the north, it was said, so it was not surprising that small villages like this had suffered such a fate. It was happening all across the Empire – people got sick, withering and falling into a comatose state before dying, at which time some foul sorcerous power makes them rise up to kill those tending them.

In grim silence the group left the village. It seemed that all of the Ostermark had suffered a similar, or worse, fate. They passed dozens of villages and small towns, once thriving communities now reduced to smoking ruins. Evidence of war was everywhere, from the skeletal corpses to broken swords, armour and arrows that they trod into the ground beneath their feet. Some were laid low by plague, others by violence and war, while others were remarkably untouched, but their inhabitants nowhere to be found.

The Ostermark was the most north-eastern state of the Empire, bordering allied Kislev to the north and the towering heights of the Worlds Edge Mountains to the east. While much of the Empire was swathed in forests, much of the Ostermark was high moorland or marshes, dangerous and bleak countryside dotted with villages and fortified road warden stations. And now, thought Grunwald, its people had been massacred.

Cut off from the Empire since they boarded the dwarf steam engine in Black Fire Pass, they had received no word of the progression of the war, and for all Grunwald knew, they were now in enemy territory, behind the Chaos lines sweeping down from the icy north.

As they skirted the smouldering remains of yet another village, he made the sign of Sigmar to ward off the Ruinous Powers. In silence they marched past a massive pile of skulls arranged carefully one on top of another to form a pyramid some fifteen feet in height. Each skull had been scorched in fire, and was bereft of skin or hair, and a blue mark had been daubed onto the forehead – a stylised, wide, staring azure eye.

As they passed, a cloud of ravens and crows launched themselves from its peak, cawing loudly as they began to circle around it, almost protectively. Other groups of birds could be seen rising in the distance, circling above other piles of skulls – eight in total, placed equidistant around the perimeter of the village, each point representing one of the tips of the cursed eight-pointed star of Chaos.

Grunwald had seen this before, and he knew it was a dedication to the heathen daemonic gods of the northern tribes – a hateful oblation of death and destruction offered up to these foul deities by their worshippers, a sacrifice to gain the attention and favour of the gods.

A ghostly silence enveloped the land like a cloying blanket, and as they left the raucous cries of the carrion birds behind them the absence of sound became oppressive. They dared not break it with talk, and so they continued on through the overcast day, each lost in their own dark thoughts.

There saw no sign of any living soul for days on end, though once at dusk they glimpsed dark shapes crawling through the ruin of yet another abandoned town. The movement of the shapes was unnatural, stooped, shuffling and inbred, and no one argued when Karl suggested they move on before setting camp, putting as many miles between them and the ghoulish figures as possible.

For a time they went along the old Kadrin road, though as they travelled they came across increasing evidence of the passage of enemy forces.

'We have to get off the road,' said Grunwald. 'For all we know we are marching straight towards an enemy army – our own forces may have pulled back to Talabecland and Stirland.'

'It certainly seems that way,' said Karl. 'The Ostermark is a dead land.'

'My clan is fighting north of Bechafen,' said Thorrik. 'And so that is where I go. I will continue on to the north, with or without you.'

'And if there is nothing left of Bechafen?' snapped Karl.

'Then I will join my ancestors,' said Thorrik.

'If the Empire forces pulled back from the Ostermark, your clan would have retreated with them,' said Grunwald.

'Aye, that is true, but we don't know that Bechafen has fallen.'

'Look around you dwarf!' snapped Karl. 'We have seen no life since leaving the foothills of the mountains. Thirteen days and not a living human soul! And yet we have seen what, a dozen villages and towns sacked by the enemy? Bechafen is over a hundred miles to the north! If the enemy are laying waste to the land this far south, Bechafen is no more.'

'Be that as it may, without solid proof that my clan is no longer there, that is where I go.'

'Then you are a stubborn fool,' said Karl. 'Bechafen is where my knights and I were due as well, but to head on blindly is folly. We must seek the armies of the Empire. I say we cut to the west and head towards Talabecland, or to the Stir.' The dwarf did not respond.

'I too will head on to Bechafen with Thorrik,' said Annaliese, breaking the tense silence.

'What?' said Karl. 'Has everyone lost their sense?'

'Why would you wish to head there?' said Grunwald. The girl's eyes were clear, fearless and confident.

'Sigmar sent me to the north,' she said with a shrug. 'And Bechafen is to the north.'

'Karl speaks the truth, girl,' said Grunwald. 'Bechafen is most likely no more. The Reiksmarshal would surely have pulled back the forces of the north to face the enemy on more favourable territory.'

'And give up this land that Sigmar united to the ravages of the enemy? This land we stand upon is the Empire. It must not be handed over to the enemy without a fight.'

'The fight has been going on here for centuries,' said Grunwald. 'And it would be folly to throw away the armies of the Empire in a fruitless war on terrain already lost.'

'Surely running away like a dog with its tail between its legs will only strengthen the foe,' said the girl, her eyes blazing with passion.

'You know nothing of what you speak,' said Grunwald, losing patience. 'You are a farm girl playing at war, but you know nothing of it. To go north blindly will lead to nothing.'

'I'm sure the thousands who have already been killed in the Ostermark, their villages destroyed, would be filled with pride to see the armies of the Empire fleeing before the enemy,' said Annaliese scathingly.

'Villages can be rebuilt,' snapped Grunwald. 'But if the Empire itself is shattered, there will be nobody *to* rebuild them.'

A shout came from up ahead, interrupting the argument, and Grunwald swung his gaze around to see the pale-skinned figure of Eldanair, his grey cloak whipping around him, gesturing to the east.

'I see nothing,' said Karl.

'Wait,' said Grunwald, shielding his eyes against the glare. 'There,' he said, seeing the flash of metal in the distance.

'I see it,' said Annaliese. 'Riders?'

'Could be the enemy,' said Karl. At a shout from him, the Knights of the Blazing Sun drew their weapons and formed up around the preceptor.

Closer the riders came, a group of around a dozen or so men riding in loose formation. As they sighted the knights, they altered their direction and turned towards them, cantering swiftly across the open ground.

Eldanair stood with an arrow nocked and readied, but as the horsemen drew nearer Grunwald saw the tension leave his body, and his bowstring slacken.

'Outriders,' said Grunwald finally, relief in his voice.

They were young men bedecked in gleaming breast-plates, plumes of feathers bobbing from their conical helmets. They rode swift unarmoured steeds, and as they drew near, the knights sheathed their swords. The young warriors wore braces of expensive pistols over their torsos, and light cavalry sabres were strapped at their sides. Their leader was a grizzled, bearded warrior who held a strange, multi-barrelled handgun loosely in one hand, its ornate butt resting on his thigh.

Karl stepped forward, his hand raised as the horsemen wheeled warily around the motionless figure of Eldanair. They drew their steeds to a halt before the preceptor.

'Hail, warriors of the Empire!' called Karl, and the leader of the horsemen dismounted to greet him. He was a stocky man, and he nodded curtly to the knight, still holding his ornate weapon in one hand. He seemed ungainly walking on the ground – truly, he was more suited to life in the saddle.

'And to you, preceptor,' replied the warrior, his accent thick. 'I am surprised to see you here, in this forsaken land. The Raven Host controls the Ostermark.'

'We travel from Kadrin,' replied Karl. 'Seeking to join the templars of the Blazing Sun in the north – the temple of Myrmidia in Bechafen.'

'Bechafen has fallen to the enemy,' replied the outrider grimly.

'The foe has crossed the Talabec, then?' asked Karl.

'It has,' replied the veteran outrider.

'And my brother templars?'

'They are falling back to Talabecland with the remainder of the armies of the Ostermark. Our forces gather there in strength, at Zurin and Unterbaum.'

'Unterbaum… the foe has pushed so deep into the Empire?' Grunwald was aghast – things were clearly much worse than he would have predicted.

'Yes, witch hunter,' said the outrider, turning his gaze towards Grunwald. His eyes flicked back towards Karl. 'Your order are amongst the last to leave the Ostermark – they are part of the army not a day's march from here – to the west.'

'Less than a day's march away?' said Karl, his eyes brightening. The outrider nodded.

'An army accompanied by the Elector of the Ostermark himself. It marches for Talabecland, heading for Hazelhof.'

'Hazelhof?' said Grunwald, not recognising the name.

'A small village at the foot of the Kolsa Hills. It is of little consequence, yet the enemy seems intent on controlling the area – agents of the Order of the Griffon are trying to ascertain what it is they seek. We are to liberate the area.'

'So you are the rearguard,' said Grunwald. The outrider nodded.

'The enemy chases us, like rabid hounds. And they are closing in on the elector's army – I fear it will not make Talabecland without battle. And it must hold, regardless of the odds. It seems that the enemy are moving against us in force – if the elector's army breaks, then the enemy will be able to move into Talabecland unopposed, and strike against the flanks of the armies there. It would be disastrous.'

'What of the dwarfs stationed at Bechafen?' said Thorrik. The outrider gazed at the dwarf for a moment.

'I know nothing of them,' admitted the outrider. Thorrik grunted, and walked away.

'A day's march,' said Karl thoughtfully. 'Tell me, man, what of the enemy? Where are their armies?'

The outrider sighed. 'They are all around,' he said. 'Vanguard forces push deeper into Talabecland already, and I have heard that Ostland too is overrun.'

'The armies of Chaos from the north, the green tide of Orcs from the east...' Grunwald shook his head.

The outrider frowned. 'Enemies from the east?'

Karl waved a hand, dismissing the question.

'We must away,' he said. 'Knights of Myrmidia! Ready yourselves! We march!'

'I will leave one of my men with you, to guide you to the Elector's army,' said the outrider. 'Helmut!' he shouted, and a young noble, probably no more than fourteen years of age, saluted sloppily. 'You will guide these templars and their companions to the army of the Elector count. Be wary of the enemy.'

Karl nodded in thanks, and extended his hand to the outrider. 'Preceptor Karl Heiden is my name,' he said as he clasped hands with the older warrior.

'Klaus Midders,' said the outrider. 'I pray to Sigmar that we shall meet again.'

'Indeed. Ride well, Klaus Midders,' said Karl. The outrider hoisted himself easily into the saddle.

Eldanair shouted again, and several of the pistolier's horses snorted and tossed their heads.

The outrider Klaus pulled a brass eyeglass from a pouch at his side and extended it, looking to the east where Eldanair was pointing.

'An enemy rider, alone on the rise to the east,' he said after a minute. 'He's motionless – watching us. They are closer than anticipated. The elector must be warned.'

With quick, sharp orders, the outrider organised his pistoliers. Two of them he sent directly back to the army, carrying messages he swiftly penned and sealed with his ornate signet ring. They galloped off to the west, riding hard.

Leaving just the young pistolier Helmut as their guide, the outrider wheeled his steed and with a wave, led his soldiers in a trot towards the lone enemy horseman.

'Thorrik,' said Grunwald, walking away from the others to speak to the ironbreaker, who was sat on a stone smoking. 'Will you join us heading east?'

The dwarf sighed and puffed on his pipe. 'I have been gone from my clan too long,' he said at last. 'I am eager to return to my people. But it seems that there is nothing at Bechafen now. Aye, I will come with you, manling. If nothing else, I should be able to learn where Clan Barad fights.'

Grunwald slapped the dwarf on the shoulder.

'I am sorry that it seems your people are not there,' the witch hunter said. 'Though I am glad you're still travelling with us.'

The dwarf nodded to him, his eyes glittering with rare humour. 'Aye,' he said. 'For a manling you are not half bad.'

'WELL, YOUNG MAN,' said Karl to the solitary pistolier. 'Lead on.'

The moorland they travelled over was bleak and eerie and thick fogs surrounded them often, wet and cloying, making their progress difficult. Strange lights seemed to shimmer in the distance at times, and the silence then was even more profound, the fog muffling even the rattle of Thorrik's armour so that it seemed dull and distant.

They travelled as swiftly as they were able. The young pistolier was clearly in awe of the knights, as well he would be, thought Grunwald. The pistolkorps was an organisation that many noble lords sent their sons to join, and it was generally regarded as a place where a young man could earn his spurs in battle. From the pistolkorps many of the men went on to join one of the knightly orders, the templars of the Blazing Sun amongst them. Still, Grunwald found the upper-class bearing of the boy irritating, and though he regarded the knights with the utmost respect, his disdain for him and Annaliese was palpable. As for Thorrik and Eldanair, the boy did not so much as glance in their direction.

'That was a sloppy salute you gave your commanding officer, boy,' he said after an hour's hard march.

The pistolier looked down at Grunwald arrogantly.

'I am the son of a baron. Klaus Midders is a lowborn – a mere drill instructor.'

'I too am a *mere* lowborn,' said Grunwald dangerously. The pistolier flushed an angry red, and opened his mouth to say something. He caught himself, his eyes flicking to the pendant hanging around the witch hunter's neck, and closed his mouth.

'Very wise,' said Grunwald.

'You are of the church of Sigmar, therefore your low birth is of lesser importance,' said the pistolier sullenly.

'Helmut!' said Karl sharply. The young pistolier straightened instantly, snapping off a sharp salute to the preceptor. 'Ride ahead and ensure the way is clear.' The boy nodded and dug his heels into his steed.

Karl smirked. 'Why bait the boy, Grunwald?'

'I don't like his type.'

'He's a spoilt brat – there are thousands of them. Never going to get ahead in the world if that is the way you treat all of your betters.'

'Do I *look* like I have any interest in getting ahead by toadying myself to the likes of his breed?'

'*His breed.* Ouch. I am of noble birth myself, you know.'

'There are two types of nobleman, Karl. And you are not *his* kind.'

The preceptor laughed. 'Perhaps. It will be beaten out of him if he is chosen to join the templars of the Blazing Sun.'

'If he lives that long,' said Grunwald. He felt suddenly rather petty for his actions, and stalked further ahead, walking alone.

Karl dropped back alongside Annaliese, glancing in irritation at the tall figure of Eldanair ghosting her footsteps.

'Nothing like a walk in the countryside, eh?' he said lightly as the girl smiled at him. She laughed at his levity, and Karl smiled broadly.

'And how is the maiden of Sigmar today?' he said.

She scowled at him, though her eyes laughed at his quip. 'I wish you would not call me that,' she said.

'I apologise,' he said, bowing and sweeping his hand before him. 'I see you are still practising at swordplay with the elf before the dawn of each day.'

'Eldanair is a fine teacher,' she said.

'A marvel, I'm sure,' said Karl. 'Your timing and balance is improved. You move well. I would suggest a blade over that hammer, as it would complement your speed more, but I don't think that anything I say could convince you not to use it.'

Annaliese smiled. 'You know me too well.'

Not nearly enough, he thought.

THE ARMY OF Wolfram Hertwig, Elector Count of the Ostermark, was encamped at Seuthes, a village some ninety miles south-west of the capital of the state, Bechafen.

Five miles out from the Empire army they were challenged by swarthy men appearing out of the mist with arrows aimed at them. They wore no uniform and had appeared silently and with great stealth – most likely militia scouts, thought Grunwald. Not part of the formal state army, but employed in times of war. At other times they might have made their way hunting, either game or bounties. Their leader, a hulking scout called Dietrich with arms as thick as Grunwald's thighs, was taken by surprise as Eldanair rose up like a wraith behind him and placed a blade to his throat.

Her hands raised, Annaliese stepped forward speaking and signing to Eldanair that these were friends, and the elf somewhat reluctantly removed his blade. Dietrich frowned, unnerved that the elf had managed to sneak up on him, rubbing at his neck.

Escorted by these scouts, they were taken down to the army, the last fighting force remaining within the state.

From the high moors, the land dropped away sharply, and the village could be seen below. Thousands of tents were picketed in the snow-covered fields beyond, and makeshift defences and emplacement were being hastily dug. Several great cannons, mighty war machines crafted in far away Nuln, were being heaved into place, and engineers were pacing out distances to ensure they knew how much powder to load.

'Looks like the elector has chosen to make his stand here,' said Grunwald.

'Why not keep the army moving towards the east?' questioned Karl. 'Get closer to reinforcements?'

The scout leader, Dietrich, answered him.

'The forces of the Raven Host are massing along the border of Talabecland and the Ostermark. If we had kept moving, then we might well have ended up caught between two enemy armies. Better to turn and face one than fight a battle on two fronts.'

'The enemy controls the border?' asked Karl. Dietrich nodded.

'The curs are gathering in strength. We fight 'em here, or we fight 'em somewhere else,' he said, shrugging. 'I reckon this elector's got some sense at least – this ain't a bad place to make our stand.'

He was a simple, down to earth and direct man, with none of the pomposity that often surrounded the military. Grunwald liked him.

It *was* a good place to face the enemy, he decided. Down the steep, rough incline the enemy would descend, down into the dip. Ice covered the murky pools in this natural marsh, and the enemy would be slowed as it pushed through it, all the while being targeted by the Empire bows and handguns.

Having struggled though the mire, the foe would then be forced to climb a steady slope of clear land towards the Empire forces. It would be long and tiring and the icy ground would likely be thick with the dead.

The state soldiers working to ready the defences wore the purple and yellow liveries of the Ostermark, though there were many pockets bedecked in the yellow and red of Talabecland, and the men heaving the cannon into place wore the black of Nuln.

It was a hive of activity, as the Empire forces readied themselves for battle.

'Still, if we can trust the word of those uptight pistolier bastards, then we are gonna be in for one hell of a fight,' said Dietrich. 'Messages came in about an hour ago, just before we headed out. They say the army heading our way spreads from one horizon to the other.'

'Sounds like great odds,' said Karl sarcastically. 'We might as well start the victory celebrations early.'

'Still, I don't trust the word of a pistolier further than I can piss,' added Dietrich. 'Excusing me language,' he added, tipping his hat in the direction of Annaliese. She laughed, finding the sight of the massive scout looking abashed comical.

'I've heard far worse in my time, Dietrich,' she assured him. 'And I'll hear far worse yet, I'm sure.'

Grunwald calculated quickly as they descended towards the village. He guessed there must have been around three thousand soldiers camped here, judging from the number of tents and lean-tos erected on the far field. Not a large force by any stretch, and if the reports of the pistoliers *were* correct, they would find themselves heavily outnumbered in the forthcoming battle. Still, that was a concern that he had no power to affect, and so he pushed it from his mind.

'Your elf there,' said Dietrich, nodding towards Eldanair, who was walking nearby, his face pale and expressionless.

'He's not *my* elf,' said Grunwald.

'Whatever. I'll be leading the boys back out before dawn,' continued Dietrich, 'and if he's willing, I'd like to have him along. Certainly showed me up earlier,' he added, rubbing at his neck where the elf's slim blade had been placed, right alongside the artery.

Grunwald shrugged. 'As I said, he isn't my man. And I don't think he would be interested in being hired. But, if he's willing, it's his own business.'

'Fair enough,' said Dietrich. He looked over at the elf. 'He speaks Reikspiel?'

'No,' answered Grunwald.

'Ah,' replied Dietrich. 'That might make things tricky, then.'

'She seems to have the knack of talking with him though,' Grunwald said, jabbing a black-gloved thumb in Annaliese's direction.

'Preceptor!' called one of the knights, a young man from Reikland.

'What is it Jarek?' said Karl.

'Look,' said the young knight eagerly, pointing down into an open field to the south of the village. Squinting his eyes against the glare of the snow, Karl could see two blocks of knights wheeling and charging across the open field, practising their movement as a cohesive unit. The banners held aloft by one knight within each of the regiments was unmistakable. Karl laughed out loud.

'Templars of Myrmidia! Finally!' he said. 'And if the goddess is looking favourably upon us, they may even have some spare warhorses. Come!' he called. 'Let us rejoin our temple!'

CHAPTER TWENTY

GRUNWALD STRODE THROUGH the village with Annaliese and Eldanair. Soldiers hefting powder kegs and lead shot gave them long looks before returning to their work, muttering amongst themselves. Eldanair had drawn his hood down low over his face once more, but no doubt rumour of the elf had already circulated amongst the soldiers – word travelled fast within an army.

Karl and his knights had made their way towards the templars of their order, and Thorrik had left to speak to one of the Imperial commanders – he knew several of them, having been stationed around Bechafen for years, fighting alongside many of these same warriors.

'There are many here who are not soldiers,' commented Annaliese.

'There are,' said Grunwald. The streets were filled with desperate looking people, families clearly dispossessed by the wars and following close to the army for protection. 'But the outcome of the coming battle will effect them as much as it will the soldiers on the field.'

Many of the ragged, dirty people were clearly trying to eke out an existence as camp followers, cooking and cleaning for the soldiers in return for food. Others prostituted themselves, their wives or their daughters to feed their families, and had a haunted look in their eyes.

Grunwald stared through the crowd of ragged, homeless Ostermarkers, and many turned away from his gaze, recognising him for what he was and fearing drawing attention to themselves. He narrowed his eyes, scanning the faces, more out of habit than any thought of possible threat. They moved through the crowd, passing crippled, malformed beggars and hastily erected stalls.

Grunwald ignored the begging hands held out towards him, pushing through the crowd of wretches and cripples. On top of a barrel a near naked flagellant screamed and ranted of redemption and death as he slowly pushed metal pokers through his own flesh. Few paid any heed at his crazed words, and dozens of the spikes already pierced the skin of his forearms, chest and thighs. As they walked past, the flagellant pointed at Annaliese and began screeching at the top of his lungs.

'The great comet will come again! From the heavens shall He hurl it, and the world will be engulfed in darkness and flame! The End Times! These are the End Times!'

Annaliese's face was pale, and Grunwald held her by her upper arm, guiding her away from the ranting madman. Something caught Grunwald's attention, a cry from somewhere nearby, and he stalked towards the sound, releasing the girl.

'Get yer blessings! Authentic fetishes of Morr! Icons of the long sleep!' came the shout, and Grunwald followed it, Annaliese and Eldanair close on his heels, until they came upon a tiny, rat-like man with long black hair trailing from his scabrous scalp. He held a long stick hung with all manner of deathly images and icons: representations of skulls carved with Morr's sign, miniature hourglasses filled with sand, dried black roses and other minor fetishes and phylacteries.

The black haired man fell silent as he saw Grunwald stalking towards him, and his eyes flicked back and forth, as if seeking an escape route.

'Priest of Morr, are you?' the witch hunter snarled, grabbing a hold of the man's shirtfront.

'No, sir,' stammered the man. Grunwald fingered through the man's items with one black-gloved hand, his scarred and brutal face hard.

'Any individual who is not a priest of Morr and identified as selling such items may be seen by some as a purveyor of necromantic curios,' the witch hunter said, his voice low and deadly. A space developed around them as other citizens backed away from the scene, and the rat-like man visibly paled, his eyes widening.

'N...no sir! I am not... I would never,' he stammered.

'One suspected of necromantic practices faces death by burning,' continued Grunwald. He pulled the staff from the man's hand violently, and hurled it to the ground, where he crushed several of the miniature icons beneath his heel, while the man quivered before him.

'You are not such a man, though are you,' said Grunwald, no question in his voice. 'You are merely an opportunistic wretch, seeking to earn a few coins through the fear of others. Correct?'

The man nodded his head quickly.

'Show me what you have earned,' said Grunwald. The man looked at him with wild eyes. 'Empty out your pouches,' the witch hunter urged. The man fumbled at his belt, and emptied the contents of a pouch into one of his hands. Grunwald cuffed the man suddenly, hard on the back his head, and he fell to his knees. 'All of it,' the witch hunter said with snarl. His hands shaking, the man pulled a hidden pouch out from beneath his shirt and emptied it upon the ground. Grunwald pushed the coins around with the toe of one boot, counting. There was more here than a soldier earned in half a year. He frowned and nodded his head slowly, his eyebrows raised.

'A good little income,' he said. Then his face hardened once more and he leant down to stare the terrified man in the face. 'I want you to take every coin here to the surgeon's tent that has been set up in the town square. Speak to the headman there, and tell him you wish to make a donation. Tell him you wish to help see the soldiers who'll be injured and slain in the battle tomorrow cared for. The donation is to go towards that – to help the men that will tomorrow walk out onto the field of battle and die so that the likes of *you* may live. I will check at the surgery myself within the hour, and ensure that every last one of these coins has been delivered. If it has not, then you are a dead man. Run away now, little man,' snarled Grunwald, 'before I change my mind and burn you here and now.'

The terrified man scrabbled in dirt, picking up his coins, and fled, his face drawn and pale. Grunwald turned around, smirking, to find Annaliese glaring at him.

'What?' he said.

'Was that really necessary?' she said scathingly. Grunwald frowned, not understanding.

'He was selling fake blessings of the god of death the day before battle. He was taking money from scared soldiers and citizens, making himself wealthy from their fear.'

'Did you really need to threaten him so?' she said.

'It would have been well within my writ as witch hunter to see the man dead for holding items such as these,' he said, indicating toward the fallen staff of trinkets and protective charms.

'Merciful Udo, that is what they should call you,' said Annaliese, her voice mocking.

Losing patience, Grunwald swung around and pointed a finger at her. His brutal face was flushed and angry, making the scars stand out in stark relief against his ruddy skin.

'Yes, damn you, I *am* merciful,' he said. 'More than you know.'

The crowd parted and a pair of flagellating doomsayers drew near them, whipping themselves with long leather flails that had nails embedded in their tips. One of them had pushed fishhooks through the skin of his cheeks, and they wore pages of holy Sigmarite script upon their bare flesh, held in place with long nails that had been hammered into their bones.

They stared up from their self-mutilation and saw Grunwald and Annaliese. One of them bared his yellow teeth, and gargled something incoherent, drool and foam dripping from his lips. The other dropped to his knees and reached for the girl, grabbing her by her robe, grinning up at her insanely. The witch hunter placed his boot on the side of the flagellant's neck and pushed him away, into the muddy slush of melted snow.

Giving the witch hunter a dark look, Annaliese dropped to her haunches to help the man back to his feet, ignoring the wet and the mud that stained her robe.

Grunwald's face was thunderous as he stared at the girl. She had no idea of the depths of his mercy.

The witch hunter sighed, and turned away, walking through the crowd as something attracted his interest. He purchased a strip of cooking meat from a dirt-covered vendor, the spit roasted animal making his mouth water. It looked like a dog, but at the moment he didn't really care, his hunger overcoming any delicate sensibilities.

As he looked around, his eyes locked onto those of a man in the crowd, standing no more than ten paces from the witch hunter. The man's eyes were different colours – his left was a dark brown but his right was a startling, brilliant blue.

Grunwald saw this stranger's face clearly for a second. It was heavily lined, and the man wore a dark, sour expression. He leant heavily on a tall staff that seemed to be hung with feathers, and Grunwald felt that time halted for a moment as he held the gaze of the man.

His years as a witch hunter had taught him to trust his instincts, and he knew with certainty that something about this man was *wrong*. Grunwald's eye twitched, and he reached for one of his pistols.

'Sigmar be praised!' came the shout behind him, and the witch hunter flicked his gaze around to see the flagellant prostrate himself before Annaliese. By the time he swung his gaze back around to the mysterious figure in the crowd, he was gone. He pulled a pistol from its holster and took a step into the crowd, pushing people out of his way roughly, trying to sight the man.

'Our lord Sigmar with us!' came another shout, and Grunwald was suddenly fighting against a surge of people moving towards Annaliese, and he swore, violently knocking people out of his path. But the man that he knew with dread was an agent of the enemy was long gone, and he turned to witness the commotion.

Grunwald swore again as he saw what was transpiring, and began to move back towards the girl. The flagellant's companion stared at the girl with wide eyes.

'Sigmar is with us in this girl! The maiden of Sigmar comes to fight the enemy!' the fanatic shouted at the top of his lungs, and more people crowded in. The second flagellant threw himself to the ground beside his companion, and Annaliese turned around frantically through the press, looking for aid.

'What have you done?' Grunwald said as he closed on her.

'Nothing!' she said quickly. 'I helped him to his feet – nothing more!'

'I felt Sigmar's divinity within her,' said the prostrate flagellant, grabbing at Grunwald's boot. 'We are blessed by her presence!'

A pair of purple and yellow liveried soldiers stepped forwards and unsheathed their swords. They dropped

to their knees before her, holding their weapons before
them like an offering.

'Give us Sigmar's blessing, holy maiden!' one of
them said. Within moments, there was a cluster of soldiers crowding around her, and Grunwald swore.

The face of the man in the crowd lingered in his
mind. Yes, he was certain of it – there was an enemy
within the Empire camp.

THE GROUND WAS trampled to muddy slush beneath
Grunwald's feet, and the smell of meat cooking over
fires made his mouth water. He pushed such thoughts
from his mind, and concentrated on not losing sight of
the purple and yellow liveried pageboy as he darted
through the bustling crowd of Ostermark soldiers,
leading him towards the impressive, opulent tent in the
centre of the army encampment.

The boy, who couldn't have been more than eleven,
had approached him as he sat warming himself by a
fire. He had been lost amongst his own thoughts when
he had appeared, requesting Grunwald's presence
within the command tent of the Empire army.

'What do they want with me?' he had asked, but the
boy had shrugged. Placing his broad brimmed hat on
his shaved head, Grunwald had stood, and let the boy
lead the way.

The tent was large, and a guard of soldiers stood to
attention at its entrance, halberds upright in their
hands. Banners of purple and yellow fluttered, and the
boy led the witch hunter past the guards, whose eyes
did not so much as flicker in his direction. A soldier
barred their way. The boy nodded to the guard, and
then ran off into the press of soldiers once more.

'Name?' said the soldier.

'Udo Grunwald, witch hunter,' he replied. The guard nodded in response, and motioning for silence, led him into the tent. The flap was dropped behind him, and it took a moment for Grunwald's eyes to adjust to the light within.

Lanterns hung from the poles of the tent, casting their yellow light across the interior, and Grunwald saw that there were around a dozen soldiers there, gathered around a table where a map was spread. Karl stood alongside a clearly more senior member of the Blazing Sun, his ornate helmet held under one arm. The preceptor inclined his head slightly to the witch hunter.

A middle-aged man dominated the room, his beardless chin cupped in one hand. A huge ring of gold was worn over the leather of one glove, and his clothes were of rich purple and yellow silk, though he wore little in the way of adornment other than the imposing ring.

A sword was strapped at his side, its scabbard beautifully ornate, and its hilt gold and magnificently inlaid. Grunwald realised this was one of the famed Runefangs – awesomely powerful magical swords forged by the dwarfs and borne by the elector counts. It was a potent symbol of their office, and they were amongst the most treasured objects in all the Empire.

Grunwald stared at the Elector Count of the Ostermark, Wolfram Hertwig. He had never been so close to such a highly ranked noble.

The other men within the tent were grizzled veterans, clearly the elector's most senior aides and military commanders. They talked in low tones, and Grunwald saw the elector count sigh and shake his head. It looked like the man had not slept in days.

Looking up, the count saw Grunwald standing in the shadows. His eyes were strong, and his face clearly bore the mark of nobility, but it was not the soft features common in upper classes of the southern states – this was a man of war.

'Who is this?' the elector said simply, his voice carrying a hint of the Ostermark accent, slightly harsher than those of other states and some of his words sounding slightly Kislevite in their pronunciation. Long had the ties between the Ostermark and Kislev been strong.

'This is the witch hunter you sent for, my lord,' replied the guard at the witch hunter's side. 'Udo Grunwald.'

'Come forward so I can see you,' ordered the elector count.

Grunwald saluted sharply and stepped into the circle of light. The elector counts were the most powerful men in the Empire, and at their word armies marched – they paid allegiance to the Emperor Karl Franz, an elector himself, but on the whole their rule was autonomous. They held the power of life and death, and the Elector of the Ostermark was said to be a hard and demanding, though fair, ruler. He held out his hand, and Grunwald crossed the tent and dropped to one knee before the man, lightly kissing the massive golden ring of office.

'Rise.'

'How may I be of service, my lord?' said Grunwald. Though he had never been comfortable around nobility, neither was he one to be cowed by any man, and his voice was strong and confident.

'I understand that you travel with a girl. A true paragon of Sigmar, so it is said.'

'So some would call her, my lord. She is in my charge.'

'The young preceptor here claims her to be quite the warrior,' said the elector, nodding his head towards Karl. Grunwald followed his gaze and stared at the knight for a moment, his face hard.

'And I have heard she has already made quite an impression with the soldiers,' said the elector evenly.

Grunwald's jaw twitched. 'A misunderstanding, my lord.'

'Oh?' said the elector count. 'How so?'

'She is not endorsed by the Temple of Sigmar,' he said, choosing his words carefully. 'She has not had any training, and is ill-equipped to act as Sigmar's emissary.'

The elector took a long swig from a silver goblet that would have cost more money than Grunwald had ever seen. The noble savoured the drink, licking his lips.

'Let me be open, witch hunter. We have no priests with us. The last of them fell against the enemy. And now, the day before battle this girl appears. *The Maiden of Sigmar*, I believe is what the men are calling her.'

Grunwald's gaze flickered to Karl, who had the grace to flush and look down.

'She is but a simple farm girl. Nothing more,' said Grunwald.

'To be frank, I do not care if she is a copper-coin whore or the Queen of Bretonnia. What I *do* care about is the fighting spirit of my soldiers. And they see her as the Maiden of Sigmar, rightly or wrongly – it matters not to me. All I care about is the men believing they can win the fight tomorrow, and that Sigmar is with us.'

'I understand, my lord,' said Grunwald.

'Good. I am sure you will do the right thing, then. Ensure that the girl is seen by the soldiers. Let her walk amongst them. Let them have hope. And tomorrow on the field of battle, make sure she stands amongst the soldiers. Make sure she stands firm against the enemy. Protect her well – I will give orders that she is to be guarded as if she were the Emperor himself.'

'She has never stood on the field of battle before, my lord,' said Grunwald.

'That matters not at all–she doesn't have to *fight* in the front ranks. She just has to be seen,' said the elector. Then he sighed, and looked hard into Grunwald's eyes.

'You were a soldier before you became a witch hunter, is that not so?'

'That is so, my lord,' said Grunwald in reply.

'I too am a soldier. And I do not exaggerate when I say that if we falter tomorrow, then the fate of the Empire hangs in the balance.'

'My lord?' said Grunwald, furrowing his brow, unable to see how this battle would effect the outcome of the war.

'Talabecland is a state under siege, witch hunter. It is attacked relentlessly from Ostland, which is under the control of the enemy. Our forces there are almost over-whelmed as they are. If we fail here, then this army facing us will march uncontested into Talabecland…'

'And strike against the rear of our forces already engaged there,' finished Grunwald, understanding.

'Indeed,' said the elector. 'Talabecland will not be able to sustain a war on two fronts.'

Grunwald nodded his head, his face dark.

'I think you understand the importance of the girl now, witch hunter. If she can strengthen the resolve of the soldiers, then we would be negligent, nay seditious, not to make use of that.'

'I understand, my lord.'

'Good. That is all.' The elector returned to his discussion of troop dispositions and enemy movements. Grunwald made no move to leave, and the guard that had announced him tapped him on the shoulder, indicating for him to back away. He ignored the man and cleared his throat, stroking his long, silver-streaked moustache. The elector looked up, clearly surprised that he was still here.

'Was there something else, witch hunter?'

'Yes, my lord. I spotted someone amongst the citizens today – I believe it was an agent of the enemy, sir.'

There was muttering amongst the advisors. The elector raised a hand for silence.

'Explain yourself, witch hunter.'

'I saw the man only briefly, my lord, but I am certain that he was a witch – a magos, a sorcerer.'

'And you were not able to… apprehend this individual?'

'No, sir. He disappeared into the press. I have been scouring the area for any sign of him, but have thus far been unable to relocate him.'

The elector pinched the base of his nose between his eyes with his fingers as if trying to alleviate a headache.

'I see,' he said finally. 'Speak to Captain Heldemund there on your way out,' he said, motioning towards the soldier at Grunwald's side. 'He will give you whatever men you need. Find him, witch hunter. An enemy launching an attack from within our camp is the last thing we need.'

Grunwald saluted and bowed low before retreating from the tent.

Stepping out into the cool air, he let out a long breath. He made his needs clear to the captain, and organised to meet the men that would be at his disposal in an hour's time. Then, shaking his head and swearing quietly to himself, he stamped back through the snow to find Annaliese.

HE FOUND HER seated outside a tent, dipping bread into a thick broth. Eldanair sat with her, though the elf did not touch any of the human food. Soldiers whispered and stared at the girl, though she seemed oblivious to the attention. She smiled at Grunwald as he approached, her cheeks stuffed with food.

'You should try this,' she said after swallowing her mouthful. Grunwald looked around, feeling prying eyes and ears all around him.

'Come with me,' he said harshly, and turned and stalked away through the press. People scrambled out of his way, and he pushed away those that were too slow for his liking. Annaliese ran after him, licking her fingers.

'What is it?' she said. The witch hunter ignored her, and walked into an open tent. A soldier lying on his back upon a simple unrolled pallet looked up from where he was in surprise.

'Get out,' Grunwald snarled. The soldier blinked, registering the witch hunter's dark garb, then scrambled to his feet and left the tent. Grunwald pulled the tent flap down behind him.

'What is the matter with you?' said Annaliese.

'Your reputation proceeds you,' Grunwald said.

'I don't understand.'

'The Maiden of Sigmar,' snarled Grunwald.

'It's just something stupid that Karl has taken to calling me,' she said.

'Well, it has drawn the attention of the Elector Count of the Ostermark.'

'What? What does that mean?'

'It means,' said Grunwald, his voice low and dangerous, 'that he wants you to live up to the name. It means you are to become the religious talisman of his army.'

'I know I am no priestess,' said Annaliese hotly. 'And I have never claimed to be one.'

'It doesn't matter what you claim to be, girl!' he barked. 'What matters is what you *appear* to be!

'Tomorrow, the enemy will be upon us. And this army believes that Sigmar is with you – and so long as you stand in the battle-lines, their faith is strong. And so, you *will* stand in the battle lines, and you will *not* falter.'

'Is this what Sigmar has sent me here to do?' she said, her face pale.

'It doesn't matter,' said Grunwald. 'You are here, and you now have a duty to do.'

'Why are you so angry? I didn't ask for this?'

'I am angry because you have never stepped foot on a true battlefield, but now you must – and you must appear strong and confident.'

'You do not think I am ready for this.'

'I *know* you are not,' said Grunwald. 'Priests of Sigmar train from childhood to face the enemy without showing fear. Only the strongest are chosen to represent Sigmar – if one of them allows fear to overcome him and he runs, the morale of the men would be shattered.'

'You think I will run?'

'I would not blame you if you did. But that cannot now be allowed to happen. And if for a second it looks like it will, I will kill you myself and claim that you are a witch. Better that than let the soldiers see their *Maiden of Sigmar* run.'

KARL SMILED AS he saw Annaliese approach through the press of soldiers. He had been dutifully oiling and shining his armour and weapons in anticipation of the coming battle, enjoying the camaraderie of being back amongst his order. He stood to greet the girl, his eyes lingering on her shapely form, and he shook his head at her beauty.

'Annaliese, you are a vision...' he began. She interrupted him by smashing her fist into his jaw, and his head rocked backwards from the sudden blow. Her eyes were blazing with simmering anger as he stared at her in shock and surprise, and not a small amount of pain. There was fear in her eyes as well, he noted.

'Why did you damn well come up with that stupid name?' she snarled.

He tongued the inside of his mouth, and spat blood onto the ground. The girl could punch, he would give her that.

'What are you talking about?' he said, bemused.

'The Maiden of Sigmar!' she spat.

'Ah,' said Karl.

'You are a self-centred fool, Karl Heiden.' Bristling with anger, Annaliese turned on her heel and stormed away from him. He rubbed at his jaw, and watched her go. He felt the amused gaze of his knights around him, and he coughed self-consciously. For a moment he stood immobile, caught between going after the girl or leaving her be.

The sun was just beginning to set, and he opted for the latter. He had no wish to be shamed by her again today.

Tomorrow I will seek her out and set things right, he thought. Tonight I will drink.

GRUNWALD FROWNED DEEPLY as he scanned the faces of the Empire citizens arrayed before him. He stared at each in turn before he shook his head to the sergeant, and the people were escorted away. With the men at his disposal he had been rounding up the hundreds of dispossessed, desperate people all afternoon. So far his search for the man he had seen amongst the crowd had proved fruitless.

He sighed heavily. It was to be a long night then, for he would allow himself no rest until the witch was discovered.

HOURS LATER ANNALIESE found the preceptor. Everywhere she went she was hailed by the soldiers who looked at her with hopeful eyes. She found it exhausting.

He was sitting away from his comrades, and it was clear he had been drinking. She hesitated for a moment. She had wished to speak to him, but seeing him morose and drunk, she decided against it, and turned away. Before she could slip away he spotted her, and she cursed inwardly.

'I'm sorry,' he said, his words slurred. 'You are right. I am a fool.'

'Yes you are,' she said, moving to sit down beside him. She pulled her legs up to her chest, hugging herself for warmth and rested her chin on her knees, staring into the fire.

He fumbled around, rising unsteadily and placed a blanket around her shoulders. She smiled her thanks.

'I'm sorry for hitting you,' she said at last.

Karl rubbed his jaw. 'It was a fine punch,' he said with a grimace. She laughed. He offered her his bottle but she got a whiff of the strong fumes and pulled back from it. 'How can you drink that poison?'

'A soldier takes what he can get,' he said, his voice heavy, and she suddenly realised just how drunk he was. A warning bell inside her rang, and she decided she wanted to get away.

'I think I will turn in,' she said. 'Tomorrow will likely be a long day.'

'It will,' said the knight, staring into the smouldering flames.

'Don't drink any more tonight, alright? Goodnight, Karl,' said Annaliese, putting her hand lightly on his shoulder as she rose.

He grabbed her trailing hand and stood, his face flushed. With one hand around her slim waist, he pulled her roughly in close to him, and kissed her passionately. She struggled against him, and he held her tighter, until she pushed back away from him violently, her eyes flashing with anger.

'Go to sleep, Karl. You've drunk too much,' she said softly, though there was a hard edge to her words.

'Just the right amount,' he said, his words slurring slightly. She took another step back and the knight's face flushed with anger.

'Damn it woman! What's the matter with you?' He stood over her, a full head-and-a-half taller than her and easily twice her weight. He reached for her again, and she punched him in the face, her fist cracking sharply against his cheek.

He reeled backwards in shock and surprise, blinking his eyes. When his eyes cleared, they were filled with anger and lust.

With a snarl he stepped in close, grabbing her wrists as she tried to strike him once more. He held her as easily as a child, and he closed his eyes, the smell of her hair intoxicating him.

The next moment he felt a sharp, cold point against his neck, and his eyes flicked open. Eldanair stood at his side, the tip of his slim blade touching his neck. A tiny bead of blood ran down the silver edge of the knife.

Karl let out a dry laugh, and pushed Annaliese away from him. The elf stepped away from the knight, his blade still raised, stepping protectively towards Annaliese.

'I see,' said Karl, nodding his head and laughing softly to himself. 'I see what's going on here.'

'There is nothing going on here except you being a lecherous drunkard,' snarled Annaliese.

'You refuse me because you already have a lover,' said Karl stabbing a finger at Annaliese.

'You are a fool,' she snapped. 'You see nothing.'

'Oh no, I see it all now, *Maiden* of Sigmar,' he said mockingly. 'You've been parading yourself as some virtuous, devout woman, and all the time you have been rutting with this one. Not even a true man!'

'You go too far, Karl,' said Annaliese dangerously.

'Was she good?' the preceptor asked the elf, speaking loudly and slowly as if he were deaf rather than did not understand Reikspiel. The elf regarded him coldly, no emotion showing on his face. The knight made a crude gesture, and Annaliese stepped towards him, her fists clenched.

He blinked then, as if realising his actions, and he wiped a hand across his brow, swaying slightly. He half-fell, half-sat back down and reached for his bottle, taking a long swig.

Annaliese and Eldanair stood there still.

'What?' Karl said eventually. 'Was there something else?'

Annaliese shook her head in disgust.

'You were a man I regarded with high esteem, Karl Heiden. It seems I was wrong to have thought so highly of you,' she spat, before turning on her heel and storming off into the night, Eldanair following.

Karl took another long swig from his bottle, staring into the fire. He gulped down the last of it and threw it onto the flames. He swung around to see if Annaliese had gone. She had.

'Well that went well,' he said to himself.

A moment later, he was on his knees, emptying the contents of his stomach onto the ground. He heaved and brought up everything, until he finally sat gasping, and wiped at his face.

He stood unsteadily and walked to a barrel of water nearby, plunging his hands into it. Ice had begun to form on its surface and it cracked beneath his fingers. He washed his face in the freezing water. Scooping water, he drank deep, until his fingers were numb. More sober now, he thought back over the last half an hour.

'You are a fool,' he said to himself, realising the damage he had done. But then the image of Eldanair's face popped into his mind, and once again he felt anger, hot and fierce.

Curse them both, he thought, and staggered back towards his tent.

DIETRICH CREPT FORWARD in the snow, worming his way through the darkness. His every sense was alert; he saw the silent form of an owl as it passed overhead and could smell the unmistakable stench of burning flesh on the wind. The glow of fires lit up the perfect darkness of the night over the hillock just ahead.

The elector had hand-picked a group of scouts and sent them out earlier to judge the strength of the enemy and gauge its approach.

The elf was somewhere up ahead, an invisible ghost in the darkness. They were in awe of his skills. They had moved out as the silver moon had reached its zenith overhead, moving swiftly into the night toward the enemy. Dietrich knew that he would never have dared to approach had the elf not been leading them – dozens of times through the night they had been saved by the elf, who urged them down into the snow. Moments later, enemies had passed by them, moving through the darkness with no torches to light their way.

They took two of these enemy bands, their shafts hurling the warriors from their horses, leaving none alive. The elf had led them through the enemy patrols and they climbed up a hillock to overlook the enemy encampment.

Dietrich crawled on, ignoring the biting cold. He almost cried out when Eldanair appeared before him like a phantom, a finger placed on his lips. Dietrich quickly signalled for his men to freeze, and they sank into the snow, motionless at his command. The elf disappeared up ahead, and Dietrich lay there unmoving for long minutes, wondering what was going on. Had they been discovered? No, there had been no warning shouts, or sounds of alarm.

A moment later the elf was back, beckoning him forwards. Edging around an ancient rock, Dietrich came upon the first corpse. The body of the enemy warrior was huge, and his powerful arms were covered in golden torcs. Countless rings of metal pierced the flesh of his bearded face, and he wore a circular black iron breastplate over his heavily muscled torso. A helmet lay in the snow beside him, tall horns cut from an animal that Dietrich did not recognise rising from it.

He saw Eldanair rise to his feet like a shadow behind another sentry and clamp his hand across the man's mouth and nose. A blade flashed in the night as he stabbed through the heavy fur cloak of the enemy warrior, again and again. The hulking figure was easily twice the weight of the elf, but he was dead in seconds, and the elf lowered the body into the snow.

Dietrich inched through the snow to the elf's side, and his eyes widened as he overlooked the enemy encampment.

The size of the army was immense. Campfires spread as far as the eye could see. There must have been tens of thousands of enemy warriors here. And not just men – chained in long pickets were massive hounds covered in thick fur, beasts almost the size of ponies. They lay sprawled on top of each other as they slept, jaws hanging open to show huge fangs and lolling tongues. Further away from the encamped warriors were other, larger shapes. Their forms were hidden in darkness, but they were huge, easily the size of the largest bears that Dietrich had even heard of, but he instinctively knew that these were not natural creatures. No, their shapes were perverted and mutated from decades of exposure to the warping effects of Chaos.

Eldanair got his attention with a light touch on his shoulder, and pointed into the distance, to the north. At first Dietrich could see nothing, squinting over the glowing remains of five thousand fires, but at last he saw movement. Mounted figures were riding across the open land away from the camp.

There must have been around three hundred of them, riding for the north. Heavy chariots pulled by midnight steeds rolled out amongst the mounted warriors, snow kicking up behind their metal-studded wheels.

Dietrich knew that this was vital information that he needed to get back to his commander, for it certainly appeared as though the enemy was sending a fast moving force to circumvent the Empire line – and quite possibly attack it from an unexpected angle once battle was met. He knew that such a move could tip the balance of the battle.

Taking one last look over the enemy encampment, estimating their number, he began to crawl backwards down the hillock away from the enemy. Once in open ground, the scouts began to move as swiftly as it was safe to do, dogging the enemy horsemen. They would follow them for a few hours to gauge their direction before turning back towards the Empire lines.

IT WAS DAWN, and Grunwald, sitting just outside his tent, was stripping down and meticulously cleaning his weapons. They were laid out on an unrolled sheet of leather, and he polished and oiled the mechanisms of first his wheel-lock pistols, then his heavy, black metal crossbow. The barrels of the guns he cleaned out with a fine cloth and a ramming rod, gazing along the barrels to ensure not a speck of dust or dirt was within.

He was angry, and the simple act of maintaining his weapons calmed him somewhat. His night's work of scouring the citizenry had garnered nothing, and the dull thumping of a pressure headache made him even more irritable and tense.

He was angry with himself for taking his eyes off the man, and was frustrated that he had been unable to discover his whereabouts. He had even begun to doubt himself – perhaps the man had been nothing more than a frightened peddler – but he knew deep inside that he was not. The fact that the man had clearly hidden himself was evidence enough of his guilt.

Annaliese found him there, and sat alongside him in silence as he worked. The witch hunter enjoyed the quietness of early morning, and made no effort to talk to the girl, and he was glad when she too seemed content to remain in silence.

'I am scared about the battle,' she said at last.

'It's only normal,' he replied, blowing an errant speck of dust out of the wheel-mechanism of one of his guns.

'You don't seem too worried.'

'It would be a fool indeed who didn't have some fear in him on the day of a battle,' said Grunwald, casting his careful gaze over his weapon, turning it in his hands, seeking any fault or tarnish. 'Either that, or a madman.' Finding no defects, he turned his attention to the black metal bolts of his crossbow, studying the tip of the first. Satisfied, he lifted the bolt and stared along its length, ensuring that it was perfectly straight, with no deviation in it that would effect his aim.

'I am neither a fool or a madman,' continued Grunwald. 'And so, I fear the coming battle. But it is what that fear does to you that is the important thing. Either you master it, and use it to your advantage, or you let it master you. Let it master you and it will grow and grow within you, until you are nothing but a slave to it.'

'Use fear to your advantage?' said Annaliese, furrowing her brow. 'How is fear an advantage?'

'Fear keeps us alive. It is fear that tells us not to walk on the cliff edge in a billowing gale.'

'But only a fool would do that.'

'Or a madman. But another example – if controlled, fear lends you strength, speed and crystal clear clarity of mind. If it is left unchecked and controls you, it will work against you – cause you to react slowly, if at all.'

Annaliese nodded. 'I remember being out hunting with my father once. We were surprised by a bear. I froze – unable to run, to shoot, to do anything but stare at it. It would have killed me had my father not been there.' Annaliese's eyes were glazed over as she remembered. She looked up at the witch hunter, snapping herself out of her reverie. 'What happens if I freeze up today?'

'Then you will die,' said Grunwald simply. 'My advice? Don't freeze up.' He lifted one of his pistols quickly, testing the wheel-lock mechanism. 'It doesn't matter if you are scared – you just must ensure that the Maiden of Sigmar does not show it.'

Thorrik appeared from amidst the bustle of soldiers busying themselves before battle, stamping heavily to get the snow off his boots. His face was thunderous, and he sat down heavily and pulled his dragon-headed pipe from a pouch.

Grunwald raised a questioning eyebrow to the dwarf.

'North!' Thorrik spluttered. 'My clan has gone to the north!'

'North? We are *in* the north,' said Grunwald.

'Kislev! They have marched into Kislev with an army from Reikland!'

'Kislev? But the war is here, in the Empire. What the hell are armies doing marching there?'

'Seems that this so-called Raven Host is massing north of Kislev. What is here already is only its vanguard. Your Emperor has sent an army into Kislev to fight it – and my kinsmen have marched with them!' The dwarf harrumphed loudly, and began muttering to himself in his own language.

'So, if we survive the day, you will march northwards then? What, to the city of Kislev itself?'

The dwarf snorted. 'Further than that – the army marches on Praag.'

Grunwald's eyes widened. Praag was far to the north of the Kislev, thousands of miles north of their current position. It would take weeks, months to travel there. He whistled in awe.

'Ah well,' said Thorrik. 'We have this battle to get through first. You will be fighting too I hear, lass?'

'I will,' said Annaliese.

'I will be in the front ranks. That's where an ironbreaker fights. I just hope you humans will stand firm alongside me.'

'We will,' said Annaliese with grim determination. 'We have to.'

CHAPTER TWENTY-ONE

THE CLEAR BLUE morning sky was slowly overtaken by the relentless, brooding dark clouds clawing their way across the heavens. Shadow engulfed the Empire lines and Grunwald shivered as the temperature dropped. He was alert and wary for the reappearance of the magos he had seen in the crowd the previous day, certain that he would rear his head before the day was out.

Lightning crackled through the heavy clouds, rippling back and forth with intense flashes, accompanied by the relentless dull rumble of thunder. Bright bolts seared down to the ground beyond the crest of the moorland, jagged lines of power and light that were followed a second later by deafening booms that made the knights' horses whinny in fear.

The storm was moving forwards like a living malevolent being, and it seemed to carry with it powerful, hateful emotions that promised death and destruction.

Grunwald noted that Annaliese was breathing heavily, her face pale, as she watched the cloudbank rolling towards them.

It was like a black mountain spur, its tip heading inexorably in their direction – a thick wedge of darkness that slid ever closer. The apex of this elemental force halted above the crest of the high moorland, just beyond the shadowed village, as if it had hit an invisible barrier. The weight of the clouds built and they darkened so that they were now almost black and began spilling around the sides of the village like a pair of giant horns, surrounding it menacingly.

A great shadow of darkness that seemed to ride before the cloud mass detached itself from the storm and flew low towards the village. Grunwald saw that it was a mass of black-feathered birds, thousands of them flying together, and they filled the air with their raucous cries. Diving low, they flew over the heads of the Empire soldiers, their harsh cawing a deafening chorus and the beating of their wings disorienting. As a single living mass flying as one, the ravens blocked out the sky completely, and they flew low enough that men were forced to duck their heads, and many of those who did not wear helmets suffered cuts from stabbing black beaks and lashing talons. The living mass wheeled again, a maddening maelstrom of black feathers, and dozens of soldiers fired crossbows and handguns into the mass before their sergeants restored order with harshly barked commands.

Scores of ravens fell to the ground, their wings shattered by bolt and lead shot, their bodies broken and flightless. They flapped on the ground uselessly, feathers drifting down in their wake, wings hanging limp behind them. One struck Annaliese as it fell, and she cried out in shock. It cawed deafeningly and its long beak and talons lashed out, drawing blood on her neck before she managed to frantically hurl the creature to the ground before her. It flopped around in a circle, its left wing and leg a bloody ruin, and it fixed Annaliese fiercely with one beady eye. Anger burnt within the shiny orb, simmering rage and malevolence projected from the raven that was as large as a small dog. Up close Grunwald could see that its feathers were not truly black, but rather a shimmer of colours could be seen on them, like the rainbow of oil on water.

It cawed and opened its beak aggressively towards Grunwald as he stepped towards the dying creature. He killed it beneath his heavy black boot, crushing its fragile bones and silencing its raucous, disturbing cries.

The ravens overhead circled once more before screaming back overhead, flying low over the land towards the rise of moorland. Like a flowing carpet of black feathers the fell birds of the enemy flowed up the rising, rocky earth and disappeared over the crest of the moors.

At that moment, the first dark figures could be seen at the crest of the highlands, standing dark and motionless, silhouetted against the flashes of lightning behind them. They stood immobile, like ancient statues of long-dead, infernal warrior-gods, a line of them that spread along the crest, dark, imposing and deadly.

It was as if the ravens had metamorphosed into these terrible warriors. Grunwald wondered if they would turn back into the hateful carrion birds at the battle's end to pick over the corpses and pluck at their eyes.

The horned helms of the motionless warriors of Chaos could be seen clearly against the backdrop of flashing light. Huge standards were held before them, and although the images upon the human-skin banners should have been hidden in shadow, they could be seen clearly – twisting, blasphemous glyph-shapes of blue fire that flickered with cold light of their own.

A ripple of fear ran through the Empire line as the soldiers saw the warriors of the Chaos gods.

The warriors were massive, each easily a head taller than any man of the Empire. They were raised as brutal fighters from birth, the weak amongst them ruthlessly culled. They were taught to hold a sword or axe from the moment they could stand, and before they had reached eight summers they were already seasoned killers, preying on those weaker than them and offering up their souls to the dark gods of Chaos.

Only the strongest and fiercest of them reached adulthood, and every one had proven himself before their daemonic gods.

But as nine bolts of lighting struck the earth below the ridge simultaneously, the figures that had been mere silhouettes were thrown into sharp focus, and the sense of terror and pervading doom amongst the Empire lines was redoubled. For these were not average warriors of Chaos, but the chosen elite of the Raven Host.

Each warrior was fully armoured in dark metal, and wore an enclosed helmet tipped with curving, daemonic horns. In the centre of every helmet was a glowing blue gem fashioned in the shape of an unblinking eye. They hefted brutal killing weapons– swords, axes and heavy spiked mauls – that a normal man would be unable to lift in two hands, let alone one as many of these warriors seemed to do effortlessly. Many bore tall shields tipped with spikes and barbs, and each of these also had an unblinking blue eye on its centre. Cloaks of raven feathers were thrown over the massive shoulders of these elite warriors, the chosen of Tzeentch, and they surveyed the village and meagre lines of quaking Empire soldiers unmoving.

To either side of the motionless chosen warriors more of the enemy appeared, and massive stakes of metal were driven into the ground along the ridge. Each of these was easily fifteen feet high, and upon each was spitted a man wearing the purple and yellow of Ostermark – clearly Empire soldiers slain in an earlier confrontation, perhaps in the fall of Bechafen itself.

No, not slain in an earlier battle, Grunwald realised – a great groan of horror rose up amongst the Empire ranks as they saw that these soldiers were not dead at all. The impaled figures twitched and flailed in agony, kept alive and in torment by the fell magics of the enemy. The moans and cries of the tormented men of the Ostermark echoed down from the ridge to the village, and Annaliese covered her mouth as she heard their agonised, desperate wailing.

A thousand stakes were raised along the ridge, and larger ones too were hefted into position with ropes and chains – each of these had five or more soldiers impaled on them. Ravens landed on many of these tortured men, tearing strips of flesh from them and pecking at their faces – but not one of them was dead.

'Why don't they attack?' said Annaliese, her voice strained.

'They are trying to scare us,' said Grunwald.

'It's working,' said Annaliese. She swallowed with difficulty, her mouth and throat dry.

'Or they are waiting for something,' said the witch hunter. He craned his neck, looking back to where the citizens crowded, back behind the lines of soldiers. His gaze passed over the mass of desperate humanity, but he did not see the face he sought – the heavily lined face of the witch he knew was lurking back there somewhere.

KARL SAT ASTRIDE a massive destrier, glad at last to be back in the saddle. He felt the horse beneath him trembling with fear and anticipation. Leaning forward he patted it heavily on its neck, talking in gentle, comforting tones. He knew how it felt.

The knights' steeds stamped their hooves, ears flat against their heads. They were uneasy and tense. Such was generally the way before a battle, but the fear that washed down over the Empire lines was almost like a living thing. It washed around them, making men sweat despite the icy chill. The sky continued to darken, the massing cloudbanks encircling the village almost completely.

Karl wished the enemy would just advance, so this waiting would end. Battle would be met, and then the killing would start, and he could lose himself in the melee.

He tried to push away the thoughts of the previous night's encounter with Annaliese, but her shocked and angry face kept appearing in his mind's eye, the look of fear as he had pulled her roughly to him haunted him. He gritted his teeth and shoved the image to the back of his mind, but it kept rearing up within him, taunting and painful.

He felt shame tear at him. What had he been thinking, he wondered? What evil had overtaken his senses?

She had brought it on herself, said a dark voice within him. She had tempted him for weeks, with her seductive looks and luscious eyes. She had led him on, making him think that there was something between them. But all the time she had been laughing at him, her and that cursed elf.

Karl closed his eyes against the maddening thoughts, striving to drive them from his mind. Had the enemy infected him with some vile sorcery? No, he answered – this was but jealousy and desire, very human emotions, and they had been enflamed by drink.

What a fool he had been! He had blown his chance with the girl, and he had no one to blame but himself.

It mattered little now though, he thought darkly, as he gazed up at the enemy standing motionless along the ridge of moorland. Soon, he would lose himself amid the cacophony of battle, and it would not matter any more.

Feathers sticking up from soft caps bobbed up and down as Karl watched around two thousand archers, handgunners and crossbowmen moving lightly forwards, angling their lines opposite the marshy dip at the foot of the moorland crest.

Phalanxes of state soldiers marched forwards more slowly behind them, halberdiers and swordsmen, their wildly fluttering banners flying. In the centre of the line were the greatswords, a block of hard-bitten soldiers with massive two-handed blades resting on their right shoulders. Great plumes topped their conical helmets, and they stepped forwards in perfect unison, for they were the elite foot troops of the army, its most seasoned and veteran soldiers.

Light cavalry hung back from the main line, and further regiments of spears, halberds and pikes stood motionless along the edge of the village. An unruly rabble of refugees was arrayed; thousands of desperate survivors from outlying villages and towns that followed the army. They stood watching over the battlefield from whatever vantage point they could find, waiting to see the outcome. Karl knew that if the day were lost, then they would all be slaughtered.

The Empire commanders had tried to force these stragglers to leave the area, but it was an impossible task. In truth, Karl could understand that they did not wish to be away from the army and the protection it gave them. Though how long that protection would last would soon be determined.

Karl wondered where Annaliese was. He turned in the saddle, looking across at the soldiers' frightened faces. He spotted the witch hunter Udo Grunwald first – he was hard to miss standing amongst the soldiery, wearing his trademark heavy black greatcoat and wide-brimmed hat. He stood with a small group of soldiers to the rear of the gathered forces. He seemed to be looking for someone, staring around him.

Karl's eyes widened as he recognised Annaliese standing alongside the witch hunter. She wore a close-fitting sallet helmet, though her face was bare, and her head was held high as she stared fiercely across the battlefield towards the motionless enemy. Her hammer was held in one hand, and she wore a circular shield upon her arm. Plates of armour protected her arms and shoulders, and the hem of her long chainmail coat could be seen beneath her red and cream travel-worn robe.

She was a shining, radiant light amongst the soldiers. The Maiden of Sigmar she was, and truly she looked the part as she waited fearlessly for the battle to commence. He stared at her in open awe and admiration. Then the shame of his actions pounded in at him, and he turned away, cursing himself.

'WHY DON'T THEY damn well come?' growled Thorrik, stamping his feet, trying to get some feeling back into his cold toes. He stood in the front rank of a phalanx of halberdiers, the other soldiers towering above him. The men around him were silent, their faces grim. Further along the line, the purple and yellow standard of the Ostermark whipped loudly in the rising winds.

At last there was movement from the ridge, as warriors lowered their heads and moved respectfully out of the way of a giant figure upon a snorting black steed. The figure wore ornate, fluted armour of gold, and its gleaming helmet was topped with coiling horns that twisted around each other. An eye of blue fire the size of a man's torso hung in the air between these horns, the flames burning fiercely with unholy light. A large black pupil hung within the centre of the burning blue iris, and as another bolt of lightning slammed into the earth before the Chaos lord, this pupil contracted sharply so that it was little more than a vertical black slit, like the pupil of a serpent.

The fell steed stamped its hooves, and its eyes blazed with pale fire. It was armoured with ornate, fluted gold barding in the same manner as its lord, and a similar array of twisting horns coiled from its head.

The massive warrior wore a long cloak of feathers, and it billowed behind him like a death-shroud. He hefted a huge bladed glaive one handed over his head as his infernal steed reared up on its hind legs, and lightning arced down from the heavens once again, striking this long weapon. Electricity coursed over the figure, crackling over its armour before it earthed itself into the ground beneath the daemon-steed's hooves.

The sound of the lightning bolt striking reached the Empire lines a second later, and it sounded like the earth had been split down the middle. Horses reared and screamed in fear, and the knights struggled to bring them back under control.

The last electric flickers of lightning coalesced across the Chaos lord, and he began to speak. His words were those of a daemon, and they rolled out before him like a deafening wave, reaching the ears of every man standing upon the field of battle, as if the fell lord of Chaos screamed in their ears.

It sounded as though there were a thousand roaring voices bellowing as one, and the Empire soldiers around Thorrik took an involuntary step backwards as the wall of sound struck them. There were screams and roars of fury and pain in that voice, and the cries of tortured souls.

The words were alien and meaningless to the men of the Empire, but great was their power. There were moans of fear amongst the soldiers around Thorrik, and several fell to their knees, covering their ears in a futile attempt to block out the horrendous din. Thorrik himself gritted his teeth and gripped the shaft of his axe tightly, grimly weathering the storm of screaming, incoherent words.

* * *

GRUNWALD FELT THE power of the words of Chaos battering against his sanity, and he resisted their power. Annaliese at his side grasped her pendant of Sigmar and began mouthing words of prayer, her face defiant. The witch hunter felt the building of power, and clenched his teeth as he felt the electric tang of magic charge the air.

A regiment of soldiers standing some fifty paces ahead of his own position were suddenly engulfed in a blurring maelstrom as the fabric of reality was shredded.

A hundred men fell to the ground as a surging wave of daemonic energy enveloped them, screaming and roaring. They convulsed madly and those nearby backed away, horror on their faces. The men began to writhe, screaming, and their flesh seemed to ripple and contort. Bones bulged beneath flesh as they grew uncontrollably, bursting through skin to form giant pointed growths. Spinal columns became twisted and erupted from men's backs, spikes of bone growing from vertebrae and impaling other wildly mutating men. Feathers sprouted along the forearms of some, bloody and covered with mucous, and tentacles burst from the chests of others, reaching to the sky like questing leeches.

Mouths were forced open far beyond their natural limits, and massive tusks of bone burst from jawbones. Other men were drawn together, their flesh merging, and eyeballs weeping blood opened up in their skin alongside fang-filled mouths that screamed in agony.

Thunder rumbled overhead as the soldiers' flesh mutated and altered maddeningly, as if the fell daemonic gods of Chaos were pleased.

Screaming and bellowing in pain and anger, the monstrous spawn-creatures created from the flesh of the Empire soldiers lashed out around them with barbed limbs and powerful claws, snapping bones and ripping their erstwhile comrades apart. Mouths filled with rows of teeth snapped out, locking onto arms and necks, crushing and killing. Upon legs broken and mal-formed, the spawn crawled and staggered, reaching towards the soldiers of the Ostermark with flipper-like appendages and whipping, worm-like tentacles.

The soldiers fell back from these monstrosities that were moments before their friends and comrades, and scores of them were killed beneath the ripping jaws and flailing limbs of the spawn.

Grunwald stepped out from the line of soldiers he had chosen to accompany him in his hunt for the witch. He turned around on the spot, his eyes flicking around.

At last he locked onto a dark figure standing in a crooked eyrie on top of one of the village buildings. A strange rotating metal globe turned on top of the building, a mechanical, clockwork contraption that showed the position of the moons and passage of the sun. The figure of the man he had been searching for all night was standing there, his staff raised above his head as he mouthed an incantation.

As the attention of the entire army was directed at the enemy lined against the sky and the monstrous, hor-rific creatures that were causing havoc, no one had looked back and seen this dire figure.

Suffer not the witch to live was one of the mantras of the witch hunters, and Grunwald had no intention of letting this one live any longer.

With a barked order for the soldiers around him to fall in behind, he began running towards the building, keeping his eyes on the morbid figure. He roared as he ran, ordering the terrified crowd of citizens out of his way. They melted back as he ran, soldiers running at his heels.

Still, the press of people was too great for a path to be cleared before him, and he bashed people out of his way in his eagerness to close in on the enemy. People fell screaming to the ground, only to be trampled beneath the press.

'There! Go!' shouted Grunwald, directing the soldiers towards the building, and he hefted his crossbow to his shoulder, taking aim at the witch who was still incanting on top of the eyrie.

The black bolt sliced through the air, thudding into the wooden banister an inch from the magos. The figure jerked, his incantation interrupted and stared down at Grunwald with hate-filled eyes.

Snarling, the witch thrust his staff in Grunwald's direction, and a searing burst of blue flame shot down towards him. The witch hunter gripped his icon of Sigmar tightly, mouthing a prayer and bracing himself. He felt the icon heat up in his hand as the hellfire roared towards him. Daemonic faces could be seen within the licking flames, snarling and hissing. People screamed and ran, and the flames burst around him like a raging inferno.

But they did not touch him. Instead they washed harmlessly around him, as if they had struck a physical barrier. He could see the malevolent forms of daemons as they clawed at him, and they hissed and spat as they were denied. Still the blue flames pushed in at him,

and he dropped to one knee as he felt the wave of evil
energy beating at him. The temperature rose sharply as
the flames burst around Grunwald, and steam rose
from his damp clothes. His face was hot from the raging conflagration just feet from him, and he shielded
his eyes against it, but it did not touch his skin and a
second later it was gone. He stood in a tight circle of
melting snow, though all around him the ground was
scorched and blackened from the fire.

Feeling a presence behind him, Grunwald turned to
see Annaliese standing there, her hammer held high.
Wrapped around her wrist was a chain from which
hung her pendant of Sigmar, and it seemed to glow
with fading light. Her eyes were locked onto the fell
sorcerer, and truly she looked like the Maiden of Sigmar that people were claiming her to be. Grunwald
wondered briefly if it had been her faith or his own
that had protected him from the enemy magic, but it
mattered not – all that mattered was that the witch was
alive – and he needed to die.

Grunwald saw that the panicked masses had halted
in their mindless flight, turning to look upon
Annaliese with awe-struck eyes.

'The Maiden of Sigmar!' someone shouted, and he
felt the raw power of their belief.

'Stay back here!' shouted Grunwald to the girl as he
saw the dark shape of the enemy sorcerer snarl and
abandon his post. His heart burning with hot fury and
anger, the witch hunter began to run once more
towards the building, pushing through the motionless
crowd who were staring at Annaliese in awe.

His soldiers were waiting for him, though they had
taken up positions around the building so that the

sorcerer could not escape. The building looked like
some kind of warehouse, its upper levels converted to
a rich abode. At Grunwald's nod, one of the soldiers, a
veteran warrior built like an ox, kicked a side door in,
the wood around the frame splintering.

Before he could shout a warning, the soldier had thundered inside the darkened warehouse, his momentum
carrying him forward. A light flared, and coruscating
energy enveloped the man, crackling through the colour
spectrum as it washed over his skin. He fell to the ground,
twitching and convulsing and bulges appeared beneath
his clothing as his flesh mutated.

One of Grunwald's pistols boomed, the shot slamming into the soldier's head and ending his torment,
but still the body shuddered and contorted with
malign magic. The soldier's face bulged as fingers
pushed impossibly from within. A pale talon ripped a
hole through his skin, and long, multi-jointed fingers
struggled to tear the flesh away. Like a suit of fine
clothes being ripped open, the man's skin was torn
from the crown of his head to his sternum, the steel of
his breastplate melting and bubbling away as if it had
been subjected to an inferno. The body of the soldier
was ripped opened before the horrified eyes of his
comrades, and the mutilated, perverted corpse
thrashed around on the ground as the foul daemonic
entity pulled itself from within.

The air was filled with the stink of ozone and cau-
terised flesh, and the infernal being rose from the still
convulsing corpse like a demented newborn, its pink-
ish flesh covered in blood and mucous.

It was crouched, and its eyes blinked open as it
unfolded its long, gangly arms. It seemed to have no

head, or rather its head was squashed into its chest, and its yellow irises were filled with insanity and unholy, manic energy. Worm-like protuberances appeared in its flesh and they waved around blindly, foul and disturbing.

A long slash of a mouth that almost bisected its torso split open, exposing thousands of tiny, coral-like teeth, each one covered in miniscule barbs. It exhaled, a long throaty breath, and a bluish mist of magical energy coiled from within the foul creature, and a demented giggle from the pit of hell erupted from the creature's lips. Like a discarded flesh-shell, the split corpse of the soldier that had birthed this foul daemon still twitched upon the ground at its feet.

With a snarl, Grunwald stepped forward and slammed the sole of his boot into the creature's face. He connected solidly, his whole weight behind the blow, and the creature was thrown backwards. It rolled, cackling hysterically, and scrambled about on the floor, gangly arms shaking above it.

'Cleanse this place in the name of Sigmar!' Grunwald roared, surging inside the warehouse, the soldiers a step behind him.

He heard a muttered incantation in the tainted dark tongue of Chaos, and threw himself into a roll as an arc of purple light reached towards him from the wooden staircase that climbed up to the second level and beyond. It impacted with the wooden table beside him, and its form was instantly altered almost beyond recognition, the curving wooden legs twisting, barbs and spines erupting through the woodgrain. Its solid surface sagged inwards like melting wax before bursting into green flames.

A blue fireball roared past Grunwald as he rose to his feet, hurled by the cackling daemonic creature that had fashioned it out of the air above its head. There was a desperate screaming behind him as the flames caught several soldiers, but Grunwald did not turn. With pistol in one hand and his flanged mace in the other, he leapt towards the fell being. The pistol boomed, taking the creature in one of its wild eyes, and it stumbled backwards, blue smoke coiling from the wound. It began to melt, its unnatural form turning to viscous liquid as it died.

Leaping over the vanquished daemon, he surged up the staircase, taking them three at a time. He could see the magos now, backing higher away from him, blue fire streaming from his eyeballs. He had a smile on his face, and Grunwald snarled as he closed in on the hated foe.

Something grabbed his leg as he leapt up the stairs, and he fell heavily, face first into the solid wood. He felt claws bite through his thick leather trousers, and turned around kicking at whatever held him. It was a smaller version of the creature he had just killed, though its flesh was blue-tinged and it wore a frowning expression rather than manic glee upon its face.

Further down the stairs a soldier was battling against another of the blue-tinged daemons that had birthed from the dying corpse of the first infernal being, and Grunwald saw him fall screaming to his knees as the creature clasped its long fingers around his face. Smoke and the stink of burning flesh rose from beneath its grasp before another purple and yellow liveried warrior clove his sword down through the creature's head.

Grunwald kicked again at the monstrosity clinging to him, and its claws bit deeper, piercing his skin. Its fanged maw opened wide to close around his leg, but then a spear tip emerged from between its eyes, and it was lifted up and away from him by one of the soldiers. A blast of blue fire consumed the man, melting his flesh to the bone.

Grunwald rose on one knee, his hand reaching into his boot. The magos stood at the top of the warehouse stairs facing him.

'Feel the power of Tzeentch, pitiful mortal,' said the magos as he lowered his staff towards Grunwald, but the witch hunter's hand flashed out and a dagger struck the man in his throat. He dropped his staff and clutched at the blade. Blood bubbled between his fingers and he stumbled forwards, falling heavily down the stairs.

As the figure rolled past, Grunwald kicked him hard, smashing the magos through the banister to fall ten feet to the hardwood floor below.

'Grab him!' he ordered, and three men leapt upon the fallen magos. 'Hold him tight,' said the witch hunter as he stalked down the stairs, each boot fall echoing loudly now that all was silent bar the witch's gargled gasps.

He stepped over bubbling masses of ichor, all that remained of the daemons summoned by the man. Unrolling a leather package he wore at his belt, Grunwald selected an implement from amongst his myriad tools, and knelt down alongside the magos. He held the pair of black iron pliers before the witch's face, enjoying the look of pain and fear there now that the blue fire had left the orbs.

'Open his mouth,' he ordered a soldier standing nearby, whose face was pale. The man nodded, and knelt down alongside the witch hunter, forcing the magos's jaws open.

Grunwald grabbed the man's tongue with his pliers and pulled it out as far as he was able. Then he brandished a knife before him.

'You shall not speak your foul incantations as you burn,' he said, and began to cut. He prayed to Sigmar that this was the only enemy within their midst.

Outside, the hideous sound of the daemonic voice had died, to be replaced by the resounding beat of a thousand enemy drums.

The ground reverberated as the Raven Host advanced.

CHAPTER TWENTY-TWO

As IF THE magos's first horrific incantation had been the signal to attack, the enemy marched down from the highlands to battle. While the Empire commanders sought to regain some order to their battle line and more of the mewling monstrosities spawned of Chaos magic from the flesh of Empire soldiers were slain, the enemy closed towards the village.

The chosen warriors of the Chaos host remained motionless on the ridge, but thousands of warriors descended around them, screaming praises to their gods and their war-drums pounding.

Dressed in furs and hefting weapons of dark steel, the marauders surged down the slope, a sea of warriors, their huge muscles daubed with swirling, tribal war paint. Some amongst them bore the favour of the gods, their flesh having been blessed by change – arms altered in form, muscles and bones warped into brutal killing appendages, or thick tusks jutting from their jaws. These warriors were revered as mighty champions, for the touch of the gods upon them was clear.

They screamed as they raced down from the high land into the mire at its base, and into the range of the guns of the Empire. As they surged into the ice-covered marsh, plunging thigh deep into the icy waters, the first cannon shots boomed. Smoke and flame burst from the barrels of the mighty weapons of Nuln, and cannonballs smashed into the first ranks of the marauders, ripping limbs from bodies.

The massive balls of steel and iron skidded off the ground and bounced through the massing warriors, tearing through legs and bodies, crushing everything in their path. Under the watchful gaze of their lord and his elite chosen warriors, the marauders continued on, uncaring of their losses, scrambling through the mire over their dying companions.

Scores were drowned in the icy, reed-choked waters, and soon the marsh was thick with the dead.

Though a section of the Empire line was in chaos, as the blood-frenzied mutated spawn continued to lay around them causing havoc, the other sections of the army were unscathed, and they advanced upon the enemy struggling through the morass in the dip below the moorland.

At a shouted signal hundreds of arrows were nocked to strings and crossbows readied. Handguns already primed were lifted to take aim.

With a shout, the barrage began, and the sky was darkened further as the first flights of arrows arced high into the air. Before they had even struck home, a second barrage of arrows was launched. They fell amongst the warriors of Chaos, and scores of men were struck. The shafts thudded into their bodies, piercing chests and necks, driving through thighs and heavily muscled arms. Men stumbled and were trampled into the marsh, but the survivors toiled on, and they reached the rising banks of the morass, struggling onto solid, snow-covered land.

The handguns and crossbows of the Empire spoke then, and great swathes of battlefield were obscured by the smoke of the guns firing. The crack of the handguns echoed sharply off the higher slopes, and hundreds of warriors fell as the wall of lead shot struck. The powerful weapons punched through shields and helmets as if they were made of paper, and more enemies were laid low as crossbow bolts drove through flesh. The cannons boomed again and they tore through the line of marauders.

Thousands of men were killed in the first moments of battle, but it was just the beginning of the slaughter that was to come.

SURROUNDED BY A circle of soldiers, Grunwald stalked out into the open, kicking the staggering, bloody figure of the enemy magos before him. The crowd were pushed out of the way with halberds and spears, and he came to a halt in their midst. The sorcerer was on his knees, his chin and front soaked in blood, and he made pathetic sounds of agony, his tongueless mouth wide and dripping with gore.

One of the soldiers stepped forward at Grunwald's order, and upended a small barrel of oil over the witch, who screamed incoherently. Another handed Grunwald a lit lantern, and he held it high above his head.

'Witness the fate of those who consort with diabolic powers!' he shouted, turning on the spot so that all could hear his words. 'Such is the fate of all who oppose our lord Sigmar! And such will be the fate of the enemy army this day!'

Grunwald brought the lantern smashing down to the ground at the feet of the oil-drenched magos, and he was instantly engulfed in flames. His clothes and hair were burnt from his body, and his flesh blackened and blistered as the searing heat of the fire did its work.

Rising to his feet and with blood gushing from his mouth, the magos stumbled towards the crowd but a solid strike from the shaft of a halberd smashed him back to the ground. His tortured screams rose to the heavens, and the gathered citizens cheered loudly, pounding the air with their fists as the enemy was burnt to death, thrashing madly.

Within moments the life had departed from the witch, and he lay still.

With blood splashed across his face, Grunwald led the soldiers from the crowd. As he broke from the heaving mass of humanity, he saw the lines of the Empire soldiers and the swarming ranks of the enemy close.

THORRIK HELD HIS gromril shield before him as the barbarian hordes ran towards the Empire line, screaming and roaring praises to their dark gods. At a barked order, the halberdiers around him braced their long weapons, their deadly spiked ends extended outwards towards the charging foe, a sea of metal that the enemy raced into.

The distance between the armies closed quickly, and Thorrik saw the faces of the men he was about to kill.

They were fierce, many covered in tattoos and war paint, and they towered over him just as they towered over the men of the Empire. They roared as they raced across the even ground, swinging massive war-axes and barbed swords back for killing blows.

'For the Emperor Karl Franz!' shouted the sergeant of the regiment. 'Now!'

The halberdiers took a step forward as one as the fur-cloaked northmen drew close, thrusting the spiked points of their weapons into the foe. The enemy struck with sickening force, and hundreds were impaled in the first onslaught as they ran headlong onto the Empire soldiers' weapons.

The men of the Ostermark were driven backwards by the sheer weight of the enemy, and the screams of the dying and the clash of weapons was deafening. In front of Thorrik, one bearded enemy warrior dropped to his knees as a halberd point took him in the throat, blood gushing from the wound, and another roared through clenched teeth as he died, spitted upon another of the long-hafted weapons. A massive broadsword smashed down onto the haft of another halberd, which splintered beneath the blow, and Thorrik stepped forward and swung his axe into the midriff of the towering warrior, cutting him down before stepping back into line with the Empire soldiers to either side of him.

The strength and weight of the enemy was immense, and they pushed forwards relentlessly, drawing within striking range of the Empire line. Some halberds were ripped from the hands of their owners as impaled enemies sank to the ground, while others were smashed apart with heavy blows. The blood of the soldier to the left of Thorrik splashed across the dwarf's armour as a

sword blade hacked into the side of his head, the
power of the blow ripping through the metal helmet
and skull with ease. To his right, a soldier was cut down
as a heavily muscled barbarian smashed his blade
down onto his collarbone, the blade driven deep into
his flesh.

Thorrik's axe blade slashed out, cutting the
marauder's neck open, and blood pumped from the
wound before he dropped and was trampled into the
ground.

The second rank of Empire soldiers lifted their
weapons high, and the axe-blades of the halberds
smashed down onto the heads and shoulders of the
enemy, cleaving through metal and crunching through
bone. Arms holding shields aloft were broken by the
force of the powerful blows, but the enemy was
amongst the soldiers of the Empire now, and the
killing began in earnest.

Fuelled with growing resentment as the men at his
side were hacked down, Thorrik hacked around him
with fury. He chopped through one marauder's forearm, the severed limb dropping to the ground, still
gripping a sword tightly. With his reverse blow, Thorrik
smashed the axe into the man's face, and he was
knocked backwards, his skull cleaved.

Blows rained in against him, but Thorrik weathered
them all with dwarfen stoicism, growling with anger as
each attack struck against his armour. His fury rose
with each impact, and he hacked around him madly,
his wrath lending him strength.

Nevertheless, in a close quarters fight, the enemy
were stronger, fiercer and had less fear of death than
the men of the Empire, and they began to drive the

Ostermarkers back. Scores of soldiers were dying, and Thorrik could sense that the battle was shifting in the enemy's favour.

'KNIGHTS OF THE Blazing Sun! Forward!'

The resplendent line of knights kicked their steeds forward, and they began to gallop across the open ground, their lances held upright. Karl rode in the lead, his face grim beneath his helmet, as they rode towards the melee.

The ground thundered beneath their hooves, and the preceptor felt a savage joy to be riding into battle once more – it had been too long. Hearing the pounding of hooves as the heavily armoured knights moved across the battlefield, the enemy turned to face this new threat, and a splinter force detached from the main force, its line wheeling to take the charge of the knights.

That was what Karl had been hoping for, and he altered the angle of the knights' approach, riding hard for the gap that was opening up in the enemy line.

The banner of the order whipped like the sails of a great ship in the wind, and Karl rejoiced at the feeling of speed and power. It had been a great honour to be placed in command of the regiment, for never had he led so many of his warrior brethren into battle. The head of the temple of Bechafen had taken the remainder of the knights to the north-east, for word had come in the early hours before dawn of a fast moving enemy strike force that was seeking to outflank the Empire army, and he had deemed the threat serious enough to ride out and meet it personally.

Turning his head to the side, he nodded to the knight riding beside him – the only knight amongst the

regiment who did not wear a full face, visored helm –
and the man lifted a horn to his lips and blew a series
of long notes upon it. The sound blared across the
battlefield before them, and Karl began to lower his
lance from its upright position.

'Myrmidia, guide my lance,' he said, invoking the
goddess of his order.

The warriors they were closing in on hurried to close
the gap in their lines, but Karl could see that they
would be too slow to react. Still, they showed no fear,
moving eagerly towards the knights thundering across
the field. As they pounded ever nearer and the knights
lowered and couched their lances, Karl picked out one
particular warrior as his target. The warrior had a
swirling blue icon painted on the left side of his face,
and the same marking was painted upon his bare chest.
In his left arm the man hefted a brutal axe, but his right
arm was what attracted Karl's attention, for it was far
from human in nature. From beneath the warrior's
heavy metal shoulder plate it emerged, the limb covered in dark feathers. There was an extra joint between
wrist and elbow, and the fingers had been reformed
into the gripping talons of a great bird, though they
were a striking yellow in colour.

The knights thundered toward the enemy, and Karl
lifted himself in the stirrups, readying for the strike.
The barbarian snarled up at him and ducked to the side
but the preceptor had fought for many years on horseback, and followed the man's sudden movement with
his lance tip.

He took the marauder high in the chest, his twelve-
foot lance driving through his body and bursting from
his back. A second man, close behind the first, was also

spitted on the lance, its length piercing his neck and killing him instantly.

Then the knights were amongst the enemy, riding hard through their midst, and Karl released his grip on his lance to draw his broad-bladed sword. His steed lashed out with flailing hooves, crushing skulls, and more were trampled beneath the weight of the warhorse. Karl slashed with his sword as the knights ploughed through the enemy formation, hacking down warriors as they sought to bring him down.

Their charge began to slow, and he saw several knights fall as their steeds were cut from beneath them. Horses screamed as axes and swords cleaved into their legs, and another knight was felled as he was impaled on a long sword blade, lifted out of the saddle by the shuddering blow.

Karl shouted, trying to maintain the momentum of the charge, urging his steed and his warriors on. An enemy grabbed his armoured leg, he slashed down with his sword, opening the man's skull, and kicked his warhorse hard, driving the stallion on.

And then they were out of the frantic melee, bursting from the rear of the enemy formation. Karl's eyes widened as he saw what was waiting there and his steed reared, whinnying in terror.

A spiked club almost the length of a wagon smashed into the head of Karl's steed, and blood splashed across the preceptor's black and bronze armour. He saw the ground come racing up towards him as his warhorse fell.

ANNALIESE STOOD WATCHING the two forces embroiled in combat, their lines blurred together in the nightmare of battle. Her breath had caught in her throat as she saw the Knights of the Blazing Sun smash through the enemy lines, and she wondered briefly if Karl was amongst them. Then they had disappeared, seemingly swallowed up by the enemy, and she saw them no more.

Her breathing was heavy, and her heart was beating wildly within her. The screams of the dying echoed dimly across the field, and the true horror of warfare washed over her. Still, she tried to maintain an exterior of calm, knowing that the soldiers around her were looking to her for strength.

The cannons continued their barrage, belching smoke and flame across the battlefield, but she could see that the lines of archers and crossbowmen were pulling back, jogging lightly towards the village, and putting more distance between them and the enemy. The handgunners still stood in their serried ranks, each line kneeling as they reloaded, allowing those behind to fire over their heads.

The secondary line of Empire soldiers was urged forwards, and they broke into a run to aide the faltering battle line. Annaliese found herself running with the bustling crowd of soldiers across the snow-covered field, her hands shaking as they clung to the haft of her hammer and her shield. She felt heavy and constricted by the armour she wore, the unfamiliar weight awkward and shifting as she ran.

Eldanair moved lightly at her side, launching arrows from his longbow as he ghosted across the snow, his white fletched arrows arcing through the air to fall amongst the dark ranks of the enemy. Even his presence did little to buoy her, but she clenched her teeth and pushed her fear down, lest it overtake her. She wished that Grunwald was with her, but she had not seen him since he had entered the building in pursuit of the enemy magos. Where was he? she thought wildly.

HOOVES FLASHED AROUND Karl as horses reared and bucked. He pushed himself up out of the mud and slush, his vision swimming before his eyes. His sight cleared as he raised himself to one knee and he looked upon the monstrous creatures before him.

They stood over ten feet in height, and their hulking bodies were covered in fur and scarred with battle-wounds and ritualised markings burnt into their flesh. Their heads were heavy and bestial, and were supported by massive necks of rippling muscle. Steam snorted from their nostrils, and giant horns extended from either side of their heads, just above bovine ears. Their eyes blazed with blood-frenzy and hatred, and they carried immense weapons in their human-like, oversized hands. True creatures of Chaos, they had emerged from the forests in the north to join the slaughter.

Karl rose to his feet as one of the monsters leapt into the air. The beast brought its massive axe smashing down onto one of the knights, splitting him from the shoulder to the waist. The dead warrior slid from the saddle as his steed reared, ripping the axe from the creature's hands and it lashed out with a balled fist. The blow caught the horse on the side of the head, and it collapsed to the ground, a tangled mess of limbs.

A knight urged his baulking steed forwards and drove the point of his sword deep into the beast's chest, and it bellowed in pain and outrage. It grabbed the knight around the throat and lifted him from the saddle before slamming him forcibly into the ground.

'Myrmidia!' shouted Karl, hefting his sword over his shoulder. He stumbled forwards and brought it down into the beast's neck, severing the arteries there. Blood fountained from the wound, but the creature did not die. It shook its heavy head from side to side, foam flying from thick lips, its red eyes focused on Karl.

With a snort it surged forwards and hooked one of its horns between his legs. In one violent motion it flicked its head up and hurled him into the air, his arms and legs flailing. He smashed into one of his fellow knights, and they both toppled to the ground.

He came up groggily, and as a massive cleaver flashed downwards he threw himself backwards. The blade smashed down into his fallen comrade, who was cut in half by the blow, Karl staggered to his feet.

A riderless horse reared next to him and blindly he reached out and grabbed at the reins. He caught hold of them, and swung himself up into the saddle. It was mayhem all around him as his knights battled the bestial creatures vainly, being butchered by the brutal monsters.

'Blazing Sun!' he cried, his voice cutting across the din of bellowing beasts and screaming horses. 'With me!' he shouted, and kicked the horse hard. It broke into a run, and Karl raced free of the one-sided battle. 'With me!' he roared again.

LESS THAN A third of the Knights of the Blazing Sun rode clear, and they rode hard back across the field. The battle-crazed minotaurs raced after then, bellowing in anger and baying for blood.

The knights veered off to the south suddenly, leaving the way clear for the handgunners. The first rank of guns barked and the soldiers dropped to their knees. The second rank of handgunners fired, and they too dropped down to their knees, frantically reloading their long weapons as the third rank opened fire.

As the smoke cleared, there were few of the minotaurs still standing, and those that were staggered unsteadily, their bodies pierced dozens of times, blood seeping from their wounds and matting their thick fur.

The knights, having wheeled around upon the open field, thundered back towards the massive beasts, and the last of them were hacked down beneath their swords.

DIETRICH BIT HIS lip, tense and alert. He knew that four miles to the south battle was underway – he could hear the pounding of cannons – and he prayed for the men there. But he had seen the scale of the army arrayed against the Empire, and he could see little chance of victory.

Such a fickle thing, chance. He thought that somewhere in the heavens above Ranald, the god of chance and trickery, was chuckling to himself, and Dietrich swore that he would dedicate a year's pay to the trickster's acolytes if the god smiled upon him today.

Luck was all that would save them, he thought. If the enemy cavalry took a wider arc around the battlefield and attacked from the rear, then any chance of victory would be dashed. If the oil of the engineers had soaked too deep, or the snow deadened its effect, then hope was lost. If the enemy noticed something strange about the snow ahead of them, if they noticed that the snow here was more melted than it was elsewhere – an unexpected side-effect of the oil – then the ambush would fail even before it had been launched. Ranald, he prayed, give us just this chance.

One of his men shouted, and he looked up.

'Dietrich! They come!'

The scout scrambled to the edge of the high ground, crawling forward to look down into the narrow defile below. It was perhaps three hundred yards wide, and the snow hid the cobbled road beneath.

In the distance to the north a shimmer of movement could be seen, and Dietrich's heart leapt. The enemy were on the road, riding hard in their direction.

'Thank you,' Dietrich muttered, casting his eyes to the sky.

He squirmed back away from the lip – scrambling and running down the slope on the other side.

'Get them fires blazing, boys!' he shouted, and dozens of braziers were stoked. Dietrich watched the sky carefully for any hint of smoke. He had instructed his men to use only the driest tinder, for any hint of smoke in the sky might warn the enemy, and they could easily avoid the trap if they suspected anything. Little smoke drifted up from the braziers, and he let out a slow breath that he had not realised he had been holding.

'They are getting close, sir!' came the shout from the lip, and Dietrich ordered the braziers to be carried up the slope. Each was borne by a pair of men, the metal urns carried on a pair of wooden poles.

One of the men slipped on his ascent and a brazier toppled sideways with a crash, the burning embers falling into the deep snow. A cloud of steam rose where they fell, and a sharp hissing filled the air. Smoke began to rise as the coals touched the wet grass beneath the snow.

Dietrich swore and leapt through the drift, whipping the cloak from his shoulders. He leapt at the steaming circle, throwing his worn cloak over it to dampen it. Leaping to his feet, he stamped on the area until the coals had been put out, soaked by the melting snows and driven into the moist earth. Standing back, Dietrich looked at his blackened, muddy cloak and turned to the scout who had stumbled with a sour expression.

'We get out of this, and I'll be having your cloak,' he said.

The other braziers were in position, just behind the lip of the hillock and Dietrich took his position. The forty men lay unmoving, just behind the rise, and he prayed that no enemy scouts had seen them. If the enemy just turned off the road and travelled for a hundred yards along the higher, rougher ground, then this risk would come to nothing.

But on they came, riding hard. In the lead were around two hundred and fifty horsemen riding stout steppes ponies, hulking hounds of terrifying size loping alongside them. The riders were cloaked in furs and carried spears. Their steeds were swift – not as fast over a short distance as the big destriers that the Knights of the Blazing Sun rode, but they could run for hours on end without tiring. Over a day, the distance these horsemen could travel would far outstrip the noble templars.

Behind them came the heavy knights of Chaos. They rode midnight steeds that stood easily twenty-five hands tall at the shoulder, massive beasts whose eyes blazed with unholy light. The knights were ensconced in black armour, and they carried deadly weapons of war. They each wore a flowing cloak of feathers, and an eye of brilliant blue shone in the centre of their black helmets.

Alongside these dread warriors of Chaos rolled deathly chariots, barbed scythes rotating on their steel-rimmed wheels. A pair of giant black steeds pulled each of these heavy war machines, and fully armoured warriors stood on their armoured platforms, nail-studded whips cracking.

There were no more than fifty of the monstrous knights of the enemy, but the aura of terror they exuded was palpable.

'Stay on the road, stay on the road,' Dietrich willed them, every muscle tense. Closer and closer they came, and he waited for the moment when they would spot something amiss, something that would alert them to the ambush. But still they came, registering no alarm or knowledge of the threat they were riding towards.

With a nod, Dietrich held his first arrow to one of the braziers, and the oil-soaked rag tied around its tip lit instantly. Along the line of the hillock, fifty archers did likewise.

'Now!' he shouted, and rose to one knee. He pulled his bowstring taut and loosed in one smooth motion. The weight of the oil-soaked rag threw the balance off the arrow, but he had compensated for this, and it flew true.

He heard yells from the enemy as they spotted the archers up on the ridge, but they had come too far to avoid what was to come next.

Fifty arrows sliced through the air around the horse-men, and around a dozen of them were struck. Other arrows sank into the flesh of their horses and the bru-tal hounds, and they bucked and kicked in pain and fear, and filled the air with their deep growls and yelps. But it was the arrows that struck the ground itself that did the real damage.

Flames raced as the oil that had been doused across the area in the hours before dawn caught. The flames burnt hot and fierce, and scores of men were thrown down as their horses bolted, their tails and the long hair around their hooves catching fire.

The long shaggy fur of the hounds caught fire, and they barked and roared, and snapped at anything nearby. Horses' legs were crushed in their massive jaws, and fallen men had their throats ripped out by the frenzied beasts. Other war hounds ripped at each other, rolling over through the blaze, further spreading the fire.

Sudden explosions erupted amongst the panicking horses, for along with the oil, the engineers of the elec-tor's army had hidden a series of small wooden caskets packed with black power just beneath the snow. As the oil caught and flames whipped up the road to the north, it ignited these oil-soaked caskets and they exploded outwards. Horses were thrown to the ground, and men screamed as their flesh was seared by the det-onations. One horse's leg was blown off, and chunks of flesh rained down upon the others.

Scores of them were killed in those first moments, but the destruction was not yet complete. As expected, the horsemen who had not been engulfed in fire pulled back away from the inferno, and it was then that the other group of scouts, positioned further to the north, launched their attack. More flaming arrows arced down onto the rear of the enemy column, and a second wall of fire reared up, blocking their retreat.

The horsemen and hounds milled in between the two barriers of fire, and they were brutally cut down by wave after wave of arrows. Dietrich went through a full quiver of arrows and moved onto his second, for the enemy had nowhere to run – the ground was too steep and rough on either side of the road for them to climb, and their passage forward and back was blocked by the fire which no horse would approach.

Dozens of men leapt from the backs of their horses and ran towards the scouts, attempting to scramble up the steep ground, but they were sitting targets to the archers, and they were mercilessly cut down, one by one.

The hounds, however, had no such trouble ascending the broken ground, and they leapt up the precipice with frightening speed. They bore dozens of scouts to the ground beneath their weight, jaws snapping, breaking limbs and ripping flesh. One man was shaken like a rabbit in the jaws of a hulking beast, and his back broke with an audible crack.

One of the monstrous war hounds leapt at Dietrich, jaws latching onto his forearm and throwing him to the ground. Its growling filled his ears, and its hot breath was on his face, and he cried out. He reversed his grip on the arrow in his free hand and stabbed its point into the beast's head, but felt the tip break against the stone-like cranium of the monster. With one final, desperate stab, he pushed the wooden arrow shaft through the creature's eye, and it released him with a snarl.

Dietrich regained his feet, his arm a bloody ruin, and drew his hunting knife. He leapt on the wounded war hound, and plunged his blade into its neck, time and time again, until at last it was still.

The heavily armoured Chaos knights urged their infernal steeds on, and continued to canter up the road, ignoring the mayhem around them. Chariots rumbled along beside them, dozens of arrows stuck in their armoured sides.

Wincing at the pain in his arm, Dietrich aimed carefully and fired, watching as his arrow cut through the smoke and fire and struck one of the knights high in the neck. The warrior barely flinched, and the arrow fell harmlessly to the ground. The scout swore.

And then the knights rode their horses straight through the flames as if they mattered not at all.

Swearing again, he reached for his last oil-soaked arrow, and lit it from the brazier. Drawing his string back hard, he fired the arrow straight up into the air.

SEEING THE ARROW that symbolised that the ploy had failed, the Knights of the Blazing Sun kicked their steeds forwards, and a hundred templars began galloping over the rough moorland, three hundred yards further south, hidden from view from the road.

They rode towards the rise, and saw the enemy knights and chariots cantering perpendicular to their position. They thundered down the clear slope before them, lowering their lances. Their horn blared, and their steeds were urged faster, and they smashed into the side of the enemy formation. Massive black armoured enemy knights were ripped from their saddles, and horses screamed as they were knocked to the ground by the force of the impact.

Spiked chariots, their wheels flaming with oil, tried to turn towards this sudden threat, but they were unwieldy machines and the Blazing Sun templars were on them in seconds. Lances smashed the warriors from their chariots, and the black, hellish steeds reared and bucked. One of the chariots hit a stone as it turned, and as one of its steeds collapsed screaming, a lance buried in its chest, the entire chariot flipped over, throwing its occupants to the ground.

The knights of Chaos fought back ferociously, their massive weapons cutting the Empire warriors from the saddle, cleaving through armour like paper. The impetus was with the templars of Myrmidia and they ploughed through the thin Chaos line, killing scores in that first charge. Almost half of their number had fallen, but they wheeled around towards the surviving, feather-cloaked despoilers of the north.

The shock of the attack was now lost, and the two cavalry forces smashed together as they both urged their horses into the charge. Within minutes, both forces were all but decimated.

THORRIK HACKED AND cleaved as he stepped backwards, keeping pace with the weakening Empire line. He hated the idea of giving anything to these enemies, but he knew that if he stood his ground he would be surrounded in seconds and cut down. How he wished he stood alongside doughty dwarf warriors rather than these manlings!

He grunted as a sword smashed into his helmet. He battered the next attack away with his shield, and carved his axe into the knee joint of an enemy, splintering the bone and sending the warrior crashing to the ground. He disappeared amongst the press, replaced by another pair as they shouldered their way through the fray.

Feeling the fragile courage of the Empire soldiers faltering, knowing that it would shatter at any moment, Thorrik roared and surged forwards. If he was going to die here then at least he would make a good account for himself, enough for him to be welcomed in the halls of his ancestors. He powered into the first man, striking with his shield rim and crushing the bones of his arm. He buried his axe into the neck of the other, and hot blood pumped from the mortal wound.

He deflected another thrusting sword blade on his shield, but a powerful blow from an axe connected with his side, and he stumbled. He could taste the sharp, metallic bite of blood on his lips, and another blow struck him, a spiked hammer that smashed into his left shoulder, bending the ancient metal out of shape. It could not breach his thick plate armour, nor the fine-meshed chainmail underneath, but he felt his bones crunch beneath the blow, and shooting pain ran down his arm.

Thorrik hacked sideways, smashing the axe into the ribs of an enemy. The blade of the weapon was lodged there for a moment, and as he struggled to pull it free, a swinging shield knocked him back a step. He lost his grip on the axe, and was spun around as a sword clipped his wounded shoulder.

Disoriented and in pain, Thorrik sank to his knees.

* * *

ANNALIESE'S HEART WAS thumping wildly as she charged into combat at the head of the Empire line. She swung at the head of a hulking bearded figure that towered above her, but her blow was easily intercepted as the warrior stepped forward and lifted his blade into the path of the descending hammer. He died as Eldanair's sword speared out, taking him in the throat, and then the lines of the Empire soldiers were blurred with those of the enemy as the two sides smashed into each other.

Annaliese was knocked to the side as she took a blow on her shield, and she cried out in fear, the battle a swirl of chaos all around her. The air was filled with screams and shouts, the deafening sound of weapons clashing and the sickening sound of swords cleaving through flesh and bone. She was bustled and knocked from every direction, and frantically kept her shield up before her, her eyes wide and panicked.

She looked into the eyes of an Empire soldier, his face covered with blood, as he fell at her knees, and a sudden calmness descended over her. Anger and a stubborn refusal to let the enemy overpower her rose within her, and she lashed out, her hammer slamming into the side of the face of one of her foes. The blow crushed bone and dislocated the man's jaw, sending him reeling, where he was impaled upon the sword of another soldier.

'For Sigmar!' Annaliese screamed, and struck again, her blow this time turned aside by a warrior's shield. Nevertheless, another Empire soldier stepped forwards and stabbed his sword into the neck of the marauder, the blade sliding easily through flesh.

'Sigmar!' roared the soldiers around her, and they stabbed and blocked furiously, blood splattering.

Dozens were hacked down beneath the brute power of the enemy, but the Ostermarkers pushed forwards, cutting and hacking.

Eldanair spun, his long sword in one hand and a knife held in a downward position in his other. He felled an enemy warrior with his flashing sword, the blade cutting deep into his neck before he slashed his knife across the face of another, then reversed the blow and stabbed the blade up into the man's sternum as he reeled backwards.

The elf spun neatly, blocking a thrust that would have impaled Annaliese, and stabbed his knife into an eye socket. Another blow that would have killed the girl was deflected by the shield of an Empire soldier who died in the next breath as a spiked hammer pulverised his head.

Annaliese smashed her hammer into the arm of a tattooed berserker, his face transformed into a hellish visage of hatred and frenzy, crushing the bone and rendering the arm useless. Ignoring the pain, the berserker swung a mailed fist into the girl's head, knocking her to the ground. She ripped the helmet, which was dented out of shape, off her head, and stared up at the manic killer looming over her.

A sword cleaved down and split the berserker's head open, and his hot blood splashed over Annaliese's face. She looked up into the face of her saviour, seeing Karl Heiden's eyes through the narrow slit in the black and gold helmet as his steed reared, hooves flashing out. For a second their eyes met, and then the knight was ploughing deeper into the enemy formation, hacking left and right.

Eldanair hefted her to her feet, and she wiped the blood from her hand to get a better grip on her hammer. Then she surged forwards once again, hurtling back into the fray.

Grunwald had seen no sign of Annaliese, but pushed on through the brutal melee, battering his way into its midst, his eyes flashing around trying to find the girl.

Through the chaos around him, he saw a short figure fall to the ground, and broke into a run, bashing a man out of his way with his shield and clubbing another to the ground with his mace.

Then he was at the dwarf's side, just as knights appeared all around, smashing through the enemy lines. There was a moment's respite in the wake of the thundering knights, and Grunwald dropped to one knee beside the ironbreaker. He was amazed at the amount of damage the dwarf seemed to have taken – his armour was dented and pierced in a dozen places, and his helmet and shield bore testament to the number of attacks that had been landed against him.

'Thorrik! Are you hurt?' he shouted over the din.

'I'm fine,' snarled the dwarf, and Grunwald tried to help him rise. He weighed a ton – it would have been as futile to try to lift a mountain.

'Get off me, manling!' Thorrik thundered. The witch hunter saw that the dwarf's left arm was hanging limply at his side.

'It's fine,' snarled the ironbreaker, seeing Grunwald's eyes.

There was a ragged cheer, and Grunwald straightened up, looking around him. He could see few enemies, and these were hacked to the ground as he watched, pierced by dozens of swords and spears. A halberd smashed down into the back of a wounded enemy marauder, felling him instantly. The ground was strewn with the dead and dying, and the soldiers set about them, smashing their weapons into the fallen bodies of the enemy.

The word passed quickly through the ranks, and there was the sound of Empire horns blowing. The enemy was in flight!

Men cheered and held their weapons up high into the air in defiance.

'Victory!' shouted one soldier, but the witch hunter shook his head, his eyes locked onto the dark ridge overlooking the battlefield.

HIGH UPON THE moorland overlooking the field of carnage below, a doom-laden pounding began. It reverberated down across the land like the heavy beating of a daemonic heart as the massive, armoured sentinels who had been overseeing the progress of the battle began to beat upon their shields with their weapons in perfect unison, the sound potent and instilling fear in the bloodied Empire soldiers below.

Mounted on the back of its snorting hell-steed, the flaming blue eye hanging in the air above its head, the warlord of this massed host of Chaos lowered his long, barbed glaive towards the weakened Empire lines.

To the beat of the reverberating sound of weapons upon shields, the elite warriors of the Chaos forces, the chosen of the dark gods, began to march down to battle. And as blue flames erupted all along the shaft of its ancient daemon-weapon, the warlord of the host descended at their head.

CHAPTER TWENTY-THREE

THE FEAR PROJECTED by the dark warriors, who had long
sold their souls to the infernal power of Chaos, was like
a tidal wave, and it burst across the Empire lines, washing over them in an all-consuming torrent. Men cried
out in horror as they felt the icy chill that came with the
wave of fear, and weapons dropped from shaking
hands as they watched the hellish figures advancing
down toward them.

Terror engulfed the Empire men and blue fire hurtled
from the tip of the warlord's glaive. It smashed
amongst the centre of the Ostermarkers, and men
screamed as their flesh was melted from their bones
and their armour was twisted out of shape. Terror
turned to panic, blind and numbing, and the Empire
line broke.

Men began to stream away from the advancing
enemy, banners were dropped into the mud and blood

and slush, and templars were thrown as their steeds
bucked and kicked.

Grunwald knew then that all was lost, all hope of victory gone as the soldiers' resolve was smashed like a
fragile crystal beneath a hammer. Ranks turned away
from the hellish foe, and men pushed and shoved at
each other in their urgency to flee. All order was broken, and the panic turned into a rout.

Men were trodden into the ground underfoot in the
frantic crush. Grunwald was knocked to his knees, and
feet trampled over him, kicking and lashing out in their
hurry to run before this infernal foe. He swore as he
fought against the crowd, and he lost his grip on his
shield as heavy feet smashed down onto it.

He was struck in the head as he tried to rise, and was
knocked down again. The threat of being killed
beneath the weight of the crush was very real, and he
fought like a cornered animal to rise above it.

He saw a flash of blonde hair and a panicked face,
and he lifted himself up, drawing one of his pistols.

ANNALIESE WAS CARRIED along with the crowd, their fear
fuelling her own, and her mind was blank, her desperate need to get away overcoming all rational thought.
Then she saw Grunwald before her, saw the anger and
strength in his face, and her whole world became
focused upon him. Her vision narrowed, and she
stared down the black barrel of the gun pointed in her
direction.

The words of the witch hunter floated through her
mind.

*I will kill you myself.... Better that than let the soldiers see
their Maiden of Sigmar run.*

She jerked to a halt, though she was knocked and pushed from behind.

It all came down to this moment, she thought. Let the fear overcome you now, and if you survive, you will be running for your whole life, a slave to its whim.

She had somehow lost her shield – she could not remember where, or how – and she clasped her hand around the pendant of Sigmar still hanging from her wrist. She held onto it like a talisman, like it would save her, something that would buoy her in this sea of terror.

She turned around slowly, her head held high, standing against the terrified flow of humanity surging around her. A shoulder struck her in the chest, and she almost fell, but she forced herself upright. A hand clutched at her leg, and she looked down to see the blood-splattered face of a soldier looking up at her with fearful hope in his eyes. Then he was dead, dropping face-first into the mud, and she saw the pole clutched in his other hand.

The banner was tattered and trod into the ground, covered with blood and mud and grime. She reached for it, prying the dead soldier's fingers loose from its grip, straining with all her might to lift it. The press of bodies was too much and she cried out in despair as the weight of failure fell on her as she realised it could not be done. But then Grunwald was at her side, and between them they managed to lift the banner up into the air.

It fluttered in the wind, rippling the heavy fabric, and then it streamed out over the heads of the fleeing warriors. In the breeze, it seemed like the griffon emblazoned on its surface was flying,

* * *

GRUNWALD FELT A profound sense of awe as the banner was lifted high, and for a moment it seemed as if a golden light surrounded Annaliese. She stood, strong and defiant, the pole of the standard held in her hand.

'For Sigmar!' he roared at the top of his lungs as faces turned to his direction. Men slowed in their rout as they saw the streaming banner of the Ostermark and saw the battered and bloodied girl holding it aloft.

'The Maiden,' someone muttered and more men slowed, drawing to a halt as they gazed in awe at the fluttering banner and the girl.

'For Sigmar!' Grunwald roared again, his voice cutting across the field.

Annaliese began to walk through the confused ranks of soldiers, her head held high and the wind ruffling her blonde hair as she strode forward, the banner held up above her head.

Like a ripple that spread across a lake from the tiniest pebble being thrown into its centre, the mindless rout was stemmed. Seeing other soldiers turning to watch the girl stride through the army, more and more warriors halted their flight and turned back towards the foe.

'The Maiden of Sigmar!' someone bellowed, and the shout was repeated, rippling along the lines and filling the hearts of the warriors with new hope.

Grunwald shook his head in disbelief as he followed in the wake of Annaliese. Soldiers pressed tightly all around, pushing and shoving as they marched behind the Maiden of Sigmar.

To the very front of the Empire army she walked, holding the banner aloft. A clear path opened up before her, and she strode through it. Then, with no more men before her she stared defiantly out across the open field, strewn with the dead, towards the infernal ranks of dark warriors drawing ever nearer.

She lifted her hammer high into the air.

'For Sigmar!' she shouted, and the entire army of the Empire echoed her.

Then, shouting her defiance, she broke into a run, heading straight for the heart of the enemy lines. With a roar, the army of the Ostermark surged forward around her.

THE MEN OF the Empire fought with inspired, devout fury, but they were as children against the massive armoured chosen warriors of the Dark Gods, and they were cut down in their hundreds.

The soldiers formed a protective shield around Annaliese, desperate to ensure the Maiden came to no harm, but they were fighting a losing battle.

One of them was cut down, his arm hacked off at the shoulder and he fell screaming. Another was smashed in the face by a massive armoured gauntlet, and he stumbled. A sword punched through his breastplate and he was lifted high into the air before being hurled from the blade with a dismissive flick.

The chosen of Chaos were like demi gods of war, and they butchered their way through the Empire lines. They strode into the breach before Annaliese, hacking down Empire soldiers to the left and right. Grunwald pushed forward and smashed his mace into the face-plate of the first, piercing the metal, but the warrior did not fall, and he back-handed the witch hunter, sending him staggering back. Thorrik bellowed a dwarfen war cry and smashed his axe into the warrior's midriff, cleaving through the thick metal and felling the mighty foe, but others laid into the soldiers surrounding Annaliese, destroying and killing everything in their path.

Then the enemy lines parted, and the fell warlord of Chaos appeared, astride his towering black infernal steed. The massive beast stamped its barbed hooves, smoke rising from beneath them, and its eyes were lit with blue flame. Tusks emerged from its equine mouth, and steam filled the air with each powerful exhalation.

The warlord was huge, and the blazing blue eye hanging in the air between the curving horns of its helmet was locked on the defiant figure of Annaliese, holding the banner in one hand and her hammer of Sigmar in the other. The lord of Chaos could see that the resolve of the Empire army centred around the girl, and he approached her with sickening finality, intending to break her and send her soul screaming to the realms of Chaos.

The battle raged on around them, but Annaliese was suddenly oblivious to anything but this awesome and terrible being.

Nausea and crippling sickness struck all who gazed upon the thrice-cursed figure. Its features were hidden beneath a full-faced helm, though brilliant azure flames blazed in its eye sockets, the startling colour reflected upon the shimmering surface of the raven-feather cloak draped over the warlord's broad shoulders.

In one huge, spiked gauntlet the dread lord held its spiked glaive, the haft easily ten feet long and covered in bony spurs. It lifted its other gauntleted hand into the air, and a crackling sphere of pale light appeared in its palm, blue sparks of electricity flickering up its arm.

Nobody moved, entranced by the power of the devil before them, and Annaliese lifted her head high, staring into the eyes of the enemy even as her soul cringed and recoiled within her.

The flaming blue eye of the gods that hung above the warlord's head flicked to the left as there was a sudden flash of movement at Annaliese's side. Eldanair, his movements swifter than the human eye, had nocked an arrow to the bow he had unslung from his back, and drew back the string to fire. Faster even than the speed of the elf, the warlord hurled the ball of light held in its hand, and it smashed Eldanair in the chest, throwing him backwards, arcing electricity engulfing his body.

Annaliese cried out.

Thorrik stepped forth hefting his axe, but was smashed aside by the powerful blow of a Chaos warrior, and Grunwald levelled his pistol at the warlord's head, and fired.

The blue eye of the gods flicked in his direction, and he felt his soul shrink. The slitted iris of the daemonic eye widened slightly as it focused on the lead shot, and it was halted a mere foot away from the warlord's head, hovering impossibly in the air before him.

The warlord swung his head in Grunwald's direction, and the shot reversed its direction. It smashed into the witch hunter's shoulder and he fell with a shout of pain.

Then the dread lord of Chaos turned his eye back towards Annaliese, and he spoke. His voice was that of a daemon, a thousand voices speaking within him, and he spoke not in any tongue that would be understood by the soldiers of the Empire.

Nevertheless, his words were understood, as if reformed in the air, making them comprehensible to all.

'I am but the herald of the Raven Host, its harbinger. Know before you die that everything you have ever known will be smashed asunder, destroyed and forgotten. Everyone you have ever known will be slaughtered and their souls tortured for all eternity for daring to resist the great gods. And now, bitch of the weakling man-god Sigmar,' he said, his voice full of madness and horror, 'you shall die.'

The warlord guided his steed forwards, looming over Annaliese, and she could feel the hot, foetid breath of the creature, smell the diabolic stink of its unnatural presence. She lifted her hammer up into the air before her, a seemingly futile, tokenistic show of defiance. She felt very small and utterly alone, and the voice of the creature pounded in her mind.

Your soul shall be a delicate morsel for the Great Changer of Ways.

She felt the edges of her sanity begin to fray, and her heart was beating so hard in her chest it blocked out all sound, blood pumping heavily in her head.

Any moment, she would be cut down, impaled upon the glaive wielded by this fell lord of destruction, her bones smashed beneath the pawing hooves of his infernal steed. Her soul would be ripped screaming from her shattered physical form and enslaved to the daemon gods of Chaos, there to exist in an eternity of torment amidst a roiling nightmare.

'Sigmar,' she whispered, her voice sounding tiny and insignificant against the inferno of hateful sounds entering her head. She prayed that their bloodthirsty enemy had been held at bay for long enough that the armies of the Emperor in Talabecland would not be overwhelmed. She prayed that her sacrifice and the sacrifice of the soldiers of the Ostermark was not in vain.

A thunderous din rose amongst the chaotic roar of battle raging around her, and she raised her face to the heavens in despair as death drew near. The deafening rumble of thunder increased in intensity, and dimly she registered the sound of brass horns blaring like infernal trumpets summoning her to hell.

The flaming blue eye flicked to the right, its slitted pupil contracting and expanding, and Annaliese looked around her in confusion.

A living wall of knights appeared, smashing through the enemy ranks and crushing the warriors of Chaos beneath them. She saw lances pierce chests daubed with infernal symbols, and swords smash down through horned helmets. The knights were armoured in gleaming silver, and mighty plumes of red and white rippled in the air on their helms. They bore shields of white emblazoned with Imperial wreathed skulls and crosses, the symbols of the Emperor himself. They ploughed through the enemy, and Annaliese stared up at them in wonder and awe.

With a roar of denial and outrage, the lord of Chaos swung his glaive, the daemon weapon wreathed in coalescing light as it ripped through the air, renting the fabric of reality. The blade sheared through the chest of the first knight as if it were paper, cleaving the warrior in two. With his return blow, the warlord thrust the blade of his weapon deep into the armoured chest of another knight's steed, lifting the screaming beast high into the air and tossing it and its rider over his shoulder.

Annaliese stumbled as knights galloped past her in a blur and she expected to be smashed to the ground and trampled at any moment. An arm steadied her, and she saw Grunwald at her side, his arm a bloody ruin. She saw the witch hunter staring up at the knights thundering around them in amazement, the pain of his wound forgotten. It was as if they were cupped in the protective hands of Sigmar Himself as they stood there unscathed by the mayhem around them.

The lord of Chaos roared again, the deafening sound filled with rage and defiance, as his bodyguard was lost beneath the lances, swords and hooves of the knights.

He speared his glaive through the lowered visor of another knight, punching him from the saddle as the blade burst from the back of his skull, and swung the butt of the weapon into the head of a steed, breaking its neck and sending its rider flying through the air.

Lances pierced the body of the warlord and he staggered, but refused to fall. Another pair of knights were hacked in two by the fell glaive. Swords struck his ornate armour, sending the warlord reeling, and another knight was decapitated. The flaming blue eye flicked left and right, seeking escape, but there was none to be had. The damned warrior ripped the head from a knight's shoulders with the flick of his wrist, but the mighty warlord was at last driven to his knees as a sword blazing with white light slashed across his chest, carving through armour and the mutated flesh beneath.

His face lit with the cold blue light emanating from the daemonic eye, Kurt Helborg, Grand Marshal of the Reiksguard knights, dismounted and stood before the broken enemy warlord. He glared down at the champion of the Raven Host in hatred and loathing.

'Know that the Empire will resist you always,' he hissed. 'Not until the last drop of blood in the last soldier of this land is spilled shall you have victory.'

With a roar of fury, the Reiksmarshal thrust his glowing sword, the Runefang of Solland, straight into the Chaos champion's face. He drove the point through the eye socket of the warlord's helmet with such force that it emerged hissing and spitting from the back of the skull, shearing through his ornate, horned helmet. The Reiksmarshal continued pushing the blade on until the hilt of the Runefang struck bone.

With a sucking sound of displaced air the blue eye flickered and disappeared, and the warlord of the Raven Host collapsed to the ground, dead.

EPILOGUE

LED BY THE mighty charge of the Reiksguard knights, the Order of the Griffon descended on the battlefield and smashed through the reeling enemy army with the force of a battering ram. Thousands on both sides were killed in the slaughter, but at last the field was clear of the foe.

'This is but the beginning,' said the Reiksmarshal Kurt Helborg, his carefully weighted words echoing across the bloodied but triumphant army.

'The armies of the Raven Host are massing. They over-run Ostland and Talabecland, and the Ostermark is in ruin. They march south, and push towards Altdorf.'

There were mutterings of shock and fear amongst the soldiers, and the Reiksmarshal raised his hand for silence.

'But there is still hope, even in this hour of darkness. Your victory this day shall be a golden light in the grim night, an inspiration that speaks of the proud fighting spirit of our nation. You have held this field – and if it were lost, then the ruin of the Empire was assured. Unchecked, this horde would have marched through Talabecland unmolested, and fallen on the flank of our armies there. In the Emperor's name, I thank you for your bravery and your resolve.'

The Reiksmarshal turned his mighty steed around, stalking back along in front of the serried ranks of weary soldiers.

'Far to the north, the great city Praag has been taken by the enemy, just as it was during the time of Magnus the Pious. But there is still hope.'

Not a sound came from the gathered army, for every soldier was intent on the words of the Reiksmarshal.

'The Order of the Griffon marches to war. Even now in Kislev, in the frozen north, our armies lay siege to Praag. They fight to reclaim it for the forces of order.

'Still there is hope!' he bellowed. 'With brave soldiers like you men of the Ostermark, the Empire *will* hold firm.

'In the name of our founder and patron god, I swear this to you, soldiers of the Ostermark: we none of us shall rest until the forces of destruction are shattered utterly!'

The Reiksmarshal's strong voice rose to a roaring fury, and he bellowed his words across the gathered army, his face set in determination and hatred.

'Together we will push them back to the north and reclaim Praag, but we shall not be content with that. No, we shall hound them like rabid wolves, and hunt them down wherever they seek to hide! We shall drive them back to the hell from whence they came and pursue them still. Far to the north we shall march, taking the fight to them directly, and we shall not rest until the Inevitable City itself lies in smoking ruin! For Sigmar!'

The roaring of the army was deafening, as men shouted their promise, praised Sigmar and bashed the hafts of their weapons against the ground.

'EVER BEEN TO Praag, manling?' said Thorrik, looking up at Grunwald. The witch hunter smiled wryly, fingering the pendant on his long black coat – a bronze emblem representing the Order of the Griffon.

Annaliese turned away from the cheering, registering the empty space beside her. She pushed her way through the cheering crowd and at last broke free of the press. She saw the grey-cloaked figure of Eldanair walking away to the south-east.

Sensing her gaze upon him, he turned, and their eyes met.

She knew now what it was that the tattoo upon his cheek meant. Vengeance. Perhaps regarding her as safe now, he was leaving to seek those that had killed his kin, and it was a path he needed to walk alone.

Without further ceremony, Eldanair pulled his hood up over his head and walked away.

Annaliese stared after him until the elf disappeared into the mist, fading away like a wraith, a shadow warrior disappearing into the gloom.

KARL WAS FILLED with bitterness as he watched from a distance. Watching the elf depart, the flames of hatred burnt fiercely in his icy blue eyes.

ABOUT THE AUTHOR

After finishing university Anthony Reynolds set sail from his homeland and ventured forth to foreign climes. He ended up settling in the UK, and managed to blag his way into Games Workshop's hallowed Design Studio. There he worked for four years as a Games Developer and two years as part of the Management team. He now resides back in his hometown of Sydney, overlooking the beach and enjoying the sun and the surf, though he finds that to capture the true darkness and horror of Warhammer and Warhammer 40,000 he has taken to writing in what could be described as a darkened cave.

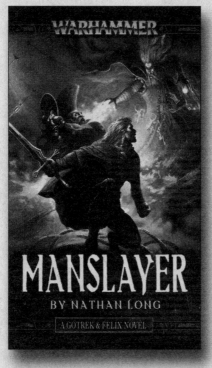

JOIN ME OR FIGHT ME!
THE CHOICE IS YOURS.

WARHAMMER ONLINE
AGE OF RECKONING

WWW.WARHAMMERONLINE.COM